TEXAS BORN

For our friends Cynthia Burton and Terry Sosebee

DIANA PALMER

Texas
BORN
& MAGGIE'S DAD

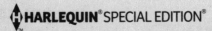

HARLEQUIN® SPECIAL EDITION®

ISBN-13: 978-0-373-83801-1

Texas Born & Maggie's Dad

Copyright © 2014 by Harlequin Books S.A.

The publisher acknowledges the copyright holder of the individual works as follows:

Texas Born
Copyright © 2014 by Diana Palmer

Maggie's Dad
Copyright © 1995 by Diana Palmer

Recycling programs
for this product may
not exist in your area.

Printed in U.S.A.

CONTENTS

Chapter 1

Michelle Godfrey felt the dust of the unpaved road all over her jeans. She couldn't really see her pants. Her eyes were full of hot tears. It was just one more argument, one more heartache.

Her stepmother, Roberta, was determined to sell off everything her father had owned. He'd only been dead for three weeks. Roberta had wanted to bury him in a plain pine box with no flowers, not even a church service. Michelle had dared her stepmother's hot temper and appealed to the funeral director.

The kindly man, a friend of her father's, had pointed out to Roberta that Comanche Wells, Texas, was a very small community. It would not sit well with the locals if Roberta, whom most considered an outsider, was disrespectful of the late Alan Godfrey's wishes that he be buried in the Methodist church cemetery beside his first wife. The funeral director was soft-spoken but eloquent. He also pointed out that the money Roberta would save with her so-called economy plans, would be a very small amount compared to the outrage she would provoke. If she planned to continue living in Jacobs County, many doors would close to her.

Roberta was irritated at the comment, but she had a shrewd mind. It wouldn't do to make people mad when she had many things to dispose of on the local market, including some cattle that had belonged to her late husband.

She gave in, with ill grace, and left the arrangements to Michelle. But she got even. After the funeral, she gathered up Alan's personal items while Michelle was at school and sent them all to the landfill, including his clothes and any jewelry that wasn't marketable.

Michelle had collapsed in tears. That is, until she saw her stepmother's wicked smile. At that point, she dried her eyes. It was too late to do anything. But one day, she promised herself, when she was grown and no longer under the woman's guardianship, there would be a reckoning.

Two weeks after the funeral, Roberta came under fire from Michelle's soft-spoken minister. He drove up in front of the house in a flashy red older convertible, an odd choice of car for a man of the cloth, Michelle thought. But then, Reverend Blair was a different sort of preacher.

She'd let him in, offered him coffee, which he refused politely. Roberta, curious because they never had visitors, came out of her room and stopped short when she saw Jake Blair.

He greeted her. He even smiled. They'd missed

Michelle at services for the past two weeks. He just wanted to make sure everything was all right. Michelle didn't reply. Roberta looked guilty. There was this strange rumor he'd heard, he continued, that Roberta was preventing her stepdaughter from attending church services. He smiled when he said it, but there was something about him that was strangely chilling for a religious man. His eyes, ice-blue, had a look that Roberta recognized from her own youth, spent following her father around the casinos in Las Vegas, where he made his living. Some of the patrons had that same penetrating gaze. It was dangerous.

"But of course, we didn't think the rumor was true," Jake Blair continued with that smile that accompanied the unblinking blue stare. "It isn't, is it?"

Roberta forced a smile. "Um, of course not." She faltered, with a nervous little laugh. "She can go whenever she likes."

"You might consider coming with her," Jake commented. "We welcome new members in our congregation."

"Me, in a church?" She burst out laughing, until she saw the two bland faces watching her. She sounded defensive when she added, "I don't go to church. I don't believe in all that stuff."

Jake raised an eyebrow. He smiled to himself, as if at some private joke. "At some point in your life, I assure you, your beliefs may change."

"Unlikely," she said stiffly.

He sighed. "As you wish. Then you won't mind if my daughter, Carlie, comes by to pick Michelle up for services on Sunday, I take it?"

Roberta ground her teeth together. Obviously the

minister knew that since Michelle couldn't drive, Roberta had been refusing to get up and drive her to church. She almost refused. Then she realized that it would mean she could have Bert over without having to watch for her stepdaughter every second. She pursed her lips. "Of course not," she assured him. "I don't mind at all."

"Wonderful. I'll have Carlie fetch you in time for Sunday school each week and bring you home after church, Michelle. Will that work for you?"

Michelle's sad face lit up. Her gray eyes were large and beautiful. She had pale blond hair and a flawless, lovely complexion. She was as fair as Roberta was dark. Jake got to his feet. He smiled down at Michelle.

"Thanks, Reverend Blair," she said in her soft, husky voice, and smiled at him with genuine affection.

"You're quite welcome."

She walked him out. Roberta didn't offer.

He turned at the steps and lowered his voice. "If you ever need help, you know where we are," he said, and he wasn't smiling.

She sighed. "It's just until graduation. Only a few more months," she said quietly. "I'll work hard to get a scholarship so I can go to college. I have one picked out in San Antonio."

He cocked his head. "What do you want to do?"

Her face brightened. "I want to write. I want to be a reporter."

He laughed. "Not much money in that, you know. Of course, you could go and talk to Minette Carson. She runs the local newspaper."

She flushed. "Yes, sir," she said politely, "I already did. She was the one who recommended that I go to college and major in journalism. She said working for a magazine, even a digital one, was the way to go. She's very kind."

"She is. And so is her husband," he added, referring to Jacobs County sheriff Hayes Carson.

"I don't really know him. Except he brought his iguana to school a few years ago. That was really fascinating." She laughed.

Jake just nodded. "Well, I'll get back. Let me know if you need anything."

"I will. Thank you."

"Your father was a good man," he added. "It hurt all of us to lose him. He was one of the best emergency-room doctors we ever had in Jacobs County, even though he was only able to work for a few months before his illness forced him to quit."

She smiled sadly. "It was a hard way to go, for a doctor," she replied. "He knew all about his prognosis and he explained to me how things would be. He said if he hadn't been so stubborn, if he'd had the tests sooner, they might have caught the cancer in time."

"Young lady," Jake said softly, "things happen the way they're meant to. There's a plan to everything that happens in life, even if we don't see it."

"That's what I think, too. Thank you for talking to her," she added hesitantly. "She wouldn't let me learn how to drive, and Dad was too sick to teach me. I don't really think she'd let me borrow the car, even if I could drive. She wouldn't get up early for anything, especially on a Sunday. So I had no way to get to church. I've missed it."

"I wish you'd talked to me sooner," he said, and smiled. "Never mind. Things happen in their own time."

She looked up into his blue eyes. "Does it…get better? Life, I mean?" she asked with the misery of someone who'd landed in a hard place and saw no way out.

He drew in a long breath. "You'll soon have more control over the things that happen to you," he replied. "Life is a test, Michelle. We walk through fire. But there are rewards. Every pain brings a pleasure."

"Thanks."

He chuckled. "Don't let her get you down."

"I'm trying."

"And if you need help, don't hold back." His eyes narrowed and there was something a little chilling in them. "I have yet to meet a person who frightens me."

She burst out laughing. "I noticed. She's a horror, but she was really nice to you!"

"Sensible people are." He smiled like an angel. "See you."

He went down the steps two at a time. He was a tall man, very fit, and he walked with a very odd gait, light and almost soundless, as he went to his car. The vehicle wasn't new, but it had some kind of big engine in it. He started it and wheeled out into the road with a skill and smoothness that she envied. She wondered if she'd ever learn to drive.

She went back into the house, resigned to several minutes of absolute misery.

"You set that man on me!" Roberta raged. "You went over my head when I told you I didn't want you to bother with that stupid church stuff!"

"I like going to church. Why should you mind? It isn't hurting you.…"

"Dinner was always late when you went, when your father was alive," the brunette said angrily. "I had to take care of him. So messy." She made a face. In fact, Roberta had never done a thing for her husband. She left it all to Michelle. "And I had to try to cook. I hate cooking. I'm not doing it. That's your job. So you'll make dinner before you go to church and you can eat when you get home, but I'm not waiting an extra hour to sit down to a meal!"

"I'll do it," Michelle said, averting her eyes.

"See that you do! And the house had better be spotless, or I won't let you go!"

She was bluffing. Michelle knew it. She was unsettled by the Reverend Blair. That amused Michelle, but she didn't dare let it show.

"Can I go to my room now?" she asked quietly.

Roberta made a face. "Do what you please." She primped at the hall mirror. "I'm going out. Bert's taking me to dinner up in San Antonio. I'll be very late," she added. She gave Michelle a worldly, patronizing laugh. "You wouldn't know what to do with a man, you little prude."

Michelle stiffened. It was the same old song and dance. Roberta thought Michelle was backward and stupid.

"Oh, go on to your room," she muttered. That wide-eyed, resigned look was irritating.

Michelle went without another word.

She sat up late, studying. She had to make the best grades she could, so that she could get a scholarship. Her father had left her a little money, but her stepmother had control of it until she was of legal age. Probably by then there wouldn't be a penny left.

Her father hadn't been lucid at the end because of the massive doses of painkillers he had to take for his condition. Roberta had influenced the way he set up his will, and it had been her own personal attorney who'd drawn it up for her father's signature. Michelle was certain that he hadn't meant to leave her so little. But she couldn't contest it. She wasn't even out of high school.

It was hard, she thought, to be under someone's thumb and unable to do anything you wanted to do. Roberta was always after her about something. She made fun of her, ridiculed her conservative clothes, made her life a daily misery. But the reverend was right. One day, she'd be out of this. She'd have her own place, and she wouldn't have to ask Roberta even for lunch money, which was demeaning enough.

She heard a truck go along the road, and glanced out to see a big black pickup truck pass by. So he was back. Their closest neighbor was Gabriel Brandon. Michelle knew who he was.

She'd seen him for the first time two years ago, the last summer she'd spent with her grandfather and grandmother before their deaths. They'd lived in this very house, the one her father had inherited. She'd gone to town with her grandfather to get medicine for a sick calf. The owner of the store had been talking to a man, a very handsome man who'd just moved down the road from them.

He was very tall, muscular, without it being obvious, and he had the most beautiful liquid black eyes she'd ever seen. He was built like a rodeo cowboy. He had thick, jet-black hair and a face off of a movie poster. He was the most gorgeous man she'd ever seen in her life.

He'd caught her staring at him and he'd laughed. She'd never forgotten how that transformed his hard face. It had melted her. She'd flushed and averted her eyes and almost run out of the store afterward. She'd embarrassed herself by staring. But he was very good-looking, after all—he must be used to women staring at him.

She'd asked her grandfather about him. He hadn't said much, only that the man was working for Eb Scott, who owned a ranch near Jacobsville. Brandon was rather mysterious, too, her grandfather had mused, and people were curious about him. He wasn't married. He had a sister who visited him from time to time.

Michelle's grandfather had chided her for her interest. At fifteen, he'd reminded her, she was much too young to be interested in men. She'd agreed out loud. But privately she thought that that Mr. Brandon was absolutely gorgeous, and most girls would have stared at him.

By comparison, Roberta's friend, Bert, always looked greasy, as if he never washed his hair. Michelle couldn't stand him. He looked at her in a way that made her skin crawl and he was always trying to touch her. She'd jerked away from him once, when he'd tried to ruffle her hair, and he made a big joke of it. But his eyes weren't laughing.

He made her uncomfortable, and she tried to stay out of his way. It would have been all right if he and Roberta didn't flaunt their affair. Michelle came home from school one Monday to find them on the sofa together, half-dressed and sweaty. Roberta had almost doubled up with laughter at the look she got from her stepdaughter as she lay half across Bert, wearing nothing but a lacy black slip.

"And what are you staring at, you little prude?" Roberta had demanded. "Did you think I'd put on black clothes and abandon men for life because your father died?"

"He's only been dead two weeks," Michelle had pointed out with choking pride.

"So what? He wasn't even that good in bed before he got sick," she scoffed. "We lived in San Antonio and he had a wonderful practice, he was making loads of money as a cardiologist. Then he gets diagnosed with terminal cancer and decides overnight to pull up stakes and move to this flea-bitten wreck of a town where he sets up a free clinic on weekends and lives on his pension and his investments! Which evaporated in less than a year, thanks to his medical bills," she added haughtily. "I thought he was rich…!"

"Yes, that's why you married him," Michelle said under her breath.

"That's the only reason I did marry him," she muttered, sitting up to light a cigarette and blow smoke in Michelle's direction.

She coughed. "Daddy wouldn't let you smoke in the house," she said accusingly.

"Well, Daddy's dead, isn't he?" Roberta said pointedly, and she smiled.

"We could make it a threesome, if you like," Bert offered, sitting up with his shirt half-off.

Michelle's expression was eloquent. "If I speak to my minister…"

"Shut up, Bert!" Roberta said shortly, and her eyes dared him to say another word. She looked back at Michelle with cold eyes and got to her feet. "Come on, Bert, let's go to your place." She grabbed him by the hand and had led him to the bedroom. Apparently their clothes were in there.

Disgusted beyond measure, Michelle went into her room and locked the door.

She could hear them arguing. A few minutes later they came back out.

"I won't be here for dinner," Roberta said.

Michelle didn't reply.

"Little torment," Roberta grumbled. "She's always watching, always so pure and unblemished," she added harshly.

"I could take care of that," Bert said.

"Shut up!" Roberta said again. "Come on, Bert!"

Michelle could feel herself flushing with anger as she heard them go out the door. Roberta slammed it behind her.

Michelle had peeked out the curtains and watched them climb into Bert's low-slung car. He pulled out into the road.

She closed the curtains with a sigh of pure relief. Nobody knew what a hell those two made of her life. She had no peace. Apparently Roberta had been seeing Bert for some time, because they were obviously obsessed with each other. But it had come as a shock to walk in the door and find them kissing the day after Michelle's father was buried, to say nothing of what she'd just seen.

The days since then had been tense and uncomfortable. The two of them made fun of Michelle, ridiculed the way she dressed, the way she thought. And Roberta was full of petty comments about Michelle's father and the illness that had killed him. Roberta had never even gone to the hospital. It had been Michelle who'd sat with him until he slipped away, peacefully, in his sleep.

She lay on her back and looked at the ceiling. It was only a few months until graduation. She made very good grades. She hoped Marist College in San Antonio would take her. She'd already applied. She was sweating out the admissions, because she'd have to have a scholarship or she couldn't afford to go. Not only that, she'd have to have a job.

She'd worked part-time at a mechanic's shop while her father was alive. He'd drop her off after school and pick her up when she finished work. But his illness had come on quickly and she'd lost the job. Roberta wasn't about to provide transportation.

She rolled over restlessly. Maybe there would be something she could get in San Antonio, perhaps in a convenience store if all else failed. She didn't mind hard work. She was used to it. Since her father had married Roberta, Michelle had done all the cooking and cleaning and laundry. She even mowed the lawn.

Her father had seemed to realize his mistake toward the end. He'd apologized for bringing Roberta into their lives. He'd been lonely since her mother died, and Roberta had flattered him and made him feel good. She'd been fun to be around during the courtship—even Michelle had thought so. Roberta went shopping with the girl, praised her cooking, acted like a really nice person. It wasn't until after the wedding that she'd shown her true colors.

Michelle had always thought it was the alcohol that had made her change so suddenly for the worse. It wasn't discussed in front of her, but Michelle knew that Roberta had been missing for a few weeks, just before her father was diagnosed with cancer. And there was gossip that the doctor had sent his young wife off to a rehabilitation center because of a drinking problem. Afterward, Roberta hadn't been quite so hard to live with. Until they'd moved to Comanche Wells, at least.

Dr. Godfrey had patted Michelle on the shoulder only days before the cancer had taken a sudden turn for the worse and he was bedridden. He'd smiled ruefully.

"I'm very sorry, sweetheart," he'd told her. "If I could go back and change things…"

"I know, Daddy. It's all right."

He'd pulled her close and kissed her forehead. "You're like your mother. She took things to heart, too. You have to learn how to deal with unpleasant people. You have to learn not to take life so seriously…."

"Alan, are you ever coming inside?" Roberta had interrupted petulantly. She hated seeing her husband and her stepdaughter together. She made every effort to keep them apart. "What are you doing, anyway, looking at those stupid smelly cattle?"

"I'll be there in a moment, Roberta," he called back.

"The dishes haven't been washed," she told Michelle with a cold smile. "Your job, not mine."

She'd gone back inside and slammed the screen.

Michelle winced.

So did her father. He drew in a deep breath. "Well, we'll get through this," he said absently. He'd winced again, holding his stomach.

"You should see Dr. Coltrain," she remarked. Dr. Copper Coltrain was one of their local physicians. "You keep putting it off. It's worse, isn't it?"

He sighed. "I guess it is. Okay. I'll see him tomorrow, worrywart."

She grinned. "Okay."

* * *

Tomorrow had ended with a battery of tests and a sad prognosis. They'd sent him back home with more medicine and no hope. He'd lasted a few weeks past the diagnosis.

Michelle's eyes filled with tears. The loss was still new, raw. She missed her father. She hated being at the mercy of her stepmother, who wanted nothing more than to sell the house and land right out from under Michelle. In fact, she'd already said that as soon as the will went through probate, she was going to do exactly that.

Michelle had protested. She had several months of school to go. Where would she live?

That, Roberta had said icily, was no concern of hers. She didn't care what happened to her stepdaughter. Roberta was young and had a life of her own, and she wasn't going to spend it smelling cattle and manure. She was going to move in with Bert. He was in between jobs, but the sale of the house and land would keep them for a while. Then they'd go to Las Vegas where she knew people and could make their fortune in the casino.

Michelle had cocked her head and just stared at her stepmother with a patronizing smile. "Nobody beats the house in Las Vegas," she said in a soft voice.

"I'll beat it," Roberta snapped. "You don't know anything about gambling."

"I know that sane people avoid it," she returned.

Roberta shrugged.

There was only one real-estate agent in Comanche Wells. Michelle called her, nervous and obviously upset.

"Roberta says she's selling the house," she began.

"Relax." Betty Mathers laughed. "She has to get the

will through probate, and then she has to list the property. The housing market is in the basement right now, sweetie. She'd have to give it away to sell it."

"Thanks," Michelle said huskily. "You don't know how worried I was…." Her voice broke, and she stopped.

"There's no reason to worry," Betty assured her. "Even if she does leave, you have friends here. Somebody will take the property and make sure you have a place to stay. I'll do it myself if I have to."

Michelle was really crying now. "That's so kind…!"

"Michelle, you've been a fixture around Jacobs County since you were old enough to walk. You spent summers with your grandparents here and you were always doing things to help them, and other people. You spent the night in the hospital with the Harrises' little boy when he had to have that emergency appendectomy and wouldn't let them give you a dime. You baked cakes for the sale that helped Rob Meiner when his house burned. You're always doing for other people. Don't think it doesn't get noticed." Her voice hardened. "And don't think we aren't aware of what your stepmother is up to. She has no friends here, I promise you."

Michelle drew in a breath and wiped her eyes. "She thought Daddy was rich."

"I see," came the reply.

"She hated moving down here. I was never so happy," she added. "I love Comanche Wells."

Betty laughed. "So do I. I moved here from New York City. I like hearing crickets instead of sirens at night."

"Me, too."

"You stop worrying, okay?" she added. "Everything's going to be all right."

"I will. And thanks."

"No thanks necessary."

Michelle was to remember that conversation the very next day. She got home from school that afternoon and her father's prized stamp collection was sitting on the coffee table. A tall, distinguished man was handing Roberta a check.

"It's a marvelous collection," the man said.

"What are you doing?" Michelle exclaimed, dropping her books onto the sofa, as she stared at the man with horror. "You can't sell Daddy's stamps! You can't! It's the only thing of his I have left that we both shared! I helped him put in those stamps, from the time I was in grammar school!"

Roberta looked embarrassed. "Now, Michelle, we've already discussed this...."

"We haven't discussed anything!" she raged, red-faced and weeping. "My father has only been dead three weeks and you've already thrown away every single thing he had, even his clothes! You've talked about selling the house... I'm still in school—I won't even have a place to live. And now this! You...you...mercenary gold digger!"

Roberta tried to smile at the shocked man. "I do apologize for my daughter...."

"I'm not her daughter! She married my father two years ago. She's got a boyfriend. She was with him while my father was dying in the hospital!"

The man stared at Michelle for a long moment,

turned to Roberta, snapped the check out of her hands and tore it into shreds.

"But...we had a deal," Roberta stammered.

The man gave her a look that made her move back a step. "Madam, if you were kin to me, I would disown you," he said harshly. "I have no wish to purchase a collection stolen from a child."

"I'll sue you!" Roberta raged.

"By all means. Attempt it."

He turned to Michelle. "I am very sorry," he said gently. "For your loss and for the situation in which you find yourself." He turned to Roberta. "Good day."

He walked out.

Roberta gave him just enough time to get to his car. Then she turned to Michelle and slapped her so hard that her teeth felt as if they'd come loose on that side of her face.

"You little brat!" she yelled. "He was going to give me five thousand dollars for that stamp collection! It took me weeks to find a buyer!"

Michelle just stared at her, cold pride crackling around her. She lifted her chin. "Go ahead. Hit me again. And see what happens."

Roberta drew back her hand. She meant to do it. The child was a horror. She hated her! But she kept remembering the look that minister had given her. She put her hand down and grabbed her purse.

"I'm going to see Bert," she said icily. "And you'll get no lunch money from me from now on. You can mop floors for your food, for all I care!"

She stormed out the door, got into her car and roared away.

Michelle picked up the precious stamp collection

and took it into her room. She had a hiding place that, hopefully, Roberta wouldn't be able to find. There was a loose baseboard in her closet. She pulled it out, slid the stamp book inside and pushed it back into the wall.

She went to the mirror. Her face looked almost blistered where Roberta had hit her. She didn't care. She had the stamp collection. It was a memento of happy times when she'd sat on her father's lap and carefully tucked stamps into place while he taught her about them. If Roberta killed her, she wasn't giving the stamps up.

But she was in a hard place, with no real way out. The months until graduation seemed like years. Roberta would make her life a living hell from now on because she'd opposed her. She was so tired of it. Tired of Roberta. Tired of Bert and his innuendoes. Tired of having to be a slave to her stepmother. It seemed so hopeless.

She thought of her father and started bawling. He was gone. He'd never come back. Roberta would torment her to death. There was nothing left.

She walked out the front door like a sleepwalker, out to the dirt road that lead past the house. And she sat down in the middle of it—heartbroken and dusty with tears running down her cheeks.

Chapter 2

Michelle felt the vibration of the vehicle before she smelled the dust that came up around it. Her back was to the direction it was coming from. Desperation had blinded her to the hope of better days. She was sick of life. Sick of everything.

She put her hands on her knees, brought her elbows in, closed her eyes, and waited for the collision. It would probably hurt. Hopefully, it would be quick....

There was a squealing of tires and a metallic jerk. She didn't feel the impact. Was she dead?

Long, muscular legs in faded blue denim came into view above big black hand-tooled leather boots.

"Would you care to explain what the hell you're doing sitting in the middle of a road?" a deep, angry voice demanded.

She looked up into chilling liquid black eyes and grimaced. "Trying to get hit by a car?"

"I drive a truck," he pointed out.

"Trying to get hit by a truck," she amended in a matter-of-fact tone.

"Care to elaborate?"

She shrugged. "My stepmother will probably beat me when she gets back home because I ruined her sale."

He frowned. "What sale?"

"My father died three weeks ago," she said heavily. She figured he didn't know, because she hadn't seen any signs of life at the house down the road until she'd watched his truck go by just recently. "She had all his things taken to the landfill because I insisted on a real funeral, not a cremation, and now she's trying to sell his stamp collection. It's all I have left of him. I ruined the sale. The man left. She hit me...."

He turned his head. It was the first time he'd noticed the side of her face that looked almost blistered. His eyes narrowed. "Get in the truck."

She stared at him. "I'm all dusty."

"It's a dusty truck. It won't matter."

She got to her feet. "Are you abducting me?"

"Yes."

She sighed. "Okay." She glanced at him ruefully. "If you don't mind, I'd really like to go to Mars. Since I'm being abducted, I mean."

He managed a rough laugh.

She went around to the passenger side. He opened the door for her.

"You're Mr. Brandon," she said when he climbed into the driver's seat and slammed the door.

"Yes."

She drew in a breath. "I'm Michelle."

"Michelle." He chuckled. "There was a song with

that name. My father loved it. One of the lines was 'Michelle, *ma belle*.'" He glanced at her. "Do you speak French?"

"A little," she said. "I have it second period. It means something like 'my beauty.'" She laughed. "And that has nothing to do with me, I'm afraid. I'm just plain."

He glanced at her with raised eyebrows. Was she serious? She was gorgeous. Young, and untried, but her creamy complexion was without a blemish. She was nicely shaped and her hair was a pale blond. Those soft gray eyes reminded him of a fog in August…

He directed his eyes to the road. She was just a child, what was he thinking? "Beauty, as they say, is in the eye of the beholder."

"Do you speak French?" she asked, curious.

He nodded. "French, Spanish, Portuguese, Afrikaans, Norwegian, Russian, German and a handful of Middle Eastern dialects."

"Really?" She was fascinated. "Did you work as a translator or something?"

He pursed his lips. "From time to time," he said, and then laughed to himself.

"Cool."

He started the truck and drove down the road to the house he owned. It wasn't far, just about a half mile. It was a ranch house, set back off the road. There were oceans of flowers blooming around it in the summer, planted by the previous owner, Mrs. Eller, who had died. Of course, it was still just February, and very cold. There were no flowers here now.

"Mrs. Eller loved flowers."

"Excuse me?"

"She lived here all her life," she told him, smiling as

they drove up to the front porch. "Her husband worked as a deputy sheriff. They had a son in the military, but he was killed overseas. Her husband died soon afterward. She planted so many flowers that you could never even see the house. I used to come over and visit her when I was little, with my grandfather."

"Your people are from here?"

"Oh, yes. For three generations. Daddy went to medical school in Georgia and then he set up a practice in cardiology in San Antonio. We lived there. But I spent every summer here with my grandparents while they were alive. Daddy kept the place up, after, and it was like a vacation home while Mama was alive." She swallowed. That loss had been harsh. "We still had everything, even the furniture, when Daddy decided to move us down here and take early retirement. She hated it from the first time she saw it." Her face hardened. "She's selling it. My stepmother, I mean. She's already talked about it."

He drew in a breath. He knew he was going to regret this. He got out, opened the passenger door and waited for her to get out. He led the way into the house, seated her in the kitchen and pulled out a pitcher of iced tea. When he had it in glasses, he sat down at the table with her.

"Go ahead," he invited. "Get it off your chest."

"It's not your problem…"

"You involved me in an attempted suicide," he said with a droll look. "That makes it my problem."

She grimaced. "I'm really sorry, Mr. Brandon…."

"Gabriel."

She hesitated.

He raised an eyebrow. "I'm not that old," he pointed out.

She managed a shy smile. "Okay."

He cocked his head. "Say it," he said, and his liquid black eyes stared unblinking into hers.

She felt her heart drop into her shoes. She swallowed down a hot wave of delight and hoped it didn't show. "Ga...Gabriel," she obliged.

His face seemed to soften. Just a little. He smiled, showing beautiful white teeth. "That's better."

She flushed. "I'm not...comfortable with men," she blurted out.

His eyes narrowed on her face, her averted eyes. "Does your stepmother have a boyfriend?"

She swallowed, hard. The glass in her hand trembled.

He took the glass from her and put it on the table. "Tell me."

It all poured out. Finding Roberta in Bert's arms just after the funeral, finding them on the couch together that day, the way Bert looked and her and tried to touch her, the visit from her minister...

"And I thought my life was complicated," he said heavily. He shook his head. "I'd forgotten what it was like to be young and at the mercy of older people."

She studied him quietly. The expression on his face was...odd.

"You know," she said softly. "You understand."

"I had a stepfather," he said through his teeth. "He was always after my sister. She was very pretty, almost fourteen. I was a few years older, and I was bigger than he was. Our mother loved him, God knew why. We'd moved back to Texas because the international company he worked for promoted him and he had to go to Dallas for the job. One day I heard my sister scream. I went into her room, and there he was. He'd tried to..."

He stopped. His face was like stone. "My mother had to get a neighbor to pull me off him. After that, after she knew what had been going on, she still defended him. I was arrested, but the public defender got an earful. He spoke to my sister. My stepfather was arrested, charged, tried. My mother stood by him, the whole time. My sister was victimized by the defense attorney, after what she'd already suffered at our stepfather's hands. She was so traumatized by the experience that she doesn't even date."

She winced. One small hand went shyly to cover his clenched fist on the table. "I'm so sorry."

He seemed to mentally shake himself, as if he'd been locked into the past. He met her soft, concerned gaze. His big hand turned, curled around hers. "I've never spoken of it, until now."

"Maybe sometimes it's good to share problems. Dark memories aren't so bad when you force them into the light."

"Seventeen going on thirty?" he mused, smiling at her. It didn't occur to her to wonder how he knew her age.

She smiled. "There are always people who are in worse shape than you are. My friend Billy has an alcoholic father who beats him and his mother. The police are over there all the time, but his mother will never press charges. Sheriff Carson says the next time, he's going to jail, even if he has to press charges himself."

"Good for the sheriff."

"What happened, after the trial?" she prodded gently.

He curled his fingers around Michelle's, as if he enjoyed their soft comfort. She might have been fascinated to know that he'd never shared these memories with any other woman, and that, as a rule, he hated having people touch him.

"He went to jail for child abuse," he said. "My mother was there every visiting day."

"No, what happened to you and your sister?"

"My mother refused to have us in the house with her. We were going to be placed in foster homes. The public defender had a maiden aunt, childless, who was suicidal. Her problems weren't so terrible, but she tended to depression and she let them take her almost over the edge. So he thought we might be able to help each other. We went to live with Aunt Maude." He chuckled. "She was not what you think of as anybody's maiden aunt. She drove a Jaguar, smoked like a furnace, could drink any grown man under the table, loved bingo parties and cooked like a gourmet. Oh, and she spoke about twenty languages. In her youth, she was in the army and mustered out as a sergeant."

"Wow," she exclaimed. "She must have been fascinating to live with."

"She was. And she was rich. She spoiled us rotten. She got my sister into therapy, for a while at least, and me into the army right after I graduated." He smiled. "She was nuts about Christmas. We had trees that bent at the ceiling, and the limbs groaned under all the decorations. She'd go out and invite every street person she could find over to eat with us." His face sobered. "She said she'd seen foreign countries where the poor were treated better than they were here. Ironically, it was one of the same people she invited to Christmas dinner who stabbed her to death."

She winced. "I'm so sorry!"

"Me, too. By that time, though, Sara and I were

grown. I was in the...military," he said, hoping she didn't notice the involuntary pause, "and Sara had her own apartment. Maude left everything she had to the two of us and her nephew. We tried to give our share back to him, as her only blood heir, but he just laughed and said he got to keep his aunt for years longer because of us. He went into private practice and made a fortune defending drug lords, so he didn't really need it, he told us."

"Defending drug lords." She shook her head.

"We all do what we do," he pointed out. "Besides, I've known at least one so-called drug lord who was better than some upright people."

She just laughed.

He studied her small hand. "If things get too rough for you over there, let me know. I'll manage something."

"It's only until graduation this spring," she pointed out.

"In some situations, a few months can be a lifetime," he said quietly.

She nodded.

"Friends help each other."

She studied his face. "Are we? Friends, I mean?"

"We must be. I haven't told anyone else about my stepfather."

"You didn't tell me the rest of it."

His eyes went back to her hand resting in his. "He got out on good behavior six months after his conviction and decided to make my sister pay for testifying against him. She called 911. The police shot him."

"Oh, my gosh."

"My mother blamed both of us for it. She moved back to Canada, to Alberta, where we grew up."

"Are you Canadian?" she asked curiously.

He smiled. "I'm actually Texas born. We moved to Canada to stay with my mother's people when my father was in the military and stationed overseas. Sara was born in Calgary. We lived there until just after my mother married my stepfather."

"Did you see your mother again, after that?" she asked gently.

He shook his head. "Our mother never spoke to us again. She died a few years back. Her attorney tracked me down and said she left her estate, what there was of it, to the cousins in Alberta."

"I'm so sorry."

"Life is what it is. I had hoped she might one day realize what she'd done to my sister. She never did."

"We can't help who we love, or what it does to mess us up."

He frowned. "You really are seventeen going on thirty."

She laughed softly. "Maybe I'm an old soul."

"Ah. Been reading philosophy, have we?"

"Yes." She paused. "You haven't mentioned your father."

He smiled sadly. "He was in a paramilitary group overseas. He stepped on an antipersonnel mine."

She didn't know what a paramilitary group was, so she just nodded.

"He was from Dallas," he continued. "He had a small ranch in Texas that he inherited from his grandfather. He and my mother met at the Calgary Stampede. He trained horses and he'd sold several to be used at the stampede. She had an uncle who owned a ranch in Alberta and also supplied livestock to the stampede."

He stared at her small hand in his. "Her people were French-Canadian. One of my grandmothers was a member of the Blackfoot Nation."

"Wow!"

He smiled.

"Then, you're an American citizen," she said.

"Our parents did the whole citizenship process. In short, I now have both Canadian and American citizenship."

"My dad loved this Canadian television show, *Due South*. He had the whole DVD collection. I liked the Mountie's dog. He was a wolf."

He laughed. "I've got the DVDs, too. I loved the show. It was hilarious."

She glanced at the clock on the wall. "I have to go. If you aren't going to run over me, I'll have to fix supper in case she comes home to eat. It's going to be gruesome. She'll still be furious about the stamp collection." Her face grew hard. "She won't find it. I've got a hiding place she doesn't know about."

He smiled. "Devious."

"Not normally. But she's not selling Daddy's stamps."

He let go of her hand and got up from his chair. "If she hits you again, call 911."

"She'd kill me for that."

"Not likely."

She sighed. "I guess I could, if I had to."

"You mentioned your minister. Who is he?"

"Jake Blair. Why?"

His expression was deliberately blank.

"Do you know him? He's a wonderful minister. Odd thing, my stepmother was intimidated by him."

He hesitated, and seemed to be trying not to laugh. "Yes. I've heard of him."

"He told her that his daughter was going to pick me up and bring me home from church every week. His daughter works for the Jacobsville police chief."

"Cash Grier."

She nodded. "He's very nice."

"Cash Grier?" he exclaimed. "Nice?"

"Oh, I know people talk about him, but he came to speak to my civics class once. He's intelligent."

"Very."

He helped her back into the truck and drove her to her front door.

She hesitated before she got out, turning to him. "Thank you. I don't think I've ever been so depressed. I've never actually tried to kill myself before."

His liquid black eyes searched hers. "We all have days when we're ridden by the 'black dog.'"

She blinked. "Excuse me?"

He chuckled. "Winston Churchill had periods of severe depression. He called it that."

She frowned. "Winston Churchill…"

"There was this really big world war," he said facetiously, with over-the-top enthusiasm, "and this country called England, and it had a leader during—"

"Oh, give me a break!" She burst out laughing.

He grinned at her. "Just checking."

She shook her head. "I know who he was. I just had to put it into context is all. Thanks again."

"Anytime."

She got out and closed the door, noting with relief that Roberta hadn't come home yet. She smiled and waved. He waved back. When he drove off, she noticed that he didn't look back. Not at all.

She had supper ready when Roberta walked in the door. Her stepmother was still fuming.

"I'm not eating beef," she said haughtily. "You know I hate it. And are those mashed potatoes? I'll bet you crammed them with butter!"

"Yes, I did," Michelle replied quietly, "because you always said you liked them that way."

Roberta's cheeks flushed. She shifted, as if the words, in that quiet voice, made her feel guilty.

In fact, they did. She was remembering her behavior with something close to shame. Her husband had only been dead three weeks. She'd tossed his belongings, refused to go to the funeral, made fun of her stepdaughter at every turn, even slapped her for messing up the sale of stamps that Alan had left to Michelle. And after all that, the child made her favorite food. Her behavior should be raising red flags, but her stepdaughter was, thankfully, too naive to notice it. Bert's doing, she thought bitterly. All his fault.

"You don't have to eat it," Michelle said, turning away.

Roberta made a rough sound in her throat. "It's all right," she managed tautly. She sat down at the table. She glanced at Michelle, who was dipping a tea bag in a cup of steaming water. "Aren't you eating?"

"I had soup."

Roberta made inroads into the meat loaf and mashed potatoes. The girl had even made creamed peas, her favorite.

She started to put her fork down and noticed her

hand trembling. She jerked it down onto the wood and pulled her hand back.

It was getting worse. She needed more and more. Bert was complaining about the expense. They'd had a fight. She'd gone storming up to his apartment in San Antonio to cry on his shoulder about her idiot step-daughter and he'd started complaining when she dipped into his stash. But after all, he was the one who'd gotten her hooked in the first place.

It had taken more money than she'd realized to keep up, and Alan had finally figured out what she was doing. They'd argued. He'd asked her for a divorce, but she'd pleaded with him. She had no place to go. She knew Bert wouldn't hear of her moving in with him. Her whole family was dead.

Alan had agreed, but the price of his agreement was that she had to move down to his hometown with him after he sold his very lucrative practice in San Antonio.

She'd thought he meant the move to be a temporary one. He was tired of the rat race. He wanted something quieter. But they'd only been in his old family homestead for a few days when he confessed that he'd been diagnosed with an inoperable cancer. He wanted to spend some time with his daughter before the end. He wanted to run a free clinic, to help people who had no money for doctors. He wanted his life to end on a positive note, in the place where he was born.

So here was Roberta, stuck after his death with a habit she could no longer afford and no way to break it. Stuck with Cinderella here, who knew about as much about life as she knew about men.

She glared at the girl. She'd really needed the money from those stamps. There was nothing left that she could liquidate for cash. She hadn't taken all of Alan's things to the landfill. She'd told Michelle that so she wouldn't look for them. She'd gone to a consignment shop in San Antonio and sold the works, even his watch. It brought in a few hundred dollars. But she was going through money like water.

"What did you do with the stamps?" Roberta asked suddenly.

Michelle schooled her features to give away nothing, and she turned. "I hitched a ride into town and asked Cash Grier to keep them for me."

Roberta sucked in her breath. Fear radiated from her. "Cash Grier?"

Michelle nodded. "I figured it was the safest place. I told him I was worried about someone stealing them while I was at school."

Which meant she hadn't told the man that Roberta had slapped her. Thank God. All she needed now was an assault charge. She had to be more careful. The girl was too stupid to recognize her symptoms. The police chief wouldn't be. She didn't want anyone from law enforcement on the place. But she didn't even have the grace to blush when Michelle made the comment about someone possibly "stealing" her stamp collection.

She got up from the table. She was thirsty, but she knew it would be disastrous to pick up her cup of coffee. Not until she'd taken what she needed to steady her hands.

She paused on her way to the bathroom, with her back to Michelle. "I'm… I shouldn't have slapped you," she bit off.

She didn't wait for a reply. She was furious with herself for that apology. Why should the kid's feelings matter to her, anyway? She pushed away memories of how welcoming Michelle had been when she first started dating Alan. Michelle had wanted to impress her father's new friend.

Well, that was ancient history now. She was broke and Alan had died, leaving her next to nothing. She picked up her purse from the side table and went into the bathroom with it.

Michelle cleaned off the table and put the dishes into the dishwasher. Roberta hadn't come out of the bathroom even after she'd done all that, so she went to her room.

Michelle had been surprised by the almost-apology. But once she thought about it, she realized that Roberta might think she was going to press charges. She was afraid of her stepmother. She had violent mood swings and she'd threatened to hit Michelle several times.

It was odd, because when she'd first married Dr. Alan Godfrey, Michelle had liked her. She'd been fun to be around. But she had a roving eye. She liked men. If they went to a restaurant, someone always struck up a conversation with Roberta, who was exquisitely groomed and dressed and had excellent manners. Roberta enjoyed masculine attention, without being either coarse or forward.

Then, several months ago, everything had changed. Roberta had started going out at night alone. She told her husband that she'd joined an exercise club at a friend's house, a private one. They did aerobics and Pilates and things like that. Just women.

But soon afterward, Roberta became more careless about her appearance. Her manners slipped, badly. She complained about everything. Alan wasn't giving her enough spending money. The house needed cleaning, why wasn't Michelle doing more when she wasn't in school? She wasn't doing any more cooking, she didn't like it, Michelle would have to take over for her. And on it went. Alan had been devastated by the change. So had Michelle, who had to bear the brunt of most of Roberta's fury.

"Some women have mood swings as they get older," Alan had confided to his daughter, but there was something odd in his tone of voice. "But you mustn't say anything about it to her. She doesn't like thinking she's getting on in years. All right?"

"All right, Daddy," she'd agreed, with a big smile.

He'd hugged her close. "That's my girl."

Roberta had gone away for a few weeks after that. Then, not too long after her return, they'd moved to Comanche Wells, into the house where Michelle had spent so many happy weeks with her grandparents every summer.

The elderly couple had died in a wreck only a few years after Michelle's mother had died of a stroke. It had been a blow. Her father had gone through terrible grief. But then, so had Michelle.

Despite the double tragedy, Comanche Wells and this house seemed far more like home than San Antonio ever had, because it was so small that Michelle knew almost every family who lived in it. She knew people in Jacobsville, too, of course, but it was much larger. Comanche Wells was tiny by comparison.

Michelle loved the farm animals that her grandparents had kept. They always had dogs and cats and chickens for her to play with. But by the time Alan moved his family down here, there was only the small herd of beef cattle. Now the herd had been sold and was going to a local rancher who was going to truck the steers over to his own ranch.

Her door opened suddenly. Roberta looked wild-eyed. "I'm going back up to San Antonio for the night. I have to see Bert."

"All…" She had started to say "all right," but the door slammed. Roberta went straight out to her car, revved it up and scattered gravel on the way to the road.

It was odd behavior, even for her.

Michelle felt a little better than she had. At least she and Roberta might be able to manage each other's company until May, when graduation rolled around.

But Gabriel had helped her cope with what she thought was unbearable. She smiled, remembering his kindness, remembering the strong, warm clasp of his fingers. Her heart sailed at the memory. She'd almost never held hands with a boy. Once, when she was twelve, at a school dance. But the boy had moved away, and she was far too shy and old-fashioned to appeal to most of the boys in her high school classes. There had been another boy, at high school, but that date had ended in near disaster.

Gabriel was no boy. He had to be at least in his mid-twenties. He would think of her as a child. She grimaced. Well, she was growing up. One day…who knew what might happen?

She opened her English textbook and got busy with her homework. Then she remembered with a start what she'd told Roberta, that lie about having Cash Grier keep the stamp book. What if Roberta asked him?

Her face flamed. It would be a disaster. She'd lied, and Roberta would know it. She'd tear the house apart looking for that collection…

Then Michelle calmed down. Roberta seemed afraid of Cash Grier. Most people were. She doubted very seriously that her stepmother would approach him. But just to cover her bases, she was going to stop by his office after school. She could do it by pretending to ask Carlie what time she would pick her up for church services. Then maybe she could work up the nerve to tell him what she'd done. She would go without lunch. That would give her just enough money to pay for a cab home from Jacobsville, which was only a few miles away. Good thing she already had her lunch money for the week, because Roberta had told her there wouldn't be any more. She was going to have to do without lunch from now on, apparently. Or get a job. And good luck to that, without a car or a driver's license.

She sighed. Her life was more complicated than it had ever been. But things might get better. Someday.

Chapter 3

Michelle got off the school bus in downtown Jacobsville on Friday afternoon. She had to stop by the newspaper office to ask Minette Carson if she'd give her a reference for the scholarship she was applying for. The office was very close to police chief Grier's office, whom she also needed to see. And she had just enough money to get the local cab company to take her home.

Minette was sitting out front at her desk when Michelle walked in. She grinned and got up to greet her.

"How's school?" she asked.

"Going very well," Michelle said. "I wanted to ask if I could put you down as a reference. I'm applying for that journalism scholarship we spoke about last month, at Marist College in San Antonio."

"Of course you can."

"Thanks. I'm hoping I can keep my grades up so I'll have a shot at it."

"You'll do fine, Michelle. You have a way with words." She held up a hand when Michelle looked as if she might protest. "I never lie about writing. I'm brutally honest. If I thought you didn't have the skill, I'd keep my mouth shut."

Michelle laughed. "Okay. Thanks, then."

Minette perched on the edge of her desk. "I was wondering if you might like to work part-time for me. After school and Saturday morning."

Michelle's jaw dropped. "You mean, work here?" she exclaimed. "Oh, my gosh, I'd love to!" Then the joy drained out of her face. "I can't," she groaned. "I don't drive, and I don't have cab fare home. I mean, I do today, but I went without lunch…." Her face flamed.

"Carlie lives just past you," she said gently. "She works until five. So do we. I know she'd let you ride with her. She works Saturday mornings, too."

The joy came back into her features. "I'll ask her!"

Minette chuckled. "Do that. And let me know."

"I will, I promise."

"You can start Monday, if you like. Do you have a cell phone?" Minette asked.

Michelle hesitated and shook her head with lowered eyes.

"Don't worry about it. We'll get you one."

"Oh, but…."

"I'll have you phoning around town for news. Junior reporter stuff," she added with a grin. "A cell's an absolute necessity."

"In that case, okay, but I'll pay you back."

"That's a deal."

"I'll go over and talk to Carlie."

"Stop back by and let me know, okay?"

"Okay!"

She didn't normally rush, but she was so excited that her feet carried her across the street like wings.

She walked into the police station. Cash Grier was perched on Carlie's desk, dictating from a paper he held in his hand. He stopped when he saw Michelle.

"Sorry," Michelle said, coloring. She clutched her textbooks to her chest almost as a shield. "I just needed to ask Carlie something. I can come back later...."

"Nonsense," Cash said, and grinned.

She managed a shy smile. "Thanks." She hesitated. "I told a lie to my stepmother," she blurted out. "I think you should know, because it involved you."

His dark eyebrows arched. "Really? Did you volunteer me for the lead in a motion picture or something? Because I have to tell you, my asking price is extremely high...."

She laughed with pure delight. "No. I told her I gave you my father's stamp collection for safekeeping." She flushed again. "She was going to sell it. She'd already thrown away all his stuff. He and I worked on the stamp collection together as long as I can remember. It's all I have left of him." She swallowed. Hard.

Cash got up. He towered over her. He wasn't laughing. "You bring it in here and I'll put it in the safe," he said gently. "Nobody will touch it."

"Thanks." She was trying not to cry. "That's so kind..."

"Now, don't cry or you'll have me in tears. What would people think? I mean, I'm a big, tough cop. I can't be seen standing around sobbing all over the place. Crime would flourish!"

That amused her. She stopped biting her lip and actually grinned.

"That's better." His black eyes narrowed quizzically. "Your stepmother seems to have some issues. I got an earful from your minister this morning."

She nodded sadly. "She was so different when we lived in San Antonio. I mean, we went shopping together, we took turns cooking. Then we moved down here and she got mixed up with that Bert person." She shivered. "He gives me cold chills, but she's crazy about him."

"Bert Sims?" Cash asked in a deceptively soft tone.

"That's him."

Cash didn't say anything else. "If things get rough over there, call me, will you? I know you're outside the city limits, but I can get to Hayes Carson pretty quick if I have to, and he has jurisdiction."

"Oh, it's nothing like that…."

"Isn't it?" Cash asked.

She felt chilled. It was as if he was able to see Roberta through her eyes, and he saw everything.

"She did apologize. Sort of. For hitting me, I mean."

"Hitting you?" Cash stood straighter. "When?"

"I messed up the sale of Daddy's stamps. She was wild-eyed and screaming. She just slapped me, is all. She's been excitable since before Daddy died, but now she's just…just…nuts. She talks about money all the time, like she's dying to get her hands on some. But she doesn't buy clothes or cosmetics, she doesn't even dress well anymore."

"Do you know why?"

She shook her head. She drew in a breath. "She doesn't drink," she said. "I know that's what you're thinking. She and Daddy used to have drinks every night, and she had a problem for a little while, but she got over it."

Cash just nodded. "You let me know if things get worse. Okay?"

"Okay, Chief. Thanks," she added.

The phone rang. Carlie answered it. "It's your wife," she said with a big grin.

Cash's face lit up. "Really? Wow. A big-time movie star calling me up on the phone. I'm just awed, I am." He grinned. Everybody knew his wife, Tippy, had been known as the Georgia Firefly when she'd been a supermodel and, later, an actress. "I'll take it in my office. With the door closed." He made a mock scowl. "And no eavesdropping."

Carlie put her hand over her heart. "I swear."

"Not in my office, you don't," he informed her. "Swearing is a misdemeanor."

She stuck out her tongue at his departing back.

"I saw that," he said without looking behind him. He went into his office and closed the door on two giggling women.

"He's a trip to work for," Carlie enthused, her green eyes sparkling in a face framed by short, dark, wavy hair. "I was scared to death of him when I interviewed for the job. At least, until he accused me of hiding his bullets and telling his men that he read fashion magazines in the bathroom."

Michelle laughed.

"He's really funny. He says he keeps files on aliens in the filing cabinet and locks it so I won't peek." The smile moderated. "But if there's an emergency, he's the toughest guy I've ever known. I would never cross him, if I was a criminal."

"They say he chased a speeder all the way to San Antonio once."

She laughed. "That wasn't the chief. That was Kilraven, who worked here undercover." She leaned forward. "He really belongs to a federal agency. We're not supposed to mention it."

"I won't tell," Michelle promised.

"However, the chief—" she nodded toward his closed door "—got on a plane to an unnamed foreign country, tossed a runaway criminal into a bag and boated him to Miami. The criminal was part of a drug cartel. He killed a small-town deputy because he thought the man was a spy. He wasn't, but he was just as dead. Then the feds got involved and the little weasel escaped into a country that didn't have an extradition treaty with us. However, once he was on American soil, he was immediately arrested by Dade County deputies." She grinned. "The chief denied ever having seen the man, and nobody could prove that it was him on the beach. And," she added darkly, "you never heard that from me. Right?"

"Right!"

Carlie laughed. "So what can I do for you?"

"I need a ride home from work."

"I've got another hour to go, but…"

"Not today," Michelle said. "Starting Monday. Minette Carson just offered me a part-time job, but I don't have a way to get home. And she said I could work part-time Saturday, but I can't drive and I don't have a car."

"You can ride with me, and I'd welcome the company," Carlie said easily.

"I'll chip in for the gas."

"That would really help! Have you seen what I drive?" She groaned. "My dad has this thing about cars. He thinks you need an old truck to keep you from speeding, so he bought me a twelve-year-old tank. At least, it looks like a tank." She frowned. "Maybe it was a tank and he had it remodeled. Anyway, it barely gets twelve miles to a gallon and it won't go over fifty." She shook her head. "He drives a vintage Ford Cobra," she added with a scowl. "One of the neatest rides on the planet and I'm not allowed to touch it, can you believe that?"

Michelle just grinned. She didn't know anything about cars. She did recall the way the minister had peeled out of the driveway, scattering gravel. That car he drove had one big engine.

"Your dad scared my stepmother." Michelle laughed. "She wasn't letting me go to church. Your dad said I could ride with you." She stopped and flushed. "I really feel like I'm imposing. I wish I could drive. I wish I had a car...."

"It's really not imposing," Carlie said softly, smiling. "As I said, I'd like the company. I go down lots of back roads getting here from Comanche Wells. I'm not spooky or anything, but this guy did try to kill my Dad with a knife." She lowered her eyes. "I got in the way."

Michelle felt guilty that she hadn't remembered. "I'll learn karate," she promised. "We can go to a class together or something, and if anybody attacks us we can fight back!"

"Bad idea," Cash said, rejoining them. "A few weeks of martial arts won't make you an expert. Even an expert," he added solemnly, "knows better than to fight if he can get away from an armed man."

"That isn't what the ads say," Carlie mused, grinning.

"Yes, I know," Cash replied. "Take it from me, disarming someone with a gun is difficult even for a black belt." He leaned forward. "Which I am."

Carlie stood up, bowed deeply from the waist, and said, "Sensei!" Cash lost it. He roared with laughter.

"You could teach us," Michelle suggested. "Couldn't you?"

Cash just smiled. "I suppose it wouldn't hurt. Just a few basics for an emergency. But if you have an armed opponent, you run," he said firmly. "Or if you're cornered, scream, make a fuss. Never," he emphasized, "get into a car with anyone who threatens to kill you if you don't. Once he's got you in a car, away from help, you're dead, anyway."

Michelle felt chills run down her spine. "Okay."

Carlie looked uncomfortable. She knew firsthand about an armed attacker. Unconsciously, she rubbed the shoulder where the knife had gone in. She'd tried to protect her father. Her assailant had been arrested, but had died soon afterward. She never knew why her father had been the target of an attack by a madman.

"Deep thoughts?" Michelle asked her.

She snapped back. "Sorry. I was remembering the guy who attacked my father." She frowned. "What sort of person attacks a minister, for goodness' sake!"

"Come on down to federal lockup with me, and I'll show you a baker's dozen who have," Cash told her. "Religious arguments quite often lead to murder, even in families. That's why," he added, "we don't discuss politics or religion in the office." He frowned. "Well, if someone died in here, we'd probably say a prayer. And if the president came to see me, and why wouldn't he, we'd probably discuss his foreign policy."

"Why would the president come to see you?" Michelle asked innocently.

Cash pursed his lips. "For advice, of course. I have some great ideas about foreign policy."

"For instance?" Carlie mused.

"I think we should declare war on Tahiti."

They both stared at him.

"Well, if we do, we can send troops, right?" he continued. "And what soldier in his right mind wouldn't want to go and fight in Tahiti? Lush tropical flowers, fire-dancing, beautiful women, the ocean…"

"Tahiti doesn't have a standing army, I don't think," Michelle ventured.

"All the better. We can just occupy it for like three weeks, let them surrender, and then give them foreign aid." He glowered. "Now you've done it. You'll repeat that everywhere and the president will hear about it and he'll never have to come and hear me explain it. You've blown my chances for an invitation to the White House," he groaned. "And I did so want to spend a night in the Lincoln bedroom!"

"Listen, break out those files on aliens that you keep in your filing cabinet and tell the president you've got them!" Carlie suggested, while Michelle giggled. "He'll come right down here to have a look at them!"

"They won't let him," Cash sighed. "His security clearance isn't high enough."

"What?" Carlie exclaimed.

"Well, he's only in the office for four years, eight tops. So the guys in charge of the letter agencies—the really secretive ones—allegedly keep some secrets to themselves. Particularly those dealing with aliens." He chuckled.

The girls, who didn't know whether to believe him or not, just laughed along with him.

Michelle stopped back by Minette's office to tell her the good news, and to thank her again for the job.

"You know," she said, "Chief Grier is really nice."

"Nice when he likes you," Minette said drily. "There are a few criminals in maximum-security prisons who might disagree."

"No doubt there."

"So, will Monday suit you, to start to work?" Minette asked.

"I'd really love to start yesterday." Michelle laughed. "I'm so excited!"

Minette grinned. "Monday will come soon enough. We'll see you then."

"Can you write me a note? Just in case I need one?" She was thinking of how to break it to Roberta. That was going to be tricky.

"No problem." Minette went to her desk, typed out an explanation of Michelle's new position, and signed it. She handed it to the younger woman. "There you go."

"Dress code?" Michelle asked, glancing around the big open room where several people were sitting at desks, to a glass-walled room beyond which big sheets of paper rested on a long section like a chalkboard.

"Just be neat," Minette said easily. "I mostly kick around in jeans and T-shirts, although I dress when I go to political meetings or to interviews with state or federal politicians. You'll need to learn how to use a camera, as well. We have digital ones. They're very user-friendly."

"This is very exciting," Michelle said, her gray eyes glimmering with delight.

Minette laughed. "It is to me, too, and I've done this since I was younger than you are. I grew up running around this office." She looked around with pure love in her eyes. "It's home."

"I'm really looking forward to it. Will I just be reporting news?"

"No. Well, not immediately, at least. You'll learn every aspect of the business, from selling ads to typing copy to composition. Even subscriptions." She leaned forward. "You'll learn that some subscribers probably used to be doctors, because the handwriting looks more like Sanskrit than English."

Michelle chuckled. "I'll cope. My dad had the worst handwriting in the world."

"And he was a doctor," Minette agreed, smiling.

The smile faded. "He was a very good doctor," she said, trying not to choke up. "Sorry," she said, wiping away a tear. "It's still hard."

"It takes time," Minette said with genuine sympathy. "I lost my mother, my stepfather, my stepmother—I loved them all. You'll adjust, but you have to get through the grief process first. Tears are healing."

"Thanks."

"If you need to talk, I'm here. Anytime. Night or day."

Michelle wiped away more tears. "That's really nice of you."

"I know how it feels."

The phone rang and one of the employees called out. "For you, boss. The mayor returning your call."

Minette grimaced. "I have to take it. I'm working on a story about the new water system. It's going to be super."

"I'll see you after school Monday, then. And thanks again."

"My pleasure."

Michelle went home with dreams of journalism dancing in her head. She'd never been so happy. Things were really looking up.

She noted that Roberta's car was in the driveway and she mentally braced herself for a fight. It was suppertime and she hadn't been there to cook. She was going to be in big trouble.

Sure enough, the minute she walked in the door, Roberta threw her hands up and glared at her. "I'm not cooking," she said furiously. "That's your job. Where the hell have you been?"

Michelle swallowed. "I was in…in town."

"Doing what?" came the tart query.

She shifted. "Getting a job."

"A job?" She frowned, and her eyes didn't seem to quite focus. "Well, I'm not driving you to work, even if somebody was crazy enough to hire you!"

"I have a ride," she replied.

"A job," she scoffed. "As if you're ever around to do chores as it is. You're going to get a job? Who's going to do the laundry and the housecleaning and the cooking?"

Michelle bit her tongue, trying not to say what she was thinking. "I have to have money for lunch," she said, thinking fast.

Roberta blinked, then she remembered that she'd said Michelle wasn't getting any more lunch money. She averted her eyes.

"Besides, I have to save for college. I'll start in the fall semester."

"Jobs. College." Roberta looked absolutely furious. "And you think I'm going to stay down here in this hick town while you sashay off to college in some big city, do you?"

"I graduate in just over three months…"

"I'm putting the house on the market," Roberta shot back. She held up a hand. "Don't even bother arguing. I'm listing the house with a San Antonio broker, not one from here." She gave Michelle a dirty look. "They're all on your side, trying to keep the property off the market. It won't work. I need money!"

For just one instant, Michelle thought about letting her have the stamps. Then she decided it was useless to do that. Roberta would spend the money and still try to sell the house. She comforted herself with what the local Realtor had told her—that it would take time for the will to get through probate. If there was a guardian angel, perhaps hers would drag out the time required for all that. And even then, there was a chance the house wouldn't sell.

"I don't imagine a lot of people want to move to a town this small," Michelle said out loud.

"Somebody local might buy it. One of those ranchers." She made it sound like a dirty word.

That made Michelle feel better. If someone from here bought the house, they might consider renting it to her. Since she had a job, thanks to Minette, she could probably afford reasonable rent.

Roberta wiped her face. She was sweating.

Michelle frowned. "Are you all right?"

"Of course I'm all right, I'm just hungry!"

"I'll make supper." She went to her room to put her books away and stopped short. The place was in shambles. Drawers had been emptied, the clothes from the shelves in the closet were tossed haphazardly all over the floor. Michelle's heart jumped, but she noticed without looking too hard that the baseboards in the closet were still where they should be. She looked around but not too closely. After all, she'd told Roberta that Chief Grier had her father's stamp collection. It hadn't stopped Roberta from searching the room. But it was obvious that she hadn't found anything.

She went back out into the hall, where her stepmother was standing with folded arms, a disappointed look on her face. She'd expected that the girl would go immediately to where she'd hidden the stamps. The fact that she didn't even search meant they weren't here. Damn the luck, she really had taken them to the police chief. And even Roberta wasn't brash enough to walk up to Cash Grier and demand the stamp collection back, although she was probably within her legal rights to do so.

"Don't tell me," Michelle said, staring at her. "Squirrels?"

Roberta was disconcerted. Without meaning to, she burst out laughing at the girl's audacity. She turned away, shaking her head. "All right, I just wanted to make sure the stamp collection wasn't still here. I guess you were telling the truth all along."

"Roberta, if you need money so much, why don't you get a job?"

"I had a job, if you recall," she replied. "I worked in retail."

That was true. Roberta had worked at the cosmetics counter in one of San Antonio's most prestigious department stores.

"But I'm not going back to that," Roberta scoffed. "Once I sell this dump of a house, I'll be able to go to New York or Los Angeles and find a man who really is rich, instead of one who's just pretending to be," she added sarcastically.

"Gosh. Poor Bert," Michelle said. "Does he know?"

Roberta's eyes flashed angrily. "If you say a word to him…!"

Michelle held up both hands. "Not my business."

"Exactly!" Roberta snapped. "Now, how about fixing supper?"

"Sure," Michelle agreed. "As soon as I clean up my room," she added in a bland tone.

Her stepmother actually flushed. She took a quick breath. She was shivering. "I need…more…" she mumbled to herself. She went back into her own room and slammed the door.

They ate together, but Michelle didn't taste much of her supper. Roberta read a fashion magazine while she spooned food into her mouth.

"Where are you getting a job? Who's going to even hire a kid like you?" she asked suddenly.

"Minette Carson."

The magazine stilled in her hands. "You're going to work for a newspaper?"

"Of course. I want to study journalism in college."

Roberta looked threatened. "Well, I don't want you working for newspapers. Find something else."

"I won't," Michelle said firmly. "This is what I want to do for a living. I have to start somewhere. And I have to save for college. Unless you'd like to volunteer to pay my tuition…."

"Ha! Fat chance!" Roberta scoffed.

"That's what I thought. I'm going to a public college, but I still have to pay for books and tuition."

"Newspapers. Filthy rags." Her voice sounded slurred. She was picking at her food. Her fork was moving in slow motion. And she was still sweating.

"They do a great deal of good," Michelle argued. "They're the eyes and ears of the public."

"Nosy people sticking their heads into things that don't concern them!"

Michelle looked down at her plate. She didn't mention that people without things to hide shouldn't have a problem with that.

Roberta took her paper towel and mopped her sweaty face. She seemed disoriented and she was flushed, as well.

"You should see a doctor," Michelle said quietly. "There's that flu still going around."

"I'm not sick," the older woman said sharply. "And my health is none of your business!"

Michelle grimaced. She sipped milk instead of answering.

"It's too hot in here. You don't have to keep the thermostat so high!"

"It's seventy degrees," Michelle said, surprised. "I can't keep it higher or we couldn't afford the gas bill." She paid the bills with money that was grudgingly supplied by Roberta from the joint bank account she'd had with Michelle's father. Roberta hadn't lifted a finger to pay a bill since Alan had died.

"Well, it's still hot!" came the agitated reply. She got up from the table. "I'm going outside. I can't breathe in here."

Michelle watched her go with open curiosity. Odd. Roberta seemed out of breath and flushed more and more lately. She had episodes of shaking that seemed very unusual. She acted drunk sometimes, but Michelle knew she wasn't drinking. There was no liquor in the house. It probably was the flu. She couldn't understand why a person who was obviously sick wouldn't just go to the doctor in the first—

There was a loud thud from the general direction of the front porch.

Chapter 4

Michelle got up from her chair and went out onto the porch. It sounded as if Roberta had flung a chair against the wall, maybe in another outburst of temper.

She opened the door and stopped. Roberta was lying there, on her back on the porch, gasping for breath, her eyes wide, her face horrified.

"It's all right, I'll call 911!" She ran for the phone and took it outside with her while she pushed in the emergency services number.

Roberta was grimacing. "The pain!" she groaned. "Hurts…so…bad! Michelle…!"

Roberta held out her hand. Michelle took it, held it, squeezed it comfortingly.

"Jacobs County 911 Center," came a gentle voice on the line. "Is this an emergency?"

"Yes. This is Michelle Godfrey. My stepmother is

complaining of chest pain. She's short of breath and barely conscious."

"We'll get someone right out there. Stay on the line."

"Yes, of course."

"Help me," Roberta sobbed.

Michelle's hand closed tighter around her stepmother's. "The EMTs are on the way," she said gently. "It will be all right."

"Bert," Roberta choked. "Damn Bert! It's…his… fault!"

"Please don't try to get up," Michelle said, holding the older woman down. "Lie still."

"I'll…kill him," Roberta choked. "I'll kill him…!"

"Roberta, lie still," Michelle said firmly.

"Oh, God, it hurts!" Roberta sobbed. "My chest… my chest…!"

Sirens were becoming noticeable in the distance.

"They're almost there, dear," the operator said gently. "Just a few more minutes."

"Yes, I hear them," Michelle said. "She says her chest hurts."

There was muffled conversation in the background, on the phone.

Around the curve, the ambulance shot toward her leaving a wash of dust behind it. Roberta's grip on Michelle's hand was painful.

The older woman was white as a sheet. The hand Michelle was holding was cold and clammy. "I'm… sorry," Roberta bit off. Tears welled in her eyes. "He said it wasn't…pure! He swore…! It was too…much…" She gasped for breath. "Don't let Bert…get away…with it…" Her eyes closed. She shivered. The hand holding Michelle's went slack.

The ambulance was in the driveway now, and a man and a woman jumped out of it and ran toward the porch.

"She said her chest hurt." Michelle faltered as she got out of the way. "And she couldn't breathe." Tears were salty in her eyes.

Roberta had never been really kind to her, except at the beginning of her relationship with Michelle's father. But the woman was in such pain. It hurt her to see anyone like that, even a mean person.

"Is she going to be all right?" Michelle asked.

They ignored her. They were doing CPR. She recognized it, because one of the Red Cross people had come to her school and demonstrated it. In between compressions one EMT ran to the truck and came back with paddles. They set the machine up and tried to restart Roberta's heart. Once. Twice. Three times. In between there were compressions of the chest and hurried communications between the EMTs and a doctor at the hospital.

After a few minutes, one EMT looked at the other and shook his head. They stood up. The man turned to Michelle. "I'm very sorry."

"Sorry. Sorry?" She looked down at the pale, motionless woman on the dusty front porch with a blank expression. "You mean, she's…?"

They nodded. "We'll call the coroner and have him come out, and we'll notify the sheriff's department, since you're outside the city limits. We can't move her until he's finished. Do you want to call the funeral home and make arrangements?"

"Yes, uh, yes." She pushed her hair back. She couldn't believe this. Roberta was dead? How could she be dead?

She just stood there, numb, while the EMTs loaded up their equipment and went back out to the truck.

"Is there someone who can stay with you until the coroner gets here?" the female EMT asked softly, staring worriedly at Michelle.

She stared back at the woman, devoid of thought. Roberta was dead. She'd watched her die. She was in shock.

Just as the reality of the situation really started to hit her, a pickup truck pulled up into the driveway, past the EMT vehicle, and stopped. A tall, good-looking man got out of it, paused to speak to the male EMT and then came right up to the porch.

Without a word, he pulled Michelle into his arms and held her, rocked her. She burst into tears.

"I'll take care of her," he told the female EMT with a smile.

"Thanks," she said. "She'll need to make arrangements...."

"I'll handle it."

"We've notified the authorities," the EMT added. "The sheriff's department and the coroner should arrive shortly." The EMTs left, the ambulance silent and grim now, instead of alive with light and sound, as when it had arrived.

Michelle drank in the scent that clung to Gabriel, the smells of soap and spicy cologne, the leather smell of his jacket. Beneath that, the masculine odor of his skin. She pressed close into his arms and let the tears fall.

Zack Tallman arrived just behind the coroner. Michelle noted the activity on the front porch, but she didn't want to see Roberta's body again. She didn't go outside.

She heard Gabriel and the lawman and the coroner discussing things, and there was the whirring sound a camera made. She imagined that they were photographing Roberta. She shivered. It was so sudden. They'd just had supper and Roberta went outside because she was hot. And then Roberta was dead. It didn't seem real, somehow.

A few minutes later, she heard the coroner's van drive away. Gabriel and Zack Tallman came in together. Zack was handsome, tall, lean and good-looking. His eyes were almost as dark as Gabriel's, but he looked older than Gabriel did.

"The coroner thinks it was a heart attack," Zack was saying. "They'll have to do an autopsy, however. It's required in cases of sudden death."

"Hayes told me that Yancy Dean went back to Florida," Gabriel said. "He was the only investigator you had, wasn't he?"

"He was," Zack said, "so when he resigned, I begged Hayes on my knees for the investigator's position. It's a peach of a job."

"Pays about the same as a senior deputy," Gabriel mused, tongue in cheek.

"Yes, but I get to go to seminars and talk to forensic anthropologists and entomologists and do hard-core investigative work," he added. He chuckled. "I've been after Yancy's job forever. Not that he was bad at it—he was great. But his parents needed him in Florida and he was offered his old job back with Dade County SO," he added, referring to the sheriff's office.

"Well, it worked out for both of you, then," Gabriel said.

"Yes." He sobered as Michelle came into the living room from the kitchen. "Michelle, I'm sorry about your stepmother. I know it must be hard, coming so close on the heels of your father passing."

"Thanks, Mr. Tallman," she replied gently. "Yes, it is." She shook her head. "I still have to talk to the funeral director."

"I'll take care of that for you," Gabriel told her.

"Thanks," she added.

"Michelle, can you tell me how it happened?" Zack asked her.

"Of course." She went through the afternoon, ending with Roberta feeling too hot and going out on the porch to cool off.

He stopped her when she mentioned what Roberta had said about Bert and had her repeat Roberta's last words. He frowned. "I'd like to see her room."

Michelle led the way. The room was a mess. Roberta never picked anything up, and Michelle hadn't had time to do any cleaning. She was embarrassed at the way it looked. But Zack wasn't interested in the clutter. He started going through drawers until he opened the one in the bedside table.

He pulled out his digital camera and shot several photos of the drawer and its contents before he put on a pair of gloves, reached into it and pulled out an oblong case. He dusted the case for fingerprints before he opened it on the table and photographed that, too, along with a small vial of white powder. He turned to Gabriel who exchanged a long look with him.

"That explains a lot," Zack said. "I'll take this up to

the crime lab in San Antonio and have them run it for us, but I'm pretty sure what it is and where she got it."

"What is it?" Michelle asked, curious.

"Something evil," Zack said.

Michelle wasn't dense. "Drugs," she said icily. "It's drugs, isn't it?"

"Hard narcotics," Zack agreed.

"That's why she was so crazy all the time," Michelle said heavily. "She drank to excess when we lived in San Antonio. Dad got her into treatment and made her quit. I was sure she was okay, because we didn't have any liquor here. But she had these awful mood swings, and sometimes she hit me…" She bit her lip.

"Well, people under the influence aren't easy to live with," Zack replied heavily. "Not at all."

Zack sat down with Michelle and Gabriel at the kitchen table and questioned Michelle further about Roberta's recent routine, including trips to see Bert Sims in San Antonio. Roberta's last words were telling. He wrote it all down and gave Michelle a form to fill out with all the pertinent information about the past few hours. When she finished, he took it with him.

There was no real crime scene, since Roberta died of what was basically a heart attack brought on by a drug overdose. The coroner's assistant took photos on the front porch, adding to Zack's, so there was a record of where Roberta died. But the house wasn't searched, beyond Zack's thorough documentation of Roberta's room.

"Bert Sims may try to come around to see if Roberta had anything left, to remove evidence," Zack said solemnly to Michelle. "It isn't safe for you to be here alone."

"I've got that covered," Gabriel said with a smile. "Nobody's going to touch her."

Zack smiled. "I already had that figured out," he mused, and Gabriel cleared his throat.

"I have a chaperone in mind," Gabriel replied. "Just so you know."

Zack patted him on the back. "I figured that out already, too." He nodded toward Michelle. "Sorry again."

"Me, too," Michelle said sadly.

Michelle made coffee while Gabriel spoke to his sister, Sara, on the phone. She couldn't understand what he was saying. He was speaking French. She recognized it, but it was a lot more complicated than, "My brother has a brown suit," which was about her level of skill in the language.

His voice was low, and urgent. He spoke again, listened, and then spoke once more. *"C'est bien,"* he concluded, and hung up.

"That was French," Michelle said.

"Yes." He sat down at the table and toyed with the thick white mug she'd put in front of him. There was good china, too—Roberta had insisted on it when she and Alan first married. But the mug seemed much more Gabriel's style than fancy china. She'd put a mug at her place, as well. She had to have coffee in the morning or she couldn't even get to school.

"This morning everything seemed much less complicated," she said after she'd poured coffee. He refused cream and sugar, and she smiled. She didn't take them, either.

"You think you're going in a straight line, and life puts a curve in the way," he agreed with a faint smile.

"I know you didn't get along with her. But she was part of your family. It must sting a bit."

"It does," she agreed, surprised at his perception. "She was nice to me when she and Daddy were dating," she added. "Taught me how to cook new things, went shopping with me, taught me about makeup and stuff." She grimaced. "Not that I ever wear it. I hate the way powder feels on my face, and I don't like gunking up my eyes and mouth with pasty cosmetics." She looked at him and saw an odd expression on his face. "That must sound strange...."

He laughed and sipped coffee before he spoke. "Actually, I was thinking how sane it sounded." He quietly studied her for a couple of moments. "You don't need makeup. You're quite pretty enough without it."

She gaped at him.

"Michelle, *ma belle,*" he said in an odd, soft, deep tone, and he smiled.

She went scarlet. She knew her heart was shaking her to death, that he could see it, and she didn't care. He was simply the most gorgeous man she'd ever seen, and he thought she was pretty. A stupid smile turned her lips up, elongating the perfect bow shape they made.

"Sorry," he said gently. "I was thinking out loud, not hitting on you. This is hardly the time."

"Would you like to schedule a time?" she asked with wide, curious eyes. "Because my education in that department is really sad. This one boy tried to kiss me and missed and almost broke my nose. After that, I didn't get another date until the junior prom." She leaned forward. "He was gay and so sweet and shy about it...well, he asked me and told me the reason very honestly. And I said I'd go with him to the prom because of the way my other date had ended. I mean, he wasn't likely to try to kiss me and break my nose and all… Why are you laughing?"

"Marshmallow," he accused, and his smile was full of affectionate amusement.

"Well, yes, I guess I am. But he's such a nice boy. Several of us know about him, but there are these two guys on the football squad that he's afraid of. They're always making nasty remarks to him. He thought if he went with a girl to a dance, they might back off."

"Did they?" he asked, curious.

"Yes, but not because he went with me," she said. She glowered at the memory. "One of them made a nasty remark to him when we were dancing, next to the refreshment table, and I filled a big glass with punch and threw it in his face." She grinned. "I got in big trouble until the gym coach was told why I did it. His brother's gay." The grin got bigger. "He said next time I should use the whole pitcher."

He burst out laughing. "Well, your attitude toward modern issues is…unique. This is a very small town," he explained when her eyebrows went up.

"Oh, I see. You think we treat anybody different like a fungus." She nodded.

"Not exactly. But we hear things about small towns," he began.

"No bigots here. Well, except for Chief Grier."

He blinked. "Your police chief is a bigot?"

She nodded. "He is severely prejudiced against people from other planets. You should just hear him talk about how aliens are going to invade us one day to get their hands on our cows. He thinks they have a milk addiction, and that's why you hear about cattle mutilations… You're laughing again."

He wiped his eyes. She couldn't know that he rarely laughed. His life had been a series of tragedies. Humor had never been part of it. She made him feel light inside, almost happy.

"I can see the chief's point," he managed.

"Cow bigot," she accused, and he almost fell on the floor.

She wrapped her cold hands around her mug. "I guess I shouldn't be cracking jokes, with Roberta dead…" Her eyes burned with tears. "I still can't believe it. Roberta's gone. She's gone." She drew in a breath and sipped coffee. "We've done nothing but argue since Daddy died. But she wanted me to hold her hand and she was scared. She said she was sorry." She looked at him. "She said it was Bert's fault. Do you think she was delirious?"

"Not really," he replied quietly.

"Why?"

"That can wait a bit." He grew somber. "You don't have any other family?"

She shook her head. She looked around. "But surely I can stay here by myself? I mean, I'm eighteen now…"

He frowned. "I thought you were seventeen."

She hesitated. Her eyes went to the calendar and she grimaced. "I just turned eighteen. Today is my birthday," she said. She hadn't even realized it, she'd been so busy. Tears ran down her cheeks. "What an awful one this is."

He caught her hand in his and held it tight. "No cousins?"

She shook her head. "I have nobody."

"Not quite true. You have me," he said firmly. "And Sara's on her way down here."

"Sara. Your sister?"

He nodded.

"She'll stay with me?" she asked.

He smiled. "Not exactly. "You'll stay with us, in my house. I won't risk your reputation by having you move in with just me."

"But…we're strangers," she pointed out.

"No, we're not," he said, and he smiled. "I told you about my stepfather. That's a memory I've never shared with anyone. And you won't mention it to Sara, right?"

"Of course not." She searched his black eyes. "Why would you do this for me?"

"Who else is there?" he asked.

She searched her mind for a logical answer and couldn't find one. She had nobody. Her best friend, Amy, had moved to New York City with her parents during the summer. They corresponded, and they were still friends, but Michelle didn't want to live in New York, even if Amy's parents, with their five children, were to offer her a home.

"If you're thinking of the local orphanage," he said, tongue in cheek, "they draw the line at cow partisans."

She managed a laugh. "Oh. Okay."

"You can stay with us until you graduate and start college."

"I can't get in until fall semester, even if they accept me," she began.

"Where do you want to go?"

"Marist College in San Antonio. There's an excellent journalism program."

He pulled out his cell phone, punched a few buttons

and made a phone call. Michelle listened with stark shock. He was nodding, laughing, talking. Then he thanked the man and hung up.

"You called the governor," she said, dumbfounded.

"Yes. We were in the same fraternity in college. He's on the board of trustees at Marist. You're officially accepted. They'll send a letter soon."

"But they don't have my grades…!"

"They will have, by the time you go. What's on the agenda for summer?" he continued.

"I… Well, I have a job. Minette Carson hired me for the rest of the school year, after school and on Saturdays. And I'm sure she'll let me work this summer, so I can save for college."

"You won't need to do that."

"What?"

He shrugged. "I drive a truck here because it helps me fit in. But I have an apartment in San Antonio with a garage. In the garage, there's a brand-new Jaguar XKE." He raised an eyebrow. "Does that give you a hint about my finances?"

She had no idea what an XKE was, but she knew what a Jaguar was. She'd priced them once, just for fun. If it was new…gosh, people could buy houses around here for less, she thought, but she didn't say it.

"But, I'm a stranger," she persisted.

"Not for long. I'm going to petition the court to become your temporary legal guardian. Sara will go with us to court. You can wear a dress and look helpless and tragic and in desperate need of assistance." He pursed his lips. "I know, it will be a stretch, but you can manage it."

She laughed helplessly.

"Then we'll get you through school."

"I'll find a way to pay you back," she promised.

He smiled. "No need for that. Just don't ever write about me," he added. It sounded facetious, but he didn't smile when he said it.

"I'd have to make up something in order to do that." She laughed.

She didn't know, and he didn't tell her, that there was more to his life than she'd seen, or would ever see. Sara knew, but he kept his private life exactly that—private.

Just for an instant, he worried about putting her in the line of fire. He had enemies. Dangerous enemies, who wouldn't hesitate to threaten anyone close to him. Of course, there was Sara, but she'd lived in Wyoming for the past few years, away from him, on a ranch they co-owned. Now he was putting her in jeopardy along with Michelle.

But what could he do? The child had nobody. Now that her idiot stepmother was dead, she was truly on her own. It was dangerous for a young woman to live alone, even in a small community. And there was Roberta's boyfriend, Bert.

Gabriel knew things about the man that he wasn't eager to share with Michelle. The man was part of a criminal organization, and he knew Michelle's habits. He also had a yen for her, if what Michelle had blurted out to him once was true—and he had no indication that she would lie about it. He might decide to come and try his luck with her now that her stepmother was out of the picture. That couldn't be allowed.

He was surprised by his own affection for Michelle. It wasn't paternal. She was, of course, far too young for anything heavy, being eighteen to his twenty-four. She was a beauty, kind and generous and sweet. She was the sort of woman he usually ran from. No, strike that, she was no woman. She was still unfledged, a dove without flight feathers. He had to keep his interest hidden. At least, until she was grown up enough that it wouldn't hurt his conscience to pursue her. Afterward...well, who knew the future?

At the moment, however, his primary concern was to make sure she had whatever she needed to get through high school and, then, through college. Whatever it took.

Sara called him back. She wouldn't be able to get a flight to Texas for two days, which meant that Michelle would be on her own at night. Gabriel wasn't about to leave her, not with Bert Sims still out there. But he couldn't risk her reputation by having her stay alone with him.

"You don't want to be alone with me," Michelle guessed when he mentioned Sara's dilemma and frowned.

"It wouldn't look right," he said. "You have a spotless reputation here. I'm not going to be the first to put a blemish on it."

She smiled gently. "You're a very nice man."

He shrugged. "Character is important, regardless of the mess some people make of theirs in public and brag about it."

"My dad used to say that civilization rested on the bedrock of morality, and that when morality went, destruction followed," she recalled.

"A student of history," he said approvingly.

"Yes. He told me that first go the arts, then goes religion, then goes morality. After that, you count down the days until the society fails. Ancient Egypt. Rome. A hundred other governments, some more recently than others," she said.

"Who's right? I don't know. I like the middle of the road, myself. We should live the way that suits us and leave others to do the same."

She grinned. "I knew I liked you."

He chuckled. He finished his coffee. "We should stop discussing history and decide what to do with you tonight."

She stared at her own cooling coffee in the thick mug. "I could stay here by myself."

"Never," he said shortly. "Bert Sims might show up, looking for Roberta's leftovers, like Zack said."

She managed a smile. "Thanks. You could sleep in Roberta's room," she offered.

"Only if there's someone else in the house, too." He pursed his lips. "I have an idea." He pulled out his cell phone.

Carlie Blair walked in the door with her overnight bag and hugged Michelle close. "I'm so sorry," she said. "I know you and your stepmother didn't get along, but it's got to be a shock, to have it happen like that."

"It was." Michelle dashed away tears. "She apologized when she was dying. She said one other thing," she added, frowning, as she turned to Gabriel. "She said don't let Bert get away with it. You never told me what you thought that meant."

Gabriel's liquid black eyes narrowed. "Did she say anything else?"

She nodded slowly, recalling the odd statement. "She

said he told her it wasn't pure and he lied. What in the world did that mean?"

Gabriel was solemn. "That white powder in the vial was cocaine," he explained. "Dealers usually cut it with something else, dilute it. But if it's pure and a user doesn't know, it can be lethal if they don't adjust the dose." He searched Michelle's eyes. "I'm betting that Bert gave her pure cocaine and she didn't know."

Carlie was surprised. "Your stepmother was using drugs?" she asked her friend.

"That's what they think," Michelle replied. She turned back to Gabriel. "Did he know it was pure? Was he trying to kill her?"

"That's something Zack will have to find out."

"I thought he cared about her. In his way," she faltered.

"He might have, even if it was only because she was a customer."

Michelle bit her lower lip. "That would explain why she was so desperate for money. I did wonder, you know, because she didn't buy new clothes or expensive cosmetics or things like she used to when Daddy was alive." She frowned. "She never bought anything, but she never had any money and she was always desperate for more. Like when she tried to sell my father's stamp collection."

"It's a very expensive habit," Gabriel said quietly.

"But…Bert might have meant to kill her…?"

"It's possible. Maybe she made threats, maybe she tried to quit or argued over the price. But, whether he meant to kill her or not, he's going to find himself in a lot of hot water pretty soon."

"Why?" Michelle asked curiously

He grimaced. "I'm sorry. That's all I can say. This is more complicated than it seems."

She sighed. "Okay. I won't pry. Keep your secrets." She managed a smile. "But don't you forget that I'm a reporter in training," she added. "One day, I'll have learned how to find out anything I want to know." She grinned.

"Now you're scaring me," he teased.

"Good."

He just shook his head. "I have to go back to my place and get a razor. I'll be right back. Lock the door," he told Michelle, "and don't open it for anybody. If Bert Sims shows up, you call me at once. Got that?"

"Got it," she said.

"Okay."

He left. Carlie got up from the sofa, where she'd been perched on the arm, and hugged Michelle. "I know this is hard for you. I'm so sorry."

"Me, too." Michelle gave way to tears. "Thanks for coming over. I hope I'm not putting you in any danger."

"Not me," Carlie said. "And neither of us is going to be in danger with that tall, dark, handsome man around. He is so good-looking, isn't he?" she added with a theatrical sigh.

Michelle dried her tears. "He really is. My guardian angel."

"Some angel."

She tried to think of something that might restore a little normalcy into her routine. Roberta was lying heavily on her mind. "I have to do dishes. Want to dry?"

"You bet!"

Chapter 5

Carlie and Michelle shared the double bed in Michelle's room, while Gabriel slept in Roberta's room. Michelle had insisted on changing the bed linen first. She put Roberta's clothes in the washing machine, the ones that had been scattered all over the room. When she'd washed them, she planned to donate them to charity. Michelle couldn't have worn them even if she'd liked Roberta's flamboyant style, which she didn't.

The next morning, Gabriel went to the local funeral home and made the arrangements for Roberta. She had an older sister in Virginia. The funeral home contacted her, but the woman wanted nothing to do with any arrangements. She and Roberta had never gotten along, and she couldn't care less, she said, whether they cremated her or buried her or what. Gabriel arranged for her to be cremated, and Reverend Blair offered a plot in the cemetery of his church for her to be interred. There would be no funeral service, just a graveside one. Michelle thought they owed her that much, at least.

Reverend Blair had invited Michelle to come and stay at his house with Carlie, but Michelle wanted familiar things around her. She also wanted Gabriel, on whom she had come to rely heavily. But she couldn't stay with Gabriel alone. It would not look right in the tiny community of Comanche Wells, where time hadn't moved into the twenty-first century yet.

"Sara will be here tomorrow," Gabriel told the girls as they sat down to supper, which Michelle and Carlie had prepared together. He smiled as he savored hash browns with onions, perfectly cooked, alongside a tender cut of beef and a salad. "You two can cook," he said with admiration. "Hash browns are hard to cook properly. These are wonderful."

"Thanks," they said in unison, and laughed.

"She did the hash browns," Carlie remarked, grinning at Michelle. "I never could get the hang of them. Mine just fall apart and get soggy."

"My mother used to make them," Michelle said with a sad smile. "She was a wonderful cook. I do my best, but I'm not in her league."

"Where do your parents live, Gabriel?" Carlie asked innocently.

Gabriel's expression went hard.

"I made a cherry pie for dessert," Michelle said, quickly and neatly deflecting Carlie's question. "And we have vanilla ice cream to go on it."

Carlie flushed, realizing belatedly that she'd made a slight faux pas with her query. "Michelle makes the best cherry pie around," she said with enthusiasm.

Gabriel took a breath. "Don't look so guilty," he told Carlie, and smiled at her. "I'm touchy about my past, that's all. It was a perfectly normal question."

"I'm sorry, just the same," Carlie told him. "I get nervous around people and I babble." She flushed again. "I don't…mix well."

Gabriel laughed softly. "Neither do I," he confessed.

Michelle raised her hand. "That makes three of us," she remarked.

"I feel better," Carlie said. "Thanks," she added, intent on her food. "I have a knack for putting my foot into my mouth."

"Who doesn't?" Gabriel mused.

"I myself never put my foot into my mouth," Michelle said, affecting a haughty air. "I have never made a single statement that offended, irritated, shocked or bothered a single person."

The other two occupants of the table looked at her with pursed lips.

"Being perfect," she added with a twinkle in her eyes, "I am unable to understand how anyone could make such a mistake."

Carlie picked up her glass of milk. "One more word…" she threatened.

Michelle grinned at her. "Okay. Just so you remember that I don't make mistakes."

Carlie rolled her eyes.

It was chilly outside. Michelle sat on the porch steps, looking up at the stars. They were so bright, so perfectly clear in cold weather. She knew it had something to do with the atmosphere, but it was rather magical. There was a dim comet barely visible in the sky. Michelle had looked at it through a pair of binoculars her father had given her. It had been winter, and most hadn't been visible to the naked eye.

The door opened and closed behind her. "School is going to be difficult on Monday," she said. "I dread it. Everyone will know…you sure you don't mind giving me rides home after work?" she added.

"That depends on where you want to go," came a deep, amused masculine voice from behind her.

She turned quickly, shocked. "Sorry," she stammered. "I thought you were Carlie."

"She found a game show she can't live without. She's sorry." He chuckled.

"Do you like game shows?" she wondered.

He shrugged. He came and sat down beside her on the step. He was wearing a thick black leather jacket with exquisite beadwork. She'd been fascinated with it when he retrieved it from his truck earlier.

"That's so beautiful," she remarked, lightly touching the colorful trim above the long fringes with her fingertips. "I've never seen anything like it."

"Souvenir from Canada," he said. "I've had it for a long time."

"The beadwork is gorgeous."

"A Blackfoot woman made it for me," he said.

"Oh." She didn't want to pursue that. The woman he mentioned might have been a lover. She didn't want to think of Gabriel with a woman. It was intensely disturbing.

"My cousin," he said, without looking down at her. "She's sixty."

"Oh." She sounded embarrassed now.

He glanced at her with hidden amusement. She was

so young. He could almost see the thoughts in her mind. "You need somebody young to cut your teeth on, kid. They'd break on my thick hide."

She flushed and started to jump up, but he caught her hand in his big, warm one, and pulled her gently back down.

"Don't run," he said softly. "No problem was ever solved by retreat. I'm just telling you how it is. I'm not involved with anyone. I haven't been for years. You're a bud, just opening on a rosebush, testing the air and the sunlight. I like my roses in full bloom."

"Oh."

He sighed. His fingers locked into hers. "These one syllable answers are disturbing," he mused.

She swallowed. The touch of his big, warm hand was causing some odd sensations in her young body. "I see."

"Two syllables. Better." He drew in a long breath. "Until you graduate, we're going to be living in close proximity, even with Sara in the house. I'll be away some of the time. My job takes me all over the world. But there are going to have to be some strict ground rules when I'm home."

"Okay," she faltered. "What?"

"No pajamas or nightgowns when you walk around the house. You put them on when you go to bed, in your room. No staying up late alone. Stuff like that."

She blinked. "I feel like Mata Hari."

"You feel like a spy? An old one, at that." He chuckled.

"A femme fatale, then," she amended. "Gosh, I don't even own pajamas or a gown…"

"You don't wear clothes in bed?" He sounded shocked.

"Oh, get real," she muttered, glad he couldn't see her face. "I wear sweats."

"To bed?" he exclaimed.

"They're comfortable," she said. "Nobody who wanted a good night's sleep ever wore a long gown, they just twist you up and constrict you. And pajamas usually have lace or thick embroidery. It's irritating to my skin."

"Sweats." Of all the things he'd pictured his young companion in at night, that was the last thing.

She looked down at his big hand in the light from the living room. It burned out onto the porch like yellow sun in the darkness, making shadows of the chairs behind them on the dusty boards of the porch. He had good hands, big and strong-looking, with square nails that were immaculate. "I guess the women you know like frilly stuff."

They did, but he wasn't walking into that land mine. He turned her hand in his. "Do you date?"

Her heart jumped. "Not since the almost-broken-nose thing."

He laughed softly. "Sorry. I forgot about that."

"There aren't a lot of eligible boys in my school who live in the dark ages like I do," she explained. "At least two of the ones who go to my church are wild as bucks and go to strip parties with drugs." She grimaced. "I don't fit in. Anywhere. My parents raised me with certain expectations of what life was all about." She turned to look at him. "Is it wrong, to have a belief system? Is it wrong to think morality is worth something?"

"Those are questions you should be asking Carlie's dad," he pointed out.

"Do you believe in...in a higher power?"

His fingers contracted around hers. "I used to."

"But not anymore?"

His drawn breath was audible. "I don't know what I believe anymore, *ma belle*," he said softly. "I live in a world you wouldn't understand, I go to places where you couldn't survive."

"What kind of work do you do?" she asked.

He laughed without humor. "That's a discussion we may have in a few years."

"Oh, I see." She nodded. "You're a cannibal."

He stilled. "I'm…a what?"

"Your work embarrasses you," she continued, unabashed, "which means you don't work in a bank or drive trucks. If I had a job that embarrassed me, it would be involved with cannibalism."

He burst out laughing. "Pest," he muttered.

She grinned.

His big thumb rubbed her soft fingers. "I haven't laughed so much in years, as I do with you."

She chuckled. "I might go on the stage. If I can make a hardcase like you laugh, I should be able to do it for a living."

"And here I thought you wanted to be a reporter."

"I do," she said. She smiled. "More than anything. I can't believe I'm actually going to work for a newspaper starting Monday," she said. "Minette is getting me my own cell phone and she's going to teach me to use a camera…it's like a dream come true. I only asked her for a reference for college. And she offered me a job." She shook her head. "It's like a dream."

"I gather you'll be riding with Carlie."

"Yes. I'm going to help with gas."

He was silent for a minute. "You keep your eyes open on the road, when you're coming home from work."

"I always do. But why?"

"I don't trust Roberta's boyfriend. He's dangerous. Even Carlie is in jeopardy because of what happened to her father, so you both have to be careful."

"I don't understand why someone would want to harm a minister," she said, shaking her head. "It makes no sense."

He turned his head toward her. "Michelle, most ministers started out as something else."

"Something else?"

"Yes. In other words, Reverend Blair wasn't always a reverend."

She hesitated, listening to make sure Carlie wasn't at the door. "What did he do before?" she asked.

"Sorry. That's a confidence. I never share them."

She curled her hand around his. "That's reassuring. If I ever tell you something dreadful in secret, you won't go blabbing it to everyone you know."

He laughed. "That's a given." His hand contracted. "The reverse is also applicable," he added quietly. "If you overhear anything while you're under my roof, it's privileged information. Not that you'll hear much that you can understand."

"You mean, like when you were talking to Sara in French," she began.

"Something like that." His eyes narrowed. "Did you understand what I said?"

"I can say, where's the library and my brother has a brown suit," she mused. "Actually, I don't have a brother, but that was in the first-year French book. And it's about the scope of my understanding. I love languages, but I have to study very hard to learn anything."

He relaxed a little. He'd said some things about Michelle's recent problems to Sara that he didn't want her to know. Not yet, anyway. It would sound as if he were gossiping about her to his sister.

"The graveside service is tomorrow," she said. "Will Sara be here in time, do you think?"

"She might. I'm having a car pick her up at the airport and drive her down here."

"A car?"

"A limo."

Her lips parted. "A limousine? Like those long, black cars you see politicians riding around in on television? I've only seen one maybe once or twice, on the highway when I was on the bus!"

He laughed softly at her excitement. "They also have sedans that you can hire to transport people," he told her. "I use them a lot when I travel."

He was talking about another world. In Michelle's world, most cars were old and had plenty of mechanical problems. She'd never even looked inside a limousine. She'd seen them on the highway in San Antonio. Her father told her that important businessmen and politicians and rich people and movie stars rode around in them. Not ordinary people. Of course, Gabriel wasn't ordinary. He'd said he owned a new Jaguar. Certainly he could afford to ride in a limousine.

"Do you think they'd let me look inside, when it brings her here?" she asked.

Gabriel was amused at her innocence. She knew nothing of the world at large. He couldn't remember being that young, or that naive about life. He hoped she wouldn't grow up too quickly. She made him feel more masculine, more capable, more intriguing than he really was. He liked her influence. She made him laugh. She made him want to be all the things she thought he was.

"Yes," he said after a minute. "Certainly you can look inside."

"Something to put in my diary," she mused.

"You keep a diary?" he asked, with some amusement.

"Oh, yes," she said. "I note all the cows I've seen abducted, and the strange little men who come out of the pasture at night…"

"Oh, cool it." He chuckled.

"Actually, it's things like how I did on tests, and memories I have of my father and mother," she confessed. "And how I feel about things. There's a lot about Roberta and Bert in there, and how disgusting I thought they were," she added.

"Well, Roberta's where she can't hurt you. And Bert is probably trying to find a way out of the country, if he's smart."

"What do you mean?" she asked.

He stood up and pulled her up beside him. "That's a conversation for another time. Let's go see if Carlie's game show is off."

"Don't you like game shows?" she wondered aloud.

"I like the History Channel, the Nature Channel, the Military Channel, and the Science Channel."

"No TV shows?"

"They're not TV shows. They're experiments in how to create attention deficit disorders in the entire population with endless commercials and ads that pop up right in the middle of programs. I only watch motion pictures or DVDs, unless I find something interesting enough to suffer through. I like programs on World War II history and science."

She pondered that. "I guess there's five minutes of program to fifteen minutes of commercials," she agreed.

"As long as people put up with it, that will continue, too." He chuckled. "I refuse to be part of the process."

"I like history, too," she began.

"There was this big war…" he began with an exaggerated expression.

She punched his arm affectionately. "No cherry pie and ice cream for you."

"I take it back."

She grinned up at him. "Okay. You can have pie and ice cream."

He smiled and opened the door for her.

She hesitated in the opening, just staring up at him, drinking in a face that was as handsome as any movie star's, at the physique that could have graced an athlete.

"Stop ogling me, if you please," he said with exaggerated patience. "You have to transfer that interest to someone less broken."

She made a face at him. "You're not broken," she pointed out. "Besides, there's nobody anywhere who could compare with you." She flushed at her own boldness. "Anyway, you're safe to cut my teeth on, and you know it." She grinned. "I'm off-limits, I am."

He laughed. "Off-limits, indeed, and don't you forget it."

"Spoilsport."

She went inside ahead of him. He felt as if he could fly. Dangerous, that. More dangerous, his reaction to her. She was years too young for anything more than banter. But, he reminded himself, the years would pass. If he lived long enough, after she graduated from college, who knew what might happen?

There was a grim memorial service at the Comanche Wells Cemetery. It was part of the land owned by the Methodist church where Reverend Blair was the minister. He stood over the small open grave, with an open Bible in his hands, reading the service for the dead. The urn containing Roberta's ashes was in the open grave, waiting for the funeral home's maintenance man, standing nearby, to close after the ceremony.

Gabriel stood beside Michelle, close, but not touching. He was wearing a suit, some expensive thing that fit him with delicious perfection. The navy darkness of the suit against the spotless white shirt and blue patterned tie only emphasized his good looks. His wavy black hair was unruly in the stiff breeze. Michelle's own hair was tormented into a bun because of the wind. But it blew tendrils down into her eyes and mouth while she tried to listen to the service, while she tried even harder to feel something for the late Roberta.

It was sad that the woman's own sister didn't care enough to even send a flower. Total strangers from Jacobs County had sent sprays and wreathes and potted plants to the funeral home that had arranged for the cremation. The flowers were spread all around the grave. Some of them would go to the local hospital and nursing home in Jacobsville, others for the evening church service here. A few of the potted plants would go home with Michelle.

She remembered her father, and how much he'd been in love with Roberta at first. She remembered Roberta in the days before Bert. More recently, she remembered horrible arguments and being slapped and having Roberta try to sell the very house under her feet. There had been more bad times than good.

But now that part of her life was over. She had a future that contained Gabriel, and the beginning of a career as a journalist. It was something to look forward to, something to balance her life against the recent death of her father and Roberta's unexpected passing.

Sara's plane had been held up due to an electrical fault. She'd phoned Gabriel just before he and Michelle went to the funeral with Carlie, to apologize and give an updated arrival time. Michelle looked forward to meeting her. From what Gabriel had said about his sister, she sounded like a very sweet and comfortable person.

Reverend Blair read the final verses, closed the Bible, bowed his head for prayer. A few minutes later, he paused to speak to Michelle, where she stood with Gabriel and Carlie, thanking the few local citizens who'd taken time to attend. There hadn't been time for the newspaper to print the obituary, so services had been announced on the local radio station. Everybody listened to it, for the obituaries and the country-western music. They also listened for the school closings when snow came. That didn't happen often, but Michelle loved the rare times when it did.

"I'm sorry for your loss," Reverend Blair said, holding Carlie's hand and smiling gently. "No matter how contrary some people are, we get used to having them in our lives."

"That's true," Michelle said gently. "And my father loved her," she added. "For a time, she made him happy." She grimaced. "I just don't understand how she changed so much, so quickly. Even when she drank too much…" she hesitated, looking around to make sure she wasn't overheard before she continued, "she was never really mean."

Gabriel and the minister exchanged enigmatic glances.

Michelle didn't notice. Her eyes were on the grave. "And she said not to let Bert get away with it," she added slowly.

"There are some things going on that you're better off not knowing about," Reverend Blair said softly. "You can safely assume that Bert will pay a price for what he did. If not in this life, then in the next."

"But what did he do?" Michelle persisted.

"Bad things." Reverend Blair smiled.

"My sister will be here in an hour," Gabriel said, reading the screen of his cell phone, with some difficulty because of the sun's glare. He grinned at the reverend. "You can have your daughter back tonight."

Reverend Blair grinned. "I must say, I miss the little touches. Like clean dishes and laundry getting done." He made a face. "She's made me lazy." He smiled with pure affection at his daughter, who grinned.

"I'll make you fresh rolls for supper," Carlie promised him.

"Oh, my, and I didn't get you anything," he quipped.

She hugged him. "You're just the best dad in the whole world."

"Pumpkin, I'm glad you think so." He let her go. "If you need anything, you let us know, all right?" he asked Michelle. "But you're in good hands." He smiled at Gabriel.

"She'll be safe, at least." Gabriel gave Reverend Blair

a complicated look. "Make sure about those new locks, will you? I've gotten used to having you around."

The other man made a face. "Locks and bolts won't keep out the determined," he reminded him. "I put my trust in a higher power."

"So do I," Gabriel replied. "But I keep a Glock by the bed."

"Trust in Allah, but tie up your camel."

Everybody looked at Michelle, who blushed.

"Sorry," she said. "I was remembering something I read in a nonfiction book about the Middle East. It was written by a former member of the French Foreign Legion."

Now the stares were more complicated, from the two males at least.

"Well, they fascinate me," she confessed, flushing a little. "I read true crime books and biographies of military men and anything I can find about the Special Air Services of Great Britain and the French Foreign Legion."

"My, my," Gabriel said. He chuckled with pure glee, a reaction that was lost on Michelle.

"I lead a sheltered life." Michelle glanced at the grave. The maintenance man, a little impatient, had started to fill the grave. "We should go."

"Yes, we should." Reverend Blair smiled. "Take care."

"Thanks. The service was very nice," Michelle said.

"I'm glad you thought so."

Gabriel took her arm and led her back to the car. He drove her home first, so that she could change back into more casual clothes and get her overnight bag. Then he drove her to his own house, where Sara was due to arrive any minute.

Michelle had this picture of Sara. That she'd be dark-haired and dark-eyed, with a big smile and a very tender nature. Remembering what Gabriel had told her in confidence, about the perils Sara had survived when they were in school, she imagined the other woman would be a little shy and withdrawn.

So it came as something of a shock when a tall, beautiful woman with long black hair and flashing black eyes stepped out of the back of the limousine and told the driver where he could go and how fast.

Chapter 6

"I am very sorry, lady," the driver, a tall lanky man, apologized. "I truly didn't see the truck coming..."

"You didn't look!" she flashed at him in a terse but sultry tone. "How dare you text on your cell phone while driving a customer!"

He was very flushed by now. "I won't do it again, I swear."

"You won't do it with me in the car, and I am reporting you to the company you work for," she concluded.

Gabriel stepped forward as the driver opened the trunk. He picked up the single suitcase that Sara had brought with her. Something in the way Gabriel looked at the man had him backing away.

"Very sorry, again," he said, flustered. "If you'd just sign the ticket, ma'am..."

He fetched a clipboard and handed it to her, eyeing

Gabriel as if he expected him to leap on him any second. Sara signed it. The man obviously knew better than to look for a tip. He nodded, turned, jumped into the car and left a trail of dust as he sped away.

"That could have gone better," Sara said with a grim smile. She hugged Gabriel. "So good to see you again."

"You, too," he replied. His face changed as he looked at the younger woman. He touched her hair. "You only grow more beautiful with age."

"You only think so because you're my brother." She laughed musically. She looked past him at Michelle, who stood silent and wary.

"And you must be Michelle." Sara went to her, smiled and hugged her warmly. "I have a nasty temper. The silly man almost killed us both, texting some woman."

"I'm so glad he didn't," Michelle said, hugging her back. "It's very kind of both of you to do this for me," she added. "I…really don't have anyplace to go. I mean, the Reverend Blair said I could stay with him and Carlie, but…"

"You certainly do have someplace to go," Gabriel said with a grin. "Sara needed the change of scenery. She was vegetating up in Wyoming."

Sara sighed. "In a sense, I suppose so, although I like it better there than in British Columbia. I left our foreman in charge at the ranch in Catelow. That's in Wyoming," Sara told Michelle with a smile. "Anything that needs doing for the sale, I can do online." Her black eyes, so like Gabriel's, had a sad cast. "The change of scenery will do me good. I love to ride. Do you?" she asked the younger woman.

"I haven't been on a horse in years," Michelle confessed. "Mostly, horses try to scrape me off or dislodge me. I'm sort of afraid of them."

"My horses are very tame," Gabriel told her. "They'll love you."

"I hope you have coffee made," Sara sighed as they made their way into the sprawling house. "I'm so tired! Flying is not my favorite mode of travel."

"I've never even been on a plane," Michelle confessed.

Sara stopped and stared at her. "Never?"

"Never."

"She wanted to look inside the limo." Gabriel chuckled. "She's never seen one of those, either."

"I'm so sorry!" Sara exclaimed. "I made a fuss…"

"You should have made a fuss," Michelle replied. "There will be other times."

"I'll make sure of that." Sara smiled, and it was like the sun coming out.

School had been rough in the days after Roberta's death. People were kind, but there were so many questions about how she died. Gossip ran rampant. One of the girls she sat near in history class told her that Roberta's boyfriend was a notorious drug dealer. At least two boys in their school got their fixes from him.

Now the things Roberta had said started to make sense. And Michelle was learning even more about the networks and how they operated from Minette since she'd started working for the Jacobsville newspaper.

"It's a vile thing, drug dealing," Minette said harshly. "Kids overdose and die. The men supplying the drugs don't even care. They only care about the profit." She hesitated. "Well, maybe some of them have good intentions…"

"A drug dealer with good intentions?" Michelle laughed. "You have got to be kidding."

"Actually, I'm not. You've heard of the man they call El Jefe?"

"Who hasn't?" Michelle replied. "We heard that he helped save you and Sheriff Carson," she added.

"He's my father."

Michelle gaped at her. "He's...?"

"My father," Minette repeated. "I didn't know who my real father was until very recently. My life was in danger, even more than Hayes's was when he was shot, because my father was in a turf war with a rival who was the most evil man I ever knew."

"Your life is like a soap opera," Michelle ventured.

Minette laughed. "Well, yes, it is."

"I wish mine was more exciting. In a good way," she clarified. She drew in a long breath. "Okay, what about this camera?" she asked. It had more dials and settings than a spaceship.

"I know, it's a little intimidating. Let me show you how it works."

She did. It took a little time, and when they finished, a phone call was waiting for Minette. She motioned to Michelle. "I have a new reporter. I'm going to let her take this down, if you don't mind. Her name is Michelle....That's right. It's a deal. Thanks!" She put her hand over the receiver so that the caller wouldn't hear. "This is Ben Simpson. He's our Jacobs County representative in District 3 for the Texas Soil and Water Conservation Board. He wants us to do a story on a local rancher who won Rancher of the Year for the Jacobs County Soil and Water Conservation District for his implementation of natural grasses and ponds. The award was made just before Christmas, but the rancher has been out of the country until now. I'm going to let you take down the details, and then I'll send you out to his ranch to take a photo of him with the natural grasses in the background. Are you up to it?" she teased.

Michelle was almost shaking, but she bit her lip and nodded. "Yes, ma'am," she said.

Minette grinned. "Go for it!"

Michelle was used to taking copious notes in school. She did well in her schoolwork because she was thorough. She took down the story, pausing to clarify the spelling of names, and when she was through she had two sheets of notes and she'd arranged a day and time to go out to photograph the rancher.

She hung up. Minette was still in the doorway. "Did I do that okay?" she asked worriedly.

"You did fine. I was listening on the other phone. I took notes, too, just in case. You write the story and we'll compare your notes to mine."

"Thanks!" Michelle said fervently. "I was nervous."

"No need to be. You'll do fine." She indicated the computer at the desk. "Get busy." She smiled. "I like the way you are with people, even on the phone. You have an engaging voice. It will serve you well in this business."

"That's nice of you to say," Michelle said.

"Write the story. Remember, short, concise sentences, nothing flowery or overblown. I'll be out front if you need me."

She started to thank Minette again, but it was going to get tedious if she kept it up, so she just nodded and smiled.

* * *

When she turned in the story, she stood gritting her teeth while Minette read it and compared it with her own notes.

"You really are a natural," she told the younger woman. "I couldn't have done better myself. Nice work."

"Thank you!"

"Now go home," she said. "It's five, and Carlie will be peeling rubber any minute to get home."

Michelle laughed. "I think she may. I'll see you tomorrow, then. Do I go out to photograph the man tomorrow, too?"

"Yes."

Michelle bit her lip. "But I don't have a license or own a car…there's only Roberta's and she didn't leave it to me. I don't think she even had a will…and I can't ask Carlie to take off from work…." The protests came in small bursts.

"I'll drive you out there," Minette said softly. "We might drop by some of the state and federal offices and I'll introduce you to my sources."

"That sounds very exciting! Thanks!" She sounded relieved, and she was.

"One more thing," Minette said.

"Yes?"

"I'm printing the conservation story under your own byline."

Michelle caught her breath. "My first one. That's so kind of you."

"You'll have others. This is just the first." She grinned. "Have a good night."

"I will. Sara's making homemade lasagna. It's my favorite."

"Sara?"

"Gabriel's sister. She's so beautiful." Michelle shook her head. "The two of them have been lifesavers for me. I didn't want to have to pick up and move somewhere else. I couldn't have stayed here to finish school without them."

"Not quite true," Minette replied. "You could have come to us. Even Cash Grier mentioned that they could make room for you, if you needed a place to stay."

"So many," Michelle said, shaking her head. "They hardly know me."

"They know you better than you think," was the reply. "In small communities like ours, there are no secrets. Your good deeds are noted by many."

"I guess I lived in the city for too long. Daddy had patients but no real friends, especially after Roberta came into our lives. It was just the three of us." She smiled. "I love living here."

"So do I, and I've been here all my life." She cocked her head. "Gabriel seems an odd choice to be your guardian. He isn't what you think of as a family man."

"He's not what he seems," Michelle replied. "He was kind to me when I needed it most." She made a face. "I was sitting in the middle of the road hoping to get hit by a car. It was the worst day of my life. He took me home with him and talked to me. He made everything better. When Roberta…died…he was there to comfort me. I owe him a lot. He even got Sara down here to live with him so that he could be my legal guardian with no raised eyebrows around us."

Minette simply said, "I see." What she did see, she

wasn't going to share. Apparently Gabriel had a little more than normal interest in this young woman, but he wasn't going to risk her reputation. It was going to be all by the book. Minette wondered what he had in mind for Michelle when she was a few years older. And she also wondered if Michelle had any idea who Gabriel really was, and how he earned his living. That was a secret she wasn't going to share, either. Not now.

"Well, I'll see you tomorrow, then," Michelle added.

"Tomorrow."

Carlie was waiting for her at the front door the next morning, which was Friday. She looked out of breath.

"Is something wrong?" Michelle asked.

"No. Of course not. Let's go."

Carlie checked all around the truck and even looked under it before she got behind the wheel and started it.

"Okay, now, what's going on?" Michelle asked.

"Daddy got a phone call earlier," Carlie said, looking both ways before she pulled carefully out of the driveway.

"What sort of call?"

"From some man who said Daddy might think he was out of the woods, but somebody else was coming to pay him a visit, and he'll never see it coming." She swallowed. "Daddy told me to check my truck out before I drove it. I forgot, so I looked underneath just in case." She shook her head. "It's like a nightmare," she groaned. "I have no idea in this world why anyone would want to harm a minister."

"It's like our police chief said," Michelle replied quietly. "There are madmen in the world. I guess you can't ever understand what motivates them to do the things they do."

"I wish things were normal again," Carlie said in a sad tone. "I hate having to look over my shoulder when I drive and look for bombs under my car." She glanced at Michelle. "I swear, I feel like I'm living in a combat zone."

"I know the feeling, although I've never been in any real danger. Not like you." She smiled. "Don't you worry. I'll help you keep a lookout."

"Thanks." She smiled. "It's nice, having someone to ride with me. These back roads get very lonely."

"They do, indeed." Michelle sighed as she looked out over the barren flat landscape toward the horizon as the car sped along. "I just wrote my first story for the newspaper," she said with a smile. "And Minette is taking me out to introduce me to people who work for the state and federal government. It's the most exciting thing that's ever happened to me," she added, her eyes starry with pleasure. "I get my own byline." She shook her head. "It really is true…"

"What's true?" Carlie asked.

"My dad said that after every bad experience, something wonderful happens to you. It's like you pay a price for great happiness."

"I see what you mean." She paused. "I really do."

Minette drove Michelle out to the Patterson ranch, to take photographs for her story and to see the rancher's award for conservation management. She also wanted a look at his prize Santa Gertrudis bull. The bull had been featured in a cattle magazine because he was considered one of the finest of his breed, a stud bull whose origins, like all Santa Gertrudis, was the famous King Ranch in Texas. It was a breed native to Texas that had resulted from breeding Shorthorn and Hereford cattle with Brahman cattle. The resulting breed was named for the Spanish land grant where Richard King founded the cattle empire in the nineteenth century: Santa Gertrudis.

Wofford Patterson was tall, intimidating. He had jet-black hair, thick and straight, and an olive complexion. His eyes, surprisingly, were such a pale blue that they seemed to glitter like Arctic ice. He had big hands and big feet and his face looked as if it had been carved from solid stone. It was angular. Handsome, in its way, but not conventionally handsome.

There were scars on his hands. Michelle stared at them as she shook his hand, and flushed when she saw his keen, intelligent eyes noting the scrutiny.

"Sorry," she said, although she hadn't voiced her curiosity.

"I did a stint with the FBI's Hostage Rescue Team," he explained, showing her the palms of both big hands. "Souvenirs from many rappels down a long rope from a hovering chopper," he added with a faint smile. "Even gloves don't always work."

Her lips fell open. This was not what she'd expected when Minette said they'd take pictures of a rancher. This man wasn't what he appeared to be.

"No need to look threatened," he told her, and his pale eyes twinkled as he shoved his hands into the pockets of his jeans. "I don't have arrest powers anymore." He scowled. "Have you done something illegal? Is that why you look intimidated?"

"Oh, no, sir," she said quickly. "It's just that I was

listening for the sound of helicopters." She smiled vacantly.

He burst out laughing. He glanced at Minette. "I believe you said she was a junior reporter? You didn't mention that she was nuts, did you?"

"I am not nuts, I have read of people who witnessed actual alien abductions of innocent cows," she told him solemnly. But her eyes were twinkling, like his.

"I haven't witnessed any," he replied, "but if I ever do, I'll phone you to come out and take pictures."

"Would you? How kind!" She glanced at Minette, who was grinning from ear to ear. "Now about that conservation award, Mr. Patterson…"

"Mr. Patterson was my father," he corrected. "And he was Mister Patterson, with a capital letter. He's gone now, God rest his soul. He was the only person alive I was really afraid of." He chuckled. "You can call me Wolf."

"Wolf?"

"Wofford…Wolf," he said. "They hung that nickname on me while I worked for the Bureau. I have something of a reputation for tracking."

"And a bit more," Minette interrupted, tongue in cheek.

"Yes, well, but we mustn't put her off, right?" he asked in return, and he grinned.

"Right."

"Come on and I'll show you Patterson's Lone Pine Red Diamond. He won a 'bull of the year' award for conformation, and I'm rolling in the green from stud fees. He has nicely marbled fat and large—" he cleared his throat "—assets."

Minette glanced at Michelle and shook her head

when Wolf wasn't looking. Michelle interpreted that as an "I'll tell you later" look.

The bull had his own stall in the nicest barn Michelle had ever seen. "Wow," she commented as they walked down the bricked walkway between the neat wooden stalls. There was plenty of ventilation, but it was comfortably warm in here. A tack room in back provided any equipment or medicines that might be needed by the visiting veterinarian for the livestock in the barn.

There were two cows, hugely pregnant, in two of the stalls and a big rottweiler, black as coal, lying just in front of the tack room door. The animal raised his head at their approach.

"Down, Hellscream," he instructed. The dog lay back down, wagging its tail.

"Hellscream?" Michelle asked.

He grinned. "I don't have a social life. Too busy with the bloodstock here. So in my spare time, I play World of Warcraft. The leader of the Horde—the faction that fights the Alliance—is Garrosh Hellscream. I really don't like him much, so my character joined the rebellion to throw him out. Nevertheless, he is a fierce fighter. So is my girl, there," he indicated the rottweiler. "Hence, the name."

"Winnie Kilraven's husband is a gaming fanatic," Minette mused.

"Kilraven plays Alliance," Wolf said in a contemptuous tone. "A Paladin, no less." He pursed his lips. "I killed him in a battleground, doing player versus player. It was very satisfying." He grinned.

"I'd love to play, but my husband is addicted to the Western Channel on TV when he's not in his office being the sheriff," Minette sighed. "He and the kids watch cartoon movies together, too. I don't really mind. But gaming sounds like a lot of fun."

"Trust me, it is." Wolf stopped in front of a huge, sleek red-coated bull. "Isn't he a beaut?" he asked the women, and actually sighed. "I'd let him live in the house, but I fear the carpets would never recover."

The women looked at each other. Then he laughed at their expressions, and they relaxed.

"I read about a woman who kept a chicken inside once," Michelle said with a bland expression. "I think they had to replace all the carpets, even though she had a chicken diaper."

"I'd like to see a cow diaper that worked." Wolf chuckled.

"That's a product nobody is likely to make," Michelle said.

"Can we photograph you with the bull?" Michelle asked.

"Why not?"

He went into the stall with the bull and laid his long arm around his neck. "Smile, Red, you're going to be even more famous," he told the big animal, and smoothed his fur.

He and the bull turned toward the camera. Michelle took several shots, showing them to Minette as they went along.

"Nice," Minette said. She took the digital camera, pulled up the shots, and showed them to Wolf.

"They'll do fine," Wolf replied. "You might want to mention that the barn is as secure as the White House, and anyone who comes here with evil intent will end up in the backseat of a patrol car, handcuffed." He pursed his lips. "I still have my handcuffs, just in case."

"We'll mention that security is tight." Minette laughed.

"He really is a neat bull," Michelle added. "Thanks for letting us come out and letting us take pictures."

He shrugged broad shoulders. "No problem. I'm pretty much available until next week."

"What happens next week?" Michelle asked.

"A World Event on World of Warcraft," he mused. "The 'Love Is in the Air' celebration. It's a hoot."

"A world event?" Michelle asked, curious.

"We have them for every holiday. It's a chance for people to observe them in-game. This is the equivalent of Valentine's Day." He laughed. "There's this other player I pal around with. I'm pretty sure she's a girl. We do battlegrounds together. She gets hung on trees, gets lost, gets killed a lot. I enjoy playing with her."

"Why did you say that you think she's a girl?" Michelle asked.

"People aren't what they seem in video games," he replied. "A lot of the women are actually men. They think of it as playing with a doll, dressing her up and stuff."

"What about women, do they play men?" she persisted.

He laughed. "Probably. I've come across a few whose manners were a dead giveaway. Women are mostly nicer than some of the guys."

"What class is your Horde character?" Minette broke in.

"Oh, you know about classes, huh?"

"Just what I overheard when Kilraven was raving about them to my husband," she replied, chuckling.

"I play a Blood Elf death knight," he said. "Two-handed sword, bad attitude, practically invincible."

"What does the woman play?" Michelle asked, curious.

"A Blood Elf warlock. Warlocks cast spells. Deadliest class there is, besides mages," he replied. "She's really good. I've often wondered where she lives. Somewhere in Europe, I think, because she's on late at night, when most people in the States are asleep."

"Why are you on so late yourself?" Michelle asked.

He shrugged. "I have sleep issues." And for an instant, something in his expression made her think of wounded things looking for shelter. He searched her eyes. "You're staying with the Brandons, aren't you?"

"Well, yes," she said hesitantly.

He nodded. "Gabriel's a good fellow." His face tautened. "His sister, however, could drop houses on people."

She stared at him. "Excuse me?"

"I was backing out of a parking space at the county courthouse and she came flying around the corner and hit the back end of my truck." He was almost snarling. "Then she gets out, cussing a blue streak, and says it's my fault! She was the one speeding!"

Michelle almost bit her tongue off trying not to say what she was thinking.

"So your husband—" he nodded to Minette "—comes down the courthouse steps and she's just charming to him, almost in tears over her poor car, that I hit!" He made a face. "I get hit with a citation for some goldarned thing, and my insurance company has to fix her car and my rates go up."

"Was that before or after you called her a broom-riding witch and indicated that she didn't come from Wyoming at all, but by way of Kansas…?"

"Sure, her and the flying monkeys," he muttered.

Michelle couldn't keep from laughing. "I'm sorry," she defended herself. "It was the flying monkey bit…" She burst out laughing again.

"Anyway, I politely asked her which way she was going and if she was coming back to town, so I could park my truck somewhere while she was on the road. Set her off again. Then she started cussing me in French. I guess she thought some dumb country hick like me wouldn't understand her."

"What did you do?" Michelle asked.

He shrugged. "Gave it back to her in fluent and formal French. That made her madder, so she switched to Farsi." He grinned. "I'm also fluent in that, and I know the slang. She called on the sheriff to arrest me for obscenity, but he said he didn't speak whatever language we were using so he couldn't arrest me." He smiled blithely. "I like your husband," he told Minette. "He was nice about it, but he sent her on her way. Her parting shot, also in Farsi, was that no woman in North America would be stupid enough to marry a man like me. She said she'd rather remain single forever than to even consider dating someone like me."

"What did you say to her then?" Michelle wanted to know.

"Oh, I thanked her."

"What?" Minette burst out.

He shrugged. "I said that burly masculine women didn't appeal to me whatsoever, and that I'd like a nice wife who could cook and have babies."

"And?" Minette persisted.

"And she said I wanted a malleable female I could chain to the bed." He shook his head.

"What did you say about that?"

"I said it would be too much trouble to get the stove in there."

Michelle almost doubled up laughing. She could picture Sara trying to tie this man up in knots and failing miserably. She wondered if she dared repeat the conversation when she got home.

Wolf anticipated her. He shook his finger at her. "No carrying tales, either," he instructed. "You don't arm the enemy."

"But she's nice," she protested.

"Nice. Sure she is. Does she keep her pointed hat in the closet or does she wear it around the house?" he asked pleasantly.

"She doesn't own a single one, honest."

"Make her mad," he invited. "Then stand back and watch the broom and the pointy hat suddenly appear."

"You'd like her if you got to know her," Michelle replied.

"No, thank you. No room in my life for a woman who shares her barn with flying monkeys."

Michelle and Minette laughed all the way back to the office.

"Oh, what Sara's missing," Minette said, wiping tears of mirth from her eyes. "He's one of a kind."

"He really is."

"I wish I could tell her what he said. I wouldn't dare. She's already scored a limousine driver. I expect she could strip the skin off Wofford Patterson at ten paces."

"A limousine?"

Michelle nodded. "The driver was texting someone at the wheel and almost wrecked the car. She reported him to the agency that sent him."

"Good for her," Minette said grimly. "There was a wreck a few months ago. A girl was texting a girlfriend and lost control of the car she was driving. She killed a ten-year-old boy and his grandmother who were walking on the side of the road."

"I remember that," Michelle said. "It was so tragic."

"It's still tragic. The girl is in jail, pending trial. It's going to be very hard on her parents, as well as those of the little boy."

"You have sympathy for the girl's parents?" Michelle ventured.

"When you work in this business for a while, you'll learn that there really are two sides to every story. Normal people can do something impulsive and wrong and end up serving a life term. Many people in jail are just like you and me," she continued. "Except they have less control of themselves. One story I covered, a young man had an argument with his friend while he was skinning a deer they'd just killed in the woods. Impulsively, he stabbed his friend with the knife. He cried at his trial. He didn't mean to do it. He had one second of insanity and it destroyed his life. But he was a good boy. Never hurt an animal, never skipped school, never did anything bad in his life. Then he killed his best friend on an impulse that he regretted immediately."

"I never thought of it like that," Michelle said, dazed.

"Convicted felons have families," she pointed out. "Most of them are as normal as people can be. They go to church, give to charity, help their neighbors, raise good children. They have a child do something stupid and land in jail. They're not monsters. Although I must confess I've seen a few parents who should be sitting in jail." She shook her head. "People are fascinating to me, after all these years." She smiled. "You'll find that's true for you, as well."

Michelle leaned back. "Well, I've learned something. I've always been afraid of people in jail, especially when they work on the roadways picking up trash."

"They're just scared kids, mostly," Minette replied. "There are some bad ones. But you won't see them out on the highways. Only the trusted ones get to do that sort of work."

"The world is a strange place."

"It's stranger than you know." Minette chuckled. She pulled up in front of the newspaper office. "Now, let's get those photos uploaded and cropped and into the galleys."

"You bet, boss," Michelle said with a grin. "Thanks for the ride, too."

"You need to learn to drive," Minette said.

"For that, you need a car."

"Roberta had one. I'll talk to Blake Kemp. He's our district attorney, but he's also a practicing attorney. We'll get him going on probate for you."

"Thanks."

"Meanwhile, ask Gabriel about teaching you. He's very experienced with cars."

"Okay," she replied. "I'll ask him." It didn't occur to her to wonder how Minette knew he was experienced with cars.

Chapter 7

"No, no, no!" Gabriel said through gritted teeth. "Michelle, if you want to look at the landscape, for God's sake, stop and get out of the car first!"

She bit her lower lip. "Sorry. I wasn't paying attention."

The truck, his truck, was an inch away from going into a deep ditch.

"Put it in Reverse, and back up slowly," he instructed, forcing his voice to seem calm.

"Okay." She did as instructed, then put it in gear, and went forward very slowly. "How's this?"

"Better," he said. He drew in a breath. "I don't understand why your father never taught you."

Mention of her father made her sad. "He was too busy at first and then too sick," she said, her voice strained. "I wanted to learn, but I didn't pester him."

"I'm sorry," he said deeply. "I brought back sad memories for you."

She managed a faint smile. "It's still not that long since he, well, since he was gone," she replied. She couldn't bring herself to say "died." It was too harsh a word. She concentrated on the road. "This is a lot harder than it looks," she said. She glanced up in the rearview mirror. "Oh, darn."

He glanced behind them. A car was speeding toward them, coming up fast. The road was straight and clear, however. "Just drive," he told her. "He's got plenty of room to pass if he wants to."

"Okay."

The driver slowed down suddenly, pulled around them and gave her a sign that made her flush.

"And that was damned well uncalled for," Gabriel said shortly. He pulled out his cell phone, called the state highway police, gave them the license plate number and offered to press charges if they caught the man. "She's barely eighteen and trying to learn to drive," he told the officer he was speaking to. "The road was clear, he had room to pass. He was just being a jerk because she was female."

He listened, then chuckled. "I totally agree. Thanks."

He closed the cell phone. "They're going to look for him."

"I hope they explain manners to him. So many people seem to grow up without any these days," she sighed. She glanced at her companion. It had made him really angry, that other man's rudeness.

He caught her staring. "Watch the road."

"Sorry."

"What's wrong?"

"Nothing. I was just…well, it was nice of you, to care that someone insulted me."

"Nobody's picking on you while I'm around," he said with feeling.

She barely turned her head and met his searching black eyes. Her heart went wild. Her hands felt like ice on the wheel. She could barely get her breath.

"Stop that," he muttered, turning his head away. "You'll kill us both."

She cleared her throat. "Okay."

He drew in a breath. "You may be the death of me, anyway," he mused, giving her a covert glance. She was very pretty, with her blond hair long, around her shoulders, with that creamy complexion and those soft gray eyes. He didn't dare pay too much attention. But when she was fully grown, she was going to break hearts. His jaw tautened. He didn't like to think about that, for some reason.

"Now make a left turn onto the next road. Give the signal," he directed. "That's right. Look both ways. Good. Very good."

She grinned. "This is fun."

"No, fun is when you streak down the interstate at a hundred and twenty and nobody sees you. That's fun."

"You didn't!" she gasped.

He shrugged. "Jags like to run. They purr when you pile on the gas."

"They do not."

"You'll see." He smiled to himself. He already had plans for her graduation day. He and Sara had planned it very well. It was only a couple of months away. He glanced at his companion. She was going to be absolutely stunned when she knew what they had in mind.

* * *

The piece on Wofford Patterson ran with Michelle's byline, along with photos of his native grasses, his water conservation project and his huge bull. People she didn't even know at school stopped her in the hall to talk to her. And not only other students. Teachers paid her more attention, as well. She felt like a minor celebrity.

"I actually had someone to sit with at lunch," she told Sara, all enthusiasm, when she got home from school that day. "Mostly I'm always by myself. But one little article in the paper with my name and just look!"

Sara managed a smile. "It was well written. You did a good job. Considering the material you had to work with," she added with smoldering black eyes.

Then Michelle remembered. Wofford Patterson. Mortal enemy. Sara's nemesis.

"Sorry," she said, flushing.

"The man is a total lunatic," Sara muttered, slamming pans around as she looked for something to boil pasta in. Her beautiful complexion was flushed. "He backed into me and tried to blame me for it! Then he said I rode a broom and kept flying monkeys in the barn!"

Michelle almost bit through her lower lip. She couldn't laugh. She couldn't laugh…

Sara glanced at her, rolled her eyes, and dragged out a big pot. "You like him, I gather?"

"Well, he didn't accuse me of keeping flying monkeys," Michelle said reasonably. "He's very handsome, in a rough-cut sort of way, and he loves animals."

"Probably because he is one," Sara said under her breath.

"He has this huge rottweiler. You wouldn't believe what he calls her!"

"Have you seen my hammer?" Gabriel interrupted suddenly.

Both women turned.

"Don't you keep it in the toolbox?" Michelle asked.

"Yes. Where's my toolbox?" he amended.

The two women looked at each other blankly. Then Sara flushed.

"I, uh, had to find a pair of pliers to turn the water spigot on outside. Not my fault," she added. "You have big hands and when you turn the water off, I can't turn it back on. I took the whole toolbox with me so I'd have access to whatever I needed."

"No problem. But where is it?" Gabriel added.

"Um," Sara frowned. "I think I remember...just a sec." She headed out the back door.

"Don't, for God's sake, tell her the name of Patterson's dog!" Gabriel said in a rough whisper.

She stared at him. "Why?"

He gave her a speaking look. "Who do you think Patterson's unknown buddy in World of Warcraft is?" he asked patiently.

Her eyes widened with glee. "You mean, they're buddies online and they don't know it?"

"In a nutshell." He grinned. "Two lonely people who can't stand each other in person, and they're soul mates online. Let them keep their illusions, for the time being."

"Of course." She shook her head. "She'd like him if she got to know him."

"I know. But first impressions die hard."

Sara was back, carrying a beat-up brown toolbox.

"Here." She set it down on the table. "Sorry," she added sheepishly.

"I don't mind if you borrow stuff. Just put it back, please." He chuckled.

She shrugged. "Sometimes I do. I'm just scatter-brained."

"Listen," he said, kissing the top of her head, "nobody who speaks six languages fluently could even remotely be called scatterbrained. You just have a lot on your mind all the time."

"What a nice way to put it. No wonder you're my favorite brother!"

He gave Michelle a droll look.

"Well, if I had other brothers, you'd still be my favorite," Sara amended.

"Are we going to drive some more today?" Michelle asked him hopefully.

"Maybe tomorrow," he said after a minute. He forced a smile. He left, quickly.

Michelle sighed. "I can't follow orders," she explained while Sara put water on to boil and got out spaghetti.

"He's just impatient," Sara replied. "He always was, even when we were kids." She shook her head. "Some habits you never grow out of."

Michelle knew a lot about Sara, and her childhood. But she was too kindhearted to mention any of what Gabriel had told her. She just smiled and asked what she could do to help.

Graduation was only days away. So much had happened to Michelle that she could hardly believe how quickly the time had gone by. Marist College had accepted her, just as Gabriel had told her. She was scheduled for orientation in August, and she'd already had a conversation online with her faculty advisor.

"I'm so excited," she told Gabriel. They were sitting on the front porch, watching a meteor shower. There were a couple of fireballs, colorful and rare. "I'll be in college. I can't believe it."

He smiled. "You'll grow. College changes people. You see the world in a different way when you've studied courses like Western Civilization and math."

"I'm not looking forward to the math," she sighed. "People say college trig is a nightmare."

"Only if you don't have a tutor."

"But I don't…"

He glanced down at her. "I made straight A's."

"Oh." She grinned. "Okay. Thanks in advance."

He stretched. "No problem. Maybe you'll do better at math than you do at driving."

She thumped his arm. "Stop that. I can drive."

"Sort of."

"It takes practice," she reminded him. "How can I practice if you're always too busy to ride in the truck with me?"

"You could ask Sara," he pointed out.

She glowered at him. "I did."

"And?"

"She's always got something ready to cook." She pursed her lips. "In fact, she has pots and pans lined up, ready, in case I look like I'm even planning to ask her to ride with me." Her eyes narrowed suspiciously. "I have reason to believe you've been filling her head with irrelevant facts about how many times I've run into ditches."

"Lies."

"It was only one ditch," she pointed out.

"That reminds me." He pulled out his cell phone and checked a text message. He nodded. "I have a professional driving instructor coming out to work with you, starting Saturday afternoon."

"Coward," she accused.

He grinned. "I don't teach."

"I thought you were doing very well, except for the nonstop cursing."

"I thought you were doing well, except for the nonstop near accidents."

She threw up her hands and sighed. "Okay. Just push me off onto some total stranger who'll have a heart attack if I miss a turn. His family will sue us and we'll end up walking everywhere…"

He held up a hand. "I won't change my mind. I can't teach you how to drive with any efficiency. These people have been doing it for a long time."

She gave in. "Okay. I'll give it a shot." She looked up at him. "You and Sara are coming to graduation, aren't you?"

He smiled down at her. "I wouldn't miss it for the whole world, *ma belle*."

Her heart jumped up into her throat. She could walk on air, because Gabriel teased her in that deep, soft tone that he used only with her.

He touched her long hair gently. "You're almost grown. Just a few more years."

"I'm eighteen."

He let go of her hair. "I know." He turned away. She was eighteen years old. Years too young for what he was thinking of. He had to let her go, let her grow, let her mature. He couldn't hold her back out of selfishness. In a few years, when she was through college, when she had a good job, when she could stand alone—then, yes, perhaps. Perhaps.

"You're very introspective tonight," she remarked.

"Am I?" He chuckled. "I was thinking about cows."

"Cows?"

"It's a clear night. If a UFO were to abduct a cow, we would probably see it."

"How exciting! Let's go looking for them. I'll drive!"

"Not on your life, and don't you have homework? Finals are coming up, I believe?"

She made a face. "Yes, they are, and I can't afford to make a bad grade." She glanced at him. "Spoilsport."

He shrugged. "I want you to graduate."

She folded her hands on her jeans-clad thighs. "I've never told you how much I appreciate all you and Sara have done for me," she said quietly. "I owe you so much…"

"Stop that. We were happy to help."

It had just occurred to her that she was going away, very soon, to college. She was going to live in the dormitory there. She wouldn't live with Sara and Gabriel again. Her holidays would be spent with fellow students, if anyone even stayed on campus—didn't the campus close for holidays?

"I can see the wheels turning," he mused, glancing down at her. "You'll come to us for holidays and vacations," he said. "Sara and I will be here. At least until you're through college. Okay?"

"But Sara has a place in Wyoming—" she began.

"We have a place in Wyoming, and we have a competent manager in charge of it," he interrupted. "Besides, she likes it here in Texas."

"I did notice she was up very late last night on the computer," she said under her breath.

"New expansion on her game," he whispered. "She and her unknown pal are running battlegrounds together. She's very excited."

Michelle laughed softly. "We should probably tell her."

"No way. It's the first time I've seen her happy, really happy, in many years," he said wistfully. "Dreams are precious. Let her keep them."

"I suppose it won't hurt," she replied. "But she's not getting a lot of sleep."

"She hasn't slept well in a long time, despite therapy and prescriptions. This gaming might actually solve a few problems for her."

"You think?"

"We can wait and see, at least." He glanced at his watch, the numbers glowing in the darkness. "I have some paperwork to get through. You coming in?"

"In just a minute. I do love meteor showers."

"So do I. If you like astronomy, we'll have to buy a telescope."

"Could we?" she asked enthusiastically.

"Of course. I'll see about it."

"I would love to look at Mars!"

"So would I."

"I would love to go there," she ventured.

He shrugged. "Not going to happen."

"It was worth a try."

He chuckled, ruffled her hair and went back inside.

* * *

Graduation day was going to be long and exciting. Michelle had gone to the rehearsal, which had to be held inside because it was pouring rain that day. She had hoped it wouldn't rain on graduation day.

Her gown and cap fit perfectly. She wasn't going to graduate with honors, but she was at least in the top 10 percent of her class. Her grades had earned her a small scholarship, which would pay for textbooks. She didn't want Gabriel and Sara to be out of pocket on her account, regardless of their financial worth.

Her gown was white. It made her look almost angelic, with her long blond hair down to her waist, her peaches-and-cream complexion delicately colored, her gray eyes glittering with excitement.

She didn't see Gabriel and Sara in the audience, but that wasn't surprising. There was a huge crowd. They were able to graduate outside because the skies cleared up. They held the graduation ceremonies on the football field, with faculty and students and families gathered for the occasion.

Michelle accepted her diploma from the principal, grinned at some of her fellow students and walked off the platform. On the way down, she remembered what a terrifying future she was stepping into. For twelve years, she'd gone to school every day—well, thirteen years if you counted kindergarten. Now, she was free. But with freedom came responsibility. She had to support herself. She had to manage an apartment. She had to pay bills....

Maybe not the bills part, totally. She would have to force Gabriel and Sara to let her pay rent. That would help her pride. She'd go off to college, to strangers, to a dormitory that might actually be unisex. That was a scary thought.

She ran to Gabriel and Sara, to be hugged and congratulated.

"You are now a free woman." Sara chuckled. "Well, mostly. Except for your job, and college upcoming."

"If it's going to be a unisex dorm…" Michelle began worriedly.

"It's not," Gabriel assured her. "Didn't you notice? It's a Protestant college. They even have a chaplain."

"Oh. Oh!" She burst out laughing, and flushed. "No, I didn't really notice, until I thought about having to share my floor with men who are total strangers."

"No way would that happen," Gabriel said solemnly, and his dark eyes flashed. "I'd have you driven back and forth first."

"So would I," Sara agreed. "Or I'd move up to San Antonio, get an apartment and you could room with me."

Tears stung Michelle's cheeks. She was remembering how proud her father had been of her grades and her ambitions, how he'd looked forward to seeing her graduate. He should have been here.

"Now, now," Gabriel said gently, as if he could see the thoughts in her mind. He brushed the tears away and kissed her eyelids closed. "It's a happy occasion," he whispered.

She was tingling all over from the unexpectedly intimate contact. Her heart went wild. When he drew back, everything she felt and thought was right there, in her eyes. His own narrowed, and his tall, muscular body tensed.

Sara coughed. She coughed again, to make sure they heard her.

"Lunch," Gabriel said at once, snapping out of it. "We have reservations."

"At one of the finest restaurants in the country, and we still have to get to the airport."

"Restaurant? Airport?" Michelle was all at sea.

Gabriel grinned. "It's a surprise. Someone's motioning to you." He indicated a female student who was waving like crazy.

"It's Yvonne," Michelle told them. "I promised to have my picture taken with her and Gerrie. They were in my geography class. Be right back!"

They watched her go, her face alive with pleasure.

"Close call, masked man," Sara said under her breath.

He stuffed his hands into his slacks and his expression hardened.

"You have to be patient," Sara added gently, and touched his chest with a small hand. "Just for a little while."

"Just for years," he said curtly. "While she meets men and falls in love...."

"Fat chance."

He turned and looked down at her, his face guarded but full of hope.

"You know how she feels," Sara said softly. "That isn't going to change. But she has to have time to grow up, to see something of the world. The time will pass."

He grimaced and then drew in a breath. "Yes. I suppose so." He laughed hollowly. "Maybe in the meantime, I can work up to how I'm going to explain my line of work to her. Another hurdle."

"By that time, she'll be more likely to understand."

He nodded. "Yes."

She hugged him impulsively. "You're a great guy. She already knows it."

He hugged her back. "I'll be her best friend."

"You already are." She drew back, smiling. The smile faded and her eyes sparked with temper as she looked past him.

"My, my, did you lose your broom?" came a deep, drawling voice from behind Gabriel.

"The flying monkeys are using it right now," Sara snarled at the tall man. "Are you just graduating from high school, too?" she added. "And I didn't get you a present."

He shrugged. "My foreman's daughter graduated. I'm her godfather."

"So many responses come to mind. But choosing just one," she pondered for a minute. She pursed her full lips. "Do you employ a full-time hit man, or do you have to manage with pickups?"

He raised his thick eyebrows. "Oh, full-time, definitely," he said easily, hands deep in his jean pockets. He cocked his head. "But he doesn't do women. Pity."

Sara was searching for a comeback when Michelle came running back.

"Oh, hi, Mr. Patterson!" she said with a grin. "How's that bull doing?"

"Eating all he can get and looking better by the day, Miss Godfrey," he replied, smiling. "That was a good piece you wrote on the ranch."

"Thanks. I had good material to work with."

Sara made a sound deep in her throat.

"What was that? Calling the flying monkeys in some

strange guttural language?" Wolf asked Sara with wide, innocent eyes.

She burst out in Farsi, things that would have made Michelle blush if she understood them.

"Oh, my, what a thing to say to someone!" Wolf said with mock surprise. He looked around. "Where's a police officer when you need one?"

"By all means, find one who speaks Farsi," Sara said with a sarcastic smile.

"Farsi?" Jacobsville police chief Cash Grier strolled up with his wife, Tippy. "I speak Farsi."

"Great. Arrest her," Wolf said, pointing at Sara. "She just said terrible things about my mother. Not to mention several of my ancestors."

Cash glanced at Sara, who was glowering at Wolf, and totally unrepentant.

"He started it," Sara said angrily. "I do not ride a broom, and I have never seen a flying monkey!"

"I did, once," Cash said, nodding. "Of course, a man threw it at me..."

"Are you going to arrest her?" Wolf interrupted.

"You'd have to prove that she said it," Cash began.

"Gabriel heard her say it," Wolf persisted.

Cash looked at Gabriel. So did Sara and Michelle and Tippy.

"I'll burn the pasta for a week," Sara said under her breath.

Gabriel cleared his throat. "Gosh, I'm sorry," he said. "I wasn't paying attention. Would you like to say it again, and this time I'll listen?" he asked his sister.

"Collusion," Wolf muttered. He glowered at Sara. "I still have my handcuffs from my FBI days..."

"How very kinky," Sara said haughtily.

Cash turned away quickly. His shoulders were shaking.

Tippy hit him.

He composed himself and turned back. "I'm sorry, but I really can't be of any assistance in this particular matter. Congratulations, Michelle," he added.

"Thanks, Chief Grier," she replied.

"Why are you here?" Wolf asked the chief.

"One of my young brother-in-law's older gaming friends is graduating," he replied with a smile. "We came to watch him graduate." He shook his head. "He's awesome at the Halo series on Xbox 360."

"So am I," Wolf said with a grin. He glanced at Gabriel. "Do you play?"

Gabriel shook his head. "I don't really have time."

"It's fun. I like console games. But I also like…" Wolf began.

"The reservations!" Gabriel interrupted, checking his watch. "Sorry, but we've got a flight to catch. Graduation present," he added with a grin and a glance at Michelle. "See you all later."

"Sure," Wolf replied. He glanced at Sara and his eyes twinkled. "An airplane, huh? Having mechanical problems with the broom…?"

"We have to go, right now," Gabriel said, catching Sara before she could move toward Wolf.

He half dragged her away, to the amusement of the others.

"You should have let me hit him," Sara fumed as they sat comfortably in the business-class section of an aircraft bound for New Orleans. "Just one little slap…"

"In front of the police chief, who would have been obliged to arrest you," Gabriel pointed out. "Not a good thing on Michelle's graduation day."

"No." She smiled at Michelle, who looked as amused as Gabriel did. "Sorry. That man just rubs me the wrong way."

"It's okay," Michelle said. "I can't believe we're flying to New Orleans for lunch." She laughed, shaking her head. "I've never been on a plane before in my life. The takeoff was so cool!" she recalled, remembering the burst of speed, the clouds coming closer, the land falling away under the plane as she looked out the window. They'd given her the window seat, so that she had a better view.

"It was fun, seeing it through your eyes," Sara replied, smiling. "I tend to take it for granted. So does he." She indicated Gabriel, who laughed.

"I spend most of my life on airplanes, of one type or another," Gabriel confessed. "I must admit, my flights aren't usually this relaxed."

"You never did tell me what you do," Michelle said.

"I'm sort of a government contractor," he said easily. "An advisor. I go lots of places in that capacity. I deal with foreign governments." He made it sound conventional. It really wasn't.

"Oh. Like businessmen do."

"Something like that," he lied. He smiled. "You have your first driving lesson tomorrow," he reminded her.

"Sure you wouldn't like to do it instead?" she asked. "I could try really hard to avoid ditches."

He shook his head. "You need somebody better qualified than I am."

"I hope he's got a good heart."

"I'm sure he'll be personable…"

"I hope he's in very good health," she amended. Gabriel just chuckled.

They ate at a five-star restaurant downtown. The food was the most exquisite Michelle had ever tasted, with a Cajun spiced fare that teased the tongue, and desserts that almost made her cry they were so delicious.

"This is one of the best restaurants I've ever frequented," Gabriel said as they finished second cups of coffee. "I always stop by when I'm in the area." He looked around at the elegant decor. "They had some problems during Hurricane Katrina, but they've remodeled and regrouped. It's better than ever."

"It was delicious," Michelle said, smiling. "You guys are spoiling me rotten."

"We're enjoying it," Sara replied. "And there's an even bigger surprise waiting when we get home," she added.

"Another one? But this was the best present I've ever had! You didn't need to…"

"Oh, but we did," Gabriel replied. He leaned back in his chair, elegant in a navy blue jacket with a black turtleneck and dark slacks. Sara was wearing a simple black dress with pearls that made her look both expensive and beautiful. Michelle, in contrast, was wearing the only good dress she had, a simple sheath of off-white, with her mother's pearls. She felt dowdy compared to her companions, but they didn't even seem to notice that the dress was old. They made her feel beautiful.

"What is it?" Michelle asked suddenly.

She was met with bland smiles.

"Wait and see," Gabriel said with twinkling black eyes.

Chapter 8

It was very late when they got back to the ranch. There, sitting in the driveway, was a beautiful little white car with a big red ribbon tied around it.

Michelle gaped at it. Her companions urged her closer.

She touched the trunk, where a sleek silver Jaguar emblem sat above the keyhole.

"It's a Jag," she stammered.

"It's not the most expensive one," Sara said quickly when Michelle gave them accusing glances. "In fact, it's a midrange automobile. But it's one of the safest cars on the road. Which is why we got it for you. Happy Graduation!"

She hugged Michelle.

"It's too much," Michelle stammered, touching the body with awe. She fought tears. "I never dreamed…

Oh, it's so…beautiful!" She turned and threw herself into Sara's arms, hugging her close. "I'll take such good care of it! I'll polish it by the inch, with my own hands…!"

"Don't I get a hug, too? It was my idea," Gabriel said.

She laughed, turned and hugged him close. "Of course you do. Thank you! Gosh, I never dreamed you'd get me a car as a present!"

"You needed one," Gabriel said at the top of her head. "You have to be able to drive to work for Minette in the summer. And you'll need one to commute from college to home on weekends. If you want to come home that often," he added.

"Why would I want to stay in the city when I can come down here and ride horses?" she asked, smiling up at him. He was such a dish, she thought dreamily.

Gabriel looked back at her with dark, intent eyes. She was beautiful. Men would want her. Other men.

"Well, try it out," Sara said, interrupting tactfully. "I'll help you untie the ribbon."

"I'm never throwing the ribbon away!" Michelle laughed. "Oh. Wait!" She pulled out her cell phone and took a picture of the car in its bow.

"Stand beside it. We'll get one of you, too," Gabriel said, pulling out his own cell phone. He took several shots, smiling all the time. "Okay. Now get inside and try it out."

"Who's riding shotgun?" Michelle asked.

They looked worriedly at each other.

"It's too late to take it out of the driveway," Gabriel said finally. "Just start it up."

Michelle stood at the door. It wouldn't open.

"The key," Sara prompted Gabriel.

"The key. Duh." He chuckled. He dug it out of his pants pocket and handed it to Michelle. It was still warm from his body.

She looked at the fob in the light from the porch. "There's no key."

"You don't need one."

She unlocked the car and got inside. "There's no gearshift!"

"See the start button?" Gabriel prompted. "Press it."

She did. Nothing happened.

"Hold down the brake with your foot and then press it," he added.

She did. The car roared to life. She caught her breath as the vents opened and the gearshift rose up out of the console. "Oh!" she exclaimed. She looked at the controls, at the instrument panel, at the leather seats. "Oh!" she said again.

Gabriel squatted by the door, on the driveway. "Its creator said something like, 'we will never come closer to building something that is alive.' Each Jaguar is unique. Each has its own little idiosyncrasies. I've been driving them for years, and I still learn new things about them. They purr when they're happy, they growl when they want the open road." He laughed self-consciously. "Well, you'll see."

She leaned over and brushed her soft mouth against his cheek, very shyly. "Thanks."

He chuckled and got to his feet. "You're welcome."

"Thanks, Sara," she called to the other woman.

"It was truly our pleasure." Sara yawned. "And now we really should get to bed, don't you think? Michelle has an early morning, and I'm quite tired." She hesitated. "Perhaps we should check to make sure the flying monkeys are locked up securely…?"

They both laughed.

The driving instructor's name was Mr. Moore. He had a small white round patch of hair at the base of his skull. Michelle wondered if his hair loss was from close calls by students.

He was very patient. She had a couple of near misses, but was able to correct in time and avoid an accident. He told her that it was something that much practice would fix. She only needed to drive, and remember her lessons.

So she drove. But it was Sara, not Gabriel, who rode with her that summer. Gabriel had packed a bag, told the women goodbye, and rushed out without another word.

"Where is he going?" Michelle had asked Sara.

The other woman smiled gently. "We're not allowed to know. Some of what he does is classified. And you must never mention it to anyone. Okay?"

"Of course not," Michelle replied. She bit her lip. "What he does—it's just office stuff, right? I mean he advises. That's talking to people, instructing, right?"

Sara hesitated only a beat before she replied, "Of course."

Michelle put it out of her mind. Gabriel didn't phone home. He'd been gone several weeks. During that time, Michelle began to perfect her driving skills, with Sara's help. She got her driver's license, passing the test easily, and now she drove alternately to work with Carlie.

"This is just so great," Carlie enthused on the way to work. "They bought you a Jaguar! I can't believe it!"

She sighed, smoothing her hand over the soft leather seat. "I wish somebody would buy me a Jaguar."

Michelle chuckled. "It was a shock to me, too, let me tell you. I tried to give it back, but they wouldn't hear of it. They said I needed something safe. Like a big Ford truck wouldn't be safe?" she mused.

"I'd love a big brand-new Ford truck," Carlie sighed. "One of those F-Series ones. Or a Dodge Ram. Or a Chevy Silverado. I've never met a truck I didn't love."

"I like cars better," Michelle said. "Just a personal preference." She glanced at her friend. "I'm going to miss riding with you when I go to college."

"I'll miss you, too." Carlie glanced out the window. "Just having company keeps me from brooding."

"Carson is still giving you fits, I gather?" Michelle asked gently.

Carlie looked down at her hands. "I don't understand why he hates me so much," she said. "I haven't done anything to him. Well, except make a few sarcastic comments, but he starts it," she added with a scowl.

"Maybe he likes you," Michelle ventured. "And he doesn't want to."

"Oh, sure, that's the reason." She shook her head. "No. That isn't it. He'd throw me to the wolves without a second thought."

"He spends a lot of time in Cash Grier's office."

"They're working on something. I'm not allowed to know what, and the chief makes sure I can't overhear him when he talks on the phone." She frowned. "My father's in there a lot, too. I can't imagine why. Carson isn't the praying sort," she added coldly, alluding to her father's profession. He was, after all, a minister.

"I wouldn't think the chief is the praying sort, either," Michelle replied. "Maybe it's something to do about that man who attacked your father."

"I've wondered about that," her companion replied. "Dad won't tell me anything. He just clams up if I mention it."

"You could ask the chief."

Carlie burst out laughing. "You try it," she replied with a grin. "He changes the subject, picks up the phone, drags someone passing by into the office to chat—he's a master at evasion."

"You might try asking Carson," she added.

The smile faded. "Carson would walk all over me."

"You never know."

"I know, all right." Carlie flushed a little, and stared out the window again.

"Sorry," Michelle said gently. "You don't want to talk about him. I understand."

"It's okay." She turned her head. "Is Gabriel coming back soon?"

"We don't know. We don't even know where he is," Michelle said sadly. "Some foreign country, I gather, but he didn't say." She shook her head. "He's so mysterious."

"Most men are." Carlie laughed.

"At least what he does is just business stuff," came the reply. "So we don't have to worry about him so much."

"A blessing," Carlie agreed.

Michelle did a story about the local fire department and its new fire engine. She learned a lot from the fire chief about how fires were started and how they were fought. She put it all into a nice article, with photos of the firemen. Minette ran it on the front page.

"Favoritism," Cash Grier muttered when she stopped by to get Carlie for the drive home that Friday afternoon.

"Excuse me?" Michelle asked him.

"A story about the fire department, on the front page," he muttered. He glared at her. "You haven't even done one about us, and we just solved a major crime!"

"A major crime." Michelle hadn't heard of it.

"Yes. Someone captured old man Jones's chicken, put it in a doll dress, and tied it to his front porch." He grinned. "We captured the perp."

"And?" Michelle prompted. Carlie was listening, too.

"It was Ben Harris's granddaughter." He chuckled. "Her grandmother punished her for overfilling the bathtub by taking away her favorite dolly. So there was this nice red hen right next door. She took the chicken inside, dressed it up, and had fun playing with it while her grandparents were at the store. Then she realized how much more trouble she was going to be in when they noticed what the chicken did, since it wasn't wearing a diaper."

Both women were laughing.

"So she took the chicken back to Jones' house, but she was afraid it might run off, so she tied it to the porch rail." He shook his head. "The doll's clothes were a dead giveaway. She's just not cut out for a life of crime."

"What did Mr. Jones do?" Michelle asked.

"Oh, he took pictures," he replied. "Want one? They're pretty cool. I'm thinking of having one blown up for my office. To put on my solved-crime wall." He grinned.

They were laughing so hard, tears were rolling down their cheeks.

"And the little girl?" Michelle persisted.

"She's assigned to menial chores for the next few days. At least, until all the chicken poop has been cleaned off the floors and furniture. They did give her back the doll, however," he added, tongue in cheek. "To prevent any future lapses. Sad thing, though."

"What is?"

"The doll is naked. If she brings it out of the house, as much as I hate it, I'll have to cite it for indecent exposure..."

The laughter could be heard outside the door now. The tall man with jet-black hair hanging down to his waist wasn't laughing.

He stopped, staring at the chief and his audience.

"Something?" Cash asked, suddenly all business.

"Something." Carson's black eyes slid to Carlie's face and narrowed coldly. "If you can spare the time."

"Sure. Come on in."

"If you don't need me, I'll go home," Carlie said at once, flushed, as she avoided Carson's gaze.

"I don't need you." Carson said it with pure venom.

She lifted her chin pugnaciously. "Thank God," she said through her teeth.

He opened his mouth, but Cash intervened. "Go on home, Carlie," he said, as he grabbed Carson by the arm and steered him into the office.

"So that's Carson," Michelle said as she drove toward Carlie's house.

"That's Carson."

Michelle drew in a breath. "A thoroughly unpleasant person."

"You don't know the half of it."

"He really has it in for you."

Carlie nodded. "Told you so."

There really didn't seem to be anything else to say. Michelle gave her a sympathetic smile and kept her silence until they pulled up in front of the Victorian house she shared with her father.

"Thanks for the ride," Carlie said. "My turn to drive tomorrow."

"And my turn to buy gas." She chuckled.

"You don't hear me arguing, do you?" Carlie sighed, smiling. "Gas is outrageously high."

"So is most everything else. Have a good night. I'll see you tomorrow."

"Sure. Thanks again."

Michelle parked her car in front of the house, noted that she really needed to take it through the car wash, and started toward the front door. Sara's car was missing. She hadn't mentioned being away. Not a problem, however, since Michelle had a key.

She started to put it into the lock, just as it opened on its own. And there was Gabriel, tanned and handsome and smiling.

"Gabriel!" She threw herself into his arms, to be lifted, and hugged, and swung around once, twice, three times, in an embrace so hungry that she never wanted to be free again.

"When did you get home?" she asked at his ear.

"About ten minutes ago," he murmured into her neck. "You smell of roses."

"New perfume. Sara bought it for me." She drew back just enough to see his face, her arms still around his neck, his arms still holding her close. She searched his eyes at point-blank range and felt her heart go into overdrive. She could barely breathe. He felt like heaven in her arms. She looked at his mouth, chiseled, perfect, and wondered, wondered so hard, how it would feel if she moved just a little, if she touched her lips to it...

His hand caught in her long hair and pulled. "No," he said through his teeth.

She met his eyes. She saw there, or thought she saw, the same burning hunger that was beginning to tauten her young body, to kindle needs she'd never known she had.

Her lips parted on a shaky breath. She stared at him. He stared back. There seemed to be no sound in the world, nothing except the soft rasp of her breathing and the increasing heaviness of his own. Against her flattened breasts, she could feel the warm hardness of his chest, the thunder of his heartbeat.

One of his hands slid up and down her spine. His black eyes dropped to her mouth and lingered there until she almost felt the imprint of them, like a hard, rough kiss. Her nails bit into him where her hands clung.

She wanted him. He could feel it. She wanted his mouth, his hands, his body. Her breath was coming in tiny gasps. He could feel her heartbeat behind the soft, warm little breasts pressed so hard to his chest. Her mouth was parted, moist, inviting. He could grind his own down into it and make her moan, make her want him, make her open her arms to him on the long, soft sofa that was only a few steps away....

She was eighteen. She'd never lived. There hadn't

been a serious romance in her young life. He could rob her of her innocence, make her a toy, leave her broken and hurting and old.

"No," he whispered. He forced himself to put her down. He held her arms, tightly, until he could force himself to let go and step back.

She was shaky. She felt his hunger. He wasn't impervious to her. But he was cautious. He didn't want to start anything. He was thinking about her age. She knew it.

"I won't…always be eighteen," she managed.

He nodded, very slowly. "One day," he promised. "Perhaps."

She brightened. It was like the sun coming out. "I'll read lots of books."

His eyebrows arched.

"You know. On how to do…stuff. And I'll buy a hope chest and fill it up with frothy little black things."

The eyebrows arched even more.

"Well, it's a hope chest. As in, I hope I'll need it one day when you think I'm old enough." She pursed her lips and her gray eyes twinkled. "I could fake my ID…."

"Give it up." He chuckled.

She shrugged. "I'll grow up as fast as I can," she promised. She glowered at him. "I won't like it if I hear about you having orgies with strange women."

"Most women are strange," he pointed out.

She hit his chest. "Not nice."

"How's the driving?" he asked, changing the subject.

"I haven't hit a tree, run off the road or approached a ditch since you left," she said smugly. "I haven't even dinged the paint."

"Good girl," he said, chuckling. "I'm proud of you. How's the job coming along?"

"It's great! I'm working on this huge story! It may have international implications!"

Odd, how worried he looked for a few seconds. "What story?"

"It involves a kidnapping," she continued.

He frowned.

"A chicken was involved," she added, and watched his face clear and become amused. "A little girl whose doll was taken away for punishment stole a chicken and dressed it in doll's clothes. I understand she'll be cleaning the house for days to come."

He laughed heartily. "The joys of small-town reporting," he mused.

"They never end. How was your trip?"

"Long," he said. "And I'm starving."

"Sara made a lovely casserole. I'll heat you up some."

He sat down at the kitchen table and watched her work. She made coffee and put a mug of it, black, at his place while she dealt with reheating the chicken casserole.

She warmed up a piece of French bread with butter to go with it. Then she sat down and watched him eat while she sipped her own coffee.

"It sure beats fried snake," he murmured.

She blinked. "What?"

"Well, we eat what we can find. Usually, it's a snake. Sometimes, if we're lucky, a big bird or some fish."

"In an office building?" she exclaimed.

He glanced at her with amusement. "It's not always in an office building. Sometimes we have to go out and look at…projects, wherever they might be. This time, it was in a jungle."

"Wow." She was worried now. "Poisonous snakes?"

"Mostly. It doesn't really affect the taste," he added.

"You could get bitten," she persisted.

"I've been bitten, half a dozen times," he replied easily. "We always carry antivenin with us."

"I thought you were someplace safe."

He studied her worried face and felt a twinge of guilt. "It was just this once," he lied, and he smiled. "What I do is rarely dangerous." Another lie. A bigger one. "Nothing to concern you. Honest."

She propped her face in her hands, her elbows on the table, and watched him finish his meal and his coffee.

"Stop that," he teased. "I can take care of myself. I've been doing it for twenty-odd years."

She grimaced. "Okay. Just checking."

"I promise not to get killed."

"If you do, I'm coming after you. Boy, will you be sorry, too."

He laughed. "I hear you."

"Want dessert? We have a cherry pie."

He shook his head. "Maybe later. Where's Sara?"

"I have no idea. She didn't even leave a note."

He pulled out his cell phone and pressed the speed dial. He got up and poured more coffee into his cup while he waited.

"Where are you?" he asked after a minute.

There was a reply. He glanced at Michelle, his lips pursed, his eyes twinkling. "Yes, she's right here."

Another silence. He sat back down. He was nodding. "No, I think it's a very good idea. But you might have asked for my input first….No, I agree, you have exquisite taste….Yes, that's true, returns are possible. I won't tell her. How long?…Okay. See you then." He smiled. "Me, too. Thanks."

He hung up.

"Where is she?" she asked.

"On her way home. With a little surprise."

"Something for me?" she asked, and her face brightened.

"I'd say so."

"But you guys have already given me so much," she began, protesting.

"You can take that up with my sister," he pointed out. "Not that it will do you much good. She's very stubborn."

She laughed. "I noticed." She paused. "What is it?"

"You'll have to wait and see."

Sara pulled up into the driveway and got out of her car. She popped the truck and dragged out several big shopping bags. She handed some to Gabriel and one to Michelle. She was grinning from ear to ear.

"What in the world…?" Michelle exclaimed.

"Just a few little odds and ends that you're going to need to start college. Come on inside and I'll show you. Gabriel, get your nose out of that bag, it's private!"

He laughed and led the way into the house.

Michelle was speechless. Sara had exquisite taste in clothing, and it showed in the items she'd purchased for their houseguest. There was everything from jeans and sweats to dresses and handbags and underwear, gossamer gowns and an evening gown that brought tears to Michelle's eyes because it was the loveliest thing she'd ever seen.

"You like them?" Sara asked, a little worried.

"I've never had things like this," she stammered. "Daddy was so sick that he never thought of shopping with me. And when Roberta took me, it was just for bras and panties, never for nice clothes." She hugged Sara impulsively. "Thank you. Thank you so much!"

"You might try on that gown. I wasn't sure about the size, but we can exchange it if it doesn't fit. I'll go have coffee with Gabriel while you check the fit." She smiled, and left Michelle with the bags.

They were sipping coffee in the kitchen when Michelle came nervously to the doorway. She'd fixed her hair, put on shoes and she was wearing the long, creamy evening gown with its tight fit and cap sleeves, revealing soft cleavage. There was faint embroidery on the bodice and around the hem. The off-white brought out the highlights in Michelle's long, pale blond hair, and accentuated her peaches-and-cream complexion. In her softly powdered face, her gray eyes were exquisite.

Gabriel turned his head when he caught movement in his peripheral vision. He sat like a stone statue, just staring. Sara followed his gaze, and her face brightened.

"It's perfect!" she exclaimed, rising. "Michelle, it's absolutely perfect! Now you have something to wear to a really formal occasion."

"Thanks," she replied. "It's the most beautiful thing I've ever owned." She glanced at Gabriel, who hadn't spoken. His coffee cup was suspended in his hand in midair, as if he'd forgotten it. "Does it…look okay?" she asked him, wanting reassurance.

He forced his eyes away. "It looks fine." He put the mug down and got to his feet. "I need to check the livestock." He went out the back door without a glance behind him.

Michelle felt wobbly. She bit her lower lip. "He didn't like it," she said miserably.

Sara touched her cheek gently. "Men are strange. They react in odd ways. I'm sure he liked it, but he's not demonstrative." She smiled. "Okay?"

Michelle relaxed. "Okay."

Out in the barn, Gabriel was struggling to regain his composure. He'd never seen anything in his life more beautiful than Michelle in that dress. He'd had to force himself out the door before he reacted in a totally inappropriate way. He wanted to sweep her up in his arms and kiss her until her mouth went numb. Not a great idea.

He stood beside one of his horses, stroking its muzzle gently, while he came to grips with his hunger. It was years too soon. He would have to manage the long wait. Meanwhile, he worried about the other men, young men, who would see Michelle in that gown and want her, as he wanted her. But they would be her age, young and untried, without his jaded past. They would be like her, full of passion for life.

It wasn't fair of him to try to keep her. He must distance himself from her, give her the chance to grow away from him, to find someone more suitable. It was going to be hard, but he must manage it. She deserved the chance.

* * *

The next morning, he was gone when Michelle went into the kitchen to help Sara fix breakfast.

"His truck's gone," Michelle said, her spirits dropping hard.

"Yes. I spoke to him late last night," Sara replied, not looking at her. "He has a new job. He said he might be away for a few weeks." She glanced at the younger woman and managed a smile. "Don't worry about him. He can take care of himself."

"I'm sure he can. It's just…" She rested her hand on the counter. "I miss him, when he's away."

"I'm sure you do." She hesitated. "Michelle, you haven't started to live yet. There's a whole world out there that you haven't even seen."

Michelle turned, her eyes old and wise. "And you think I'll find some young man who'll sweep me off my feet and carry me off to a castle." She smiled. "There's only one man I'll ever want to do that, you know."

Sara grimaced. "There are so many things you don't know."

"They won't matter," Michelle replied very quietly. She searched Sara's eyes. "None of it will matter."

Sara couldn't think of the right words. So she just hugged Michelle instead.

Chapter 9

Michelle was very nervous. It was the first day of the semester on campus, and even with a map, it was hard to find all her classes. Orientation had given the freshmen an overview of where everything was off the quad, but it was so confusing.

"Is Western Civilization in Sims Hall or Waverly Hall?" she muttered to herself, peering at the map.

"Waverly," came a pleasant male voice from just behind her. "Come on, I'll walk you over. I'm Randy. Randy Miles."

"Michelle Godfrey," she said, shaking his hand and smiling. "Thanks. Are you in my class?"

He shook his head. "I'm a junior."

"Should you be talking to me?" she teased. "After all, I'm pond scum."

He stopped and smiled. He had dark hair and pale

eyes. He was a little pudgy, but nice. "No. You're not pond scum. Trust me."

"Thanks."

"My pleasure. Are you from San Antonio?"

"My family is from Jacobsville, but I lived here with my parents while they were alive."

"Sorry."

"They were wonderful people. The memories get easier with time." She glanced around. "This is a huge campus."

"They keep adding to it," he said. "Sims Hall is brand-new. Waverly is old. My father had history with old Professor Barlane."

"Really?"

He nodded. "Just a word of warning, never be late for his class. You don't want to know why."

She grinned. "I'll remember."

On the way to Waverly Hall, Randy introduced Michelle to two of his friends, Alan Drew and Marjory Wills. Alan was distantly pleasant. Marjory was much more interested in talking to Randy than being introduced to this new student.

"You're going to be late for class, aren't you?" Alan asked Michelle, checking his watch. "I'll walk you the rest of the way."

"Nice to have met you," Randy said pleasantly. Marjory just nodded.

Michelle smiled and followed Alan to the towering building where her class was located.

"Thanks," she said.

He shrugged and smiled. "Those two." He rolled his eyes. "They're crazy about each other, but neither one will admit it. Don't let them intimidate you, especially Marjory. She has…issues."

"No problem. I guess I'll see you around."

"You will." He leaned forward, grinning. "I'm in the class you're going to right now. And we'd better hurry!"

They barely made it before the bell. The professor, Dr. Barlane, was old and cranky. He gave the class a dismissive look and began to lecture. Michelle was grateful that she'd learned how to take notes, because she had a feeling that this class was going to be one of the more demanding ones.

Beside her, Alan was scribbling on scraps of paper instead of a notebook, like Michelle. He wasn't bad-looking. He had dark hair and eyes and a nice smile, but in her heart, there was only Gabriel. She might like other men as friends, but there was never going to be one to compare with Gabriel.

After class, Alan left her with a smile and whistled as he continued on to his next class. Michelle looked at her schedule, puzzled out the direction to go and went along the walkway to the next building.

"Well, how was it?" Sara asked that night on the phone.

"Very nice," she replied. "I made a couple of friends."

"Male ones?" Sara teased.

"What was that?" Gabriel spoke up in the background.

"She made friends," Sara called to him. "Don't have a cow."

He made a sarcastic sound and was quiet.

"How do you like your roommate?" Sara continued.

Michelle glanced into the next room, where Darla was searching frantically for a blouse she'd unpacked and couldn't find, muttering and ruffling her red hair.

"She's just like me. Disorganized and flighty," Michelle said, a little loudly.

"I heard that!" Darla said over her shoulder.

"I know!" Michelle laughed. Darla shook her head, laughing, too.

"We're going to get along just fine," Michelle told Sara. "Neither of us has half a mind, and we're so disorganized that we're likely to be thrown out for creating a public eyesore."

"Not likely," Sara replied. "Well, I'm glad things are going well. If you need us, you know where we are, sweetie."

"I do. Thanks. Thanks for everything."

"Keep in touch. Good night."

"Good night."

"Your family?" Darla asked, poking her head into the room.

Michelle hesitated, but only for a second. She smiled. "Yes. My family."

Michelle adjusted to college quite easily. She made some friends, mostly distant ones, and one good one— her roommate, Darla. She and Darla were both religious, so they didn't go to boozy parties or date promiscuous boys. That meant they spent a lot of time watching rented movies and eating popcorn in their own dorm room.

One thing Sara had said was absolutely true; college changed her. She learned things that questioned her own view of the world and things about other cultures. She saw the rise and fall of civilizations, the difference in religions, the rise of science, the fascination of history. She continued her study of French—mainly because she wanted to know what Sara and Gabriel spoke about that they didn't want her to hear—and she sweated first-year biology. But by and large, she did well in her classes.

All too soon, final exams arrived. She sat in the library with other students, she and Darla trying to absorb what they needed to know to pass their courses. She'd already lived in the biology lab for several days after school with a study group, going over material that was certainly going to come up when they were tested.

"I'm going to fail," she moaned softly to Darla. "I'll go home in disgrace. I'll have to hide my head in a paper sack…."

"Shut up," Darla muttered. "You're going to pass! So am I. Be quiet and study, girl!"

Michelle sighed. "Thanks. I needed that."

"I'm going to fail," one of the boys nearby moaned to Darla. "I'll go home in disgrace…"

She punched him.

"Thanks." He chuckled, and went back to his books.

Michelle did pass, with flying colors, but she didn't know it when she went back to Comanche Wells for the holidays.

"I'll have to sweat it out until my grades come through," she said to Sara, hugging her warmly. "But I think I did okay." She looked past Sara and then at her, curious.

"He's out of the country," Sara said gently. "He was

really sorry, he wanted to be home for the holidays. But it wasn't possible. This was a rush thing."

Michelle's heart fell. "I guess he has to work."

"Yes, he does. But he got your presents, and mine, and wrapped them before he left." Her dark eyes twinkled. "He promised that we'd love the gifts."

"I'd love a rock, if he picked it out for me," Michelle sighed. "Can we go shopping? Minette said I could work for her over the holidays while I'm home, so I'll have a little money of my own."

"Whenever you like, dear," Sara promised.

"Thanks!"

"Now come and have hot chocolate. I want to hear all about college!"

Minette had some interesting assignments for Michelle. One was to interview one of Jacobsville's senior citizens about Christmas celebrations in the mid-twentieth century, before the internet or space travel. It had sounded rather boring, honestly. But when she spoke to Adelaide Duncan, the old woman made the past come alive in her soft, mellow tones.

"We didn't have fancy decorations for the Christmas tree," Mrs. Duncan recalled, her pale blue eyes dancing with delightful memories. "We made them from construction paper. We made garlands of cranberries. We used candles set on the branches to light the tree, and we used soap powder mixed with a little water for snow. Presents were practical things, mostly fruit or nuts or handcrafted garments. One year I got oranges and a knit cap. Another, I got a dress my mother had made me in a beautiful lemon color. My husband kissed me under the mistletoe when we were still in school together, long before we married." Her face was wistful. "He was seventeen and I was fifteen. We danced to music that our parents and relatives made with fiddles and guitars. I wore the lemon-yellow dress, ruffled and laced, and I felt like I had possession of the whole world's treasures." She sighed. "We were married for fifty-five years," she added wistfully. "And one day, not too long away now, I'll see him again. And we'll dance together...."

Michelle had to fight tears. "Fifty-five years," she repeated, and couldn't imagine two people staying together for so long.

"Oh, yes. In my day, people got married and then had children." She shook her head. "The world has changed, my dear. Marriage doesn't seem to mean the same as it used to. History tends to repeat itself, and I fear when the stability of a civilization is lost, society crumbles. You'll study the results in your history classes in college," she added, nodding. "Do you have Dr. Barlane for history by any chance?"

"Yes," Michelle said, stunned.

The old woman laughed. "He and I graduated together from Marist College, both with degrees in history. But he went on to higher education and I got married and had a family. By and large, I think my life was happier than his. He never married."

"Do your children live here?" she asked.

"Oh, no, they're scattered around the world." She laughed. "I visit with them on Skype and we text back and forth every day, though. Modern technology." She shook her head. "It really is a blessing, in this day and time."

Michelle was surprised. "You text?" she asked.

"My dear," the old lady mused, laughing, "I not only

text, I tweet and surf, and I am hell on wheels with a two-handed sword in World of Warcraft. I own a guild."

The younger woman's idea of elderly people had gone up in a blaze of disbelief. "You…play video games?"

"I eat them up." She shrugged. "I can't run and jump and play in real life, but I can do it online." She grinned from ear to ear. "Don't you dare tell Wofford Patterson, but I creamed one of his Horde toons last night on a battleground."

Michelle almost fell over laughing.

"And you thought you were going to interview some dried up old hulk who sat in a rocking chair and knitted, I bet," the woman mused with twinkling eyes.

"Yes, I did," Michelle confessed, "and I am most heartily sorry!"

"That's all right, dear," Mrs. Duncan said, patting her hand. "We all have misconceptions about each other."

"Mine were totally wrong."

"How nice of you to say so!"

Michelle changed gears and went back to the interview. But what she learned about elderly people that day colored her view of them forever.

"She plays video games," Michelle enthused to Minette, back at the office. She'd written her story and turned it in, along with her photos, while Minette was out of the office. Now she was elaborating on the story, fascinated with what she'd learned.

"Yes, there have been a lot of changes in the way we perceive the elderly," Minette agreed. "I live with my great-aunt. She doesn't play video games, but I did catch her doing Tai Chi along with an instructor on public television. And she can text, too."

"My grandparents sat and rocked on the porch after supper," Michelle recalled. "He smoked a pipe and she sewed quilt tops and they talked." She shook her head. "It's a different world."

"It is." She hesitated. "Has Gabriel come home?"

Michelle shook her head. "It's almost Christmas, too. We don't know where he is, or what he's doing."

Minette, who did, carefully concealed her knowledge. "Well, he might surprise you and show up on Christmas day. Who knows?"

Michelle forced a smile. "Yes."

She and Sara decorated the tree. Two of the men who worked for Gabriel part-time, taking care of the horses and the ranch, had come in earlier with a big bucket, holding a tree with the root ball still attached.

"I can't bear to kill a tree," Sara confided as the men struggled to put it in place in the living room. "Sorry, guys," she added.

"Oh, Miss Sara, it's no trouble at all," the taller of the two cowboys said at once, holding his hat to his heart. He grinned. "It was our pleasure."

"Absolutely," the shorter one agreed.

They stood smiling at Sara until one thumped the other and reminded him that they had chores to do. They excused themselves, still smiling.

"You just tie them up in knots." Michelle laughed, when they were out of the room. "You're so pretty."

Sara made a face. "Nonsense."

"Hide your head in the sand, then. What are we going to decorate it with?" she added.

"Come with me."

Sara pulled down the ladder and the two women climbed carefully up into the attic.

Michelle caught her breath when she saw the heart of pine rafters. "My goodness, it's almost a religious experience to just look at them!" she exclaimed. "Those rafters must be a hundred years old!"

Sara glanced at her with amusement. "I believe they are. Imagine you, enthralled by rafters!"

"Heart of pine rafters," she replied. "My grandfather built houses when he was younger. He took me with him a time or two when he had to patch a roof or fix a leak. He was passionate about rafters." She laughed. "And especially those made of heart of pine. They're rare, these days, when people mostly build with green lumber that hasn't been properly seasoned."

"This house has a history," Sara said. "You probably already know it, since your people came from Jacobs County."

Michelle nodded, watching Sara pick up two boxes of ornaments and stack them together. "It belonged to a Texas Ranger."

"Yes. He was killed in a shoot-out in San Antonio. He left behind two sons, a daughter and a wife. There's a plaque in city hall in Jacobsville that tells all about him."

"I'll have to go look," Michelle said. "I haven't done any stories that took me there, yet."

"I'm sure you will. Minette says you're turning into a very good reporter."

"She does?" Michelle was all eyes. "Really?"

Sara looked at her and smiled. "You must have more confidence in yourself," she said gently. "You must believe in your own abilities."

"That's hard."

"It comes with age. You'll get the hang of it." She handed Michelle a box of ornaments. "Be careful going down the steps."

"Okay."

They spent the afternoon decorating the tree. When they finally plugged in the beautiful, colored fairy lights, Michelle caught her breath.

"It's the most breathtaking tree I've ever seen," she enthused.

"It is lovely, isn't it?" Sara asked. She fingered a branch. "We must keep it watered, so that it doesn't die. When Christmas is over, I'll have the men plant it near the front steps. I do so love white pines!"

"Do you ever miss Wyoming?" Michelle asked, a little worried because she knew Sara was only here so that Michelle could come home, so that she wouldn't be alone with Gabriel.

Sara turned to her. "A little. I lived there because Gabriel bought the ranch and one of us needed to run it. But I had no real friends. I'm happier here." Her dark eyes were soft. She smoothed over an ornament. "This belonged to my grandmother," she said softly. It was a little house, made of logs, hanging from a red silk ribbon. "My grandfather whittled it for her, when they were dating." She laughed. "Wherever I am, it always makes me feel at home when the holidays come."

"Your mother's parents?"

Sara's face went hard. "No. My father's."

"I'm sorry."

Sara turned back to her. In her lovely face, her dark

eyes were sad. "I don't speak of my mother, or her people. I'm sorry. It's a sore spot with me."

"I'll remember," Michelle said quietly. "It's like my stepmother."

"Exactly."

Michelle didn't betray her secret knowledge of Sara's early life, of the tragedy she and Gabriel had lived through because of their mother's passion for their stepfather. She changed the subject and asked about the other ornaments that Sara had placed on the tree.

But Sara wasn't fooled. She was very quiet. Later, when they were sipping hot chocolate in the kitchen, her dark eyes pinned Michelle.

"How much did he tell you?" she asked suddenly.

In her hands, the mug jumped, almost enough to spill the hot liquid on her fingers.

"Careful, it's hot," Sara said. "Come on, Michelle. How much did Gabriel tell you?"

Michelle grimaced.

Sara took in a long breath. "I see." She sipped the liquid gingerly. "He never speaks of it at all. Yet he told you." Her soft eyes lifted to Michelle's worried gray ones. "I'm not angry. I'm surprised."

"That he told me?"

"Yes." She smiled sadly. "He doesn't warm to people. In fact, he's cold and withdrawn with almost everyone. You can't imagine how shocked I was when he phoned me and asked me to come down here because of a young girl he was going to get custody of." She laughed, shaking her head. "I thought he was joking."

"But he's not. Cold and withdrawn, I mean," Michelle faltered.

"Not with you." She stared into Michelle's eyes earnestly. "I haven't heard Gabriel laugh in years," she added softly. "But he does it all the time with you. I don't understand it. But you give him peace, Michelle."

"That would be nice, if it were true. I don't know if it is," Michelle replied.

"It's fairly obvious what you feel for him."

She flushed. She couldn't lift her eyes.

"He won't take advantage of it, don't worry," Sara added gently. "That's why I'm here." She laughed. "He's taking no chances."

"He doesn't want to get involved with a child," Michelle said heavily.

"You won't be a child for much longer," the other woman pointed out.

"I'm sure he meets beautiful women all the time," Michelle said.

"I'm sure it doesn't matter what they look like," Sara replied. She smiled. "You'll see."

Michelle didn't reply to that. She just sipped her hot chocolate and felt warm inside.

It was the week before Christmas, a Friday about lunchtime, when the women heard a truck pull up in the driveway.

Michelle, who was petting one of the horses in the corral, saw the truck and gasped and ran as fast as she could to the man getting out of it.

"Gabriel!" she cried.

He turned. His face lit up like floodlights. He held out his arms and waited until she ran into them to pick her up and whirl her around, holding her so close that she felt they were going to be joined together forever.

"Oh, I've missed you," she choked.

"I've missed you." His voice was deep at her ear. He lifted his head and set her on her feet. His black eyes were narrow, intent on her face. He touched her mouth with just the tip of his forefinger, teasing it apart. His eyes fell to it and lingered there while her heart threatened to jump right out of her throat.

"Ma belle," he whispered roughly.

He framed her oval face in his big hands and searched her eyes. *"Ma belle,"* he repeated. His eyes fell to her mouth. "It's like falling into fire…"

As he spoke, his head started to bend. Michelle's heart ran away. She could hear her own breathing, feel his breath going into her mouth, taste the coffee and the faint odor of tobacco that came from him, mingled with some masculine cologne that teased her senses.

"Gabriel," she whispered, hanging at his mouth, aching to feel it come crashing down on her lips, crushing them, devouring him, easing the ache, the hunger that pulsed through her young, untried body…

"Gabriel!"

Sara's joyful cry broke them apart just in the nick of time. Gabriel cleared his throat, turned to his sister and hugged her.

"It's good to have you home," Sara said against his chest.

"It's good to be home." He was struggling to sound normal. His mind was still on Michelle's soft mouth and his hunger to break it open under his lips, back her into a wall and devour her.

"Have you eaten? I just made soup," Sara added.

"No. I'm starved." He made an attempt not to look at Michelle when he said that. He even smiled.

"I could eat, too," Michelle said, trying to break the tension.

"Let's go in." Sara took his arm. "Where did you come from?"

"Dallas, this time," he said. "I've been in the States for a couple of days, but I had business there before I could get home." He hesitated. "I got tickets to the ballet in San Antonio when I came through there this morning." He glanced at Michelle. "Want to go see *The Nutcracker* with me?" he added with a grin.

"Oh, I'd love to," she said fervently. "What do we wear?"

"A very dressy evening outfit," Sara said. "I bought you one once, and you never even wore it."

Michelle grinned. "Well, I haven't been anywhere I'd need to wear it," she replied, not guessing what it told Gabriel, whose eyes twinkled brightly.

Michelle flushed and then grinned at him. "No, I'm not dating anybody at college," she said. She shrugged. "I'm too busy studying."

"Is that so?" Gabriel laughed, and was relieved.

"When are you leaving?" Sara asked.

"At six, and you'd better start dressing as well, because we're all three going," Gabriel added, and he exchanged a speaking look with Sara.

"All of us? Oh. Oh! That's nice!" Michelle worked at sounding enthusiastic.

Sara just winked at her. "I'd better go through my closet."

Gabriel looked down at Michelle with the Christmas tree bright and beautiful behind her. "I wouldn't dare take you out alone, *ma belle,*" he said under his breath. "You know it. And you know why."

Her eyes searched his hungrily. She knew. She'd felt it, when he held her beside the truck. She knew that he wanted her.

She'd had no idea what wanting really was, until Gabriel had come into her life. Now she was aware of a hunger that came around when he was close, that grew and surged in her when he looked at her, when he spoke to her, when he touched her....

"Yes, you know, don't you?" he breathed, standing a little too close. He rubbed his thumb against her lips, hard enough to make her gasp and shiver with delight. His black eyes narrowed. "It's too soon. You know that, too."

She ground her teeth together as she looked at him. He was the most perfect thing in her life. He was preaching caution when all she wanted to do was push him down on the floor and spread her body over him and...

She didn't know what would come next. She'd read books, but they were horribly lacking in preliminaries.

"What are you thinking about so hard?" he asked.

"About pushing you down on the floor," she blurted out, and flushed. "But I don't know what comes next, exactly..."

He burst out laughing.

"You stop that," she muttered. "I'll bet you weren't born knowing what to do, either."

"I wasn't," he confessed. He touched her nose with the tip of his finger. "It's just as well that you don't know. Yet. And we aren't going to be alone. Yet."

She drew in a long sigh and smiled. "Okay."

He chuckled.

"I've never been to the ballet," she confessed.

"High time you went," he replied, and he laughed. "Go on."

* * *

Sara had laid out the most beautiful black velvet dress Michelle had ever seen. It had a discreet rounded neckline and long sleeves, and it fell to the ankles, with only a slight tuck where the waistline was.

"It's gorgeous!" Michelle enthused.

"And you'll look gorgeous in it," Sara replied. She hugged Michelle. "It's yours. I have shoes and a purse to match it."

"But, I have a dress," Michelle began.

"A summer dress," Sara said patiently, and smiled. "This one is more suitable for winter. I have one similar to it that I'm wearing. We'll look like twins." She grinned.

"Okay, then. And thank you!" Michelle said heartily.

"You're very welcome."

Chapter 10

Gabriel wore a dress jacket with dark slacks and a black turtleneck sweater. He looked classy and elegant. Sara wore a simple sheath of navy blue velvet with an expensive gold necklace and earrings and looked exquisite, with her silky black hair loose almost to her waist and her big, dark eyes soft in her beautiful face.

Michelle in her black velvet dress felt like royalty. The trio drew eyes as they filed into the auditorium where the ballet was being performed.

Up front, in the orchestra pit, the musicians were tuning up their instruments. Gabriel found their seats and let the women go in first before he took his place on the aisle.

"There's quite a crowd," Michelle remarked as more people filed in.

"Oh, dear." Sara's voice was full of consternation.

Before Michelle could ask what was wrong, she saw it for herself. Wofford Patterson, in a dinner jacket with a white tie and black slacks was escorting a beautiful blonde, in an elegant green velvet gown, down the aisle—directly to the seats beside Sara.

"Mr. Brandon," Wolf said, nodding. "This is Elise Jorgansen. Elise, Gabriel Brandon. That's his sister, Sara. And that's his ward, Michelle."

"Nice to meet you," Elise said, and smiled at them all with genuine warmth.

"I believe our seats are right there," Wolf told the pretty woman. He escorted her past Gabriel and the women with apologies, because it was a tight squeeze. He sat next to Sara, with Elise on his other side.

Sara tensed and glared straight ahead. Wolf grinned.

"I didn't know that you liked the ballet, Miss Brandon," Wolf said politely.

"I like this one. It's *The Nutcracker,*" she added with a venomous look at the man beside her.

He pursed his lips. "Left the flying monkeys at home, did we?"

"I'd love to drop a house on you, dear man," she said under her breath.

"Now, now, it's the ballet," he pointed out. "We must behave like civilized people."

"You'd need so much instruction for that, Mr. Patterson," Sara said, her voice dripping honey.

"Isn't the music lovely?" Michelle broke in.

The music was the instruments being tuned, but it shattered the tension and everyone laughed.

"Behave," Gabriel whispered to his sister.

She gave him an irritated look, but she kept her hands in her lap and sat quietly as the ballerinas came onstage one by one and the performance began, to Michelle's utter fascination and delight. She'd never seen a live performance of the ballet, which was her favorite.

At intermission, Sara excused herself and left the row.

"I'm not getting up," Wolf said. "I'd never get back in here."

"Neither am I," Gabriel mused. "It's quite a crowd."

"You seem to be enjoying the music, Miss Godfrey," Wolf said politely.

"I've never been to a ballet before," she replied, laughing. "It's so beautiful!"

"You should see it in New York City, at the American Ballet Company," Gabriel said gently.

"They do an excellent performance," Wolf agreed. "Have you seen it at the Bolshoi?" he added.

"Yes," Gabriel agreed. "Theirs is unbelievably beautiful."

"That's in Russia, isn't it?" Michelle asked, wide-eyed.

"Yes," Gabriel said. He smiled down at her. "One day, Sara and I will have to take you traveling."

"You should see the world," Elise agreed, from beside Wolf. "Or at least, some of it. Travel broadens your world."

"I can't think of anything I'd love more," Michelle replied, smiling back at the woman.

"Elise studied ballet when she was still in school," Wolf said. "She was in line to be a prima ballerina with the company she played with in New York."

"Don't," Elise said gently.

"Sorry," Wolf said, patting her hand. "Bad memories. I won't mention it again."

"That life is long over," she replied. "But I still love going to see the ballet and the theater and opera. We have such a rich cultural heritage here in San Antonio."

"We do, indeed," Gabriel agreed.

The musicians began tuning their instruments again, just as Sara came back down the aisle, so graceful and poised that she drew male eyes all the way.

"Your sister has an elegance of carriage that is quite rare," Elise said to Gabriel as she approached.

"She also studied ballet," Gabriel replied quietly. "But the stress of dancing and trying to get through college became too much. She gave up ballet and got her degree in languages." He laughed. "She still dances, though," he added. "She just doesn't put on a tutu first."

"It wouldn't go with the broom," Sara said to Wolf, and smiled coldly as she sat down.

"Broom?" Elise asked, curious.

"Never mind. I'll explain it to you later," Wolf replied.

Sara gave him a look that might have curdled milk and turned her attention to the stage as the curtain began to rise.

"Well, it was a wonderful evening," Michelle said dreamily as she followed them out to the car. "Thank you so much for taking us," she added to Gabriel.

He studied her in the lovely dress, smiling. "It was my pleasure. We'll have to do this more often."

"Expose you to culture, he means," Sara said in a stage whisper. "It's good for you."

"I really had a good time."

"I would have, except for the company," Sara muttered. She flushed. "Not you two," she said hastily when they gaped at her. "That…man! And his date."

"I thought Elise was very nice," Michelle ventured.

Sara clammed up.

Gabriel just chuckled.

Christmas Eve was magical. They sat around the Christmas tree, watching a program of Christmas music on television, sipping hot chocolate and making s'mores in the fireplace, where a sleepy fire flamed every now and then.

In all her life, Michelle couldn't remember being so happy. Her eyes kept darting to Gabriel, when she thought he wasn't looking. Even in jeans and a flannel shirt, he was the stuff of dreams. It was so hard not to appear starstruck.

They opened presents that night instead of the next morning, because Sara announced that she wasn't getting up at dawn to see what Santa had left.

She gave Michelle a beautiful scarf of many colors, a designer one. Michelle draped it around her neck and raved over it. Then she opened Gabriel's gift. It was pearls, a soft off-white set in a red leather box. They were Japanese. He'd brought them home from his last trip and hidden them to give at Christmas. The necklace was accompanied by matching drop earrings.

"I was right," he mused as Michelle tried them on enthusiastically. "They're just the right shade."

"They are, indeed. And thank you for mine, also, my sweet." Sara kissed his tan cheek, holding a strand of white ones in her hand. They suited her delicate coloring just as the off-white ones suited Michelle's.

"I like mine, too." He held up a collection of DVDs

of shows he particularly liked from Michelle and a black designer turtleneck from Sara.

Sara loved her handmade scarf from Michelle. It was crocheted and had taken an age to finish. It was the softest white knit, with tassels. "I'll wear it all winter," she promised Michelle, and kissed her, too.

Michelle had hung mistletoe in strategic places, but she hadn't counted on Gabriel's determined reticence. He kissed her on the cheek, smiled and wished her the happiest of Christmases and New Years. She pretended that it didn't matter that he didn't drag her into an empty room and kiss her half to death. He was determined not to treat her as an adult. It was painful. But in some sense, she did understand.

So three years went by, more quickly than Michelle had dreamed they would. She got a job part-time with a daily newspaper in San Antonio and did political pieces for it while she got through her core courses and into serious journalism in college.

She went to class during summer to speed up her degree program, although she came home for the holidays. Gabriel was almost always away now. Sara was there, although she spent most of her time in Wyoming at the ranch she and Gabriel owned. Michelle had gone up there with her one summer for a couple of weeks during her vacation. It was a beautiful place. Sara was different somehow. Something had happened between her and Wofford Patterson. She wouldn't talk about it, but she knew that it had changed Sara. Gabriel had mentioned something about Sara going back into therapy and there had been an argument in French that Michelle couldn't follow.

Wofford Patterson had also moved up to Catelow, Wyoming. He bought a huge ranch there near Sara's. He kept his place in Comanche Wells, but he put in a foreman to manage it for him. He had business interests in Wyoming that took up much of his time, he said, and it was hard to commute. Sara didn't admit that she was glad to have him as a neighbor. But Michelle suspected that she did.

Sara was still playing her online game with her friend, and they fought battles together late into the night. She still didn't know who he really was, either. Gabriel had made sure of it.

"He's such a gentleman," Sara mused over coffee one morning, her face bright with pleasure. "He wants to meet me in person." She hesitated. "I'm not sure about that."

"Why not, if you like him?" Michelle asked innocently, although she didn't dare let on that she knew exactly who Sara's friend was, and she knew that Sara would have a stroke if she saw him in person. It would be the end of a lovely online relationship.

"People aren't what they seem," Sara replied, and pain was in her eyes. "If it seems too good to be true, it usually is."

"He might be a knight in shining armor," Michelle teased. "You should find out."

"He might be an ogre who lives in a cave with bats, too." Sara chuckled. "No. I like things the way they are. I really don't want to try to have a relationship with a man in real life." Her face tensed. "I never wanted to."

Michelle grimaced. "Sara, you're so beautiful…"

"Beautiful!" She laughed coldly. "I wish I'd been born ugly. It would have made my life so much easier.

You don't know…" She drew in a harsh breath. "Well, actually, you do know." She managed a soft smile. "We're all prisoners of our childhoods, Michelle. Mine was particularly horrible. It warped me."

"You should have been in therapy," Michelle said gently.

"I tried therapy. It only made things worse. I can't talk to total strangers."

"Maybe you just talked to the wrong person."

Sara's eyes were suddenly soft and dreamy and she flushed. "I think I did. So much has changed," she added softly.

Michelle, who had a good idea what was going on up in Wyoming, just grinned.

Sara's eyes took on an odd, shimmering softness. "Life is so much sweeter than I dreamed it could be." She smiled to herself and looked at her watch. "I have some phone calls to make. I love having you around." She added, "Thanks."

"For what?"

"For caring," Sara said simply.

Michelle was looking forward to her last Christmas in college. She got talked into a blind date with Darla's boyfriend's friend. He turned out to be a slightly haughty man who worked as a stockbroker and never stopped talking on his cell phone for five seconds. He was at it all through dinner. Bob, Darla's boyfriend, looked very uncomfortable and apologetic.

"Bob feels awful," Darla whispered to Michelle in the restroom after they'd finished eating. "Larry seemed to be a normal guy."

"He just lives and breathes his job. Besides," she

added, "you know there's only one man who interests me at all. And it's never going to be someone like Larry."

"Having seen your Mr. Brandon, I totally understand." Darla giggled. She shook her head. "He is a dreamboat."

"I think so."

"Well, we'll stop by the bar for a nightcap and go home. Maybe we can pry Larry away from his phone long enough to say good-night."

"I wish I was riding with you and Bob." Michelle sighed. "At least he stops talking while he's driving."

"Curious, that he didn't want to ride with Bob," Darla said. "Well, that's just men, I guess."

But Larry had an agenda that the girls weren't aware of. He knew that Bob and Darla were going dancing and wouldn't be home soon. So when he walked Michelle to the door of the apartment she and Darla shared, he pushed his way in and took off his jacket.

"Finally, alone together," he enthused, and reached for her. "Now, sweetie, let's have a little payback for the meal and the drinks…"

"Are you out of your mind?" she gasped, avoiding his grasping arms.

"I paid for the food," he said, almost snarling. "You owe me!"

"I owe you? Like hell I owe you!" She got to the door and opened it. "I'll send you a check for my part of the meal! Get out!"

"I'm not leaving. You just want to play hard to get." He started to push the door closed. And connected with a steely big hand that caught him by the arm, turned him around and booted him out into the night.

"Gabriel!" Michelle gasped.

"You can't do that to me…!" Larry said angrily, getting to his feet.

Gabriel fell into a fighting stance. "Come on," he said softly. "I could use the exercise."

Larry came to his senses. He glanced at Michelle. She went back inside, got his jacket, and threw it at him.

"Dinner doesn't come with bed," she told him icily.

Larry started to make a reply, but Gabriel's expression was a little too unsettling. He muttered something under his breath, turned, slammed into his car and roared away.

Gabriel went inside with Michelle, who was tearing up now that the drama had played itself out.

"Ah, no, *ma belle,*" he whispered. "There's no need for tears." He pulled her into his arms, bent his head, and kissed her so hungrily that she forgot to breathe.

He lifted his head. His black eyes were smoldering, so full of desire that they mesmerized Michelle. She tasted him on her mouth, felt the heavy throb of his heart under her hands.

"Finally," he breathed, pulling her close. He brushed his lips over her soft mouth. "Finally!"

She opened her mouth to ask what he meant, and the kiss knocked her so off balance that she couldn't manage a single word in reply. She held on with all her might, clung to him, pushed her body into his so that she could feel every movement of his powerful body against her. He was aroused, very quickly, and even that didn't intimidate her. She moaned. Which only made matters worse.

He picked her up, still kissing her, and laid her out on the couch, easing his body down over hers in a silence that throbbed with frustrated desire.

"Soft," he whispered. "Soft and sweet. All mine."

She would have said something, but he was kissing her again, and she couldn't think at all. She felt his big, rough hands go under her dress, up and up, touching and exploring, testing softness, finding her breasts under the lacy little bra.

"You feel like silk all over," he murmured. He found the zipper and eased her out of the dress and the half slip under it, then out of the bra, so that all she had left on were her briefs. He kissed his way down her body, lingering on her pert breasts with their tight little crowns, savoring her soft, helpless cries of pleasure.

It excited him to know that she'd never done this. He ate her up like candy, tasting her hungrily. He nuzzled her breasts, kissing their soft contours with a practiced touch that made her rise up in an aching arch to his lips.

Somehow, his jacket and shirt ended up on the floor. She felt the rough, curling hair on his chest against her bare breasts as his body covered hers. His powerful legs eased between her own, so that she could feel with him an intimacy she'd never shared with anyone.

She cried out as he moved against her. Sensations were piling on each other, dragging her under, drowning her in pleasure. She clung to him, pleading for more, not even knowing exactly what she wanted, but so drawn with tension that she was dying for it to ease.

She felt hot tears run down her cheeks as his mouth moved back onto hers. He touched her as he never had before. She shivered. The touch came again. She sobbed, and opened her mouth under his. She felt his tongue go into her mouth, as his hands moved on her more intimately.

Suddenly, like a fall of fire, a flash of agonized pleasure convulsed the soft body under his. He groaned and had to fight the instinctive urge to finish what he started, to go right into her, push inside her, take what was his, what had always been his.

But she was a virgin. His exploration had already told him that. He'd known already, by her reactions. She was very much a virgin. He didn't want to do this. Not yet. She was his. It must be done properly, in order, in a way that wouldn't shame her to remember somewhere down the line.

So he forced his shivering body to bear the pain. He held her very close while she recovered from her first ecstasy. He wrapped her up tight, and held her while he endured what he must to spare her innocence.

She wept. He kissed away the tears, so tenderly that they fell even harder, hot and wet on her flushed cheeks.

She was embarrassed and trying not to let him see.

He knew. He smiled and kissed her eyes shut. "It had to be with me," he whispered. "Only with me. I would rather die than know you had such an experience with any other man."

She opened her eyes and looked up into his. "Really?"

"Really." He looked down at her nudity, his eyes hungry again at the sight of her pink-and-peach skin, silky and soft and fragrant. He touched her breasts tenderly. "You are the most beautiful woman I will ever see."

Her lips parted on a shaky breath.

He bent and kissed her breasts. "And now we have to get up."

She stared at him.

"Or not get up," he murmured with a laugh. "Because I can't continue this much longer."

"It would be…all right," she whispered. "If you wanted to," she added.

"I want to," he said huskily. "But you won't be happy afterward. And you know it. Not like this, *ma belle*. Not our first time together. It has to be done properly."

"Properly?"

"You graduate from college, get a job, go to work. I come to see you bringing flowers and chocolates," he mused, tracing her mouth. "And then, eventually, a ring."

"A ring."

He nodded.

"An…engagement…ring?"

He smiled.

"People do it all the time, even before they get engaged," she said.

He got to his feet. "They do. But we won't."

"Oh."

He dressed her, enjoying the act of putting back onto her lovely body the things he'd taken off it. He laughed at her rapt expression. "You have a belief system that isn't going to allow a more modern approach to sex," he said blandly. "So we do it your way."

"I could adjust," she began, still hungry.

"Your happiness means a lot to me," he said simply. "I'm not going to spoil something beautiful with a tarnished memory. Not after I've waited so long."

She stared up into his black eyes. "I've waited for you, too," she whispered.

"I know." He smoothed back her hair just as they heard a car door slam and footsteps approaching.

Michelle looked horrified, thinking what could have happened, what condition they could have been in as Darla put her key into the lock.

Gabriel burst out laughing at her expression. "Now was I right?" he asked.

The door opened. Darla stopped with Bob in tow and just stared at Gabriel. Then she grinned. "Wow," she said. "Look what Larry changed into!"

And they all burst out laughing.

Michelle graduated with honors. Gabriel and Sara were both there for the ceremony, applauding when she walked down the aisle to accept her diploma. They went out to eat afterward, but once they were home, Gabriel couldn't stay. He was preoccupied, and very worried, from the look of things.

"Can you tell me what's wrong?" Michelle asked.

He shook his head. He bent to kiss her, very gently. "I'm going to have to be out of the country for two or three months."

"No!" she exclaimed.

"Only that. Then I have a job waiting, one that won't require so much travel," he promised. "Bear with me. I'm sorry. I have to do this."

She drew in a long breath. "Okay. If you have to go."

"You've got a job waiting in San Antonio, anyway," he reminded her with a smile. "On a daily newspaper. It has a solid reputation for reporting excellence. Make a name for yourself. But don't get too comfortable there," he added enigmatically. "Because when I get back, we need to talk."

"Talk." She smiled.

"And other things."

"Oh, yes, especially, other things," she whispered, dragging his mouth down to hers. She kissed him hungrily. He returned the kiss, but drew back discreetly when Sara came into the room. He hugged her, too.

He paused in the doorway and looked back at them, smiling. "Take care of each other." He grinned at his sister. "Happy?" he asked, referring to the changes in her life.

Sara laughed, tossing her long hair. "I could die of it." She sighed.

"I'll be back before you miss me," he told Michelle, who was looking sad. He wanted to kiss her, right there in front of the world. But it wasn't the time. And he wasn't sure he could stop.

"Impossible," Michelle said softly. "I miss you already."

He winked and closed the door.

Michelle liked the job. She had a desk and three years of solid education behind her to handle the assignments she was given.

A big story broke the second month she'd been with the newspaper. There was a massacre of women and children in a small Middle Eastern nation, perpetrated, it was said, by a group of mercenaries led by a Canadian national named Angel Le Veut. He had ties to an antiterrorism school run by a man named Eb Scott in, of all places, Jacobsville, Texas.

Michelle went on the offensive at once, digging up everything she could find about the men in the group who had killed the women and children in the small

Muslim community that was at odds with a multinational occupation force.

The name of the man accused of leading the assault was ironic. One of the languages she'd studied was French. And if loosely translated, the man's name came out as "Angel wants it." It was an odd play on words that was used most notably in the sixteenth century by authorities when certain cases were tried and a guilty verdict was desired. The phrase *"Le Roi le Veut"* meant that the king wanted the accused found guilty—whether or not he really was, apparently. The mysterious Angel was obviously an educated man with a knowledge of European history. Michelle was puzzled over why such a man would choose a lifestyle that involved violence.

Her first stop was Jacobsville, Texas, where she arranged an interview with Eb Scott, the counterterrorism expert, whose men had been involved in the massacre. Michelle knew him, from a distance.

Her father had gone to school with him and they were acquaintances. Her father had said there wasn't a finer man anywhere, that Eb was notorious for backing lost causes and fighting for the underdog. That didn't sound like a man who would order the murder of helpless women and children.

Eb shook her hand and invited her into his house. His wife and children were gone for the day, shopping in San Antonio for summer clothing. It was late spring already.

"Thank you for seeing me," Michelle said when they were seated. "Especially under the circumstances."

"Hiding from the press is never a good idea, but at times, in matters like this, it's necessary, until the truth can be ferreted out," Eb said solemnly. His green eyes searched hers. "You're Alan Godfrey's daughter."

"Yes," she said, smiling.

"You used to spend summers in Comanche Wells with your grandparents." He smiled back. "Minette Carson speaks well of you. She did an interview with me yesterday. Hopefully, some of the truth will trickle down to the mass news media before they crucify my squad leader."

"Yes. This man, Angel," she began, looking over her notes while Eb Scott grimaced and tried not to reveal what he really knew about the man, "his name is quite odd."

"Le Veut?" He smiled again. "He gets his way. He's something of an authority on sixteenth-century European history. He and Kilraven, one of the feds who's married to a local girl, go toe-to-toe over whether or not Mary Queen of Scots really helped Lord Bothwell murder her husband."

"Has this man worked for you, with you, for a long time?" she asked.

He nodded. "Many years. He's risked his life time and time again to save innocents. I can promise you that when the truth comes out, and it will, he'll be exonerated."

She was typing on her small notebook computer as he spoke. "He's a Canadian national?"

"He has dual citizenship, here and in Canada," he corrected. "But he's lived in the States most of his life."

"Does he live in Jacobsville?"

Eb hesitated.

She lifted her hands from the keyboard. "You wouldn't want to say, would you?" she asked perceptibly. "If he has family, it could hurt them, as well. There wouldn't be a place they could go where the media wouldn't find them."

"The media can be like a dog after a juicy bone," Eb said with some irritation. "They'll get fed one way or the other, with truth or, if time doesn't permit, with lies. I've seen lives ruined by eager reporters out to make a name for themselves." He paused. "Present company excepted," he added gently. "I know all about you from Minette."

She smiled gently. "Thanks. I always try to be fair and present both sides of the story without editorializing. I don't like a lot of what I see on television, presented as fair coverage. Most of the commentators seem quite biased to me. They convict people and act as judge, jury and executioner." She shook her head. "I like the paper I work for. Our editor, even our publisher, are fanatics for accurate and fair coverage. They fired a reporter last month whose story implicated an innocent man. He swore he had eyewitnesses to back up the facts, and that he could prove them. Later, when the editor sent other reporters out to recheck—after the innocent man's attorneys filed a lawsuit—they found that the reporter had ignored people who could verify the man's whereabouts at the time of the crime. The reporter didn't even question them."

Eb sighed, leaning back in his recliner. "That happens all too often. Even on major newspapers," he added, alluding to a reporter for one of the very large East Coast dailies who'd recently been let go for fabricating stories.

"We try," Michelle said quietly. "We really try. Most

reporters only want to help people, to point out problems, to help better the world around us."

"I know that. It's the one bad apple in the barrel that pollutes the others," he said.

"This man, Angel, is there any way I could interview him?"

He almost bit through his lip. He couldn't tell her that. "No," he said finally. "We've hidden him in a luxury hotel in a foreign country. The news media will have a hell of a time trying to ferret him out. We have armed guards in native dress everywhere. Meanwhile, I've hired an investigative firm out of Houston—Dane Lassiter's—to dig out the truth. Believe me, there's no one in the world better at it. He's a former Houston policeman."

"I know of him," she replied. "His son was involved in a turf war between drug lords in the area, wasn't he?"

"Yes, he was. That was a while back."

"Well, tell me what you can," she said. "I'll do my best not to convict the man in print. The mercenaries who were with Angel," she added, "are they back in the States?"

"That's another thing I can't tell you right now," he replied. "I'm not trying to be evasive. I'm protecting my men from trial by media. We have attorneys for all of them, and our investigator hopes to have something concrete for us, and the press, very soon."

"That's fair enough."

"Here's what we know right now," Eb said. "My squad leader was given an assignment by a State Department official to interview a local tribesman in a village in Anasrah. The man had information about a group of terrorists who were hiding in the village—protected by a high-ranking government official, we were told. My squad leader, in disguise, took a small team in to interview him, but when he and his men arrived, the tribesman and his entire family were dead. One of the terrorists pointed the finger at Angel and accused his team of the atrocity. I'm certain the terrorist was paid handsomely to do it."

Michelle frowned. "You believe that?"

Eb stared her down with glittering green eyes. "Miss Godfrey, if you knew Angel, you wouldn't have to ask me that question."

"Sorry," she said. "It's my job, Mr. Scott."

He let out a breath. "You can't imagine how painful this is for me," he said. "Men I trained, men I've worked with, accused of something so inhuman." His face hardened. "Follow the money. It's all about the money, I assure you," he added curtly. "Someone stands to lose a lot of it if the truth comes out."

"I can only imagine how bad it must be," she said, and not without sympathy.

She asked questions, he answered them. She was impressed by him. He wasn't at all the sort of person that she'd pictured when she heard people speak of mercenaries. Even the word meant a soldier for hire, a man who sold his talents to the highest bidder. But Eb Scott's organization trained men in counterterrorism. He had an enormous operation in Jacobsville, and men and women came from around the world to learn from his experts. There were rumors that a few government agents had also availed themselves of his expertise.

The camp was state-of-the-art, with every electronic gadget known to modern science—and a few things that were largely experimental. They taught everything from evasive driving techniques to disarming bombs, improvised weapons, stealth, martial arts, the works. Michelle was allowed to photograph only a small section of the entire operation, and she wasn't allowed to photograph any of his instructors or the students. But even with the reservations on what she was shown, what she learned fascinated her.

"Well, I'll never think of mercenaries the same way again, Mr. Scott," she said when she was ready to leave. "This operation is very impressive."

"I'm glad you think so."

She paused at the door and turned. "You know, the electronic media have resources that those of us in print journalism don't. I mean, we have a digital version of our paper online, like most everyone does. But the big networks employ dozens of experts who can find out anything. If they want to find your man, they will. And his family."

"Miss Godfrey, for the sake of a lot of innocent people, I hope you're wrong."

The way he said it stayed on her mind for hours after she left.

Chapter 11

Michelle wrote the story, and she did try to be fair. But when she saw the photographs of the massacre, the bodies of small children with women and men weeping over them, her heart hardened. If the man was guilty, he should be hanged for this.

She didn't slant the story. She presented the facts from multiple points of view. She interviewed a man in Saudi Arabia who had a friend in Anasrah with whom he'd recently spoken. She interviewed a representative of the State Department, who said that one of their staff had been led into the village by a minor government official just after the attack and was adamant that the mercenaries had been responsible for the slaughter. She also interviewed an elder in the village, through an interpreter, who said that an American had led the attack.

There was another man, also local, who denied that

a foreigner was responsible. He was shouted down by the others, but Michelle managed to get their representative in Saudi Arabia to go to Anasrah, a neighboring country, and interview the man in the village. His story contradicted the others. He said that it was a man well-known in terrorist circles who had come into the village and accused the tribesmen of betraying their own people by working with the government and foreigners. He said that if it continued, an example, a horrible example, would be made, he would see to it personally.

The local man said that he could prove that the terrorists themselves had perpetrated the attack, if he had time.

Michelle made the first big mistake of her career in journalism by discounting the still, small voice in the wilderness. The man's story didn't ring true. She took notes, and filed them on her computer. But when she wrote the story, she left out what sounded like a made-up tale.

The story broke with the force of bombs. All of a sudden, it was all anyone heard on the media. The massacre in Anasrah, the children murdered by foreigners, the mercenaries who had cut them down with automatic weapons while their parents pleaded for mercy. On television, the weeping relatives were interviewed. Their stories brought even hardened commentators to tears on-screen.

Michelle's story, with its unique point of view and Eb Scott's interview—which none of the national media had been able to get, because he refused to talk to them—put her in the limelight for the first time. Her story was reprinted partially in many national papers, and she was interviewed by the major news networks, as well. She respected Eb Scott, she added, and she thought he was sincere, but she wept for the dead children and she thought the mercenary responsible should be tried in the world court and imprisoned for the rest of his life.

Her impulsive comment was broadcast over and over. And just after that came the news that the mercenary had a sister, living in Wyoming. They had her name, as well. Sara.

It could have been a coincidence. Except that suddenly she remembered that the man, Angel, had both American and Canadian citizenship. Now she learned that he had a sister named Sara. Gabriel was gone for long periods of time overseas on jobs. Michelle still tried to persuade herself that it wasn't, couldn't, be Gabriel.

Until Sara called her on the phone.

"I couldn't believe it when they said you broke the story," she said in a cold tone. "How could you do this to us?"

"Sara, it wasn't about anyone you know," she said quickly. "It was about a mercenary who gunned down little children in a Middle Eastern village…!"

"He did nothing of the sort," Sara said, her voice dripping ice. "It was the tribesman's brother-in-law, one of the terrorists, who killed the man and his family and then blamed it on Angel and his men."

"Do you know this man Angel?" Michelle asked, a sick feeling in her stomach because Sara sounded so harsh.

"Know him." Her laugh was as cold as death. "We both know him, Michelle. He uses Angel as an alias when he goes on missions for Eb Scott's clients. But his name is Gabriel."

Michelle felt her blood run cold. Images flashed through her mind. Dead children. The one dissenting voice, insisting that it was the terrorists not the Americans who perpetrated the horror. Her refusal to listen, to print the other side of the story. Gabriel's side. She'd convinced herself that it couldn't be Gabriel. Now she had to face facts.

"I didn't know," she said, her voice breaking. "Sara, believe me, I didn't know!"

"Eb told you it wasn't him," Sara said furiously. "But you wouldn't listen. I had a contact in the State Department send a man to tell your newspaper's agent about the dead man's brother-in-law. And you decided not to print it. Didn't you? God forbid you should run against the voice of the world press and risk your own glowing reputation as a crusader for justice by dissenting!"

"I didn't know," Michelle repeated through tears.

"You didn't know! If Gabriel ends up headfirst in a ditch somewhere, it will be all right, because you didn't know! Would you like to see the road in front of our ranch here in Wyoming, Michelle?" she added. "It looks like a tent city, surrounded by satellite trucks. They're certain they'll wear me down and I'll come out and accuse my brother for them!"

"I'm so sorry." Michelle didn't have to be told that Gabriel was innocent. She knew he was. But she'd helped convict him.

"You're sorry. I'll be certain to tell him when, and if, I see him again." There was a harshly indrawn breath. "He phoned me two days ago," she said in a haunted voice. "They're hunting him like an animal, thanks to you. When I told him who sold him out, he wouldn't believe me. It wasn't until I sent him a link to your story that he saw for himself."

Michelle felt every drop of blood draining out of her face. "What…did he say?"

"He said," Sara replied, enunciating every word, "that he'd never been so wrong about anyone in his life. He thought that you, of all people, would defend him even against the whole world. He said," she added coldly, "that he never wanted to see you or hear from you again as long as he lived."

The words were like bullets. She could actually feel their impact.

"I loved you like my own sister," Sara said, her voice breaking. "And I will never, never forgive you!" She slammed down the phone.

Michelle realized after a minute that she hadn't broken the connection. She hung up her own telephone. She sat down heavily and heard the recriminations break over her head again and again.

She remembered Eb Scott's certainty that his man would never do such a thing. Sara's fierce anger. It had been easy to discount them while Angel was a shadowy figure without substance. But Michelle knew Gabriel. And she was certain, absolutely certain, that the man who'd saved her from suicide would never put another human being in harm's way.

It took two days for the effects of Sara's phone call to wear off enough that she could stop crying and blaming herself. The news media was having a field day with the story, running updates about it all day, every day, either in newscasts or in banners under the anchor people. Michelle finally had to turn off the television to escape it, so that she could get herself back together.

She wanted, so desperately, to make up for what she'd done. But she didn't even know where to start. The story was everywhere. People were condemning the American mercenaries on every news program in the world.

But Gabriel was innocent. Michelle had helped convict him in the press, without knowing who she was writing about. Now it was her turn to do her job properly, and give both sides of the story, however unpopular. She had to save him, if she could, even if he hated her forever for what she'd done.

So she went back to work. Her first act was to contact the newspaper's man in Saudi Arabia and ask him to repeat the story his informant in Anasrah had told him. Then she contacted Eb Scott and gave him the information, so that he could pass it on to his private investigator. Before she did that, she asked him to call her back on a secure line, because she knew how some of the tabloid news bureaus sometimes had less scrupulous agents digging out information.

"You're learning, Miss Godfrey," Eb said solemnly.

"Not soon enough. I know who Angel is now," she added heavily. "His sister hates me. He told her that he never wanted to see or speak to me again, either. And I deserve that. I wasn't objective, and people are paying for my error. But I have to do what I can to undo the mess I helped make. I'm sorry I didn't listen."

"Too little, and almost too late," he said brutally.

"Learn from it. Sometimes the single dissenting voice is the right one."

"I won't forget," she said.

He hung up.

She tried to phone Sara back and apologize once again, to tell her she was trying to repair the damage. But Sara wouldn't accept the first phone call and after that, her number was blocked. She was heartsick. The Brandons had been so good to her. They'd made sacrifices to get her through school, through college, always been there when she needed help. And she'd repaid them like this. It wounded her as few things in life ever had.

When she tried to speak to her editor in confidence, to backtrack on the story she'd written, he laughed it off. The man was obviously guilty, he said, why make waves now? She'd made a name for herself in investigative reporting, it was all good.

She told him that Angel wasn't the sort of person to ever harm a child. Then he wanted to know how she knew that. She wouldn't reveal her source, she said, falling back on a tried and true response. But the man was innocent.

Her editor had just laughed. So she thought the guy was innocent, what did it matter? The news was the thing that mattered, scooping all the other media and being first and best at delivering the story. She'd given the facts of the matter, that was the end of it. She should just enjoy her celebrity status while it lasted.

Michelle went back to her apartment that night saddened and weary, with a new sense of disillusionment about life and people.

* * *

The next morning, she phoned Minette Carson and asked if she had an opening for a reporter who was certain she wasn't cut out for the big dailies.

Minette was hesitant.

"Look, never mind," Michelle said gently. "I know I've made a lot of enemies in Jacobsville with the way I covered the story. It's okay. I can always teach journalism. I'll be a natural at showing students what not to do."

"We all have to start somewhere when we learn how to do a job," Minette replied. "Usually, it's a painful process. Eb Scott called and asked me, before you did the interview, if you knew who Gabriel really was. I told him no. I knew you'd have said something long before this. I should have told you."

"I should have suspected something," came the sad reply. "He was away from home for long stretches, he spoke a dozen impossible languages, he was secretive about what sort of work he did—I just wasn't paying attention."

"It amused everyone when he took you in as his ward," Minette said. "He was one of the coldest men Eb Scott ever hired—well, after Carson, who works for Cy Parks, that is." She chuckled. "But once you came along, all of a sudden Gabriel was smiling."

"He won't be anymore," Michelle said, feeling the pain to the soles of her feet.

"Give it time," was the older woman's advice. "First, you have some work to do."

"I know. I'm going to do everything in my power to prove him innocent. Whatever it takes," Michelle added firmly.

"That's more like it. And about the job," she replied. "Once you've proven that you aren't running away from an uncomfortable assignment, we'll have a place for you here. That's a promise."

"Thanks."

"You're welcome."

Michelle convinced Eb Scott to let her talk to his detective. It worked out well, because Dane Lassiter was actually in San Antonio for a seminar that week and he agreed to meet with her in a local restaurant.

He wasn't exactly what she'd expected. He was tall, dark-haired and dark-eyed, with an easygoing manner and a wife who was thirtysomething and very attractive. She, like Michelle, was blonde.

"We always go together when he has to give seminars." Tess laughed. "At least once I've had to chase a pursuing woman out of his room." She shook her head, sighing as she met her husband's amused gaze. "Well, after all, I know he's a dish. Why shouldn't other women notice?"

Michelle laughed with them, but her heart wasn't in it. There had been a snippet of news on television the night before, showing a camp of journalists on the road that led to the Brandons' Wyoming property. They were still trying to get Sara to talk to them. But this time they were met with a steely-eyed man Michelle recognized as Wofford Patterson, who was advising them to decamp before some of Sara's friends loosed a few bears on the property in a conservation project. Patterson had become Sara's personal protector and much more, after many years of antagonism.

"I've been watching the press reports on Brandon,"

Dane said, having guessed the train of her thoughts. "You watch six different reports and get six different stories."

"Yes," Michelle said sadly. "Not everyone tries for accuracy. And I can include myself in that company, because I should have gone the extra mile and presented the one dissenting opinion. It was easy to capitulate, because I didn't think I had any interest in the outcome," she added miserably.

Tess's pale eyes narrowed. "Mr. Brandon was your guardian."

She nodded. He was more, but she wasn't sharing that news with a virtual stranger. "I sold him out. I didn't mean to. I had no idea Angel was Gabriel. It was hard, going against a majority opinion. Everyone said he was guilty as sin. I saw the photographs of the women and children." Her face hardened. "It was easy to believe it, after that."

"I've seen similar things," Dane said, sipping black coffee. "But I can tell you that things are rarely what they seem."

She told him about her contacts, and he took notes, getting names and telephone numbers and putting together a list of people to interview.

He put up his pen and notebook. "This is going to be a lot of help to the men who were blamed for the tragedy," he said finally. "There's a violent element in the country in question, dedicated to rooting out any hint of foreign influence, however beneficial. But at the same time, in their ranks are a few who see a way to quick profit, a way to fund their terrorism and inflict even more horror on our overseas personnel. This group that put your friend in the middle of the controversy is made up of a few money-hungry profiteers. Our State Department has worked very hard to try to stifle them. We have several oil corporations with offices there, and a good bit of our foreign oil is shipped from that country. We depend on the goodwill of the locals to keep the oil companies' officials and workers safe. The terrorists know that, and they see a way to make a quick profit through kidnappings and other attacks. Except that instead of holding people for ransom, they threaten violence if their demands aren't met. It's almost like a protection racket…"

"That's what he meant," Michelle said suddenly.

"Excuse me?"

"Eb Scott said, 'follow the money,'" she recalled.

"Eb's sharp. Yes, that's apparently what's behind all this. The terrorist leader wanted millions in bribes to protect oil company executives in his country. The brother-in-law of the leader was selling him out to our State Department. A lot of local men work for the oil companies and don't want any part of the terrorist's plans. It's a poor country, and the oil companies provide a secure living for the village. But nobody makes waves and gets away with it. The terrorist leader retaliated, in the worst possible way, and blamed it on Angel and his men—a way of protecting his own men, whom he ordered to kill his brother-in-law to keep him from talking. It was also a way of notifying foreigners that this is how any future attempts to bypass his authority would be handled."

"I'm not telling you anything you didn't already know," she said suddenly.

"I knew it. I couldn't prove it," he added. "But you've given me contacts who can back up the protester's story.

I'll have my investigators check them out and our attorneys will take depositions that will hold up in court. It will give the State Department's representatives the leverage they need to deal with the terrorists. And it will provide our news media with a week of guaranteed stories," he added coldly.

She sighed. "I think I'm in the wrong business."

"Good reporters can do a lot of good in the world," Tess interrupted. "It's just that there's more profit in digging up dirt on people."

"Amen," Dane said.

"Well, if I can help dig Gabriel out of the hole I put him into, I'll be happy," Michelle told him. "It's little enough in the way of apology."

"If you hear anything else, through your sources, you can call me anytime," he told her.

"I'll remember."

Dane went to pay the check, against Michelle's protests.

Tess smiled at her. "You really care about the mercenary, don't you?" she asked.

"More than you know," Michelle replied. "He and his sister sacrificed a lot for me. I'll never be able to pay them back. And now, this has happened...."

"At least you're trying to make up for it," she replied. "That's worth something."

"I hope it's worth enough. I'm grateful to you and your husband for meeting with me."

"It was a nice interlude between the rehashing of horrible cases." Tess laughed. "I work as a skip tracer, something Dane would never let me do before. My father planned to marry his mother, but they were killed in a wreck, so Dane became sort of responsible for me," she added surprisingly. "He wasn't very happy about it. We had a rocky road to the altar." She smiled. "But a son and a daughter later, we're very content."

"You don't look old enough to have two children." Michelle laughed. "Either of you."

"Thanks. But believe me, we are."

Dane was back, putting away his wallet. He handed Michelle a business card. "My cell's on there, as well as the office number."

"I'll cross my fingers, that our contacts can help you get Gabriel and his men off the hook," Michelle said.

His eyes narrowed. "I'm surprised that the national news media hasn't been camped on your doorstep," he remarked.

"Gabriel didn't advertise his involvement with me," she replied. "And nobody in Jacobsville, Texas, will tell them a thing, believe me."

He smiled. "I noticed the way the locals shut them out when they waltzed into town with their satellite trucks. Amazing, that the restaurants all ran out of food and the motels were all full and nobody had a single room to rent out at any price."

She smiled angelically. "I'm sure that was mostly true."

"They did try Comanche Wells, I hear," Dane added.

"Well, see, Comanche Wells doesn't have a restaurant or a motel at all."

"That explains it."

She went back to work, only to find her desk piled high with notes.

"Hey, Godfrey, can't you get your answering machine to work?" Murphy, one of the older reporters whose desk was beside hers, asked. "My old hands are too gnarled to take notes from all your darned callers."

"Sorry, Murph," she said. She was frowning when she noticed who the notes were from. "They want to send a limo for me and have me stay at the Plaza?" she exclaimed.

"What it is to be a celebrity," Murph shook his head. "Hey, there was this cool video that Brad Paisley did, about being a celebrity…!"

"I saw it. Thanks," she said, waving the notes at him. She picked up her purse and left the building, just avoiding her editor on the way out the door.

Apparently the news media had found somebody in Jacobsville who was willing to talk to them. She wondered with droll cynicism what the informant had been paid.

She discovered that if she agreed to do an exclusive interview with just one station, the others would have to leave her alone. Before she signed any papers, she spoke with an attorney and had him check out the agreement.

"It says that I agree to tell them my story," she said.

"Exactly," he replied.

She pursed her lips. "It doesn't specify which story."

"I think they'll assume it means the story they want to hear," he replied. "Although that's implied rather than stated."

"Ah."

"And I would advise caution when they ask you to name the person overseas whom your newspaper provided as a reference regarding the informer," he added. "That may be a protected source."

"I was hoping you'd notice that. It is a protected source."

He only smiled.

She sat down in front of the television cameras with a well-known, folksy interviewer who was calm, gentle and very intelligent. He didn't press her for details she couldn't give, and he understood that some sources of information that she had access to were protected.

"I understand from what you told our correspondent that you don't believe the men in question actually perpetrated the attack, which resulted in the deaths of several women and small children," he began.

"That's correct."

"Would you tell me why?"

"When I first broke the story, I went on the assumption that because the majority of the interviewees placed the blame on the American mercenaries, they must be guilty. There was, however, one conflicting opinion. A villager, whom I cannot name, said that extortion was involved and that money was demanded for the protection of foreign workers. When a relative of the extortionist threatened to go to the authorities and reveal the financial aspect, he and his family were brutally murdered as a warning. These murders were blamed on the Americans who had, in fact, been working for the government trying to uncover a nest of terrorists threatening American oil company employees there."

The interviewer was frowning. "Then the massacre was, in fact, retaliation for the villager's threat to expose the extortionist."

"That is my information, yes."

He studied a sheet of paper. "I see here that the newspaper which employs you used its own foreign sources to do interviews about this story."

"Those sources are also protected," Michelle replied. "I can't name them."

He pursed his lips and, behind his lenses, his blue eyes twinkled. "I understand. But I believe the same sources have been named, in the press, by attorneys for the men allegedly implicated by the international press for the atrocities."

She smiled. "I believe so."

"In which case," he added, "we have elicited permission to quote one of the sources. He has signed an affidavit, which is in the hands of our State Department. Please welcome Mr. David Arbuckle, who is liaison for the U.S. Department of State in Anasrah, which is at the center of this matter. Mr. Arbuckle, welcome."

"Thank you, Mr. Price," a pleasant-looking, middle-aged man replied. He was in a studio in Washington, D.C., his image provided via satellite.

"Now, from what Ms. Godfrey has told us—and we have validated her story—a terrorist cell had infiltrated the village in question and made threats against foreign nationals including ours. Is this true?"

"It is," Mr. Arbuckle said solemnly. "We're very grateful to Ms. Godfrey for bringing this matter to our attention. We were told that a group of mercenaries muscled their way into the village, demanding tribute and killed people when their demands were not met. This is a very different story than we were able to verify by speaking, under offer of protection, to other men in the same village."

He coughed, then continued, "We were able to ascertain that a terrorist cell with links to another notorious international organization was going to fund itself by extorting money from oil corporations doing business near the village. They were using the village itself for cover, posing as innocent tribesmen."

"Abominable," the host replied.

"Yes, killing innocents to prove a point is a particularly bloodthirsty manner in which to operate. The local people were terrified to say anything, after the massacre, although they felt very sad that innocent men were blamed for it. In fact, the so-called mercenaries had provided medical supplies and treatment for many children and elderly people and even helped buy food for them."

"A laudable outreach effort."

"Indeed," Mr. Arbuckle replied grimly. "Suffice it to say that we have used our influence to make sure that the terrorists no longer have a foothold in the village, and the international community has moved people in to assure the safety of the tribesmen who provided us with this information."

"Then the American mercenaries are being cleared of any involvement with the massacre?"

"I can assure you that they have been," Mr. Arbuckle replied. "We were provided with affidavits and other documents concerning the massacre by an American private detective working in concert with the mercenaries' attorneys. They were allowed to leave the country last night and are en route to a secure location while we deal with the terrorists in question. The terrorists responsible for the massacre will be brought to trial for the murders and held accountable. And the mercenaries will return to testify against them."

"I'm sure our viewers will be happy to hear that."

"We protect our people overseas," Mr. Arbuckle

replied. "All of them. And in fact, the mercenaries in question were private contractors working for the United States government, not the sort of soldiers for hire that often involve themselves in foreign conflicts."

"Another surprise," Mr. Price said with a smile.

"In this day and time, we all have to be alert about our surroundings abroad," Mr. Arbuckle said. "We take care of our own," he added with a smile.

"Thank you for your time, Mr. Arbuckle."

"Thank you for yours, Mr. Price."

Mr. Price turned back to Michelle. "It was a very brave thing you did, Ms. Godfrey, going up against the weight of the international press to defend these men. I understand that you know some of them."

"I know Eb Scott, who runs an international school of counterterrorism," Michelle corrected, unwilling to say more. "He has great integrity. I can't imagine that any agents he trained would ever go against basic humanitarianism."

"He has a good advocate here." He chuckled.

"I learned a lesson from this, as well," she replied quietly. "That you don't discount the single small voice in the wilderness when you write a story that can cost lives and reputations. It is one I hope I never have to repeat." She paused. "I'd like to thank my editor for standing by me," she added, lying because he hadn't, "and for teaching me the worth of integrity in reporting."

Mr. Price named the newspaper in San Antonio and thanked her for appearing on his program.

Back in the office, her editor, Len Worthington, was ecstatic. "That was the nicest plug we ever got from anybody! Thanks, kid!" he told her, shaking her hand.

"You're welcome. Thanks for not firing me for messing up so badly."

"Hey, what are friends for?"

He'd never know, she thought, but she only smiled. She'd seen a side of journalism that left her feeling sick. It wasn't pretty.

She didn't try to call Sara again. The poor woman probably hadn't seen the program Michelle was on. It was likely that she was avoiding any sort of press coverage of what had happened. That wasn't hard anymore, because there was a new scandal topping the news now, and all the satellite trucks had gone in search of other prey. Michelle's phone had stopped ringing. There were no more notes on her desk, no more offers of limos and five-star hotels. She didn't mind at all.

She only hoped that one day Sara and Gabriel would forgive her. She went back to work on other stories, mostly political ones, and hoped that she'd never be in a position again where she'd have to sell out her nearest and dearest for a job. Not that she ever would. Nor would she have done it, if she'd had any idea who Gabriel really was.

Michelle had thought about asking Minette for a job again. She wasn't really happy living in the city and she cringed every time someone mentioned her name in connection with the past big news story.

She still hadn't heard from Gabriel or Sara. She didn't expect to. She'd hoped that they might contact her. But that was wishful thinking.

She now owned the home where her father and, before him, her grandparents had lived in Comanche

Wells. She couldn't bear to drive the Jaguar that Gabriel and Sara had given her...driving it made her too sad. So she parked it at Gabriel's house and put the key in the mail slot. One day, she assumed, he'd return and see it. She bought a cute little VW bug, with which she could commute from Jacobsville to work in San Antonio. She moved back home.

At first, people were understandably a little standoffish. She was an outsider, even though she was born in Jacobs County. Perhaps they thought she was going to go all big-city on them and start poking her nose into local politics.

When she didn't do that, the tension began to ease a little. When she went into Barbara's Café to have lunch on Saturdays, people began to nod and smile at her. When she went grocery shopping in the local supermarket, the cashier actually talked to her. When she got gas at the local station, the attendant finally stopped asking for identification when she presented her credit card. Little by little, she was becoming part of Jacobs County again.

Carlie came to visit occasionally. She was happily married, and expecting her first child. They weren't as close as they had been, but it made Michelle feel good to know that her friend was settled and secure.

She only wished that she could be, settled and secure. But as months went by with no word of or from the Brandons, she gave up all hope that she might one day be forgiven for the things she'd written.

She knew that Sara had a whole new life in Wyoming from the cashier at the grocery store who had known her. Michelle didn't blame her for not wanting to come back to Texas. After all, she'd only lived in Comanche Wells as a favor to Gabriel, so that he could be Michelle's guardian.

Guardian no more, obviously. He'd given up that before, of course, when she turned twenty-one. But sometimes Michelle wished that she still had at least a relationship with him. She mourned what could have been, before she lost her way. Gabriel had assured her that they had a future. But that was before.

She was hanging out sheets in the yard, fighting the fierce autumn breeze to keep them from blowing away, when she heard a vehicle coming down the long road. It was odd, because nobody lived out this way except Michelle. It was Saturday. The next morning, she'd planned to go to church. She'd missed it for a couple of Sundays while she worked on a hot political story.

These days, not even the Reverend Blair came visiting much. She didn't visit other people, either. Her job occupied much of her time, because a reporter was always on call. But Michelle still attended services most Sundays.

So she stared at the truck as it went past the house. Its windows were tinted, and rolled up. It was a new truck, a very fancy one. Perhaps someone had bought the old Brandon place, she concluded, and went back to hanging up clothes. It made her sad to think that Gabriel would sell the ranch. But, after all, what would he need it for? He only had a manager there to care for it, so it wasn't as if he needed to keep it. He had other things to do.

She'd heard from Minette that Gabriel was part of an international police force now, one that Eb Scott had contracted with to provide security for those Middle Eastern oilmen who had played such a part in Gabriel's close call.

She wondered if he would ever come back to Comanche Wells. But she was fairly certain he wouldn't. Too many bad memories.

Chapter 12

Michelle finished hanging up her sheets in the cool breeze and went back into the house to fix herself a sandwich.

There were rumors at work that a big story was about to break involving an oil corporation and a terrorist group in the Middle East, one that might have local ties. Michelle, now her editor's favorite reporter for having mentioned him on TV, was given the assignment. It might, he hinted, involve some overseas travel. Not to worry, the paper would gladly pay her expenses.

She wondered what sort of mess she might get herself into this time, poking her nose into things she didn't understand. Well, it was a job, and she was lucky to even have one in this horrible economy.

She finished her sandwich and drank a cup of black coffee. For some reason she thought of Gabriel, and how

much he'd enjoyed her coffee. She had to stop thinking about him. She'd almost cost him his life. She'd destroyed his peace of mind and Sara's, subjected them
both to cameras and reporters and harassment. It was
not really a surprise that they weren't speaking to her
anymore. Even if she'd gone the last mile defending
them, trying to make up for her lack of foresight, it
didn't erase the damage she'd already done.

She was bored to death. The house was pretty. She'd
made improvements—she'd redecorated Roberta's old
room and had the whole place repainted. She'd put up
new curtains and bought new furniture. But the house
was cold and empty.

Back when her father was alive, it still held echoes of
his parents, of him. Now, it was a reminder of old tragedies, most especially her father's death and Roberta's.

She carried her coffee into the living room and
looked around her. She ought to sell it and move into
an apartment in San Antonio. She didn't have a pet,
not even a dog or cat, and the livestock her father had
owned were long gone. She had nothing to hold her
here except a sad attachment to the past, to dead people.

But there was something that kept her from letting
go. She knew what it was, although she didn't want to
remember. It was Gabriel. He'd eaten here, slept here,
comforted her here. It was warm with memories that
no other dwelling place would ever hold.

She wondered if she couldn't just photograph the
rooms and blow up the photos, make posters of them,
and sacrifice the house.

Sure, she thought hollowly. Of course she could.

She finished her coffee and turned on the television.
Same old stories. Same programs with five minutes of

commercials for every one minute of programming. She switched it off. These days she only watched DVDs or streamed movies from internet websites. She was too antsy to sit through a hundred commercials every half hour.

She wondered why people put up with it. If everyone stopped watching television, wouldn't the advertisers be forced to come up with alternatives that compromised a bit more? Sure. And cows would start flying any day.

That reminded her of the standing joke she'd had with Grier and Gabriel about cows being abducted by aliens, and it made her sad.

Outside, she heard the truck go flying past her house. It didn't even slow down. Must be somebody looking at Gabriel's house. She wondered if he'd put it on the market without bothering to put a for-sale sign out front. Why not? He had no real ties here. He'd probably moved up to Wyoming to live near Sara.

She went into the kitchen, put her coffee cup in the sink, and went back to her washing.

She wore a simple beige skirt and a short-sleeved beige sweater to church with pretty high heels and a purse to match. She left her hair long, down her back, and used only a trace of makeup on her face.

She'd had ample opportunities for romance, but all those years she'd waited for Gabriel, certain that he was going to love her one day, that she had a future with him. Now that future was gone. She knew that one day, she'd have to decide if she really wanted to be nothing more than a career woman with notoriety and money taking the place of a husband and children and a settled life.

There was nothing wrong with ambition. But the few career women she'd known seemed empty somehow, as if they presented a happy face to the world but that it was like a mask, hiding the insecurities and loneliness that accompanied a demanding lifestyle. What would it be like to grow old, with no family around you, with only friends and acquaintances and business associates to mark the holidays? Would it make up for the continuity of the next generation and the generation after that, of seeing your features reproduced down through your children and grandchildren and great-grandchildren? Would it make up for laughing little voices and busy little hands, and soft kisses on your cheek at bedtime?

That thought made her want to cry. She'd never thought too much about kids during her school days, but when Gabriel had kissed her and talked about a future, she'd dreamed of having his children. It had been a hunger unlike anything she'd ever known.

She had to stop tormenting herself. She had to come to grips with the world the way it was, not the way she wanted it to be. She was a grown woman with a promising career. She had to look ahead, not behind her.

She slid into her usual pew, listened to Reverend Blair's sermon and sang along with the choir as they repeated the chorus of a well-loved old hymn. Sometime during the offering, she was aware of a tingling sensation, as if someone were watching her. She laughed silently. Now she was getting paranoid.

As the service ended, and they finished singing the final hymn, as the benediction sounded in Reverend Blair's clear, deep voice, she continued to have the sensation that someone was watching her.

Slowly, as her pew filed out into the aisle, she glanced toward the back of the church. But there was no one there, no one looking at her. What a strange sensation.

Reverend Blair shook her hand and smiled at her. "It's nice to have you back, Miss Godfrey," he teased.

She smiled back. "Rub it in. I had a nightmare of a political story to follow. I spent so much time on it that I'm thinking I may run for public office myself. By now, I know exactly what not to do to get elected," she confided with a chuckle.

"I know what you mean. It was a good story."

"Thanks."

"See you next week."

"I hope." She crossed her fingers. He just smiled.

She walked to her car and clicked the smart key to unlock it when she felt, rather than saw, someone behind her.

She turned and her heart stopped in her chest. She looked up into liquid black eyes in a tanned, hard face that looked as if it had never known a smile.

She swallowed. She wanted to say so many things. She wanted to apologize. She wanted to cry. She wanted to throw herself into his arms and beg him to hold her, comfort her, forgive her. But she did none of those things. She just looked up at him hopelessly, with dead eyes that looked as if they had never held joy.

His square chin lifted. His eyes narrowed on her face. "You've lost weight."

She shrugged. "One of the better consequences of my profession," she said quietly. "How are you, Gabriel?"

"I've been better."

She searched his eyes. "How's Sara?"

"Getting back to normal."

She nodded. She swallowed again and dropped her eyes to his chest. It was hard to find something to say that didn't involve apologies or explanations or pleas for forgiveness.

The silence went on for so long that she could hear pieces of conversation from other churchgoers. She could hear the traffic on the highway, the sound of children playing in some yard nearby. She could hear the sound of her own heartbeat.

This was destroying her. She clicked the key fob again deliberately. "I have to go," she said softly.

"Sure."

He moved back so that she could open the door and get inside. She glanced at him with sorrow in her face, but she averted her eyes so that it didn't embarrass him. She didn't want him to feel guilty. She was the one who should feel that emotion. In the end she couldn't meet his eyes or even wave. She just started the car and drove away.

Well, at least the first meeting was over with, she told herself later. It hadn't been quite as bad as she'd expected. But it had been rough. She felt like crying, but her eyes were dry. Some pain was too deep to be eased by tears, she thought sadly.

She changed into jeans and a red T-shirt and went out on the front porch to water her flowers while a TV dinner microwaved itself to perfection in the kitchen.

Her flowers were going to be beautiful when they bloomed, she decided, smiling as they poked their little heads up through the dirt in an assortment of ceramic pots all over the wooden floor.

She had three pots of chrysanthemums and one little bonsai tree named Fred. Gabriel had given it to her when she first moved in with them, a sort of welcome present. It was a tiny fir tree with a beautiful curving trunk and feathery limbs. She babied it, bought it expensive fertilizer, read books on how to keep it healthy and worried herself to death that it might accidentally die if she forgot to water it. That hadn't happened, of course, but she loved it dearly. Of all the things Gabriel had given her, and there had been a lot, this was her favorite. She left it outside until the weather grew too cold, then she carried it inside protectively.

The Jaguar had been wonderful. But she'd still been driving it when she did the story that almost destroyed Gabriel's life and after that, she could no longer bear to sit in it. The memories had been killing her.

She missed the Jag. She missed Gabriel more. She wondered why he'd come back. Probably to sell the house, she decided, to cut his last tie with Comanche Wells. If he was working for an international concern, it wasn't likely that he'd plan to come back here. He'd see the Jag in the driveway, she thought, and understand why she'd given it back. At least, she hoped he would.

That thought, that he might leave Comanche Wells forever, was really depressing. She watered Fred, put down the can, and went back into the house. It didn't occur to her to wonder what he'd been doing at her church.

When she went into the kitchen to take her dinner out of the microwave, a dark-haired man was sitting at the table sipping coffee. There were two cups, one for him and one for her. The dinner was sitting on a plate with a napkin and silverware beside it.

He glanced up as she came into the room. "It's getting cold," he said simply.

She stood behind her chair, just staring at him, frowning.

He raised an eyebrow as he studied her shirt. "You know, most people who wore red shirts on the original *Star Trek* ended up dead."

She cocked her head. "And you came all this way to give me fashion advice?"

He managed a faint smile. "Not really." He sipped coffee. He let out a long breath. "It's been a long time, Michelle."

She nodded. Slowly, she pulled out the chair and sat down. The TV dinner had the appeal of mothballs. She pushed it aside and sipped the black coffee he'd put at her place. He still remembered how she took it, after all this time.

She ran her finger around the rim. "I learned a hard lesson," she said after a minute. "Reporting isn't just about presenting the majority point of view."

He lifted his eyes to hers. "Life teaches very hard lessons."

"Yes, it does." She drew in a breath. "I guess you're selling the house."

His eyebrows lifted. "Excuse me?"

"I saw a truck go out there yesterday. And I read that you're working with some international police force now. So since Sara's living in Wyoming, I assumed you'd probably be moving up there near her. For when you're home in the States, I mean."

"I'd considered it," he said after a minute. He sipped more coffee.

She wondered if her heart could fall any deeper into her chest. She wondered how in the world he'd gotten into the house so silently. She wondered why he was there in the first place. Was he saying goodbye?

"Did you find the keys to the Jag?" she asked.

"Yes. You didn't want to keep it?"

She swallowed hard. "Too many bad memories, of what I did to you and Sara," she confessed heavily.

He shook his head. After a minute, he stared at her bent head. "I don't think you've really looked at me once," he said finally.

She managed a tight smile. "It's very hard to do that, after all the trouble I caused you," she said. "I rehearsed it, you know. Saying I was sorry. Working up all sorts of ways to apologize. But there really isn't a good way to say it."

"People make mistakes."

"The kind I made could have buried you." She said it tautly, fighting tears. It was harder than she'd imagined. She forced down the rest of the coffee. "Look, I've got things to do," she began, standing, averting her face so he couldn't see her eyes.

"Ma belle," he whispered, in a voice so tender that her control broke the instant she heard it. She burst into tears.

He scooped her up in his arms and kissed her so hungrily that she just went limp, arching up to him, so completely his that she wouldn't have protested anything he wanted to do to her.

"So it's like that, is it?" he whispered against her soft, trembling mouth. "Anything I want? Anything at all?"

"Anything," she wept.

"Out of guilt?" he asked, and there was an edge to his tone now.

She opened her wet eyes and looked into his. "Out of…love," she choked.

"Love."

"Go ahead. Laugh…"

He buried his face in her throat. "I thought I'd lost you for good," he breathed huskily. "Standing there at your car, looking so defeated, so depressed that you couldn't even meet my eyes. I thought, I'll have to leave, there's nothing left, nothing there except guilt and sorrow. And then I decided to have one last try, to come here and talk to you. You walked into the room and every single thing you felt was there, right there, in your eyes when you looked at me. And I knew, then, that it wasn't over at all. It was only beginning."

Her arms tightened around his neck. Her eyes were pouring with hot tears. "I loved you…so much," she choked. "Sara said you never wanted to see me again. She hated me. I knew you must hate me, too…!"

He kissed the tears away. He sat down on the sofa with Michelle in his lap and curled her into his chest. "Sara has a quick, hot temper. She loses it, and it's over. She's sorry that she was so brutal with you. She was frightened and upset and the media was hunting her. She's had other problems as well, that you don't know about. But she's ashamed that she took it all out on you, blamed you for something you didn't even do deliberately." He lifted his head and smoothed the long, damp hair away from her cheek. "She wanted to apologize, but she's too ashamed to call you."

"That's why?" she whispered. "I thought I would never see her again. Or you."

"That would never happen," he said gently. "You're part of us."

She bit her lower lip. "I sold you out…!"

"You did not. You sold out a mercenary named Angel, someone you didn't know, someone you thought had perpetrated a terrible crime against innocent women and children," he said simply. He brushed his mouth over her wet eyes. "You would never have sold me out in a million years, even if you had thought I was guilty as sin." He lifted his head and looked into her eyes. "Because you love me. You love me enough to forgive anything, even murder."

The tears poured out even hotter. She couldn't stop crying.

He wrapped her up close, turned her under him on the sofa, slid between her long legs and began to kiss her with anguished hunger. The kisses grew so long and so hard and so hot that she trembled and curled her legs around the back of his, urging him into greater intimacy, pleading with him to ease the tension that was putting her young body on the rack.

"If you don't stop crying," he threatened huskily, "this is going to end badly."

"No, it isn't. You want to," she whispered, kissing his throat.

"Yes, I do," he replied deeply. "But you're going to need a lot of time that I can't give you when I'm out of control," he murmured darkly. "You won't enjoy it."

"Are you sure?" she whispered.

He lifted his head. His eyes were hot and hungry on her body. His hands had pushed up the red shirt and the bra, and he was staring at her pert, pretty breasts with aching need. "I am absolutely sure," he managed.

"Oh."

The single word and the wide-eyed, hopeless look in her eyes broke the tension and he started laughing. "That's it? 'Oh'?"

She laughed, too. "Well, I read a lot and I watch movies, but it's not quite the same thing…"

"Exactly."

He forced himself to roll off her. "If you don't mind, could you pull all this back down?" he asked, indicating her breasts. He averted his eyes. "And I'll try deep breaths and mental imagery of snow-covered hills."

"Does it work?"

"Not really."

She pulled down her shirt and glanced at him with new knowledge of him and herself, and smiled.

"That's a smug little look," he accused.

"I like knowing I can throw you off balance," she said with a wicked grin.

"I'll enjoy letting you do it, but not until we're used to each other," he replied. He pulled her close. "The first time has to be slow and easy," he whispered, brushing his mouth over hers. "So that it doesn't hurt so much."

"If you can knock me off balance, I won't care if it hurts," she pointed out.

His black eyes twinkled. "I'll remember that."

She lay back on the sofa and looked up at him with wide, wondering eyes. "I thought it was all over," she whispered. "That I had nothing left, nothing to live for…"

"I felt the same way," he returned, solemn and quiet.

"Thank God I decided to make one more attempt to get through to you."

She smiled gently. "Fate."

He smiled back. "Yes. Fate."

"Where are you going? Come back here." She pulled him back down.

He pursed his lips. "We need to discuss things vertically, not horizontally."

"I'm not going to seduce you, honest. I have something very serious I need to talk to you about."

"Okay. What?"

She pursed her own lips and her eyes twinkled. "Cow abductions."

He burst out laughing.

They were married in the Methodist church two weeks later by Reverend Blair. Michelle wore a conventional white gown with lace inserts and a fingertip veil, which Gabriel lifted to kiss her for the first time as his wife. In the audience were more mercenaries and ex-military and feds than anyone locally had seen in many a year.

Eb Scott and his wife, along with Dr. Micah Steele and Callie, and Cy Parks and Lisa, were all in the front row with Minette Carson and her husband Hayes. Carlie and her husband were there, too.

There was a reception in the fellowship hall and Jacobsville police chief Cash Grier kept looking around restlessly.

"Is something going on that we should know about?" Gabriel asked with a grin.

"Just waiting for the riot to break out."

"What riot?" Michelle asked curiously.

"You know, somebody says something, somebody else has too much to drink and takes offense, blows are exchanged, police are called in to break up the altercation..."

"Chief Grier, just how many riots at weddings have you seen?" she wanted to know.

"About half a dozen," he said.

"Well, I can assure you, there won't be any here," Michelle said. "Because there's no booze!"

Cash gaped at her. "No booze?"

"No."

"Well, damn," he said, glowering at her.

"Why do you say that?" she asked.

"How can you have altercations without booze?" He threw up his hands. "And I had so looked forward to a little excitement around here!"

"I could throw a punch at Hayes," Gabriel offered, grinning at the sheriff. "But then he'd have to arrest me, and Michelle would spend our honeymoon looking for bail bondsmen...."

Cash chuckled. "Just kidding. I like the occasional quiet wedding." He leaned forward. "When you're not busy, you might want to ask Blake Kemp about *his* wedding reception, though," he added gleefully. "Jacobsville will never forget that one, I swear!"

Michelle lay trembling in Gabriel's arms, hot and damp in the aftermath of something so turbulent and thrilling that she knew she could live on the memory of it for the rest of her life.

"I believe the chief wanted a little excitement?" She laughed hoarsely. "I don't think anyone could top this. Ever."

He trailed his fingers up her body, lingering tenderly on a distended nipple. He stroked it until she arched and gasped. "I don't think so, either." He bent his head and slipped his lips over the dusky peak, teasing it until it grew even harder and she shivered. He suckled it, delighting in the sounds that came out of her throat.

"You like that, do you?" he whispered. He moved over her. "How about this?"

"Oh...yes," she choked. "Yes!"

He slid a hand under her hips and lifted her into the slow penetration of his body, moving restlessly as she accepted him, arched to greet him, shivered again as she felt the slow, hungry depth of his envelopment.

"It's easier now," he whispered. "Does it hurt?"

"I haven't...noticed yet," she managed, shuddering as he moved on her.

He chuckled.

"I was afraid," she confessed in a rush of breath.

"I know."

She clung to him as the rhythm lifted her, teased her body into contortions of pure, exquisite pleasure. "I can't believe...I was afraid!"

His hips moved from side to side and she made a harsh, odd little cry that was echoed in the convulsion of her hips.

"Yes," he purred. "I can make you so hungry that you'll do anything to get me closer, can't I, *ma belle?*"

"Any...thing," she agreed.

He ground his teeth together. "It works...both ways... too," he bit off. He groaned harshly as the pleasure bit into him, arched him down into her as the rhythm grew hard and hot and deep. He felt his heartbeat in his head, slamming like a hammer as he drove into her welcoming body, faster and harder and closer until suddenly, like a storm breaking, a silver shaft of pleasure went through him like a spear, lifting him above her in an arch so brittle that he thought he might shatter into a thousand pieces.

"Like...dying," he managed as the pleasure took him.

She clung to him, too involved to even manage a reply, lifting and pleading, digging her nails into his hard back as she welcomed the hard, heavy push of his body, welcomed the deep, aching tension that grew and swelled and finally burst like rockets going off inside her.

She cried out helplessly, sobbing, as the ecstasy washed over her like the purest form of pleasure imaginable and then, just as quickly, was gone. Gone. Gone!

They clung together, damp with sweat, sliding against each other in the aftermath, holding on to the echoes of the exquisite satisfaction that they'd shared.

"Remind me to tell you one day how rare it is for two people to find completion at the same time," he whispered, sliding his mouth over her soft, yielding body. "Usually, the woman takes a long time, and the man only finds his satisfaction when hers is over."

She lifted an eyebrow. "And you would know this, how?" she began.

He lifted his head and looked into her eyes with a rakish grin. "Oh, from the videos I watched and the books I read and the other guys I listened to...."

"Is that so?" she mused, with a suspicious look.

He kissed her accusing eyes shut. "It was long before I knew you," he whispered. "And after the first day I saw you, sitting in the road waiting for me to run over you, there was no one. Ever."

Her eyes flew open. "Wh-what?"

He brushed the hair from her cheeks. "I knew then that I would love you one day, forever," he said quietly.

"So there were no other women."

Her face flushed. "Gabriel," she whispered, overcome.

He kissed her tenderly. "The waiting was terrible," he groaned. "I thought I might die of it, waiting until you grew up, until you knew something of the world and men so that I didn't rob you of that experience." He lifted his head. "Always, I worried that you might find a younger man and fall in love…"

She put her fingers over his chiseled mouth. "I loved you from the day I met you," she whispered. "When I stared at you, that day in town with my grandfather, before I was even sixteen." She touched his cheek with her fingertips. "I knew, too, that there could never be anyone else."

He nibbled her fingers. "So sweet, the encounter after all the waiting," he whispered.

"Sweeter than honey," she agreed, her eyes warm and soft on his face.

"There's just one thing," he murmured.

She raised her eyebrows.

He opened a drawer and pulled out an item that he'd placed there earlier. An item that they'd forgotten to use.

She just smiled.

After a minute, he smiled back and dropped the item right back into the drawer.

Sara was overjoyed. "I can't wait to come down there and see you both," she exclaimed. "But you've only been married six weeks," she added.

Gabriel was facing the computer with Michelle at his side, holding her around the waist, his big hands resting protectively over her slightly swollen belly as they talked on Skype with Sara in Wyoming. "We were both very sure that it was what we wanted," he said simply.

"Well, I'm delighted," Sara said. She smiled. "The only way I could be more delighted is if it was me who was pregnant. But, that will come with time," she said complacently, and smiled. "I'm only sorry I couldn't be at the wedding," she added quietly. "I was very mean to you, Michelle. I couldn't face you, afterward."

"I understood," Michelle said gently. "You're my sister. Really my sister now," she added with a delighted laugh. "We're going to get a place near yours in Wyoming so that we can be nearby when the baby comes."

"I can't wait!"

"Neither can I," Michelle said. "We'll talk to you soon."

"Very soon." Sara smiled and cut the connection.

"Have you ever told her?" Michelle asked after a minute, curling up in Gabriel's lap.

He kissed her. "We did just tell her, my love…"

"Not about the baby," she protested. "About Wolf. About who he really is."

"You mean, her gaming partner for the past few years?" He grinned. "That's a story for another day."

"If you say so."

He kissed her. "I do say so. And now, how about a nice pickle and some vanilla ice cream?"

Her eyebrows lifted. "You know, that sounds delicious!"

He bent his head and kissed the little bump below her waist. "He's going to be extraordinary," he whispered.

"Yes. Like his dad," she replied with her heart in her eyes.

And they both grinned.

* * * * *

In November, from Harlequin HQN,
don't miss Sara and Wolf's romance in
WYOMING STRONG
by Diana Palmer.
Available in stores and through e-tailers
wherever books are sold.

MAGGIE'S DAD

With this book's reprint,
I remember my Torch sisters and fellow Alpha Chi
members at Piedmont College in Demorest, GA.

This book is fondly dedicated to all of them,
especially Melissa, Cindy and Penny, and to the
educators among my readers. God bless you for
the worthwhile job you do and for the sacrifices
you make in order to give our children the best
education possible. You are very special people.

Prologue

Rain was peppering down on the roof of the small house where Antonia Hayes's parents lived. It was a cold rain, and Antonia thought absently that she was very glad it was summer, because by early autumn that soft rain would turn to sleet or snow. Bighorn, a small town in northwestern Wyoming, was not an easy town to leave once it was covered in ice. It was rural and despite having three thousand inhabitants, it was too small to offer the transportation choices of a larger town. There wasn't even an airport; only a bus station. The railroad ran through it, too, but the trains were spaced too far apart to do Antonia much good.

She was about to begin her sophomore year in college, at the University of Arizona in Tucson, and snow was fairly rare in that area in winter, except up in the mountains. The desert floor had light dustings, but not

enough to inconvenience anyone. Besides, Antonia—
having just finished her first year there—had been
much too busy trying to pass her core courses and heal
a broken heart to notice the weather. She did notice the
summer heat now, though, she mused, and thanked God
for air-conditioning.

The clock sounded and Antonia turned, her short,
blond hair perky and her gray eyes full of sadness at
having to leave. But fall semester started in less than
a week, and she had to get back into her dorm room
and set up some sort of schedule. The only comforting
thing about going back was that George Rutherford's
stepdaughter, Barrie Bell, was her dorm roommate, and
they got along very well indeed.

"It's been lovely having you home for a whole week,"
her mother, Jessica, said warmly. "I do wish you could
have stayed the whole summer…."

Her voice trailed off. She knew, as did Antonia and
Ben, her husband, why Antonia couldn't stay in Bighorn very long. It was a source of great sadness to all
of them, but they didn't discuss it. It still hurt too much,
and the gossip hadn't quite died down even now, almost
a year after the fact. George Rutherford's abrupt move
to France a few months after Antonia's departure had
quelled the remaining gossip.

Despite what had happened, George had remained a
good, true friend to Antonia and her family. Her college
education was his gift to her. She would pay him back
every penny, but right now the money was a godsend.
Her parents were well regarded in the community, but
lacked the resources to swing her tuition. George had
been determined to help, and his kindness had cost
them both so much.

But George's son, Dawson, and his stepdaughter, Barrie, had rallied around Antonia, defending her against the talk.

It was comforting to know that the two people closest to George didn't believe he was Antonia's sugar daddy. And of course, it helped that Dawson and Powell Long were rivals for a strip of land that separated their respective Bighorn ranch holdings. George had lived on his Bighorn ranch until the scandal. Then he went back to the family home he shared with Dawson in Sheridan, hoping to stem the gossip. It hadn't happened. So he'd moved to France, leaving more bitterness between Dawson and Powell Long. There was no love lost there.

But even with George out of the country, and despite the support of friends and family, Sally Long had done so much damage to Antonia's reputation that she was sure she would never be able to come home again.

Her mind came back to the remark her mother had just made. "I took classes this summer," she murmured absently. "I'm really sorry, but I thought I'd better, and some of my new friends went, too. It was nice, although I do miss being home. I miss both of you."

Jessica hugged her warmly. "And we miss you."

"That damn fool Sally Long," Ben muttered as he also hugged his daughter. "Spreading lies so that she could take Powell away from you. And that damn fool Powell Long, believing them, marrying her, and that baby born just seven months later…!"

Antonia's face went pale, but she smiled gamely. "Now, Dad," she said gently. "It's all over," she added with what she hoped was a reassuring smile, "they're married and they have a daughter now. I hope he's happy."

"Happy! After the way he treated you?"

Antonia closed her eyes. The memories were still painful. Powell had been the center of her life. She'd never imagined she could feel a love so sweeping, so powerful. He'd never said he loved her, but she'd been so sure that he did. Looking back now, though, she knew that he'd never really loved her. He wanted her, of course, but he had always drawn back. *We'll wait for marriage,* he'd said.

And waiting had been a good thing, considering how it had all turned out.

At the time, Antonia had wanted him desperately, but she'd put him off. Even now, over a year later, she could still see his black eyes and dark hair and thin, wide mouth. That image lived in her heart despite the fact that he'd canceled their wedding the day before it was to take place. People who hadn't been notified in time were sitting in the church, waiting. She shuddered faintly, remembering her humiliation.

Ben was still muttering about Sally.

"That's enough, Ben." Jessica laid a hand on her husband's arm. "It's water under the bridge," she said firmly. Her voice was so tranquil that it was hard for Antonia to believe that the scandal had caused her mother to have heart problems. She'd done very well, and Antonia had done everything possible to avoid the subject so that her mother wouldn't be upset.

"I wouldn't say Powell was happy," Ben continued, unabashed. "He's never home, and we never see him out with Sally in public. In fact, we never see Sally much at all. If she's happy, she doesn't let it show." He studied his daughter's pale, rigid face. "She called here one day before Easter and asked for your address. Did she write to you?"

"She wrote me."

"Well?" he prompted, curious.

"I returned the letter without opening it," Antonia said tightly, even paler now. She looked down at her shoes. "It's ancient history."

"She might have wanted to apologize," Jessica ventured.

Antonia sighed. "Some things go beyond apologies," she said quietly. "I loved him, you know," she added with a faint smile. "But he never loved me. If he did, he didn't say so in all the time we went together. He believed everything Sally told him. He just told me what he thought of me, called off the wedding and walked away. I had to leave. It hurt too much to stay." She could picture in her mind that long, straight back, the rigid set of his dark head. The pain had been terrible. It still was.

"As if George was that sort of man," Jessica said wearily. "He's the kindest man in the world, and he adores you."

"Not the sort to play around with young girls," Ben agreed. "Idiots, people who could believe that about him. I know that's why he moved out of the country, to spare us any more gossip."

"Since he and I are both gone, there's not much to gossip about," Antonia said pointedly. She smiled. "I'm working hard on my grades. I want George to be proud of me."

"He will be. And we already are," Jessica said warmly.

"Well, it serves Powell Long right that he ended up with that selfish little madam," Ben persisted irritably. "He thinks he's going to get rich by building up that cattle ranch, but he's just a dreamer," Ben scoffed. "His father was a gambler, and his mother was a doormat. Imagine him thinking he's got enough sense to make money with cattle!"

"He does seem to be making strides," his wife said gently. "He just bought a late-model truck, and they say a string of ranches up in Montana have given him a contract to supply them with seed bulls. You remember, Ben, when his big purebred Angus bull was in the paper, it won some national award."

"One bull doesn't make an empire," Ben scoffed.

Antonia felt the words all the way to her heart. Powell had told her his dreams, and they'd planned that ranch together, discussed having the best Angus bulls in the territory...

"Could we not...talk about him, please?" Antonia asked finally. She forced a smile. "It still stings a little."

"Of course it does. We're sorry," Jessica said, her voice soft now. "Can you come home for Christmas?"

"I'll try. I really will."

She had one small suitcase. She carried it out to the car and hugged her mother one last time before she climbed in beside her father for the short ride to the bus depot downtown.

It was morning, but still sweltering hot. She got out of the car and picked up her suitcase as she waited on the sidewalk for her father to get her ticket from the office inside the little grocery store. There was a line. She'd just turned her attention back to the street when her eyes froze on an approaching pedestrian; a cold, quiet ghost from the past.

He was just as lean and dark as she remembered him. The suit was better than the ones he'd worn when they were dating, and he looked thinner. But it was the same Powell Long.

She'd lost everything to him except her pride. She still had it, and she forced her gray eyes up to his as he walked down the sidewalk with that slow, elegant stride that was particularly his own. She wouldn't let him see how badly his distrust had hurt her, even now.

His expression gave away nothing that he was feeling. He paused when he reached her, glancing at the suitcase.

"Well, well," he drawled, watching her face. "I heard you were here. The chicken came home to roost, did she?"

"I'm not here to stay," she replied coolly. "I've been to visit my parents. I'm on my way to Arizona, back to college."

"By bus?" he taunted. "Couldn't your sugar daddy afford a plane ticket? Or did he leave you high and dry when he hightailed it to France?"

She kicked him right in the shin. It wasn't premeditated, and he looked as shocked as she did when he bent to rub the painful spot where her shoe had landed.

"I wish I'd been wearing steel-toed combat boots like one of the girls in my dorm," she said hotly. "And if you ever so much as speak to me again, Powell Long, I'll break your leg the next time!"

She brushed past him and went into the depot.

Her father had just paid for the ticket when his attention was captured by the scene outside the depot. He started outside, but Antonia pushed him back into the building.

"We can wait for the bus in here, Dad," she said, her face still red and hot with anger.

He glanced past her to where Powell had straightened to send a speaking look toward the depot.

"Well, he seems to have learned to control that hot temper, at least. A year ago, he'd have been in here, right through the window," Ben Hayes remarked coldly. "I hope you crippled him."

She managed a wan smile. "No such luck. You can't wound something that ornery."

Powell had started back down the street, his back stiff with outrage.

"I hope Sally asks him how he hurt his leg," Antonia said under her breath.

"Here, girl, the bus is coming." He shepherded her outside, grateful that the ticket agent hadn't been paying attention and that none of the other passengers seemed interested in the byplay out the window. All they needed was some more gossip.

Antonia hugged her father before she climbed aboard. She wanted to look down the street, to see if Powell was limping. But even though the windows were dark, she wouldn't risk having him catch her watching him. She closed her eyes as the bus pulled away from the depot and spent the rest of the journey trying to forget the pain of seeing Powell Long again.

Chapter 1

"That's very good, Martin, but you've left out something, haven't you?" Antonia prompted gently. She smiled, too, because Martin was very shy even for a nine-year-old and she didn't want to embarrass him in front of her other fourth graders. "The secret weapon the Greeks used in battle...a military formation?"

"Secret weapon," he murmured to himself. Then his dark eyes lit up and he grinned. "The phalanx!" he said at once.

"Yes," she replied. "Very good!"

He beamed, glancing smugly at his worst enemy in the second row over, who was hoping Martin would miss the question and looked very depressed indeed that he hadn't.

Antonia glanced at her watch. It was almost time to dismiss class for the day, and the week. Odd, she thought, how loose that watch was on her wrist.

"It's time to start putting things away," she told her students. "Jack, will you erase the board for me, please? And, Mary, please close the windows."

They rushed to obey, because they liked Miss Hayes. Mary glanced at her with a smile. Miss Hayes smiled back. She wasn't as pretty as Miss Bell down the hall, and she dressed in a very backward sort of way, always wearing suits or pantsuits, not miniskirts and frilly blouses. She had pretty long blond hair, though, when she took it out of that awful bun, and her gray eyes were like the December sky. It would be Christmas soon, and in a week they could all go home for the holidays. Mary wondered what Miss Hayes would do. She never went anywhere exciting for holidays. She never talked about her family, either. Maybe she didn't have one.

The bell rang and Antonia smiled and waved as her students marched out to waiting buses and cars. She tidied her desk with steady hands and wondered if her father would come for Christmas this year. It was very lonely for both of them since her mother's death last year. It had been hard, coping with the loss. It had been harder having to go home for the funeral. He was there. He, and his daughter. Antonia shivered just remembering the look on his dark, hard face. Powell hadn't softened even then, even when her mother was being buried. He still hated Antonia after nine years. She'd barely glanced at the sullen, dark-haired little girl by his side. The child was like a knife through her heart, a reminder that Powell had been sleeping with Sally even while he and Antonia were engaged to be married; because the little girl had been born only seven months after Powell married Sally. Antonia had glanced at them once, only once, to meet Powell's hateful stare. She hadn't looked toward the pew where they sat again.

Incredible how he could hate Antonia after marriage and a child, when everyone must have told him the truth ten times over in the years between. He was rich now. He had money and power and a fine home. His wife had died only three years after their wedding, and he hadn't remarried. Antonia imagined it was because he missed Sally so much. She didn't. She hated even the memory of her one-time best friend. Sally had cost her everything she loved, even her home, and she'd done it with deliberate lies. Of course, Powell had believed the lies. That was what had hurt most.

Antonia was over it now. It had been nine years. It hardly hurt at all, in fact, to remember him.

She blinked as someone knocked at the door, interrupting her train of thought. It was Barrie, her good friend and the Miss Bell of the miniskirt who taught math, grinning at her. Barrie was gorgeous. She was slender and had beautiful long legs. Her hair was almost black, like a wavy curtain down her back. She had green eyes with mischief in them, and a ready smile.

"You could stay with me at Christmas," Barrie invited merrily, her green eyes twinkling.

"In Sheridan?" she asked idly, because that was where Barrie's stepfather's home was, where George Rutherford and her stepbrother Dawson Rutherford, and Barrie and her late mother had lived before she left home and began teaching with Antonia in Tucson.

"No," Barrie said tightly. "Not ever there. In my apartment here in Tucson," she added, forcing a smile to her face. "I have four boyfriends. We can split them, two each. We'll have a merry whirl!"

Antonia only smiled. "I'm twenty-seven, too old for merry whirls, and my father will probably come here for Christmas. But thanks anyway."

"Honestly, Annie, you're not old, even if you do dress like someone's maiden aunt!" she said explosively. "Look at you!" she added, sweeping her hand toward the gray suit and white blouse that was indicative of the kind of clothes Antonia favored. "And your hair in that infernal bun...you look like a holdover from the Victorians! You need to loose that glorious blond hair and put on a miniskirt and some makeup and look for a man before you get too old! And you need to eat! You're so thin that you're beginning to look like skin and bones."

Antonia knew that. She'd lost ten pounds in the past month or so and she'd finally gotten worried enough to make an appointment with her doctor. It was probably nothing, she thought, but it wouldn't hurt to check. Her iron might be low. She said as much to Barrie.

"That's true. You've had a hard year, what with losing your mother and then that awful scare with the student who brought his dad's pistol to school and held everybody at bay for an hour last month."

"Teaching is becoming the world's most dangerous profession," Antonia agreed. She smiled sadly at Barrie. "Perhaps if we advertised it that way, we'd attract more brave souls to boost our numbers."

"That's an idea," came the dry agreement. "Want adventure? Try teaching! I can see the slogan now—"

"I'm going home," Antonia interrupted her.

"Ah, well, I suppose I will, too. I have a date tonight."

"Who is it this time?"

"Bob. He's nice and we get along well. But sometimes I think I'm not cut out for a conventional sort of man. I need a wild-eyed artist or a composer or a drag racer."

Antonia chuckled. "I hope you find one."

"If I did, he'd probably have two wives hidden in another country or something. I do have the worst luck with men."

"It's your liberated image," Antonia said in a conspiratorial tone. "You're devil-may-care and outrageous. You scare off the most secure bachelors."

"Bunkum. If they were secure enough, they'd rush to my door," Barrie informed her. "I'm sure there's a man like that somewhere, just waiting for me."

"I'm sure there is, too," her friend said kindly, and didn't for a minute let on that she thought there was already one waiting in Sheridan.

Beneath Barrie's outrageous persona, there was a sad and rather lonely woman. Barrie wasn't at all what she seemed. Barrie basically was afraid of men—especially her stepbrother, Dawson. He was George's blood son. Dear George, the elderly man who'd been another unfortunate victim of Sally Long's lies. The tales hadn't fazed Dawson, though, who not only knew better, but who was one of the coldest and most intimidating men Antonia had ever met where women were concerned. Barrie never mentioned Dawson, never talked about him. And if his name was mentioned, she changed the subject. It was common knowledge that they didn't get along. But secretly, Antonia thought there was something in their past, something that Barrie didn't talk about.

She never had, and now that poor George was dead and Dawson had inherited his estate, there was a bigger rift between them because a large interest in the cattle empire that Dawson inherited had been willed to Barrie.

"I've got to phone Dad and see what his plans are," Antonia murmured, dragging herself back from her memories.

"If he can't come down here, will you go home for Christmas?"

She shook her head. "I don't go home."

"Why not?" She grimaced. "Oh. Yes. I forget from time to time, because you never talk about him. I'm sorry. But it's been nine years. Surely he couldn't hold a grudge for that long? After all, he's the one who called off the wedding and married your best friend less than a month later. And she caused the scandal in the first place!"

"Yes, I know," Antonia replied.

"She must have loved him a lot to take such a risk. But he did eventually find out the truth," she added, tugging absently on a strand of her long, wavy black hair.

Antonia sighed. "Did he? I suppose someone told him, eventually. I don't imagine he believed it, though. Powell likes to see me as a villain."

"He loved you…"

"He wanted me," Antonia said bitterly. "At least that's what he said. I had no illusions about why he was marrying me. My father's name carried some weight in town, even though we were not rich. Powell needed the respectability. The love was all on my side. As it worked out, he got rich and had one child and a wife who was besotted with him. But from what I heard, he didn't love her either. Poor Sally," she added on a cold laugh, "all that plotting and lying, and when she got what she wanted, she was miserable."

"Good enough for her," Barrie said curtly. "She ruined your reputation and your parents'."

"And your stepfather's," she added, sadly. "He was very fond of my mother once."

Barrie smiled gently. "He was very fond of her up until the end. It was a blessing that he liked your father, and that they were friends. He was a good loser when she married your father. But he still cared for her, and that's why he did so much to help you."

"Right down to paying for my college education. That was the thing that led to all the trouble. Powell didn't like George at all. His father lost a lot of land to George—in fact, Dawson is still at odds with Powell over that land, even today, you know. He may live in Sheridan, but his ranch covers hundreds of acres right up against Powell's ranch, and I understand from Dad that he gives him fits at any opportunity."

"Dawson has never forgotten or forgiven the lies that Sally told about George," came the quiet reply. "He spoke to Sally, you know. He cornered her in town and gave her hell, with Powell standing right beside her."

"You never told me that," Antonia said on a quick breath.

"I didn't know how to," Barrie replied. "It hurts you just to have Powell's name mentioned."

"I suppose Powell stood up for her," she said, fishing.

"Even Powell is careful about how he deals with Dawson," Barrie reminded her. "Besides, what could he say? Sally told a lie and she was caught, red-handed. Too late to do you any good, they were already married by then."

"You mean, Powell's known the truth for nine years?" Antonia asked, aghast.

"I didn't say he believed Dawson," the other woman replied gently, averting her eyes.

"Oh. Yes. Well." Antonia fought for composure. How ridiculous, to think Powell would have accepted the word of his enemy. He and Dawson never had gotten along. She said it aloud even as she thought it.

"Is it likely that they would? My stepfather beat Old Man Long out of everything he owned in a poker game when they were both young men. The feud has gone on from there. Dawson's land borders Powell's, and they're both bent on empire building. If a tract comes up for sale, you can bet both men will be standing on the Realtor's doorstep trying to get first dibs on it. In fact, that's what they're butting heads about right now, that strip of land that separates their ranches that the widow Holton owns."

"They own the world between them," Antonia said pointedly.

"And they only want what joins theirs." Barrie chuckled. "Ah, well, it's no concern of ours. Not now. The less I see of my stepbrother, the happier I am."

Antonia, who'd only once seen the two of them together, had to agree. When Dawson was anywhere nearby, Barrie became another person, withdrawn and tense and almost comically clumsy.

"Well, if you change your mind about the holidays, my door is open," Barrie reminded her.

Antonia smiled warmly. "I'll remember. If Dad can't come down for the holidays, you could come home with me," she added.

Barrie shivered. "No, thanks! Bighorn is too close to Dawson for my taste."

"Dawson lives in Sheridan."

"Not all the time. Occasionally he stays at the ranch

in Bighorn. He spends more and more time there these days." Her face went taut. "They say the widow Holton is the big attraction. Her husband had lots of land, and she hasn't decided who she'll sell it to."

A widow with land. Barrie had mentioned that Powell was also in competition with Dawson for the land. Or was it the widow? He was a widower, too, and a long-standing one. The thought made her sad.

"You need to eat more," Barrie remarked, concerned by her friend's appearance. "You're getting so thin, Annie, although it does give you a more fragile appearance. You have lovely bone structure. High cheekbones and good skin."

"I inherited the high cheekbones from a Cheyenne grandmother," she said, remembering sadly that Powell had called her Cheyenne as a nickname—actually meant as a corruption of "shy Ann," which she had been when they first started dating.

"Good blood," Barrie mused. "My ancestry is black Irish—from the Spanish armada that was blown off course to the coast of Ireland. Legend has it that one of my ancestors was a Spanish nobleman, who ended up married to a stepsister of an Irish lord."

"What a story."

"Isn't it, though? I must pursue historical fiction one day—in between stuffing mathematical formulae into the heads of innocents." She glanced at her watch. "Heavens, I'll be late for my date with Bob! Gotta run. See you Monday!"

"Have fun."

"I always have fun. I wish you did, once in a while." She waved from the door, leaving behind a faint scent of perfume.

Antonia loaded her attaché case with papers to grade and her lesson plan for the following week, which badly needed updating. When her desk was cleared, she sent a last look around the classroom and went out the door.

Her small apartment overlooked "A" mountain in Tucson, so-called because of the giant letter *A* that was painted at its peak and was repainted year after year by University of Arizona students. The city was flat and only a small scattering of tall buildings located downtown made it seem like a city at all. It was widespread, sprawling, sandy and hot. Nothing like Bighorn, Wyoming, where Antonia's family had lived for three generations.

She remembered going back for her mother's funeral less than a year ago. Townspeople had come by the house to bring food for every meal, and to pay their respects. Antonia's mother had been well-loved in the community. Friends sent cartloads of the flowers she'd loved so much.

The day of the funeral had dawned bright and sunny, making silver lights in the light snow covering, and Antonia thought how her mother had loved spring. She wouldn't see another one now. Her heart, always fragile, had finally given out. At least, it had been a quick death. She'd died at the stove, in the very act of putting a cake into the oven.

The service was brief but poignant, and afterward Antonia and her father had gone home. The house was empty. Dawson Rutherford had stopped to offer George's sympathy, because George had been desperately ill, far too ill to fly across the ocean from France for the funeral. In fact, George had died less than two weeks later.

Dawson had volunteered to drive Barrie out to the airport to catch her plane back to Arizona, because Barrie had come to the funeral, of course. Antonia had noted even in her grief how it affected Barrie just to have to ride that short distance with her stepbrother.

Later, Antonia's father had gone to the bank and Antonia had been halfheartedly sorting her mother's unneeded clothes and putting them away when Mrs. Harper, who lived next door and was helping with the household chores, announced that Powell Long was at the door and wished to speak with her.

Having just suffered the three worst days of her life, she was in no condition to face him now.

"Tell Mr. Long that we have nothing to say to each other," Antonia had replied with cold pride.

"Guess he knows how it feels to lose somebody, since he lost Sally a few years back," Mrs. Harper reminded her, and then watched to see how the news would be received.

Antonia had known about Sally's death. She hadn't sent flowers or a card because it had happened only three years after Antonia had fled Bighorn, and the bitterness had still been eating at her.

"I'm sure he understands grief," was all Antonia said, and waited without saying another word until Mrs. Harper got the message and left.

She was back five minutes later with a card. "Said to give you this," she murmured, handing the business card to Antonia, "and said you should call him if you needed any sort of help."

Help. She took the card and, without even looking at it, deliberately tore it into eight equal parts. She handed them back to Mrs. Harper and turned again to her clothes sorting.

Mrs. Harper looked at the pieces of paper in her hand. "Enough said," she murmured, and left.

It was the last contact Antonia had had with Powell Long since her mother's death. She knew that he'd built up his purebred Angus ranch and made a success of it. But she didn't ask for personal information about him after that, despite the fact that he remained a bachelor. The past, as far as she was concerned, was truly dead. Now, she wondered vaguely why Powell had come to see her that day. Guilt, perhaps? Or something more? She'd never know.

She found a message on her answering machine and played it. Her father, as she'd feared, was suffering his usual bout of winter bronchitis and his doctor wouldn't let him go on an airplane for fear of what it would do to his sick lungs. And he didn't feel at all like a bus or train trip, so Antonia would have to come home for Christmas, he said, or they'd each have to spend it alone.

She sat down heavily on the floral couch she'd purchased at a local furniture store and sighed. She didn't want to go home. If she could have found a reasonable excuse, she wouldn't have, either. But it would be impossible to leave her father sick and alone on the holidays. With resolution, she picked up the telephone and booked a seat on the next commuter flight to Billings, where the nearest airport to Bighorn was located.

* * *

Because Wyoming was so sparsely populated, it was lacking in airports. Powell Long, now wealthy and able to afford all the advantages, had an airstrip on his ranch. But there was nowhere in Bighorn that a commercial aircraft, even a commuter one, could land. She knew that Barrie's stepbrother had a Learjet and that he had a landing strip near Bighorn on his own ranch, but she would never have presumed on Barrie's good nature to ask for that sort of favor. Besides, she admitted to herself, she was as intimidated by Dawson Rutherford as Barrie was. He, like Powell, was high-powered and aggressively masculine. Antonia felt much safer seated on an impersonal commuter plane.

She rented a car at the airport in Billings and, with the easy acceptance of long distances on the road from her time in Arizona, she set out for Bighorn.

The countryside was lovely. There were scattered patches of snow, something she hadn't thought about until it was too late and she'd already rented the car. There was snow on the ground in Billings, quite a lot of it, and although the roads were mostly clear, she was afraid of icy patches. She'd get out, somehow, she told herself. But she did wish that she'd had the forethought to ask her father about the local weather when she'd phoned to say she was leaving Tucson on an early-morning flight. But he was hoarse and she hadn't wanted to stress his voice too much. He knew when she was due to arrive, though, and if she was too long overdue, she was certain that he'd send someone to meet her.

She gazed lovingly at the snow-covered mountains, thinking of how she'd missed this country that was home to her, home to generations of her family. There was so much of her history locked into these sweeping mountain ranges and valleys, where lodgepole pines stood like sentinels over shallow, wide blue streams. The forests were green and majestic, looking much as they must have when mountain men plied their trade here. Arizona had her own forests, too, and mountains. But Wyoming was another world. It was home.

The going got rough the closer to home she went. It was just outside Bighorn that her car slipped on a wide patch of ice and almost went into a ditch. She knew all too well that if she had, there would have been no way she could get the vehicle out, because the slope was too deep.

With a prayer of thanks, she made it into the small town of Bighorn, past the Methodist Church and the post office and the meat locker building to her father's big Victorian house on a wide street off the main thoroughfare. She parked in the driveway under a huge cottonwood tree. How wonderful to be home for Christmas!

There was a decorated tree in the window, all aglow with the lights and ornaments that had been painstakingly purchased over a period of years. She looked at one, a crystal deer, and remembered painfully that Powell had given it to her the Christmas they'd become engaged. She'd thought of smashing it after his desertion, but she couldn't bring herself to do it. The tiny thing was so beautiful, so fragile; like their destroyed relationship. So long ago.

Her father came to the door in a bathrobe and pajamas, sniffling.

He hugged her warmly. "I'm so glad you came, girl,"

he said hoarsely, and coughed a little. "I'm much better, but the damn doctor wouldn't let me fly!"

"And rightly so," she replied. "You don't need pneumonia!"

He grinned at her. "I reckon not. Can you stay until New Year's?"

She shook her head. "I'm sorry. I have to go back the day after Christmas." She didn't mention her upcoming doctor's appointment. There was no need to worry him.

"Well, you'll be here for a week, anyway. We won't get to go out much, I'm afraid, but we can keep each other company, can't we?"

"Yes, we can."

"Dawson said he might come by one evening," he added surprisingly. "He's just back from Europe, some convention or other he said he couldn't miss."

"At least he never believed the gossip about George and me," she said wistfully.

"Why, he knew his father too well," he replied simply.

"George was a wonderful man. No wonder you and he were friends for so long."

"I miss him. I miss your mother, too, God rest her soul. She was the most important person in my life, next to you."

"You're the most important person in mine," she agreed, smiling. "It's good to be home!"

"Still enjoy teaching?"

"More than ever," she told him warmly.

"There's some good schools here," he remarked. "They're always short of teachers. And two of them are expecting babies any day. They'll have problems

getting supply teachers in for that short little period."
He eyed her. "You wouldn't consider…?"

"I like Tucson," she said firmly.

"The hell you do," he muttered. "It's Powell, isn't
it? Damn fool, listening to that scatterbrained woman
in the first place! Well, he paid for it. She made his
life hell."

"Would you like some coffee?" she asked, changing the subject.

"Oh, I suppose so. And some soup. There's some
canned that Mrs. Harper made for me."

"Does she still live next door?"

"She does," he murmured with a wicked smile, "and
she's a widow herself. No need to ask why she brought
the soup, is there?"

"I like Mrs. Harper," she said with a grin. "She and
Mother were good friends, and she's like family already.
Just in case you wondered what I thought," she added.

"It's only been a year, girl," he said, and his eyes
were sad.

"Mother loved you too much to want you to go
through life alone," she said. "She wouldn't want you
to grieve forever."

He shrugged. "I'll grieve as long as I please."

"Suit yourself. I'll change clothes and then I'll see
about the soup and coffee."

"How's Barrie?" her father asked when Antonia
came out of her bedroom dressed in jeans and a white
sweatshirt with golden sequined bells and red ribbon
on it.

"She's just fine. Spunky as ever."

"Why didn't you bring her with you?"

"Because she's juggling four boyfriends," she said, chuckling as she went about warming soup.

"Dawson won't wait forever."

She glanced at him. "Is that what you think, too? She won't talk about him."

"He won't talk about her, either."

"What's this rumor about him and the widow Holton?"

He sat down in a chair at the table with a painful breath. "The widow Holton is redheaded and vivacious and a man-killer," he said. "She's after Dawson. And Powell Long. And any other man with money and a passable face."

"I see."

"You don't remember her, do you? Came here before you went off to college, but she and her husband traveled a lot. She was some sort of actress. She's been home more since he died."

"What does she do?"

"For a living, you mean?" He chuckled and had to fight back a cough. "She's living on her inheritance. Doesn't have to do anything, lucky girl."

"I wouldn't want to do nothing," Antonia remarked thoughtfully. "I like teaching. It's more than just a job."

"Some women aren't made for purposeful employment."

"I guess not."

She finished heating the soup and poured the coffee she'd made. They ate in silence.

"I wish your mother was here," he said.

She smiled sadly. "So do I."

"Well, we'll make the most of what we have and thank God for it."

She nodded. "We have more than some people do."

He smiled, seeing her mother's face in her own. "And a lot more than most," he added. "I'm glad you came home for Christmas."

"So am I. Eat your soup." She poured him some more, and thought that she was going to make this Christmas as happy for him as she could.

Chapter 2

Dawson Rutherford was tall, lean and drop-dead gorgeous with blond, wavy hair and eyes that seemed to pierce skin. Even if he hadn't been so handsome, his physical presence was more than enough to make him attractive, added to a deep voice that had the smoothness of velvet, even in anger. But he was as icy a man as she'd ever known, especially with women. At his father's funeral, she'd actually seen him back away from a beautiful woman to avoid being touched. Odd, that, when she knew for a fact that he'd been quite a rounder with women in his checkered past.

If Antonia hadn't given her heart to Powell Long so many years before, she wouldn't have minded setting her cap at Dawson, intimidating though he was. But he was plainly meant for another type of woman altogether. Barrie, perhaps.

It was Christmas Eve, and he'd stopped by with a pipe for her father. Antonia walked him out a few minutes later.

"Shame on you," she muttered, pausing on the porch.

Dawson's green eyes twinkled. "He'll get over the bronchitis. Besides, you know he won't quit smoking, whether or not I give him a new pipe. You've tried and I've tried for years to break him. The best we can do is make him smoke it outdoors."

"I know that," she agreed, and smiled. "Well, it was a nice gesture."

"Want to see what he gave me?" he asked, and produced a smooth silver lighter with inlaid turquoise.

"I didn't know you smoked," she observed.

"I don't."

Her eyes widened.

"I did, just briefly, smoke cigars." He corrected himself. "I gave it up months ago. He doesn't know, so don't tell him."

"I won't. But good for you!" she said approvingly.

He shrugged. "I don't know any smokers who don't want to quit." His eyes narrowed, and he watched her without blinking. "Except one, maybe."

She knew he was talking about Powell, who always had smoked cigars, and presumably still did. Her face began to close up. "Don't say it."

"I won't. You look tortured."

"It was nine years ago."

"Somebody should have shot him for the way he treated you," he replied. "I've never liked him, but that didn't win him any points with me. I loved my father. It was a low thing, for Sally to make him out a foolish old man with a lust for young girls."

"She wanted Powell."

His eyes narrowed. "She got him. But he made her pay for it, let me tell you. She took to alcohol because he left her alone so much, and from all accounts, he hated their daughter."

"But why?" Antonia asked, shocked. "Powell loved children, surely…!"

"Sally trapped him with the child," he replied. "Except for that, he'd have left her. Don't you think he knew what a stupid thing he'd done? He knew the truth, almost from the day he married Sally."

"But he stayed with her."

"He had to. He was trying to build a ranch out of nothing, and this is a small town. How would it look for a man to walk out on a pregnant woman, or on his own newborn daughter?" He pursed his lips. "He hates you, you know," he added surprisingly. "He hates you for not making him listen, for running. He blames his misery on you."

"He's your worst enemy, so how do you know so much?" she retorted.

"I have spies." He sighed. "He can't admit that the worst mistake was his own, that he wouldn't believe Sally capable of such underhanded lies. It wasn't until he married her that he realized how she'd conned him." He shrugged. "She wasn't a bad woman, really. She was in love and she couldn't bear losing him, even to you. Love does crazy things to people."

"She destroyed my reputation, and your father's, and made it impossible for me to live here," Antonia said without pity. "She was my enemy, and he still is. Don't think I'm harboring any tender feelings for him. I'd cut his throat given the slightest opportunity."

His eyebrows levered up. Antonia was a gentle soul herself for the most part, despite an occasional outburst of temper and a keen wit that surprised people. She hadn't ever seemed vindictive, but she harbored a long-standing grudge against her former best friend, Sally. He couldn't really blame her.

He fingered the lighter her father had given him. "How's Barrie?" he asked with deliberate carelessness.

"Fending off suitors," she said with a grin, her soft gray eyes twinkling. "She was juggling four of them when I left."

He laughed coldly. "Why doesn't that surprise me? One man was never enough for her, even when she was a teenager."

She was curious about his antagonism toward Barrie. It seemed out of place. "Why do you hate her so?" she asked bluntly.

He looked surprised. "I don't…hate her," he said. "I'm disappointed at the way she behaves, that's all."

"She isn't promiscuous," she said, defending her colleague. "She may act that way, but it's only an act. Don't you know that?"

He looked at the lighter, frowning slightly. "Maybe I know more than you think," he said curtly. His eyes came up. "Maybe you're the one wearing blinders."

"Maybe you're seeing what you want to see," she replied gently.

He pocketed the lighter with a curt gesture. "I'd better go. I've got a deal cooking. I don't want the client to get cold feet."

"Thanks for coming to see Dad. You cheered him up."

"He's my friend." He smiled. "So are you, even when you stick your nose in where you shouldn't."

"Barrie's my friend."

"Well, she's not mine," he said flatly. "Merry Christmas, Annie."

"You, too," she replied with a warm smile. He was kind, in his way. She liked him, but she felt sorry for Barrie. He was a heartbreaker. And unless she missed her guess, Barrie was in love with him. His feelings were much less readable.

After he left, she went back to join her father in the kitchen, where he was fixing hot chocolate in a double boiler. He glanced over his shoulder.

"Did he leave?"

"Yes. Can I help?"

He shook his head. He poured hot chocolate into two mugs and nodded for her to take one while he put the boiler in water to soak.

"He gave me a pipe," he told her when they were seated at the small kitchen table, sipping the hot liquid. He grinned. "Didn't have the heart to tell him that I've finally given it up."

"Dad!" She reached across and patted his hand. "Oh, that's great news!"

He chuckled. "Figured you'd like it. Maybe I won't have so much trouble with my lungs from now on."

"Speaking of lungs," she said, "you gave Dawson a lighter. Guess what he's just given up, and didn't have the heart to tell you?"

He burst out laughing. "Well, maybe he can use it to light fires under his beef cattle when he throws barbecues out on the Rutherford spread."

"What a good idea! I'll suggest it to him the next time we see him."

"I wouldn't hold my breath," he replied. "He travels

a lot these days. I hardly ever see him." He lifted his eyes to hers. "Powell came by last week."

Her heart fluttered, but her face was very composed. "Did he? Why?"

"Heard I was sick and came to check on me. Wanted to know where you were."

Her frozen expression grew darker. "Did he?"

"I told him you didn't know about the bronchitis and that he should mind his own business."

"I see."

He sipped hot chocolate and put the mug down with a thud. "Had his daughter with him. Quiet, sullen little thing. She never moved a muscle the whole time, just sat and glared. She's her mother all over."

Antonia was dying inside. She stared into her hot chocolate. That woman's child, here, in her home! She could hardly bear the thought. It was like a violation to have Powell come here with that child.

"You're upset," he said ruefully. "I guessed you would be, but I thought you'd better know. He said he'd be back to check on me after Christmas. Wouldn't want him to just show up without my telling you he was expected sooner or later. Not that I invited him," he added curtly. "Surprised me, too, that he'd come to see about me. Of course, he was fond of your mother. It hurt him that the scandal upset her so much and caused her to have that first heart attack. Anyway, he's taken it upon himself to be my guardian angel. Even sent the doctor when I first got sick, conspired with Mrs. Harper next door to look after me." He sounded disgusted, but he smiled, too.

"That was nice of him," she said, although Powell's actions surprised her. "But thanks for warning me." She forced a smile to her lips. "I'll arrange to do something in the kitchen if he turns up."

"It's been nine years," he reminded her.

"And you think I should have forgotten." She nodded. "You forgive people, Dad. I used to, before all this. Perhaps I should be more charitable, but I can't be. He and Sally made my life hell." She stopped, dragging in a long breath.

"No other suitors, in all that time," he remarked. "No social life, no dating. Girl, you're going to die an old maid, with no kids of your own, no husband, no real security."

"I enjoy my own company," she said lightly. "And I don't want a child." That was a lie, but only a partial one. The children she had wanted were Powell's, no one else's.

Christmas Day passed uneventfully, except for the meager gifts she and her father exchanged and their shared memories of her late mother to keep them company.

The next day, she was packed and dressed for travel in a rose knit suit, her hair carefully coiffed, her long legs in hose and low-heeled shoes on her feet. Her burgundy velvet, full-length coat was slung over one arm, its dark lining gleaming in the overhead light, as she put her suitcase down and went to find her father to say goodbye.

Voices from the living room caught her attention and she moved in that direction. But at the doorway, she froze in place, and in time. That deep, gravelly voice was as familiar as her own, despite the many years since she'd last heard it. And then a tall, lean man turned, and cast narrow black eyes on her face. Powell!

She lifted her face slowly, not allowing a hint of emotion to show either in her posture or her eyes. She simply looked at him, reconciling this man in his thirties with the man who'd wanted to marry her. The memories were unfavorable, because he was definitely showing his age, in the new lines beside his mouth and eyes, in the silver that showed at his temples.

He was doing his share of looking, too. The girl he'd jilted was no longer visible in this quiet, conservatively dressed woman with her hair in a bun. She looked schoolmarmish, and he was surprised that the sight of her was still like a knife through the heart, after all these years. He'd been curious about her. He'd wanted to see her again, God knew why. Maybe because she refused to see him at her mother's funeral. Now here she was, and he wasn't sure he was glad. The sight of her touched something sensitive that he'd buried inside himself.

Antonia was the first to look away. The intensity of his gaze had left her shaking inside, but that reaction was quickly hidden. It would never do to show any weakness to him. "Sorry," she told her father. "I didn't realize you had company. If you'll come and see me off, I'll be on my way."

Her father looked uncomfortable. "Powell came by to see how I was doing."

"You're leaving so soon?" Powell asked, addressing her directly for the first time in so many long years.

"I have to report back to work earlier than the students," she said, pleased that her voice was steady and cool.

"Oh, yes. You teach, don't you?"

She couldn't quite meet his eyes. Her gaze fell somewhere between his aggressive chin and his thin but sensuous mouth, below that straight, arrogant nose and the high cheekbones of his lean face. He wasn't handsome, but five minutes after they met him, most women were enchanted with him. He had an intangible something, authority perhaps, in the sureness of his movements, even in the way he held his head. He was overwhelming.

"I teach," she agreed. Her eyes hadn't quite met his. She turned to her father. "Dad?"

He excused himself and came forward to hug her. "Be careful. Phone when you get there, to let me know that you made it all right, will you? It's been snowing again."

"I'll be fine. I have a phone in the car, if I get stuck."

"You're driving to Arizona, in this weather?" Powell interrupted.

"I've been driving in this weather most of my adult life," she informed him.

"You were terrified of slick roads when you were in your teens," he recalled solemnly.

She smiled coldly at him. "I'm not a teenager now."

The way she looked at him spoke volumes about her feelings. He didn't avert his gaze, but his eyes were dark and quiet, full of secrets and seething accusation.

"Sally left a letter for you," he said unexpectedly. "I never got around to posting it. Over the years, I'd forgotten about it."

Her chest rose in a quick, angry breath. It reminded her of the letter that Sally had sent soon after Antonia had left town, the one she'd returned unopened. "Another one?" she asked in a frozen tone. "Well, I want nothing from your late wife, not even a letter."

He bristled. "She was your friend once," he reminded her curtly.

"She was my enemy." She corrected him. "She ruined my reputation and all but killed my mother! Do you really believe I'd want any reminder of what she did?"

He didn't seem to move for a minute. His face hardened. "She did nothing to hurt you deliberately," he said tersely.

"Really? Will her good intentions bring back George Rutherford or my mother?" she demanded hotly, because George himself had died so soon after her mother had. "Will it erase all the gossip?"

He turned away and bent his head to light a cigar, apparently unconcerned. Antonia fought for control. Her hands were icy cold as she picked up her suitcase and winced at her father's worried expression.

"I'll phone you, Dad. Please take care of yourself," she added.

"You're upset," he said distractedly. "Wait a bit..."

"I won't...I can't..." Her voice choked on the words and she averted her eyes from the long back of the man who was turned away from her. "Bye, Dad!"

She was out the door in a flash, and within two minutes she'd loaded her cases into the trunk and opened the door. But before she could get in, Powell was towering over her.

"Get a grip on yourself," he said curtly, forcing her to look at him. "You won't do your father any favors by landing in a ditch in the middle of nowhere!"

She shivered at the nearness of him and deliberately backed away, her gray eyes wide, accusing.

"You look so fragile," he said, as if the words were torn from him. "Don't you eat?"

"I eat enough." She steadied herself on the door. "Goodbye."

His big hand settled beside hers on the top of the door. "Why was Dawson Rutherford here a couple of nights ago?"

The question was totally unexpected. "Is that your business?" she asked coldly.

He smiled mockingly. "It could be. Rutherford's father ruined mine, or didn't you remember? I don't intend to let his son ruin me."

"My father and George Rutherford were friends."

"And you and George were lovers."

She didn't say a word. She only looked at him. "You know the truth," she said wearily. "You just don't want to believe it."

"George paid your way through college," he reminded her.

"Yes, he did," she agreed, smiling. "And I rewarded him by graduating with honors, second in my graduating class. He was a philanthropist and the best friend my family ever had. I miss him."

"He was a rich old man with designs on you, whether you'll admit it or not!"

She searched his deep-set black eyes. They never smiled. He was a hard man, and the passing years had only added to his sarcastic, harsh demeanor. He'd grown up dirt poor, looked down on in the community because of his parents. He'd struggled to get where he was, and she knew how difficult it had been. But his hard life had warped his perception of people. He looked for the worst, always. She'd known that, somehow, even when they were first engaged. And now, he was the sum of all the tragedies of his life. She'd loved him so much, she'd tried to make up to him for the love he'd never had, the life his circumstances had denied him. But even while he was courting her, he'd loved Sally most. He'd told Antonia so, when he broke their engagement and called her a streetwalker with a price tag....

"You're staring," he said irritably, ramming his hands into the pockets of his dark slacks.

"I was remembering the way you used to be, Powell," she said simply. "You haven't changed. You're still the loner who never trusted anyone, who always expected people to do their worst."

"I believed in you," he replied solemnly.

She smiled. "No, you didn't. If you had, you wouldn't have swallowed Sally's lies without—"

"Damn you!"

He had her by both shoulders, his cigar suddenly lying in the snow at their feet. He practically shook her, and she winced, because she was willow thin and he had the grip of a horseman, developed after long years of back-breaking ranch work long before he ever made any money at it.

She looked up into blazing eyes and wondered dimly why she wasn't afraid of him. He looked intimidating with his black eyes flashing and his straight black hair falling down over his thick eyebrows.

"Sally didn't lie!" he reiterated. "That's the hell of it, Antonia! She was gentle and kind and she never lied to me. She cried when you had to leave town over what happened. She cried for weeks and weeks, because she hadn't wanted to tell me what she knew about you and George! She couldn't bear to see you two-timing me!"

She pulled away from him with a strength she didn't know she had. "She deserved to cry!" she said through her teeth.

He called her a name that made her flush. She only smiled.

"Sticks and stones, Powell," she said in a steady, if husky, tone. "But if you say that again, you'll get the same thing I gave you the summer after I started college."

He remembered very well the feel of her shoe on his shin. Even through his anger, he had to stifle a mental smile at the memory. Antonia had always had spirit. But he remembered other things, too; like her refusal to talk to him after her mother's death, when he'd offered help. Sally had been long dead by then, but Antonia wouldn't let him close enough to see if she still felt anything for him. She wouldn't even now, and it caused him to lose his temper when he'd never meant to. She wouldn't let go of the past. She wouldn't give him a chance to find out if there was anything left of what they'd felt for each other. She didn't care.

The knowledge infuriated him.

"Now, if you're quite through insulting me, I have to go home," she added firmly.

"I could have helped, when your mother died," he said curtly. "You wouldn't even see me!"

He sounded as if her refusal to speak to him had hurt. What a joke that would be. She didn't look at him again. "I had nothing to say to you, and Dad and I didn't want your help. One way or another, you had enough help from us to build your fortune."

He scowled. "What the hell do you mean by that?"

She did look up, then, with a mocking little smile.

"Have you forgotten already? Now if you'll excuse me...?"

He didn't move. His big fists clenched by his sides as she just walked around him to get into the car.

She started it, put it into Reverse, and pointedly didn't look at him again, not even when she was driving off down the street toward the main highway. And if her hands shook, he couldn't see them.

He stood watching, his boots absorbing the freezing cold of the snow around them, snowflakes touching the wide brim of his creamy Stetson. He had no idea what she'd meant with that last crack. It made him furious that he couldn't even get her to talk to him. Nine years. He'd smoldered for nine years with seething outrage and anger, and he couldn't get the chance to air it. He wanted a knock-down, drag-out argument with her, he wanted to get everything in the open. He wanted... second chances.

"Do you want some hot chocolate?" Ben Hayes called from the front door.

Powell didn't answer him for a minute. "No," he said in a subdued tone. "Thanks, but I'll pass."

Ben pulled his housecoat closer around him. "You can damn her until you die," he remarked quietly. "But it won't change one thing."

Powell turned and faced him with an expression that wasn't easily read. "Sally didn't lie," he said stubbornly. "I don't care what anyone says about it. Innocent people don't run, and they both did!"

Ben studied the tormented eyes in that lean face for a long moment. "You have to keep believing that, don't you?" he asked coldly. "Because if you don't, you've got nothing at all to show for the past nine years. The hatred you've saved up for Antonia is all that's left of your life!"

Powell didn't say another word. He strode angrily back to his four-wheel-drive vehicle and climbed in under the wheel.

Chapter 3

Antonia made it back to Tucson without a hitch, although there had been one or two places along the snow-covered roads that gave her real problems. She was shaken, but it never affected her driving. Powell Long had destroyed enough of her life. She wasn't going to give him possession of one more minute of it, not even through hatred.

She kept busy for the remainder of her vacation and spent New Year's Eve by herself, with only a brief telephone call to her father for company. They didn't mention Powell.

Barrie stopped by on New Year's Day, wearing jeans and a sweatshirt and trying not to look interested in Dawson's visit to Antonia's father's house. It was always the same, though. Whenever Antonia went to Wyoming, Barrie would wait patiently until her friend said something about Dawson. Then she pretended that she wasn't interested and changed the subject.

But this time, she didn't. She searched Antonia's eyes. "Does he…look well?" she asked.

"He's fine," Antonia replied honestly. "He's quit smoking, so that's good news."

"Did he mention the widow?"

Antonia smiled sympathetically and shook her head. "He doesn't have much to do with women, Barrie. In fact, Dad says they call him 'the iceman' around Bighorn. They're still looking for a woman who can thaw him out."

"Dawson?" Barrie burst out. "But he's always had women hanging on him…!"

"Not these days. Apparently all he's interested in is making money."

Barrie looked shocked. "Since when?"

"I don't know. For the past few years at least," Antonia replied, frowning. "He's your stepbrother. You'd know more about that than I would. Wouldn't you?"

Barrie averted her eyes. "I don't see him. I don't go home."

"Yes, I know, but you must hear about him…."

"Only from you," the other woman said stiffly. "I don't…we don't have any mutual friends."

"Doesn't he ever come to see you?"

Barrie went pale. "He wouldn't." She bit off the words and forced a smile to her face. "We're poison to each other, didn't you know?" She looked at her watch. "I'm going to a dance. Want to come?"

Antonia shook her head. "Not me. I'm too tired. I'll see you back at work."

"Sure. You look worse than you did when you left. Did you see Powell?"

Antonia flinched.

"Sorry," came the instant reply. "Listen, don't tell me anything about Dawson even if I beg, and I swear I won't mention Powell again, okay? I'm really sorry. I suppose we both have wounds too raw to expose. See you!"

Barrie left, and Antonia quickly found something to do, so that she wouldn't have to think any more about Powell.

But, oh, it was hard. He'd literally jilted her the day before the wedding. The invitations had been sent out, the church booked, the minister ready to officiate at the ceremony. Antonia had a dress from Neiman Marcus, a heavenly creation that George had helped her buy—which had become part of the fiasco when she admitted it to Powell. And then, out of the blue, Sally had dropped her bombshell. She'd told Powell that George Rutherford was Antonia's sugar daddy and he was paying for her body. Everyone in Bighorn knew it. They probably did, Sally had worked hard enough spreading the rumor. The gossip alone was enough to send Powell crazy. He'd turned on Antonia in a rage and canceled the wedding. She didn't like remembering the things he'd said to her.

Some of the guests didn't get notified in time and came to the church, expecting a wedding. Antonia had had to face them and tell them the sad news. She had been publicly humiliated, and then there was the scandal that involved poor George. He'd had to move back to Sheridan, to the headquarters ranch of the Rutherford chain. It had been a shame, because the Rutherford

Bighorn Ranch had been his favorite. He'd escaped a lot of the censure and spared Antonia some of it, especially when he exiled himself to France. But Antonia and her father and mother got the whole measure of local outrage. Denial did no good, because how could she defend herself against knowing glances and haughty treatment? The gossip had hurt her mother most, leaving her virtually isolated from most of the people who knew her. She'd had a mild heart attack from the treatment of her only child as a social outcast. Ironically that had seemed to bring some people to their senses, and the pressure had been eased a bit. But Antonia had left town very quickly, to spare her mother any more torment, taking her broken heart with her.

Perhaps if Powell had thought it through, if the wedding hadn't been so near, the ending might have been different. He'd always been quick-tempered and impulsive. He hated being talked about. Antonia knew that at least three people had talked to him about the rumors, and one of them was the very minister who was to marry them. Later, Antonia had discovered that they were all friends of Sally and her family.

To be fair to Powell, he'd had more than his share of public scandal. His father had been a hopeless gambler who lost everything his mother slaved at housekeeping jobs to provide. In the end he'd killed himself when he incurred a debt he knew he'd never be able to repay. Powell had watched his mother be torn apart by the gossip, and eventually her heart wore out and she simply didn't wake up one morning.

Antonia had comforted Powell. She'd gone to the funeral home with him and held his hand all through the ordeal of giving up the mother he'd loved. Perhaps

grief had challenged his reason, because although he'd
hidden it well, the loss had destroyed something in him.
He'd never quite recovered from it, and Sally had been
behind the scenes, offering even more comfort when
Antonia wasn't around. Susceptible to her soft voice,
perhaps he'd listened when he shouldn't have. But in
the end, he'd believed Sally, and he'd married her. He'd
never said he loved Antonia, and it had been just after
they'd become engaged that Powell had managed several loans, on the strength of her father's excellent ref-
erences, to get the property he'd inherited out of hock.
He was just beginning to make it pay when he'd called
off the wedding.

The pain was like a knife. She'd loved Powell more
than her own life. She'd been devastated by his defec-
tion. The only consolation she'd had was that she'd put
him off physically until after the wedding. Perhaps that
had hurt him most, thinking that she was sleeping with
poor old George when she wouldn't go to bed with him.
Who knew? She couldn't go back and do things differ-
ently. She could only go forward. But the future looked
much more bleak than the past.

She went back to work in the new year, apparently
rested and unworried. But the doctor's appointment
was still looming at the end of her first week after she
started teaching.

She didn't expect them to find anything. She was
run-down and tired all the time, and she'd lost a lot of
weight. Probably she needed vitamins or iron tablets
or something. When the doctor ordered a blood test,
a complete blood count, she went along to the lab and
sat patiently while they worked her in and took blood

for testing. Then she went home with no particular intuition about what was about to happen.

It was early Monday morning when she had a call at work from the doctor's office. They asked her to come in immediately.

She was too frightened to ask why. She left her class to the sympathetic vice principal and went right over to Dr. Claridge's office.

They didn't make her wait, either. She was hustled right in, no appointment, no nothing.

He got up when she entered his office and shook hands. "Sit down, Antonia. I've got the lab results from your blood test. We have to make some quick decisions."

"Quick...?" Her heart was beating wildly. She could barely breathe. She was aware of her cold hands gripping her purse like a life raft. "What sort of decisions?"

He leaned forward, his forearms on his legs. "Antonia, we've known each other for several years. This isn't an easy thing to tell someone." He grimaced. "My dear, you've got leukemia."

She stared at him without comprehension. Leukemia. Wasn't that cancer? Wasn't it...fatal?

Her breath suspended in midair. "I'm...going to die?" she asked in a hoarse whisper.

"No," he replied. "Your condition is treatable. You can undergo a program of chemotherapy and radiation, which will probably keep it in remission for some years."

Remission. Probably. Radiation. Chemotherapy. Her aunt had died of cancer when Antonia was a little girl. She remembered with terror the therapy's effects on her aunt. Headaches, nausea...

She stood up. "I can't think."

Dr. Claridge stood up, too. He took her hands in his. "Antonia, it isn't necessarily a death sentence. We can start treatment right away. We can buy time for you."

She swallowed, closing her eyes. She'd been worried about her argument with Powell, about the anguish of the past, about Sally's cruelty and her own torment. And now she was going to die, and what did any of that matter?

She was going to die!

"I want...to think about it," she said huskily.

"Of course you do. But don't take too long, Antonia," he said gently. "All right?"

She managed to nod. She thanked him, followed the nurse out to reception, paid her bill, smiled at the girl and walked out. She didn't remember doing any of it. She drove back to her apartment, closed the door and collapsed right there on the floor in tears.

Leukemia. She had a deadly disease. She'd expected a future, and now, instead, there was going to be an ending. There would be no more Christmases with her father. She wouldn't marry and have children. It was all...over.

When the first of the shock passed, and she'd exhausted herself crying, she got up and made herself a cup of coffee. It was a mundane, ordinary thing to do. But now, even such a simple act had a poignancy. How many more cups would she have time to drink in what was left of her life?

She smiled at her own self-pity. That wasn't going to do her any good. She had to decide what to do. Did she want to prolong the agony, as her aunt had, until every penny of her medical insurance ran out, until she bankrupted herself and her father, put herself and him through the long drawn-out treatments when she might still lose the battle? What quality of life would she have if she suffered as her aunt had?

She had to think not what was best for her, but what was best for her father. She wasn't going to rush into treatment until she was certain that she had a chance of surviving. If she was only going to be able to keep it at bay for a few painful months, then she had some difficult decisions to make. If only she could think clearly! She was too shocked to be rational. She needed time. She needed peace.

Suddenly, she wanted to go home. She wanted to be with her father, at her home. She'd spent her life running away. Now, when things were so dire, it was time to face the past, to reconcile herself with it, and with the community that had unjustly judged her. There would be time left for that, to tie up all the loose ends, to come to grips with her own past.

Her old family doctor, Dr. Harris, was still in Bighorn. She'd get Dr. Claridge to send him her medical files and she'd go from there. Perhaps Dr. Harris might have some different ideas about how she could face the ordeal. If nothing could be done, then at least she could spend her remaining time with the only family she had left.

Once the decision was made, she acted on it at once. She turned in her resignation and told Barrie that her father needed her at home.

"You didn't say that when you first came back," Barrie said suspiciously.

"Because I was thinking about it," she lied. She smiled. "Barrie, he's so alone. And it's time I went back and faced my dragons. I've been running too long already."

"But what will you do?" Barrie asked.

"I'll get a job as a relief teacher. Dad said that two of the elementary school teachers were expecting and they didn't know what they'd do for replacements. Bighorn isn't exactly Tucson, you know. It's not that easy to get teachers who are willing to live at the end of the world."

Barrie sighed. "You really have thought this out."

"Yes. I'll miss you. But maybe you'll come back one day," she added. "And fight your own dragons."

Barrie shivered. "Mine are too big to fight," she said with an enigmatic smile. "But I'll root for you. What can I help you do?"

"Pack," came the immediate reply.

As fate would have it, when she contacted her old school system in Bighorn, one of the pregnant teachers had just had to go into the hospital with toxemia and they needed a replacement desperately for a fourth-grade class. It was just what Antonia wanted, and she accepted gratefully. Best of all, there had been no discussion of the reason she'd left town in the first place. Some people would remember, but she had old friends there, too, friends who wouldn't hold grudges. Powell would be there. She refused to even entertain the idea that he had any place in her reasons for wanting to go home.

She arrived in Bighorn with mixed emotions. It made her feel wonderful to see her father's delighted expression when he was told she was coming back there to live permanently. But she felt guilty, too, because he couldn't know the real reason for her return.

"We'll have plenty of time to visit, now," she said. "Arizona was too hot to suit me, anyway," she added mischievously.

"Well, if you like snow, you've certainly come home at a good time," he replied, grinning at the five feet or so that lay in drifts in the front yard.

Antonia spent the weekend unpacking and then went along to work the following Monday. She liked the principal, a young woman with very innovative ideas about education. She remembered two of her fellow teachers, who had been classmates of hers in high school, and neither of them seemed to have any misgivings about her return.

She liked her class, too. She spent the first day getting to know the children's names. But one of them hit her right in the heart. Maggie Long. It could have been a coincidence. But when she called the girl's name and a sullen face with blue eyes and short black hair looked up at her, she knew right away who it was. That was Sally's face, except for the glare. The glare was Powell all over again.

She lifted her chin and stared at the child. She passed over her and went on down the line until she reached Julie Ames. She smiled at Julie, who smiled back sweetly. She remembered Danny Ames from school, too, and his redheaded daughter was just like him. She'd have known Danny's little girl anywhere.

She pulled out her predecessor's lesson plan and looked over it before she took the spelling book and began making assignments.

"One other thing I'd like you to do for Friday is write a one-page essay about yourselves," she added with a smile. "So that I can learn something about you, since I've come in the middle of the year instead of the first."

Julie raised her hand. "Miss Hayes, Mrs. Donalds always assigned one of us to be class monitor when she was out of the room. Whoever she picked got to do it for a week, and then someone else did. Are you going to do that, too?"

"I think that's a good idea, Julie. You can be our monitor for this week," she added pleasantly.

"Thanks, Miss Hayes!" Julie said enthusiastically.

Behind her, Maggie Long glared even more. The child acted as if she hated Antonia, and for a minute, Antonia wondered if she knew about the past. But, then, how could she? She was being fanciful.

She dismissed the class at quitting time. It had been nice to have her mind occupied, not to have to think about herself. But with the end of the day came the terror again. And she still hadn't talked to Dr. Harris.

She made an appointment to see him when she got home, smiling at her father as she told him glibly that it was only because she needed some vitamins.

Dr. Harris, however, was worried when she told him Dr. Claridge's diagnosis.

"You shouldn't wait," he said flatly. "It's always best to catch these things early. Come here, Antonia."

He examined her neck with skilled hands, his eyes on the wall behind her. "Swollen lymph nodes, all right. You've lost weight?" he asked as he took her pulse.

"Yes. I've been working rather hard," she said lamely.

"Sore throat?"

She hesitated and then nodded.

He let out a long sigh. "I'll have him fax me your medical records," he said. "There's a specialist in Sheridan who's done oncology," he added. "But you should go back to Tucson, Antonia."

"Tell me what to expect," she said instead.

He was reluctant, but when she insisted, he drew in a deep breath and told her.

She sat back in her chair, pale and restless.

"You can fight it," he persisted. "You can hold it at bay."

"For how long?"

"Some people have been in remission for twenty-five years."

She narrowed her eyes as she gazed at him. "But you don't really believe I'll have twenty-five years."

His jaw firmed. "Antonia, medical research is progressing at a good pace. There's always, always, the possibility that a cure will be discovered…."

She held up a hand. "I don't want to have to decide today," she said wearily. "I just need…a little time," she added with a pleading smile. "Just a little time."

He looked as if he were biting his tongue to keep from arguing with her. "All right. A little time," he said emphatically. "I'll look after you. Perhaps when you've considered the options, you'll go ahead with the treatment, and I'll do everything I can. But, Antonia," he added as he stood up to show her out, "there aren't too many miracles in this business where cancer is concerned. If you're going to fight, don't wait too long."

"I won't."

She shook hands and left the office. She felt more at peace with herself now than she could ever remember feeling. Somehow in the course of accepting the diagnosis, she'd accepted something much more. She was stronger now. She could face whatever she had to. She was so glad she'd come home. Fate had dealt her some severe blows, but being home helped her to withstand the worst of them. She had to believe that fate would be kinder to her now that she was home.

But if fate had kind reasons for bringing her back to Bighorn, Maggie Long wasn't one of them. The girl was unruly, troublesome and refused to do her schoolwork at all.

By the end of the week, Antonia kept her after class and showed her the zero she'd earned for her nonattempt at the spelling test. There was another one looming, because Maggie hadn't done one word of the essay Antonia had assigned the class to write.

"If you want to repeat the fourth grade, Maggie, this is a good start," she said coolly. "If you won't do your schoolwork, you won't pass."

"Mrs. Donalds wasn't mean like you," the girl said snappily. "She never made us write stupid essays, and if there was a test, she always helped me study for it."

"I have thirty-five students in this class," Antonia heard herself saying. "Presumably you were placed in this grade because you were capable of doing the work."

"I could do it if I wanted to," Maggie said. "I just don't want to. And you can't make me, either!"

"I can fail you," came the terse, uncompromising reply. "And I will, if you keep this up. You have one last chance to escape a second zero for the essay you haven't done. You can do it over the weekend and turn it in Monday."

"My daddy's coming home today," she said haughtily. "I'm going to tell him that you're mean to me, and he'll come and cuss you out, you just wait and see!"

"What will he see, Maggie?" she asked flatly. "What does it say about you if you won't do your work?"

"I'm not lazy!"

"Then do your assignment."

"Julie didn't do all of her test, and you didn't give her a zero!"

"Julie doesn't work as fast as some of the other students. I take that into account," Antonia explained.

"You like Julie," she accused. "That's why you never act mean to her! I'll bet you wouldn't give her a zero if she didn't do her homework!"

"This has nothing to do with your ability to do your work," Antonia interrupted. "And I'm not going to argue with you. Either do your homework or don't do it. Now run along."

Maggie gave her a furious glare. She jerked up her books and stomped out of the room, turning at the door. "You wait until I tell my daddy! He'll get you fired!"

Antonia lifted an eyebrow. "It will take more than your father to do that, Maggie."

The girl jerked open the door. "I hate you! I wish you'd never come here!" she yelled.

She ran down the hallway and Antonia sat back and caught her breath. The child was a holy terror. She was a little surprised that she was so unlike her mother in that one way. Sally, for all her lying, had been sweet in the fourth grade, an amiable child, not a horror like Maggie.

Sally. The name hurt. Just the name. Antonia had come home to exorcise her ghosts and she wasn't doing a very good job of it. Maggie was making her life miserable. Perhaps Powell would interfere, at least enough to get his daughter to do her homework. She hated that it had come to this, but she hadn't anticipated the emotions Maggie's presence in her class had unleashed. She was sorry that she couldn't like the child. She wondered if anyone did. She seemed little more than a sullen, resentful brat.

Powell probably adored the child and gave her everything she wanted. But she did ride the bus to and from school and more often than not, she showed up for class in torn jeans and stained sweatshirts. Was that deliberate, and didn't her father notice that some of her things weren't clean? Surely he had a housekeeper or someone to take care of such things.

She knew that Maggie had been staying with Julie this week, because Julie had told her so. The little red-headed Ames girl was the sweetest child Antonia had ever known, and she adored her. She really was the image of her father, who'd been in Antonia's group of friends in school here in Bighorn. She'd told Julie that, and the child had been a minor celebrity for a day. It gave her something to be proud of, that her father and her teacher had been friends.

Maggie hadn't liked that. She'd given Julie the cold shoulder yesterday and they weren't speaking today. Antonia wondered at their friendship, because Julie was outgoing and generous, compassionate and kind... all the things Maggie wasn't. Probably the child saw qualities in Julie that she didn't have and liked her for them. But what in the world did Julie see in Maggie?

Chapter 4

Powell Long came home from his cattle-buying trip worn out from the long hours on the plane and the hectic pace of visiting three ranches in three states in less than a week. He could have purchased his stud cattle after watching a video, and he sometimes did if he knew the seller, but he was looking over new territory for his stock additions, and he wanted to inspect the cattle in person before he made the acquisition. It was a good thing he had, because one of the ranches had forwarded a video that must have been of someone else's cattle. When he toured the ranch, he found the stock were underfed, and some were lacking even the basic requirements for good breeding bulls.

Still, it had been a profitable trip. He'd saved several thousand dollars on seed bulls simply by going to visit the ranchers in person. Now he was home again and he didn't want to be. His house, like his life, was full of painful memories. Here was where Sally had lived, where her daughter still lived. He couldn't look at Maggie without seeing her mother. He bought the child expensive toys, whatever her heart desired. But he couldn't give her love. He didn't think he had it in him to love the product of such a painful marriage. Sally had cost him the thing he'd loved most in all the world. She'd cost him Antonia.

Maggie was sitting alone in the living room with a book. She looked up when he entered the room with eyes that avoided his almost at once.

"Did you bring me something?" she asked dully. He always did. It was just one more way of making her feel that she was important to him, but she knew better. He didn't even know what she liked, or he wouldn't bring her silly stuffed toys and dolls. She liked to read, but he hadn't noticed. She also liked nature films and natural history. He never brought her those sort of things. He didn't even know who she was.

"I brought you a new Barbie," he said. "It's in my suitcase."

"Thanks," she said.

Never a smile. Never laughter. She was a little old woman in a child's body, and looking at her made him feel guilty.

"Where's Mrs. Bates?" he asked uncomfortably.

"In the kitchen cooking," she said.

"How's school?"

She closed the book. "We got a new teacher last week. She doesn't like me," she said. "She's mean to me."

His eyebrows lifted. "Why?"

She shrugged, her thin shoulders rising and falling restlessly. "I don't know. She likes everybody else. She glares at me all the time. She gave me a zero on my test, and she's going to give me another zero on my homework. She says I'm going to fail fourth grade."

He was shocked. Maggie had always made good grades. One thing she did seem to have was a keen intelligence, even if her perpetual frown and introverted nature made her enemies. She had no close friends, except for Julie. He'd left Maggie with Julie's family, in fact, last week. They were always willing to keep her while he was out of town.

He glowered at her. "Why are you here instead of at Julie's house?" he demanded suddenly.

"I told them you were coming home and I wanted to be here, because you always bring me something," she said.

"Oh."

She didn't add that Julie's friendship with the detestable Miss Hayes had caused friction, or that they'd had a terrible argument just this morning, precipitating Maggie's return home. Fortunately Mrs. Bates was working in the house, so that it was possible for her to be here.

"The new teacher likes Julie," she said sullenly. "But she hates me. She says I'm lazy and stupid."

"She says what?"

That was the first time her father had ever reacted in such a way, as if it really mattered to him that someone didn't like her. She looked at him fully, seeing that angry flash of his black eyes that always meant trouble for somebody. Her father intimidated her. But, then, he intimidated everyone. He didn't like most people any more than she did. He was introverted himself, and he had a bad temper and a sarcastic manner when people irritated him. Over the years Maggie had discovered that she could threaten people with her father, and it always worked.

Locally he was a legend. Most of her teachers had bent over backward to avoid confrontations with him. Maggie learned quickly that she didn't have to study very hard to make good grades. Not that she wasn't bright; she simply didn't try, because she didn't need to. She smiled. Wouldn't it be nice, she thought, if she could use him against Miss Hayes?

"She says I'm lazy and stupid," she repeated.

"What's this teacher's name?" he asked coldly.

"Miss Hayes."

He was very still. "Antonia Hayes?" he asked curtly.

"I don't know her first name. She came on account of Mrs. Donalds quit," she said. "Mrs. Donalds was my friend. I miss her."

"When did Miss Hayes get here?" he asked, surprised that he'd heard nothing about her returning to Bighorn. Of course, he'd been out of town for a week, too.

"I told you—last week. They said she used to live here." She studied his hard face. It looked dangerous. "Did she, Daddy?"

"Yes," he said with icy contempt. "Yes, she used to live here. Well, we'll see how Miss Hayes handles herself with another adult," he added.

He went to the telephone and picked it up and dialed the principal of the Bighorn Elementary School.

Mrs. Jameson was surprised to hear Powell Long on the other end of the phone. She'd never known him to interfere in school matters before, even when Maggie was up to her teeth in trouble with another student.

"I want to know why you permit an educator to tell a child that she's lazy and stupid," he demanded.

There was a long pause. "I beg your pardon?" the principal asked, shocked.

"Maggie said that Miss Hayes told her she was lazy and stupid," he said shortly. "I want that teacher talked to, and talked to hard. I don't want to have to come up there myself. Is that clear?"

Mrs. Jameson knew Powell Long. She was intimidated enough to agree that she'd speak to Antonia on Monday.

And she did. Reluctantly.

"I had a call from Maggie Long's father Friday afternoon after you left," Mrs. Jameson told Antonia, who was sitting rigidly in front of her in her office. "I don't believe for a minute that you'd deliberately make insulting remarks to that child. Heaven knows, every teacher in this school except Mrs. Donalds has had trouble with her, although Mr. Long has never interfered. It's puzzling that he would intervene, and that Maggie would say such things about you."

"I haven't called her stupid," Antonia said evenly. "I have told her that if she refuses to do her homework and write down the answers on tests, she will be given a failing grade. I've never made a policy of giving undeserved marks, or playing favorites."

"I'm sure you haven't," Mrs. Jameson replied. "Your record in Tucson is spotless. I even spoke to your principal there, who was devastated to have lost you. He speaks very highly of your intelligence and your competence."

"I'm glad. But I don't know what to do about Maggie," she continued. "She doesn't like me. I'm sorry about that, but I don't know what I can do to change her attitude. If she could only be helpful like her friend Julie," she added. "Julie is a first-rate little student."

"Everyone loves Julie," the principal agreed. She folded her hands on her desk. "I have to ask you this, Antonia. Is it possible that unconsciously you might be taking out old hurts on Maggie? I know that you were engaged to her father once…. It's a small town," she added apologetically when Antonia stiffened, "and one does hear gossip. I also know that Maggie's mother broke you up and spread some pretty terrible lies about you in the community."

"There are people who still don't think they were lies," Antonia replied tersely. "My mother eventually died because of the pressure and censure the community put on her because of them."

"I'm sorry. I didn't know that."

"She had a bad heart. I left town, to keep the talk to a minimum, but she never got over it." Her head lifted, and she forced a weak smile. "I was innocent of everything I had been accused of, but I paid the price anyway."

Mrs. Jameson looked torn. "I shouldn't have brought it up."

"Yes, you should," Antonia replied. "You had the right to know if I was deliberately persecuting a student. I despised Sally for what she did to me, and I have no more love for Maggie's father than for his late wife. But

I hope I'm not such a bad person that I'd try to make a child suffer for something she didn't do."

"Nor do I believe you would, consciously," Mrs. Jameson replied. "It's a touchy situation, though. Mr. Long has enormous influence in the community. He's quite wealthy and his temper is legendary in these parts. He has no compunction about making scenes in public, and he threatened to come up here himself if this situation isn't resolved." She laughed a little unsteadily. "Miss Hayes, I'm forty-five years old. I've worked hard all my life to achieve my present status. It would be very difficult for me to find another job if I lost this one, and I have an invalid husband to support and a son in college. I plead with you not to put my job in jeopardy."

"I never would do that," Antonia promised. "I'd quit before I'd see an innocent person hurt by my actions. But Mr. Long is very wrong about the way his daughter is being treated. In fact, she's causing the problems. She refuses to do her work and she knows that I can't force her to."

"She certainly does. She'll go to her father, and he'll light fires under members of the school board. I believe at least one of them owes him money, in fact, and the other three are afraid of him." She cleared her throat. "I'll tell you flat that I'm afraid of him, myself."

"No freedom of speech in these parts, I gather?"

"If your freedom impinges on his prejudices, no, there isn't," Mrs. Jameson agreed. "He's something of a tyrant in his way. We certainly can't fault him for being concerned about his child, though."

"No," Antonia agreed. She sighed. Her own circumstances were tenuous, to say the least. She had her own problems and fear gnawed at her all the time. She wasn't afraid of Powell Long, though. She was more afraid of what lay ahead for her.

"You will try...about Maggie?" Mrs. Jameson added.

Antonia smiled. "Certainly I will. But may I come to you if the problem doesn't resolve itself and ask for help?"

"If there's any to give, you may." She grimaced. "I have my own doubts about Maggie's cooperation. And we both have a lot to lose if her father isn't happy."

"Do you want me to pass her anyway?" Antonia asked. "To give her grades she hasn't earned, because her father might be upset if she fails?"

Mrs. Jameson flushed. "I can't tell you to do that, Miss Hayes. We're supposed to educate children, not pass them through favoritism."

"I know that," Antonia said.

"But you wondered if I did," came the dry reply. "Yes, I do. But I'm job scared. When you're my age, Miss Hayes," she added gently, "I can guarantee that you will be, too."

Antonia's eyes were steady and sad. She knew that she might never have the problem; she might not live long enough to have it. She thanked Mrs. Jameson and went back to her classroom, morose and dejected.

Maggie watched her as she sat down at her desk and instructed the class to proceed with their English lesson. She didn't look very happy. Her father must have shaken them up, Maggie thought victoriously. Well, she wasn't going to do that homework or do those tests. And when she failed, her father would come storming up here, because he never doubted his little girl's word. He'd have Miss Hayes on the run in no time. Then maybe Mrs.

Donalds would have her baby and come back, and everything would be all right again. She glared at Julie, who just ignored her. She was sick of Julie, kissing up to Miss Hayes. Julie was a real sap. Maggie wasn't sure who she disliked more—Julie or Miss Hayes.

There was one nice touch, and that was that Miss Hayes coolly told her that she had until Friday to turn in her essay and the other homework that Antonia had assigned the class.

The next four days went by, and Antonia asked for homework papers to be turned in that she'd assigned at the beginning of the week. Maggie didn't turn hers in.

"You'll get a zero if you don't have all of it by this afternoon, including the essay you owe me," Antonia told her, dreading the confrontation she knew was coming, despite all her hopes. She'd done her best to treat Maggie just like the other students, but the girl challenged her at every turn.

"No, I won't," Maggie said with a surly smile. "If you give me a zero, I'll tell my daddy, and he'll come up here."

Antonia studied the sullen little face. "And you think that frightens me?"

"Everybody's scared of my dad," she returned proudly.

"Well, I'm not," Antonia said coldly. "Your father can come up here if he likes and I'll tell him the same thing I've told you. If you don't do the work, you don't pass. And there's nothing he can do about it."

"Oh, really?"

Antonia nodded. "Oh, really. And if you don't turn

in your homework by the time the final bell sounds, you'll find out."

"So will you," Maggie replied.

Antonia refused to argue with the child. But when the end of class came and Maggie didn't turn the homework in, she put a zero neatly next to the child's name.

"Take this paper home, please," she told the child, handing her a note with her grade on it.

Maggie took it. She smiled. And she didn't say a word as she went out the door. Miss Hayes didn't know that her daddy was picking her up today. But she was about to find out.

Antonia had chores to finish before she could go home. She didn't doubt that Powell would be along. But she wasn't going to back down. She had nothing to lose now. Even her job wasn't that important if it meant being blackmailed by a nine-year-old.

Sure enough, it was only minutes since class was dismissed and she was clearing her desk when she heard footsteps coming down the hall. Only a handful of teachers would still be in the building, but those particular steps were heavy and forceful, and she knew who they belonged to.

She turned as the door opened and a familiar tall figure came into the room with eyes as dark as death.

He didn't remove his hat, or exchange greetings. In his expensive suit and boots and Stetson, he looked very prosperous. But her eyes were seeing a younger man, a ragged and lonely young man who never fit in anywhere, who dreamed of not being poor. Sometimes she remembered that young man and loved him with a passion that even in dreams was overpowering.

"I've been expecting you," she said, putting the past away in the back drawers of her mind. "She did get a zero, and she deserved it. I gave her all week to produce her homework, and she didn't."

"Oh, hell, you don't have to pretend noble motives. I know why you're picking on the kid. Well, lay off Maggie," he said shortly. "You're here to teach, not to take out old grudges on my daughter."

She was sitting at her desk. She folded her hands together on its worn surface and simply stared at him, unblinking. "Your daughter is going to fail this grade," she said composedly. "She won't participate in class discussions, she won't do any homework, and she refuses to even attempt answers on pop tests. I'm frankly amazed that she's managed to get this far in school at all." She smiled coldly. "I understand from the principal, who is also intimidated by you, that you have the influence to get anyone fired who doesn't pass her."

His face went rigid. "I don't need to use any influence! She's a smart child."

She opened her desk drawer, took out Maggie's last test paper and slid it across the desk to him. "Really?" she asked.

He moved into the classroom, to the desk. His lean, dark hand shot down to retrieve the paper. He looked at it with narrow, deep-set eyes, black eyes that were suddenly piercing on Antonia's face.

"She didn't write anything on this," he said.

She nodded, taking it back. "She sat with her arms folded, giving me a haughty smile the whole time, and she didn't move a muscle for the full thirty minutes."

"She hasn't acted that way before."

"I wouldn't know. I'm new here."

He stared at her angrily. "And you don't like her."

She searched his cold eyes. "You really think I came all the way back to Wyoming to take out old resentments on Sally's daughter?" she asked, and hated the guilt she felt when she asked the question. She knew she wasn't being fair to Maggie, but the very sight of the child was like torture.

"Sally's and mine," he reminded her, as if he knew how it hurt her to remember.

She felt sick to her stomach. "Excuse me. Sally's and yours," she replied obligingly.

He nodded slowly. "Yes, that's what really bothers you, isn't it?" he said, almost to himself. "It's because she looks just like Sally."

"She's her image," she agreed flatly.

"And you still hate her, after all this time."

Her hands clenched together. She didn't drop her gaze. "We were talking about your daughter."

"Maggie."

"Yes."

"You can't even bring yourself to say her name, can you?" He perched himself on the edge of her desk. "I thought teachers were supposed to be impartial, to teach regardless of personal feelings toward their students."

"We are."

"You aren't doing it," he continued. He smiled, but it wasn't the sort of smile that comforted. "Let me tell you something, Antonia. You came home. But this is my town. I own half of it, and I know everybody on the school board. If you want to stay here, and teach here, you'd better be damn sure that you maintain an impartial attitude toward all the students."

"Especially toward your daughter?" she asked.

He nodded. "I see you understand."

"I won't treat her unfairly, but I won't play favorites, either," she said icily. "She's going to receive no grades that she doesn't earn in my classroom. If you want to get me fired, go ahead."

"Oh, hell, I don't want your job," he said abruptly. "It doesn't matter to me if you stay here with your father. I don't even care why you suddenly came back. But I won't have my daughter persecuted for something that she didn't do! She has nothing to do with the past."

"Nothing?" Her eyes glittered up into his. "Sally was pregnant with that child when you married her, and she was born seven months later," she said huskily, and the pain was a living, breathing thing. Even the threat of leukemia wasn't that bad. "You were sleeping with Sally while you were swearing eternal devotion to me!"

Antonia didn't have to be a math major to arrive at the difference. He'd married Sally less than a month after he broke up with Antonia, and Maggie was born seven months later. Which meant that Sally was pregnant when they married.

He took a slow, steady breath, but his eyes, his face, were terrible to see. He stared down at her as if he'd like to throw something.

Antonia averted her gaze to the desk, where her hands were so tightly clasped now that the knuckles were white. She relaxed them, so that he wouldn't notice how tense she was.

"I shouldn't have said that," she said after a minute. "I had no right. Your marriage was your own business, and so is your daughter. I won't be unkind to her. But I will expect her to do the same work I assign to the other students, and if she doesn't, she'll be graded accordingly."

He stood up and shoved his hands into his pockets. The eyes that met hers were unreadable. "Maggie's paid a higher price than you know already," he said enigmatically. "I won't let you hurt her."

"I'm not in the habit of taking out my personal feelings on children, whatever you think of me."

"You're twenty-seven now," he said, surprising her. "Yet you're still unmarried. You have no children of your own."

She smiled evenly. "Yes. I had a lucky escape."

"And no inclination to find someone else? Make a life for yourself?"

"I have a life," she said, and the fear came up into her mouth as she realized that she might not have it for much longer.

"Do you?" he asked. "Your father will die one day. Then you'll be alone."

Her eyes, full of fear, fell to the desk again. "I've been alone for a long time," she said quietly. "It's something…one learns to live with."

He didn't speak. After a minute, she heard his voice, as if from a distance. "Why did you come back?"

"For my father."

"He's getting better day by day. He didn't need you."

She looked up, searching his face, seeing the young man she'd loved in his dark eyes, his sensuous mouth. "Maybe I needed someone," she said. She winced and dropped her eyes.

He laughed. It had an odd sound. "Just don't turn your attention toward me, Antonia. You may need someone. I don't. Least of all you."

Before she could say a word, he'd gone out the door, as quietly as he'd come in.

Maggie was waiting at the door when he walked in. He'd taken her home before he had his talk with Antonia.

"Did you see her? Did you tell her off?" she asked excitedly. "I knew you'd show her who's boss!"

His eyes narrowed. She hadn't shown that much enthusiasm for anything in years. "What about that homework?"

She shrugged. "It was stupid stuff. She wanted us to write an essay about ourselves and do math problems and make up sentences to go with spelling words."

He scowled. "You mean, you didn't do it—any of it?"

"You told her I didn't have to, didn't you?" she countered.

He tossed his hat onto the side table in the hall and his eyes flashed at her. "Did you do any of the homework?"

"Well…no," she muttered. "It was stupid, I told you."

"Damn it! You lied!"

She backed up. She didn't like the way he was looking at her. He frightened her when he looked that way. He made her feel guilty. She didn't lie as a rule, but this was different. Miss Hayes was hurting her, so didn't she have the right to hurt back?

"You'll do that homework, do you hear me?" he demanded. "And the next time you have a test, you won't sit through it with your arms folded. Is that clear?"

She compressed her lips. "Yes, Daddy."

"My God." He bit off the words, staring at her furiously. "You're just like your mother, aren't you? Well, this is going to stop right now. No more lies—ever!"

"But, Daddy, I don't lie…!"

He didn't listen. He just turned and walked away. Maggie stared after him with tears burning her eyes, her small fists clenched at her sides. Just like her mother. That's what Mrs. Bates said when she misbehaved. She knew that her father hadn't cared about her mother. Her mother had cried because of it, when she drank so much. She'd said that she told a lie and Powell had hated her for it. Did this mean that he hated Maggie, too?

She followed him out into the hall. "Daddy!" she cried.

"What?"

He turned, glaring at her.

"She doesn't like me!"

"Have you tried cooperating with her?" he replied coldly.

She shrugged, averting her eyes so that he wouldn't see the tears and the pain in them. She was used to hiding her hurts in this cold house. She went up the staircase to her room without saying anything else.

He watched her walk away with a sense of hopelessness. His daughter had used him to get back at her teacher, and he'd let her. He'd gone flaming over to the school and made all sorts of accusations and charges, and Antonia had been the innocent party. He was furious at having been so gullible. It was because he didn't really know the child, he imagined. He spent as little time with her as possible, because she was a walking, talking reminder of his failed marriage.

Next time, he promised himself, he'd get his facts straight before he started attacking teachers. But he wasn't sorry about what he'd said to Antonia. Let her stew on those charges. Maybe it would intimidate her enough that she wouldn't deliberately hurt Maggie. He knew how she felt about Sally, he couldn't help but know. Her resentments were painfully visible in her thin face.

He wondered why she'd come back to haunt him. He'd almost pushed her to the back of his mind over the years. Almost. He'd gone to see her father finally to get news of her, because the loneliness he felt was eating into him like acid. He'd wondered, for one insane moment, if there was any chance that they might recapture the magic they'd had together when she was eighteen.

But she'd quickly disabused him of any such fancies. Her attitude was cold and hard and uncaring. She seemed to have frozen over in the years she'd been away.

How could he blame her? All of Antonia's misfortunes could be laid at his door, because he was distrustful of people, because he'd jumped to conclusions, because he hadn't believed in Antonia's basic innocence and decency. One impulsive decision had cost him everything he held dear. He wondered sometimes how he could have been so stupid.

Like today when he'd let Maggie stampede him into attacking Antonia for something she hadn't done. It was just like old times. Sally's daughter was already a master manipulator, at age nine. And it seemed that he was just as impulsive and dim as he'd ever been. He hadn't really changed at all. He was just richer.

Meanwhile, there was Antonia's reappearance and her disturbing thinness and paleness. She looked unwell. He wondered absently if she'd had some bout with disease. Perhaps that was why she'd come home, and not because of her father at all. But, wouldn't a warm climate be the prescription for most illnesses that caused problems? Surely no doctor sent her into northern Wyoming in winter.

He had no answers for those questions, and it would do him well to stop asking them, he thought irritably. It was getting him nowhere. The past was dead. He had to let it go, before it destroyed his life all over again.

Chapter 5

Antonia didn't move for a long time after Powell left
the classroom. She stared blindly at her clasped hands.
Of course she knew that he didn't want her. Had she
been unconsciously hoping for something different?
And even if she had, she realized, there was no future
at all in that sort of thinking.

She got up, cleared her desk, picked up her things
and went home. She didn't have time to sit and groan,
even silently. She had to use her time wisely. She had
a decision to make.

While she cooked supper for her father and herself,
she thought about everything she'd wanted to do that
she'd never made time for. She hadn't traveled, which
had been a very early dream. She hadn't been involved
in church or community, she hadn't planned past the
next day except to make up lesson plans for her classes.

She'd more or less drifted along, assuming that she had forever. And now the line was drawn and she was close to walking across it.

Her deepest regret was losing Powell. Looking back, she wondered what might have happened if she'd challenged Sally, if she'd dared Powell to prove that she'd been two-timing him with her mother's old suitor. She'd only been eighteen, very much in love and trusting and full of dreams. It would have served her better to have been suspicious and hard-hearted, at least where Sally was concerned. She'd never believed that her best friend would stab her in the back. How silly of her not to realize that strongest friends make the best enemies; they always know where the weaknesses are hidden.

Antonia's weakness had been her own certainty that Powell loved her as much as she loved him, that nothing could separate them. She hadn't counted on Sally's ability as an actress.

Powell had never said that he loved Antonia. How strange, she thought, that she hadn't realized that until they'd gone their separate ways. Powell had been ardent, hungry for her, but never out of control. No wonder, she thought bitterly, since he'd obviously been sleeping with Sally the whole time. Why should he have been wild for any women when he was having one on the side?

He'd asked Antonia to marry him. Her parents had been respected in the community, something his own parents hadn't been. He'd enjoyed being connected to Antonia's parents and enjoyed the overflow of their acceptance by local people in the church and community. He'd spent as much time with them as he had with Antonia. And when he talked about building up his little cattle ranch that he'd inherited from his father, it had been her own father who'd advised him and opened doors for him so that he could get loans, financing. On the strength of his father's weakness for gambling, nobody would have loaned Powell the price of a theater ticket. But Antonia's father was a different proposition; he was an honest man with no visible vices.

Antonia had harbored no suspicions that an ambitious man might take advantage of an untried girl in his quest for wealth. Now, from her vantage point of many years, she could look back and see the calculation that had led to Powell's proposal of marriage. He hadn't wanted Antonia with any deathless passion. He'd wanted her father's influence. With it, he'd built a pitiful little fifty-acre ranch into a multimillion-dollar enterprise of purebred cattle and land. Perhaps breaking the engagement was all part of his master plan, too. Once he'd had what he wanted from the engagement, he could marry the woman he really loved—Sally.

It wouldn't have surprised Antonia to discover that Sally had worked hand in glove with Powell to help him achieve his goals. The only odd thing was that he hadn't been happy with Sally, from all accounts, nor she with him.

She wondered why she hadn't considered that angle all those years ago. Probably the heartbreak of her circumstances had blinded her to any deeper motives. Now it seemed futile and unreal. Powell was ancient history. She had to let go of the past. Somehow, she had to forgive and forget. It would be a pity to carry the hatred and resentment to her grave.

Grave. She stared into the pan that contained the stir-fry she was making for supper. She'd never thought about where she wanted to rest for eternity. She had insurance, still in effect, although it wasn't much. And she'd always thought that she'd rest beside her mother in the small Methodist church cemetery. Now she had to get those details finalized, just in case the treatment wasn't successful—if she decided to have it—and without her father knowing. He wasn't going to be told until the last possible minute.

She finished preparing supper and called her father to the table, careful to talk about mundane things and pretend to be happy at being home again.

But he wasn't fooled. His keen eyes probed her face. "Something's upset you. What is it?"

She grimaced. "Maggie Long," she said, sidestepping the real issue.

"I see. Just like her father when he was a kid, I hear," he added. "Little hellion, isn't she?"

"Only to me," Antonia mused. "She liked Mrs. Donalds."

"No wonder," he replied, finishing his coffee. "Mrs. Donalds was one of Sally's younger cousins. So Maggie was related to her. She petted the kid, gave her special favors, did everything but give her answers to tests. She was teacher's pet. First time any teacher treated her that way, so I guess it went to her head."

"How do you know?"

"It's a small town, girl," he reminded her with a chuckle. "I know everything." He stared at her levelly. "Even that Powell came to see you at school this afternoon. Gave you hell about the kid, didn't he?"

She shifted in her chair. "I won't give her special favors," she muttered. "I don't care if he does get me fired."

"He'll have a hard time doing that," her father said easily. "I have friends on the school board, too."

"Perhaps they could switch the girl to another class," she wondered aloud.

"It would cause gossip," Ben Hayes said. "There's been enough of that already. You just stick to your guns and don't give in. She'll come around eventually."

"I wouldn't bet on it," she said heavily. She ran a hand over her blond hair. "I'm tired," she added with a wan smile. "Do you mind if I go to bed early?"

"Of course not." He looked worried. "I thought you went to see the doctor. Didn't he give you something to perk you up?"

"He said I need vitamins," she lied glibly. "I bought some, but they haven't had time to take effect. I need to eat more, too, he said."

He was still scowling. "Well, if you don't start getting better soon, you'd better go back and let him do some tests. It isn't natural for a woman your age to be so tired all the time."

Her heart skipped. Of course it wasn't, but she didn't want him to suspect that she was so ill.

"I'll do that," she assured him. She got up and collected the plates. "I'll just do these few dishes and then I'll leave you to your television."

"Oh, I hate that stuff," he said. "I'd much rather read in the evenings. I only keep the thing on for the noise."

She laughed. "I do the same thing in Tucson," she confessed. "It's company, anyway."

"Yes, but I'd much rather have you here," he confessed. "I'm glad you came home, Antonia. It's not so lonely now."

She had a twinge of conscience at the pleasure he

betrayed. He'd lost her mother and now he was going to lose her. How would he cope, with no relatives left in the world? Her mother had been an only child, and her father's one sister had died of cancer years ago. Antonia bit her lip. He was in danger of losing his only child, and she was too cowardly to tell him.

He patted her on the shoulder. "Don't you do too much in here. Get an early night. Leave those if you want, and I'll wash them later."

"I don't mind," she protested, grinning. "I'll see you in the morning, then."

"Don't wake me up when you leave," he called over his shoulder. "I'm sleeping late."

"Lucky devil," she called back.

He only laughed, leaving her to the dishes.

She finished them and went to bed. But she didn't sleep. She lay awake, seeing Maggie Long's surly expression and hating eyes, and Powell's unwelcoming scrutiny. They'd both love to see her back in Arizona, and it looked as if they were going to do their combined best to make her life hell if she stayed here. She'd be walking on eggshells for the rest of the school year with Maggie, and if she failed the child for not doing her homework, Powell would be standing in her classroom every day to complain.

She rolled over with a sigh. Things had been so uncomplicated when she was eighteen, she thought wistfully. She'd been in love and looking forward to marriage and children. Her eyes closed on a wave of pain. Maggie would have been her child, her daughter. She'd have had blond hair and gray eyes, perhaps, like Antonia. And if she'd been Antonia's child, she'd have been loved and wanted and cared for. She wouldn't have a surly expression and eyes that hated.

Powell had said something about Maggie…what was it? That Maggie had paid a higher price than any of them. What had he meant? Surely he cared for the child. He certainly fought hard enough when he felt she was attacked.

Well, it wasn't her problem, she decided finally. And she wasn't going to let it turn into her problem. She still hadn't decided what to do about her other problem.

Julie was the brightest spot in Antonia's days. The little girl was always cheerful, helpful, doing whatever she could to smooth Antonia's path and make it easy for her to teach the class. She remembered where Mrs. Donalds had kept things, she knew what material had been covered and she always eager to do anything she was asked.

Maggie on the other hand was resentful and ice-cold. She did nothing voluntarily. She was still refusing to turn in her homework. Talking to her did no good. She just glared back.

"I'll give you one more chance to make up this work," Antonia told her at the end of her second week teaching the class. "If you don't turn it in Monday, you'll get another zero."

Maggie smiled haughtily. "And my daddy will cuss you out again. I'll tell him you slapped me, too."

Antonia's gray eyes glittered at the child. "You would, wouldn't you?" she asked coldly. "I don't doubt that you can lie, Maggie. Well, go ahead. See how much damage you can do."

Maggie's reaction was unexpected. Tears filled her blue eyes and she shivered.

She whirled and ran out of the classroom, leaving Antonia deflated and feeling badly for the child. She clenched her hands on the desk to keep them from shaking. How could she have been so hateful and cold?

She cleaned up the classroom, waiting for Powell to storm in and give her hell. But he didn't show up. She went home and spent a nerve-rackingly quiet weekend with her father, waiting for an explosion that didn't come.

The biggest surprise arrived Monday morning, when Maggie shoved a crumpled, stained piece of paper on the desk and walked back to her seat without looking at Antonia. It was messy, but it was the missing homework. Not only that, it was done correctly.

Antonia didn't say a word. It was a small victory, of sorts. She wouldn't admit to herself that she was pleased. But the paper got an A.

Julie began to sit with her at recess, and shared cupcakes and other tidbits that her mother had sent to school with her.

"Mom says you're doing a really nice job on me, Miss Hayes," Julie said. "Dad remembers you from school, did you know? He said you were a sweet girl, and that you were shy. Were you, really?"

Antonia laughed. "I'm afraid so. I remember your father, too. He was the class clown."

"Dad? Really?"

"Really. Don't tell him I told you, though, okay?" she teased, smiling at the child.

From a short distance away, Maggie glared toward

them. She was, as usual, alone. She didn't get along with the other children. The girls hated her, and the boys made fun of her skinny legs that were always bruised and cut from her tomboyish antics at the ranch. There was one special boy, Jake Weldon. Maggie pretended not to notice him. He was one of the boys who made fun of her, and it hurt really bad. She was alone most of the time these days, because Julie spent her time with the teacher instead of Maggie.

Miss Hayes liked Julie. Everyone knew it, too. Julie had been Maggie's best friend, but now she seemed to be Miss Hayes's. Maggie hated both of them. She hadn't told her father what Miss Hayes had said about her homework. She wanted her teacher to know that she wasn't bad like her mother. She knew what her mother had done, because she'd heard them talking about it once. She remembered her mother crying and accusing him of not loving her, and him saying that she'd ruined his life, she and her premature baby. There had been something else, something about him being drunk and out of his mind or Maggie wouldn't have been born at all.

It hadn't made sense then. But when she was older, she'd heard him say the same thing to the housekeeper, that Maggie had been born prematurely.

After that, she'd stopped listening. That was when she knew her father didn't love her. That was when she'd stopped trying to make him notice her by being good.

Her daddy knew Miss Hayes. She heard him tell the housekeeper that Antonia had come to Bighorn to make his life miserable and that he didn't want her here. If she'd been able to talk to Miss Hayes, she'd have told her that her father hated both of them, and that it made them sort of related.

She wondered if her dad hadn't wanted to marry her mother, and why he had. Maybe it had something to do with why her daddy hated her. People had said that Sally didn't love her little child, that Maggie was just the rope she'd used to tie up Powell Long with. Maybe they were right, because her mother never spent any time doing things with her. She never liked Maggie, either.

She slid down against the tree into the dirt, getting her jeans filthy. Mrs. Bates, the housekeeper, would rage and fuss about that, and she didn't care. Mrs. Bates had thrown away most of her clothes, complaining that they were too dirty to come clean. She hadn't told her dad. When she ran out of clothes, maybe somebody would notice.

She wished Mrs. Bates liked her. Julie did, when she wasn't fawning over teachers to make them give her special privileges. She liked Julie, she did, but Julie was a kiss-up. Sometimes she wondered why she let Julie be her friend at all. She didn't need any friends. She could make it all by herself. She'd show them all that she was somebody special. She'd make them love her one day. She sighed and closed her eyes. Oh, if only she knew Julie's secret; if only she knew how to make people like her.

"There's Maggie," Julie commented, grimacing as she glanced toward her friend. "Nobody likes her except me," she confided to Miss Hayes. "She beats up the boys and she can bat and catch better than any of them, so they don't like her. And the girls think she's too rough to play with. I sort of feel sorry for her. She says her daddy doesn't like her. He's always going away somewhere. She stays with us when he's gone, only she doesn't want to this week because—" She stopped, as if she was afraid she'd already said too much.

"Because?" Antonia prompted curiously.

"Oh, nothing," Julie said. She couldn't tell Miss Hayes that she'd fought with Maggie over their new teacher. "Anyway, Maggie mostly stays with us if her dad's away longer than overnight."

Involuntarily, Antonia glanced toward the child and found her watching them with those cold, sullen eyes. The memories came flooding back—Sally jealous of Antonia's pretty face, jealous of Antonia's grades, jealous of Antonia having any other girlfriends, jealous... of her with Powell.

She shivered faintly and looked away from the child. God forgive her, it was just too much. She wondered if she could possibly get Maggie transferred to another class. If she couldn't then there was no other option. The only teaching job available was the one she had. She couldn't wait for another opening. Her eyes closed. She was running out of time. Why, she asked herself, why was she wasting it like this? She'd told herself she was coming home to cope with her memories, but they were too much for her. She couldn't fight the past. She couldn't even manage to get through the present. She had to consider how she would face the future.

"Miss Hayes?"

Her eyes opened. Julie was looking worried. "Are you all right?" the little girl asked, concerned.

"I'm tired, that's all," Antonia said, smiling. "We'd better go in now."

She called the class and led them back into the building.

* * *

Maggie was worse than ever for the rest of the day. She talked back, refused to do a chore assigned to her, ignored Antonia when she was called on in class. And at the end of the day, she waited until everyone else left and came back into the room, to stand glaring at Antonia from the doorway.

"My dad says he wishes you'd go away and never come back," she said loudly. "He says you make his life miserable, and that he can't stand the sight of you! He says you make him sick!"

Antonia's face flushed and she looked stunned.

Maggie turned and ran out the door. Her father had said something like that, to himself, and it made her feel much better that she'd told Miss Hayes about it. That had made her look sick, all right! And it wasn't a lie. Well, not a real lie. It was just something to make her feel as bad as Maggie had felt when Miss Hayes looked at her on the playground and shuddered. She knew the teacher didn't like her. She didn't care. She didn't like Miss Hayes, either.

Maggie was smug the next day. She didn't have any more parting shots for Antonia, and she did her work in class. But she refused to do her homework, again, and dared Antonia to give her a zero. She even dared her to send a note home to her father.

Antonia wanted to call her bluff, but she was feeling sicker by the day and it was increasingly hard for her to get up in the mornings and go to work at all. The illness was progressing much more quickly than she'd foreseen. And Maggie was making her life hell.

For the rest of the week, Antonia thought about the

possibility of getting Maggie moved out of her class. Surely she could approach the principal in confidence.

And that was what she did, after school.

Mrs. Jameson smiled ruefully when Antonia sat down beside her desk and hesitated.

"You're here about Maggie Long again," she said at once.

Antonia's eyes widened. "Why...yes."

"I was expecting you," the older woman said with resignation. "Mrs. Donalds got along quite well with her, but she's the only teacher in the past few years who hasn't had trouble with Maggie. She's a rebel, you see. Her father travels a good deal. Maggie is left with Julie's family." She grimaced. "We heard that he was thinking of marrying again, but once that rumor started, Maggie ran away from home. She, uh, isn't keen on the widow Holton."

Antonia was wondering if anyone was keen about the widow Holton, from what she'd already heard from Barrie. It was a surprise to hear that Powell had considered marrying the woman—if it was true and not just gossip.

The principal sighed, her attention returning to the task at hand. "You want Maggie moved, I suppose. I wish I could oblige you, but we only have one fourth-grade class, because this is such a small school, and you're teaching it." She lifted her hands helplessly. "There it is. I'm really sorry. Perhaps if you spoke with her father?"

"I already have," Antonia replied calmly.

"And he said...?"

"That if I pushed him, he'd do his best to have me removed from my position here," she said bluntly.

The older woman pursed her lips. "Well, as we've

already discussed, he wouldn't have to work that hard to do it. It's a rather ticklish situation. I'm sorry I can't be more optimistic."

Antonia leaned back in her seat with a long sigh. "I shouldn't have come back to Bighorn," she said, almost to herself. "I don't know why I did."

"Perhaps you were looking for something."

"Something that no longer exists," Antonia replied absently. "A lost part of my life that I won't find here."

"You are going to stay, aren't you?" Mrs. Jameson asked. "After this school term, I mean. Your students say wonderful things about you. Especially Julie Ames," she added with a grin.

"I went to school with her father," Antonia confessed. "To this school, as a matter of fact. She's just like her dad."

"I've met him, and she is a lot like him. What a pity all our students can't be as energetic and enthusiastic as our Julie."

"Yes, indeed."

"Well, I'll give you all the moral support I can," Mrs. Jameson continued. "We do have a very good school counselor. We've sent Maggie to her several times, but she won't say a word. We've had the counselor talk to Mr. Long, but he won't say a word, either. It's a difficult situation."

"Perhaps it will work itself out," Antonia replied.

"Do think about staying on," the older woman said seriously.

Antonia couldn't promise that. She forced a smile. "I'll certainly think about it," she agreed.

But once out of the principal's office, she was more depressed than ever. Maggie hated her, and obviously would not cooperate. It was only a matter of time before she had to give Maggie a failing grade for her non-effort, and Powell would either come back for some more heated words or get her fired. She didn't know if she could bear another verbal tug-of-war with him, especially after the last one. And as for getting fired, she wondered if that really mattered anymore. At the rate her health was failing, it wasn't going to matter for much longer, anyway.

She wandered back to her schoolroom and found Powell sitting on the edge of her desk, looking prosperous in a dark gray suit and a red tie, with a gray Stetson and hand-tooled leather boots that complemented his suit. He was wearing the same signet ring on his little finger that he'd worn when they were engaged, a script letter L. The ring was very simple, 10K gold and not very expensive. His mother had given it to him when he graduated from high school, and Antonia knew how hard the woman had had to work to pay for it. The Rolex watch on his left wrist was something he'd earned for himself. The Longs had never had enough money at any time in their lives to pay for a watch like that. She wondered if Powell ever thought back to those hard days of his youth.

He heard her step and turned his head to watch her enter the classroom. In her tailored beige dress, with her blond hair in a bun, she looked thinner than ever and very dignified.

"How you've changed," he remarked involuntarily.

"I was thinking the same thing about you," she said wearily. She sat down behind the desk, because just the walk to the office had made her tired. She looked up at him with the fatigue in her face. "I really need to go home. I know why you're here. She can't be moved to another class, because there isn't one. The only alternative is for me to leave...."

"That isn't why I came," he said, surprised.

"No?"

He picked up a paper clip from the desk and looked at it intently. "I thought you might have something to eat with me," he said. "We could talk about Maggie."

She was nauseated and trying not to let it overwhelm her. She barely heard him. "What?"

"I said, let's get together tonight," he repeated, frowning. "You look green. Put your head down."

She turned sideways and lowered her head to the hands resting on her knees, sucking in air. She felt nauseous more and more these days, and faint. She didn't know how much longer she was going to be mobile. The thought frightened her. She would have to make arrangements to get on with the therapy, while there was still time. It was one thing to say that dying didn't matter, but it was quite another when the prospect of it was staring her in the face.

"You're damn thin." He bit off the words. "Have you seen a doctor?"

"If one more person asks me that...!" She erupted. She took another breath and lifted her head, fighting the dizziness as she pushed back a wisp of hair from her eyes. "Yes, I've seen a doctor. I'm just run-down. It's been a hard year."

"Yes, I know," he said absently, watching her.

She met his concerned eyes. If she'd been less feeble, she might have wondered at the expression in them. As it was, she was too tired to care.

"Maggie's been giving everyone fits," he said unexpectedly. "I know you're having trouble with her. I thought if we put our heads together, we might come up with some answers."

"I thought my opinion didn't matter," she replied dully.

He averted his gaze. "I've had a lot on my mind," he said noncommittally. "Of course your opinion matters. We need to talk."

She wanted to ask what good he thought it would do to talk, when he'd told his daughter that he was sick of Miss Hayes and wanted her out of town because she was making his life miserable. She wasn't going to mention that. It would be like tattling. But it hurt more than anything else had in recent days.

"Well?" he persisted impatiently.

"Very well. What time shall I meet you, and where?"

The question seemed to surprise him. "I'll pick you up at your home, of course," he said. "About six."

She really should refuse. She looked into his dark eyes and knew that she couldn't. One last date, she was thinking sadly. She could have one last date with him before the ordeal began....

She managed a smile. "All right."

He watched her sort out the papers on her desk and put them away methodically. His eyes were on her hands, on the unusual thinness of them. She looked unwell. Her mother's death surely had affected her, but this seemed much more than worry. She was all but skeletal.

"I'll see you at six," she said when she'd put up the classroom and walked out into the hall with him.

He looked down at her, noting her frailty, her slenderness. He still towered over her, as he had years before. She was twenty-seven, but his eyes saw a vivacious, loving girl of eighteen. What had happened to change her whole personality so drastically? She was an old soul in a young body. Had he caused all that?

She glanced up at him curiously. "Was there something else?"

He shrugged. "Maggie showed me an A on her homework paper."

"I didn't give her the grade," she replied. "She earned it. It was good work."

He stuck his hands into his pockets. "She has a bright mind, when she wants to use it." His eyes narrowed. "I said some harsh things the last time I was here. Now's as good a time as any to apologize. I was out of line." He couldn't go further and admit that Maggie had lied to him. He was still raw, as Antonia surely was, about Sally's lies. It was too much to admit that his daughter was a liar as well.

"Most parents who care about their children would have challenged a zero," she said noncommittally.

"I haven't been much of a parent," he said abruptly. "I'll see you at six."

She watched him with sad eyes as he walked away, the sight of his long back reminding her poignantly of the day he'd ended their engagement.

He paused at the door, sensing her eyes, and he turned unexpectedly to stare at her. It was so quick that she didn't have time to disguise her grief. He actually winced, because he knew that she'd looked like that nine years ago. He hadn't looked back, so he hadn't known.

She drew in a steadying breath and composed her features. She didn't say anything. There was nothing to say that he hadn't already read in her face.

He started to speak, but apparently he couldn't find the words, either.

"At six," she repeated.

He nodded, and this time he went through the doorway.

Chapter 6

Antonia went through every dress she had in her closet before she settled on a nice but simple black crepe dress with short sleeves and a modest neckline. It reached just below her knees and although it had once fit her very nicely, it now hung on her. She had nothing that looked the right size. But it was cold and she could wear a coat over it, the one good leather one she'd bought last season on sale. It would cover the dress and perhaps when she was seated, it wouldn't look so big on her. She paired the dress with a thin black leather belt, gold stud earrings and a small gold cross that her mother had given her when she graduated from high school. She wore no other jewelry, except for the serviceable watch on her wrist. She saw the engagement ring that Powell had bought for her, a very modest little diamond in a thin gold setting. She'd sent it back to him, but he'd refused to accept it from her father. It had found its way back to her, and she kept it here in her jewelry box, the only keepsake she had except for the small cross she always wore.

She picked the ring up and looked at it with sad gray eyes. How different her life, and Powell's, might have been if he hadn't jumped to conclusions and she hadn't run away.

She put the ring back into the box, into the past, where it belonged, and closed it up. This would be the last time she'd go out with Powell. He only wanted to talk about Maggie. If he was serious about the widow Holton, of whom she'd heard so much, then this would certainly not be an occasion he'd want to repeat. And even if he asked, Antonia knew that she would have to refuse a second evening out with him. Her heart was still all too vulnerable. But for tonight, she took special care with her makeup and left her blond hair long around her shoulders. Even thin, she looked good. She hoped Powell would think so.

She sat in the living room with her curious but silent father, waiting for the clock to chime six. He had ten minutes left to make it on time. Powell had been very punctual in the old days. She wondered if he still was.

"Nervous?" her father asked gently.

She smiled and nodded. "I don't know why he wanted to take me out to talk about Maggie. We could have talked here, or at school."

He smoothed a hand over his boot, crossed over his other leg. "Maybe he's trying to make things up with you."

"I doubt that," she replied. "I hear he's been spending time with the widow Holton...."

"So has Dawson. But love isn't the reason. They both want her south pasture. It borders on both of theirs."

"Oh. Everybody says she's very pretty."

"So she is. But Dawson won't have anything to do with women in a romantic way, and Powell is playing her along."

"I heard that he was talking marriage."

"Did you?" He frowned. "Well…that's surprising."

"Mrs. Jameson said his daughter ran away when she thought he was going to marry Mrs. Holton."

Her father shook his head. "I'm not surprised. That child doesn't get along with anyone. She'll end up in jail one day if he doesn't keep a better eye on her."

She traced a pattern in the black crepe purse that matched her dress. "I haven't been quite fair to her," she confessed. "She's so much like Sally." She grimaced. "She must miss her."

"I doubt it. Her mother left her with any available babysitter and stayed on the road until the drinking started taking its toll on her. She never was much of a driver. That's probably why she went into the river."

Into the river. Antonia remembered hearing about the accident on the news. Powell had been rich enough that Sally's tragic death made headlines. She'd felt sorry for him, but she hadn't gone to the funeral. There was no point. She and Sally had been enemies for so long. For so long.

The sound of a car in the driveway interrupted her musings. She got up and reached the door just as Powell knocked.

She felt embarrassed when she saw how he was dressed. He was wearing jeans and a flannel shirt with a heavy denim jacket and old boots. If she was surprised, so was he. She looked very elegant in that black dress and the dark leather coat she wore with it.

His face drew in sharply at the sight of her, because even in her depleted condition, she took his breath away.

"I'm running late." She improvised to explain the way she was dressed. "I've just now come back from town," she lied, redfaced. "I'll hurry and change and be ready in a jiffy. Dad can talk to you while I get ready. I'm sorry…!"

She dashed back into the bedroom and closed the door. She could have died of shame. So much for her dreams of the sort of date they'd once shared. He was dressed for a cup of coffee and a sandwich at a fast-food joint, and here she was rigged out for a restaurant. She should have asked him where they were going in the first place, and not tried to second-guess him!

She quickly changed into jeans and a sweatshirt and put her hair up in its usual bun. At least the jeans fit her better than the dress, she thought dryly.

Powell stared after her and grimaced. "I had an emergency on the ranch with a calving heifer," he murmured. "I didn't realize she'd be dressed up, so I didn't think about changing…."

"Don't make it worse," her father said curtly. "Spare her pride and go along with what she said."

He sighed heavily. "I never do the right thing, say the right thing." His dark eyes were narrow and sad. "She's the one who was hurt the most, and I just keep right on adding to the pain."

Ben Hayes was surprised at the remark, but he had no love for Powell Long. He couldn't forget the torment the man had caused his daughter, nor what Antonia had said about Powell using his influence to open financial doors for him. All Powell's pretended concern for his health hadn't changed what he thought of the man. And tonight his contempt knew no bounds. He hated seeing Antonia embarrassed like that.

"Don't keep her out long," Ben said coldly. "She isn't well."

Powell's eyes cut around to meet the older man's. "What's wrong with her?" he asked.

"Her mother's barely been dead a year," he reminded him. "Antonia misses her a lot."

"She's lost weight, hasn't she?" he asked Ben.

Ben shifted in the chair. "She'll pick back up, now that she's home." He glared at Powell. "Don't hurt her again, boy," he said evenly. "If you want to talk to her about your daughter, fine. But don't expect anything. She's still raw about the past, and I don't blame her. You were wrong and you wouldn't listen. But she's the one who had to leave town."

Powell's jaw went taut. He stared at the older man with eyes that glittered, and he didn't reply.

It was a tense silence that Antonia walked back into. Her father looked angry, and Powell looked...odd.

"I'm ready," she said, sliding into her leather coat.

Powell nodded. "We'll go to Ted's Truck Stop. It's open all night and he serves good coffee, if that suits you."

She read an insult into the remark, and flushed. "I told you I was dressed up because I'd just come back from town," she began. "Ted's suits me fine."

He was stunned by the way she emphasized that, until he realized what he'd said. He turned on his heel and opened the front door for her. "Let's go," he said.

She told her father goodbye and went through the door. Powell closed it behind them, shutting them in the cold, snowy night. A metallic gold Mercedes-Benz was sitting in the driveway, not the four-wheel-drive vehicle he usually drove. Although it had chains to get through snow and ice, it was a luxury car and a far cry from the battered old pickup truck Powell had driven when they'd been engaged.

Flakes of snow fell heavily on the windshield as he drove the mile down the highway to Ted's, which was a bar and grill, just outside the Bighorn city limits. Ted's sold beer and wine and good food, but Antonia had never been inside the place before. It wasn't considered a socially respectable place, and she wondered if Powell had a reason for taking her there. Perhaps he was trying to emphasize the fact that this wasn't a routine date. It was to be a business discussion, but he didn't want to take her anyplace where they might be recognized. So if that was the case, maybe he really was serious about the widow Holton after all. It made her sad, even though she knew she had no future with him, or with anyone.

"You're quiet," he remarked as he pulled up in the almost deserted parking lot. It was early for Ted's sort of trade, although a couple of tractor trailers were sitting apart in the lot.

"I suppose so," she replied.

He felt the unease about her, the muted sadness. He felt guilty about bringing her here. She'd dressed up for him, and he'd slapped her down unintentionally. He hadn't even considered that she might think of this as a date. She was as sensitive now as she had been at eighteen.

He went around the car to open her door, but she was

already out of it and standing in the snow when he got there. She joined him at the fender and walked toward the bar. Her sneakers were getting wet and the snow was deep enough that it leaked in past her socks, but it didn't matter. She was so miserable already that cold feet just seemed to go with her general mood.

Powell noticed, though, and his lips compressed. It was already a bust of an evening, and it was his own damn fault.

They sat down in a booth and the waitress, a big brunette named Darla, smiled and handed them a menu.

"Just coffee for me," Antonia said with a quiet smile.

Powell's eyes flashed. "I brought you here for a meal," he reminded her firmly.

She evaded his angry eyes. "I'll have a bowl of chili, then. And coffee."

He ordered steak and salad and coffee and handed the menu back to the waitress. He couldn't remember a time when he'd felt as helpless, or as ashamed.

"You need more than that," he said softly.

The tone of his voice brought back too many memories. They'd gone out to eat very rarely in the old days, in his old Ford pickup truck with the torn seat and broken dash. A hamburger had been a treat, but it was being together that had made their dates perfect. They'd wolf down their food and then drive out to the pasture near Powell's house. He'd shut off the engine and turn to her, and she'd go into his arms like a homing pigeon.

She could still taste those hot, deep, passionate kisses they'd shared so hungrily. It was amazing that he'd had the restraint to keep their dates innocent. She'd rushed headlong into desire with no self-preservation at all, wanting him so much that nothing else had mattered.

But he'd put on the brakes, every time. That hadn't bothered her at the time. She'd thought it meant that he respected her enough to wait for the wedding ceremony. But after he'd called off the wedding and married Sally, and Maggie was born seven months later, his restraint had made a terrible sort of sense. He hadn't really wanted Antonia. He'd wanted her father's influence. She'd been too much in love to realize it.

"I said, you need to eat more than that," he repeated.

She looked up into his dark eyes with the memories slicing through her. She swallowed. "I haven't felt too good today," she said evasively. "I'm not really hungry."

He saw the shadows under her eyes and knew that lack of sleep had certainly added to her depleted health.

"I wanted to talk to you about Maggie," he said suddenly, because it bothered him to be with Antonia and remember their old relationship. "I know she's given you problems. I hope we can work out something."

"There's nothing to work out," Antonia said. "She's done her homework. I think she'll adjust to me eventually."

"She had a lot to say about you last night," he continued, as if she hadn't spoken. "She said that you threatened to hit her."

She looked him right in the eye. "Did she?"

He waited, but she didn't offer any defense. "And she said that you told her that you hated her and that you didn't want her in your class, because she reminded you too much of her mother."

Her eyes didn't fall. It wasn't the truth, but there was enough truth in it to twist. Maggie certainly was perceptive, she thought ruefully. And Powell sat there with his convictions so plain on his lean face that he might as well have shouted them.

She knew then why he'd invited her here, to this bar. He was showing her that he thought too little of her to take her to a decent place. He was putting her down in a cold, subtle way, while he raked her over the coals of his anger for upsetting his little girl.

She managed a smile. "Does the city cab run out this far?" she asked in a tone that was tight enough to sound choked. "Then I won't even have to ask you to take me home." She started to get up, but he rose, too, and blocked her way out of the booth.

"Here it is." The waitress interrupted them, bringing steaming black coffee in two mugs. "Sorry I took so long. Is anything wrong?" she added when Powell didn't move.

"No," he said after a minute, his eyes daring Antonia to move as he sat back down. "Nothing at all. But we'll just have the coffee, if it isn't too late to change the order."

"It's all right, I'll take care of it," the waitress said quickly. She'd seen the glint of tears in Antonia's eyes, and she recognized a kindling argument when she saw one starting. She put down the cream pitcher and wrote out the check. If she was any judge of angry women, there would barely be time for them to drink their one cup each before the explosion.

She thanked them, put down the check and got out of the line of fire.

"Don't cry," Powell said through his teeth as he stared at Antonia's white face. "Don't!"

She took a steadying breath and put both hands

around the coffee cup. She stared at it instead of him, but her hands trembled.

He closed his eyes, fighting memories and prejudices and gossip and pain. He'd forgotten nothing. Forgiven nothing. Seeing her alone like this brought it all back.

She was fighting memories of her own. She lifted the coffee to her lips and burned them trying to drink it.

"Go ahead," he invited coldly. "Tell me she's lying."

"I wouldn't tell you the time of day," she said in a voice like warmed-over death. "I never learn. You said we'd discuss the problem, but this isn't a discussion, it's an inquisition. I'll tell you flat-out—I've already asked Mrs. Jameson to move Maggie out of my class. She can't do that, and the only option I have left is to quit my job and go back to Arizona."

He stared at her without speaking. He hadn't expected that.

She met his startled eyes. "Do you think she's a little angel?" she asked. "She's rebellious, haughty and she lies better than her mother ever did."

"Damn you!"

The whip of his voice made her sick inside. She reached for her purse and this time she got up. She pushed past him, and ran out into the snow with tears streaming down her face. She'd walk back to town, she would...!

Her foot slipped on a patch of ice, and she went down hard. She felt the snow on her hot face and lifted it, to the cooling moisture of fresh snowflakes, just as a pair of steely hands jerked her back to her feet and propelled her toward the car.

She didn't react as he unlocked the door and put her inside. She didn't look at him or say a word, even when he fastened her shoulder harness and sat glaring at her before he finally started the car and headed it back toward town.

When they arrived at her father's house, she reached for the catch that would unfasten the harness, but his hand was there, waiting.

"Why can't you admit the truth?" he demanded. "Why do you keep lying about your relationship with George Rutherford? He bought your wedding dress, he paid your college tuition. The whole damn town knew you were sleeping with him, but you've convinced everyone from your father to George's own son that it was perfectly innocent! Well, you never convinced me and you never will!"

"I know that," she said without looking at him. "Let me go, Powell."

His hand only tightened. "You slept with him!" he accused through his teeth. "I would have died for you…!"

"You were sleeping with my best friend!" she accused hotly. "You got her pregnant while you were engaged to me! Do you think I give a damn about your opinion or your feelings? You weren't jealous of George! You never even loved me! You got engaged to me so that my father's influence could get you a loan that you needed to save your family ranch!"

The accusation startled him so much that he didn't have the presence of mind to retaliate. He stared at her in the dim light from the front porch as if she'd gone mad.

"Sally's people didn't have that kind of clout," she continued, tears of anger and pain running down her cheeks like tiny silver rivers. "But mine did. You used me! The only decent thing you did was to keep from seducing me totally, but then, you didn't need to go that far, because you were already sleeping with Sally!"

He couldn't believe what he was hearing. It was the first time in his life that he'd been at a loss for words, but he was literally speechless.

"And you can accuse me of lying?" she demanded in a choked tone. "Sally lied. But you wanted to believe her because it got you out of our engagement the day before the wedding. And you still believe her, because you can't admit that I was only a means to an end for your ambition. It isn't a broken heart you're nursing, it's broken pride because you couldn't get anywhere without a woman's family name to get you a loan!"

He took a short breath. "I got that loan on my own collateral," he said angrily.

"You got it on my father's name," she countered. "Mr. Sims, the bank president, said so. He even laughed about it, about how you were already making use of your future father-in-law to help you mend your family fortunes!"

He hadn't known that. He'd put the land up for security and he'd always assumed that it had been enough. He should have realized that his father's reputation as a gambler would have made him a dangerous risk as a borrower.

"Antonia," he began hesitantly, reaching out a hand.

She slapped it away immediately. "Don't you touch me," she said hotly. "I've had the Longs to hell and back! You can take this for gospel—if your daughter doesn't study, she won't pass. And if that costs me my job, I don't care!"

She jerked open the door and got out, only to find Powell there waiting for her, dark-eyed and glowering.

"I'm not going to let you take out any sort of vengeance on Maggie," he said shortly. "And if you don't stop giving her hell because of grudges against her mother, you'll be out of a job, I promise you."

"Do your worst," she invited with soft venom, her gray eyes flashing at him. "You can't hurt me more than you already have. Very soon now, I'll be beyond the reach of any vengeance you like to pursue!"

"Think so?" With a lightning-quick movement, he jerked her against his lean, hard body and bent to her mouth.

The kiss was painful, and not just physically. He kissed her without tenderness, with nothing more than a need to punish. His tongue insinuated itself past her lips in a cold, calculating parody of sex, while his hands twisted her body against his lean hips.

She stiffened, trying to fight, but she was too weak to force him to let go. She opened her eyes and looked at him, stared at him, until he thought she'd had enough. Just at the last, he relented. His mouth became soft and slow and sensuous, teasing, testing. His hands slid up to her waist and he nibbled at her lower lip with something like tenderness. But she refused him even the semblance of response. She stood like a statue in his grasp, her eyes open, wet with tears, her mouth rigid.

When his eyes opened again, he looked oddly guilty. Her mouth was swollen and her face was very pale.

He winced. "I shouldn't have done that," he said curtly.

She laughed coldly. "No, it wasn't necessary," she agreed. "I'd already gotten the message. You held me in such contempt that you didn't even change out of your working clothes. You took me to a bar...." She pulled away from him, a little shakily. "You couldn't have made your opinion of me any plainer."

He pushed his hat back on his head. "I didn't mean it to turn out like this," he said angrily.

"Didn't you?" She stared up at him with eyes that hated him and loved him, with eyes that would soon lose the ability to see him at all. She took a breath and it ended on a sob.

"Oh, God, don't," he groaned. He pulled her into his arms, but this time without passion, without anger. He held her against his heart with hands that protected, cherished, and she felt his lips in her hair, at her temple. "I'm sorry. I'm sorry, Annie." He bit off the words.

It was the first time he'd used the nickname he'd called her when she was eighteen. The sound of his deep voice calmed her. She let him hold her. It would be the last time. She closed her eyes and it was as if it was yesterday—she was a girl in love, and he was the beginning of her world.

"It was...so long ago," she whispered brokenly.

"A lifetime," he replied in a hushed tone. His arms cradled her and she felt his cheek move tenderly against her blond hair. "Why didn't I wait?" he whispered almost to himself, and his eyes closed. "Another day, just one more day..."

"We can't have the past back," she said. His arms were warm against the cold, and strong, comforting. She savored the glory of them around her for one last time. No matter how he felt about her, she would have this memory to take down into the dark with her.

She fought tears. Once, he would have done anything

for her. Or she'd thought that he would. It was cruel to think that he had only used her as a means to an end.

"You're skin and bones," he said after a minute.

"I've had a hard year."

He nuzzled his cheek against her temple. "They've all been hard years, one way or another." He sighed heavily. "I'm sorry about tonight. God, I'm sorry!"

"It doesn't matter. Maybe we needed to clear the air."

"I'm not sure we cleared anything." He drew back and looked down at her sad face. He touched her swollen mouth tenderly, and he looked repentant. "In the old days, I never hurt you deliberately," he said quietly. "I've changed, haven't I, Annie?"

"We've both changed. We've grown older."

"But not wiser, in my case. I'm still leading with my chin." He pushed a few wisps of blond hair away from her mouth. "Why did you come home? Was it because of me?"

She couldn't tell him that. "My father hasn't been well," she said, evading a direct answer. "He needs me. I never realized how much until Christmas."

"I see."

She looked up into his black eyes with grief already building in her face.

"What's wrong?" he asked gently. "Can't you tell me?"

She forced a smile. "I'm tired. That's all, I'm just tired." She reached up and smoothed her hand slowly over his lean cheek. "I have to go inside." On an impulse, she stood on tiptoe. "Powell...would you kiss me, just once...the way you used to?" she asked huskily, her gray eyes pleading with him.

It was an odd request, but the stormy evening had

robbed him of the ability to reason properly. He didn't answer. He bent, nuzzling her face, searching for her lips, and he kissed her as he had on their very first date, so long ago. His mouth was warm and searching and cautious, as if he didn't want to frighten her. She reached up to him and held him close. For a few precious seconds, there was no dreaded future, no painful past. She melted into the length of him, moaning softly when she felt the immediate response of his body to hers. He half lifted her against him, and his mouth became demanding, insistent, intimate. She gave what he asked, holding him close. For this moment, he belonged to her and she loved him so…!

An eternity later, she drew gently away without looking at him, pulling her arms from around his neck. The scent of his cologne was in her nostrils, the taste of him was in her mouth. She hoped that she could remember this moment, at the end.

She managed a smile as she stood on shaky legs. "Thanks," she said huskily. She stared up at him as if she wanted to memorize his face. In fact, she did.

He scowled. "I took you out because I wanted to talk to you," he said heavily.

"We talked," she replied, moving back. "Even if nothing got settled. There are too many scars, Powell. We can't go back. But I won't hurt Maggie, even if it means leaving the job, okay?"

"You don't have to go that far," he snapped.

She just smiled. "It will come to that," she replied. "She's got the upper hand, you see, and she knows it. It doesn't matter," she added absently as she stared at him. "In the long run, it doesn't matter at all. Maybe it's even for the best." She took a long, slow breath, drinking in the sight of him. "Goodbye, Powell. I'm glad you've been so successful. You've got everything you ever wanted. Be happy."

She turned and went into the house. She hadn't thanked him for the coffee. But, then, he probably didn't expect it. She was glad that her father was watching a television program intently, because when she called good-night, he didn't ask how it had gone. It saved her the pain of telling him. It spared her his pity when he saw the tears she couldn't stem.

Powell's step was slow and leaden as he went into his house. He was drained of emotion, tired and disheartened. Always he'd hoped that one day he and Antonia would find their way back together again, but he couldn't seem to get past the bitterness, and she'd closed doors tonight. She'd kissed him as if she were saying goodbye. Probably she had been. She didn't like Maggie, and that wouldn't change. Maggie didn't like her, either. Sally was gone, but she'd left a barrier between them in the person of one small belligerent girl. He couldn't get to Antonia because Maggie stood in the way. It was a sad thought, when he'd realized tonight how much Antonia still meant to him.

Surprisingly he found his daughter sitting on the bottom step of the staircase in her school clothes, waiting for him when he walked into his house.

"What are you doing up? Where's Mrs. Bates?" he asked.

She shrugged. "She had to go home. She said I'd be okay since you weren't supposed to be gone long." She studied his face with narrowed, resentful eyes. "Did you tell Miss Hayes that she'd better be nice to me from now on?"

He frowned. "How did you know I took Miss Hayes out?"

"Mrs. Bates said you did." She glared harder. "She said Miss Hayes was sweet, but she's not. She's mean to me. I told her that you hated her. I told her that you wanted her to go away and never come back. You did say that, Daddy, you know you did."

He felt frozen inside. No wonder Antonia had been so hostile, so suspicious! "When did you tell Miss Hayes that?" he demanded.

"Last week." Her lower lip protruded. "I want her to go away, too. I hate her!"

"Why?" he asked.

"She's so stupid," she muttered. "She goes all gooey when Julie brings her flowers and plays up to her. She doesn't even know that Julie's just doing it so she can be teacher's pet. Julie doesn't even come over to play with me anymore, she's too busy drawing pictures for Miss Hayes!"

The resentment in his daughter's face was a revelation. He remembered Sally being that way about Antonia. When they'd first been married, she'd been scathing about Antonia going to college and getting a job as a teacher. Sally hadn't wanted to go away to school. She'd wanted to marry Powell. She'd said that Antonia had laughed about his calling off the wedding and saying that she'd marry George who was richer anyway…lies, all lies!

"I want you to do your homework from now on," Powell told the child. "And stop behaving badly in class."

"I do not behave badly! And I did my homework! I did!"

He wiped a hand over his brow. Maggie was a disagreeable child. He bought her things, but he couldn't bear to spend any time around her. She always made him feel guilty.

"Did she tell you I wasn't behaving?" she demanded.

"Oh, what does it matter what she said?" He glared at her angrily, watching the way she backed up when he looked at her. "You'll toe the line or else."

He stormed off, thoroughly disgusted. He didn't think how the impulsive outburst might hurt a sensitive child who carefully hid her sensitivity from the cold adults around her. All her belligerence was nothing more than a mask she wore to keep people from seeing how much they could hurt her. But now, the mask was down. She stared up after her father with blue eyes brimming with tears, her small fists clenched at her sides.

"Daddy," she whispered to herself, "why don't you love me? Why can't you love me? I'm not bad. I'm not bad, Daddy!"

But he didn't hear her. And when she went to bed, her head was full of wicked Miss Hayes and ways to make her sorry for the way her daddy had just treated her.

Chapter 7

The class had a test the following Monday. Maggie didn't answer a single question on it. As usual, she sat with her arms folded and smiled haughtily at Antonia. When Antonia stopped beside her desk and asked if she wasn't going to try to answer any of the questions, things came to a head.

"I don't have to," she told Antonia. "You can't make me, either."

Antonia promptly took Maggie to the principal's office and decided to let Powell carry through with his threat to get her fired. It no longer mattered very much. She was tired of the memories and the future, and she was no closer to an answer about her own dilemma. Part of her wanted to take the chance that drastic therapy might save her. Another part was scared to death of it.

"I'm sorry," she said when Mrs. Jameson came out

into the waiting room, "but Maggie refuses to do the test I'm giving the class. I thought perhaps if you explained the seriousness of the situation to her…"

This was Maggie's best chance, and she took it at once. "She hates me!" Maggie cried piteously, pointing at Antonia. "She said I was just like my mommy and that she hated me!" She actually sobbed. Real tears welled in her blue eyes.

Antonia's face went red. "I said no such thing, and you know it!" she said huskily.

"Yes, you did," Maggie lied. "Mrs. Jameson, she said that she was going to fail me and there was nothing I could do about it. She hates me 'cause my daddy married my mommy instead of her!"

Antonia leaned against the door facing for support, staring at the child with eyes that were full of disbelief. The attack was so unexpected that she had no defense for it. Had Powell been merciless enough to tell the child that? Had he been that angry?

"Antonia, surely this isn't true," Mrs. Jameson began hesitantly.

"No, it's not true," Antonia said in a stilted tone. "I don't know who's been saying such things to her, but it wasn't me."

"My daddy told me," Maggie lied. Actually she'd overheard Mrs. Bates telling that to one of her friends last night on the telephone. It had given Maggie a trump card that she was playing for all it was worth.

Antonia felt the blow all the way to her heart. She'd known that Powell was angry, but she hadn't realized that he was heartless enough to tell Maggie such a painful truth, knowing that she'd use it as a weapon against her despised teacher. And it was a devastating remark to make in the school office. One of the mothers was in there to pick up a sick child, and the two secretaries were watching with wide, eager eyes. What Maggie had just said would be all over town by nightfall. Another scandal. Another humiliation.

"She's awful to me," Maggie continued, letting tears fall from her eyes. It wasn't hard to cry; all she had to do was think about how her father hated her. Choking, she pointed at Antonia. "She says she can be as mean to me as she wants to, because nobody will believe me when I tell on her! I'm scared of her! You won't let her hit me, will you, Mrs. Jameson?" she added, going close to the older woman to look up at her helplessly. "She said she was going to hit me!" she wailed.

Mrs. Jameson had been wavering. But Maggie's eyes were overflowing with tears and she wasn't a hard enough woman to ignore them. She opened her office door. "Go inside and sit down, please, dear," she said. "Don't cry, now, it will be all right. No one will hurt you."

The little girl sniffed back more tears and wiped her eyes on the back of her hand. "Yes, ma'am," she said, keeping her eyes down so that Antonia wouldn't see the triumph in them. *Now you'll have to go away,* she thought gleefully, *and Mrs. Donalds will come back.*

She closed the door behind her. Antonia just stared at Mrs. Jameson.

"Antonia, she's never been that upset," Mrs. Jameson said reluctantly. "I've never seen her cry. I think she's really afraid of you."

Hearing the indecision in the other woman's voice, Antonia knew what she was thinking. She'd heard all the old gossip, and she didn't know Antonia well. She was afraid of Powell's influence. And Maggie had cried. It didn't take a mind reader to figure the outcome. Antonia knew she was beaten. It was as if fate had taken a hand here, forcing her to go back to Arizona. Perhaps it was for the best, anyway. She couldn't have told her father the truth. It would have been too cruel, and very soon now her health was going to break. She couldn't be a burden on the man she loved most.

She met the older woman's eyes tiredly. "It's just as well," she said gently. "I wouldn't have been able to work much longer, anyway."

"I don't understand," Mrs. Jameson said, frowning.

She only smiled. She would understand one day. "I'll save you the trouble of firing me. I quit. I hope you'll release me without proper notice, and I'll forfeit my pay in lieu of it," she said. "Maybe she was right," she said, nodding toward the office. "Maybe I could have been kinder to her. I'll clear out my desk and leave at once, if you can have someone take over my class."

She turned and walked out of the office, leaving a sad principal staring after her.

When Maggie came back to the classroom, after a long talk with Mrs. Jameson and then lunch, Miss Hayes was no longer there. Julie was crying quietly while the assistant principal put the homework assignment on the board.

Julie glared at Maggie for the rest of the day, and she even refused to speak to her until they left the building to catch the bus home.

"Miss Hayes left," Julie accused. "It was because of you, wasn't it? I heard Mr. Tarleton say they fired her!"

Maggie's face flushed. "Well, of course you liked

her, teacher's pet! But she was mean to me!" Maggie snapped. "I hated her. I'm glad she's gone!"

"She was so kind," Julie sobbed. "You lied!"

Maggie went even redder. "She deserved it! She would have failed me!"

"She should have!" Julie said angrily. "You lazy, hateful girl!"

"Well, I don't like you, either," Maggie yelled at her. "You're a kiss-up, that's all you are! Mrs. Donalds doesn't like you, she likes me, and she's coming back!"

"She's having a baby, and she isn't coming back!" Julie raged at her.

"Why did Miss Hayes have to leave?" one of the boys muttered as he and his two friends joined them at the bus queue.

"Because Maggie told lies about her and she got fired!" Julie said.

"Miss Hayes got fired? You little brat!" the boy, Jake, said to Maggie, and pushed her roughly when the bus started loading. "She was the best teacher we ever had!"

"She wasn't, either!" Maggie said defensively. She hadn't realized that people were going to know that she got Miss Hayes fired, or that the teacher had been so well liked by her class.

"You got her fired because she didn't like you," Jake persisted, holding up the line. "Well, they ought to fire the whole school, then, because nobody likes you! You're ugly and stupid and you look like a boy!"

Maggie didn't say a word. She ignored him and the others and got on the bus, but she sat alone. Nobody spoke to her. Everybody glared and whispered. She huddled in her seat, trying not to look at Jake. She was crazy about him, and he hated her, too. It was a good thing that nobody knew how she felt.

At least, Miss Hayes was gone, she thought victoriously. That was one good thing that had come out of the horrible day.

Antonia had to tell her father that she'd lost her job and she was leaving town again. It was the hardest thing she'd ever had to do.

"That brat!" he raged. He went to the telephone. "Well, she's not getting away with those lies. I'll call Powell and we'll make her tell the truth!"

Antonia put her hand over his on the receiver and held it in place. She coaxed him back into his easy chair and she sat on the very edge of the sofa with her hands clenched together.

"Powell believes her," she said firmly. "He has no reason not to. Apparently she doesn't tell lies as a rule. He won't believe you any more than he believed me. He'll side with Maggie and nothing will change. Nothing at all."

"Oh, that child," Ben Hayes said through his teeth.

She smoothed down her skirt. "I disliked her and it showed. That wasn't her fault. Anyway, Dad, it doesn't matter. I'll still come back and visit and you can come and see me. It won't be so bad. Really."

"I'd only just got you home again," he said heavily.

"And maybe I'll come back one day," she replied, smiling. She'd spared him the truth, at least. She hugged him. "I'll leave in the morning. It's best if I don't drag it out."

"What will they do about a teacher?" he demanded.

"They'll hire the next person on their list," she said simply. "It isn't as if I'm not expendable."

"You are to me."

She kissed him. "And you are to me. Now, I'd better go pack."

She phoned Barrie that night and was invited to share her apartment for the time being. She didn't tell Barrie what was wrong. That could wait.

She said goodbye to her father, climbed into her car and drove off toward Arizona. He'd wanted her to take the bus, but she wanted to be alone. She had plenty of thinking to do. She had to cope with her fears. It was time for that hard decision that she might already have put off for too long.

Back in Arizona, Barrie fed her cake and coffee and then waited patiently for the reason behind her best friend's return.

When Antonia told her about Powell's daughter's lies, she was livid.

Barrie bit her lower lip, a nervous habit that sometimes left them raw. "I could shake them both," she said curtly. "You're so thin, Annie, so worn. Maybe it's for the best that you came back here. You look worse than ever."

"I'll perk up now that I'm back. I need to see about my job, if they've got something open."

"Your replacement, Miss Garland, was offered a job in industry at three times the pay and she left without notice," Barrie told her. "I expect they'd love you to replace her. There aren't many people who'll work as hard as we do for the pay."

That made Antonia smile. "Absolutely. That's a bit of luck at last! I'll phone first thing tomorrow."

"It's good to have you back," Barrie said. "I've really missed you."

"I've missed you, too. Have you heard from Dawson…Barrie!"

Barrie had bitten right through her lip.

Antonia handed her a tissue. "You have to stop doing that," she said, glad to be talking about something less somber than her sudden departure from Bighorn.

"I do try, you know." She dabbed at the spot of blood and then stared miserably at her friend. "Dawson came to see me. We had an argument."

"About what?"

Barrie clammed up.

"All right, I won't pry. You don't mind if I stay here? Really?"

"Idiot," Barrie muttered, hugging her. "You're family. You belong here."

Antonia fought tears. "You're family, too."

She patted the other woman's back. "I know. Now let's eat something before we start wailing, and I'll tell you about the expansion plans they've just announced for the math department. I may be offered the head teaching position in the department!"

"I'm so happy for you!"

"So am I. Oh, I'm so lucky!" Her enthusiasm was catching. Antonia closed her eyes and leaned silently on Barrie's strength. She had to keep going, she told herself. There must be a reason why she was here, now, instead of happily teaching for what was left of her life in Bighorn. There had to be some purpose to the chain of events that had brought her back to Arizona. The thought of the treatments still frightened her, but not as much as they had only three weeks before. She would go back and see the doctor, and discuss those options.

Maggie was spending the weekend without any company. Julie wouldn't speak to her, and she had no other friends. Mrs. Bates, having heard all about why Miss Hayes had to leave, was avoiding the child as well. She'd moved into the house just to take care of Maggie, because she refused to stay with Julie. But it was a very tense arrangement, and Mrs. Bates muttered while she kept house.

Powell had gone to a business meeting in Denver on Thursday. He'd been out of town when the trouble started. He arrived back without knowing about Antonia's sudden departure. He'd thought about nothing except his disastrous date with Antonia and the things she'd said to him. He'd finally admitted to himself that she really was innocent of any affair with George Rutherford. Her accusations that he'd only used her for financial gain had clinched it.

Of course that wasn't true; he'd never thought of doing such a thing. But if she believed it, it would explain why she hadn't tried to defend herself. She'd never thought he cared one way or the other about her. Presumably she thought he'd been in love with Sally all along, and the fact that Maggie had been premature had helped convince her that he was sleeping with Sally during their engagement. It wasn't true. In fact, he'd only ever slept with Sally once, the night after Antonia left town. He'd been heartbroken, betrayed and so drunk he hardly knew what he was doing.

When he woke the next morning beside Sally, the

horror of what he'd done had killed something inside him. He'd known that there was no going back. He'd seduced Sally, and he'd had to marry her, to prevent another scandal. He'd been trapped, especially when she missed her regular period only two weeks later and turned to him to protect her from scandal. Ironically, he had.

Antonia didn't know that. She didn't know he'd loved her, because he'd never told her so. He hadn't been able to bring himself to say the words. Only when it was too late did he realize what he'd lost. The years between had been empty and cold and he'd grown hard. Sally, knowing he didn't love her at all, knowing he hated her for breaking up his engagement to Antonia, had paid the price, along with her daughter.

Sally had turned to alcohol to numb her pain, and once she'd started, she'd become an alcoholic. Powell had sent her to one doctor after another, to treatment centers. But nothing had worked. His total rejection had devastated her, and even after she'd died he hadn't been able to mourn her.

Neither had Maggie. The child had no love for either of her parents, and she was as cold a human being as Powell had ever known. Sometimes he wondered if she was his child, because there seemed to be nothing of him in her. Sally had hinted once that Powell hadn't been her first lover. She'd even hinted that Powell wasn't Maggie's father. He'd wondered ever since, and it had colored his relationship with the gloomy child who lived in his house.

He tossed his suitcase onto the floor in the hall and looked around. The house was empty, or seemed to be. He looked up the staircase and Maggie was sitting there, by herself, in torn jeans and a stained sweatshirt. As usual, she was glowering.

"Where's Mrs. Bates?" he asked.

She shrugged. "She went to the store."

"Don't you have anything to do?"

She lowered her eyes to her legs. "No."

"Well, go watch television or something," he said irritably when she didn't look up. A thought struck him. "You didn't get in trouble at school again, did you?" he asked.

Her shoulder moved again. "Yes."

He moved to the bottom step and stared at her. "Well?"

She shifted restlessly. "Miss Hayes got fired."

He didn't feel his heart beating. His eyes didn't move, didn't blink. "Why did she get fired?" he asked in a soft, dangerous tone.

Maggie's lower lip trembled. She clenched her hands around her thin knees. "Because I lied," she said under her breath. "I wanted her…to go away, because she didn't like me. I lied. And they fired her. Everybody hates me now. Julie especially." She swallowed. "I don't care!" She looked up at him belligerently. "I don't care! She didn't like me!"

"Well, whose fault is that?" he asked harshly.

She hid the pain, as she always did. Her stubborn little chin came up. "I want to go live somewhere else," she said with a pathetic kind of pride.

He fought down guilt. "Where would you go?" he asked, thinking of Antonia. "Sally's parents live in California and they're too old to take care of you, and there isn't anybody else."

She averted her wounded eyes. He sounded as if he wanted her to leave, too. She was sick all over.

"You'll go to school with me in the morning, and you'll tell the principal the truth, do you understand?" he asked flatly. "And then you'll apologize to Miss Hayes."

She clenched her teeth. "She's not here," she said.

"What?"

"She left. She went to Arizona." She winced at the look in his dark eyes.

He took an unsteady breath. The expression in his eyes was like a whiplash to Maggie.

"You don't like her," she accused in a broken voice. "You said so! You said you wished she'd go away!"

"You had no right to cost her that job," he said coldly. "Not liking people doesn't give you the right to hurt them!"

"Mrs. Bates said I was bad like my mama," she blurted out. "She said I was a liar like my mama." Tears filled her eyes. "And she said you hate me like you hated my mama."

He didn't speak. He didn't know what to say, how to deal with this child, his daughter. He hesitated, and in that split second, she got up and ran up the stairs with a heart that broke in two, right inside her. Mrs. Bates was right. Everybody hated her! She ran into her room and closed the door and locked it.

"I'm bad," she whispered to herself, choking on the words. "I'm bad! That's why everybody hates me so."

It had to be true. Her mother had gotten drunk and told her how much she hated her for trapping her in a loveless marriage, for not looking like her father, for being a burden. Her father didn't know that. She couldn't talk to him, she couldn't tell him things. He didn't want to spend any time with her. She was unlovable and unwanted. And she had no place at all to go. Even if she ran away, everybody knew her and they'd just bring her back. Only it would make things worse, because her dad would be even madder at her if she did something like that.

She sat down on the carpeted floor and looked around at the pretty, expensive things that lined the spacious room. All those pretty things, and not one of them was purchased with love, was given with love. They were substitutes for affectionate hugs and kisses, for trips to amusement parks and zoos and carnivals. They were guilt offerings from a parent who didn't love her or want her. She stared at them with anguish in her eyes, and wondered why she'd ever been born.

Powell got into his car and drove over to Antonia's father's house. He didn't expect to be let in, but Ben opened the door wide.

"I won't come in," Powell said curtly. "Maggie told me what she did. She and I will go to Mrs. Jameson in the morning and she'll tell the truth and apologize. I'm sure they'll offer Antonia her job back."

"She won't come," Ben replied in a lackluster tone. "She said it was just as well that things worked out that way, because she didn't want to live here."

Powell took off his hat and smoothed back his black hair. "I can only say I'm sorry," he said. "I don't know why Maggie dislikes her so much."

"Yes, you do," Ben said unexpectedly. "And you know why she dislikes Maggie, too."

His chest rose and fell in a soundless breath. "Maybe

I do. I've made a hell of a lot of mistakes. She said I wouldn't believe the truth because I couldn't admit that." His shoulders shifted. "I suppose she was right. I knew it wasn't true about her and George. But admitting it meant admitting that I had ruined not only her life, but mine and Sally's as well. My pride wouldn't let me do that."

"We pay a high price for some mistakes," Ben said. "Antonia's still paying. After all these years, she's never looked at another man."

His heart jumped. He searched Ben's eyes. "Is it too late?"

Ben knew what the other man was asking. "I don't know," he said honestly.

"Something's worrying her," Powell said. "Something more than Maggie, or the past. She looks ill."

"I made her go see Dr. Harris. She said he prescribed vitamins."

Powell stared at him. He recognized the suspicion in the other man's eyes, because he'd felt it himself. "You don't buy that, Ben. Neither do I." He took a long breath. "Look, why don't you call Dr. Harris and ask him what's going on?"

"It's Sunday."

"If you don't, I will," the younger man said.

Ben hesitated only for a minute. "Maybe you're right. Come in."

He phoned Dr. Harris. After a few polite words, he asked him point-blank about Antonia.

"That's confidential, Ben," the doctor said gently. "You know that."

"Well, she's gone back to Arizona," Ben said hotly.

"And she looks bad. She said you told her all she needed was vitamins. I want the truth."

There was a hesitation. "She asked me not to tell anyone. Not even you."

Ben glanced at Powell. "I'm her father."

There was a longer hesitation. "She's under the care of a doctor in Tucson," Dr. Harris said after a minute. "Dr. Harry Claridge. I'll give you his number."

"Ted, tell me," Ben pleaded.

There was a heavy sigh. "Ben, she's taking too long to make up her mind about having treatment. If she doesn't hurry, it…may be too late."

Ben sat down heavily on the sofa, his face pale and drawn. "She needs treatment…for what?" he asked, while Powell stood very still, listening, waiting.

"God, I hate having to tell you this!" the doctor said heavily. "I'm violating every oath I ever took, but it's in her best interest…."

"She's dragging her feet over treatment for what?" Ben burst out, glancing at Powell, whose face was rigid with fear.

"For cancer, Ben. The blood work indicates leukemia. I'm sorry. You'd better speak with Dr. Claridge. And see if you can talk some sense into her. She could stay in remission for years, Ben, years, if she gets treatment in time! They're constantly coming up with new medicines, they're finding cures for different sorts of cancer every day! You can't let her give up now!"

Ben felt tears stinging his eyes. "Yes. Of course. Give me…that number, will you, Ted?"

The phone number of the doctor in Arizona was passed along.

"I won't forget you for this. Thank you," Ben said, and hung up.

Powell was staring at him with dawning horror. "She refused treatment. For what?"

"Leukemia," Ben said heavily. "She didn't come home to be with me. She came home to die." He looked up into Powell's white, drawn face, furiously angry. "And now she's gone, alone, to face that terror by herself!"

Chapter 8

Powell didn't say a word. He just stared at Ben while all the hurtful things he'd said to Antonia came rushing back to haunt him. He remembered how brutally he'd kissed her, the insulting things he'd said. And then, to make it worse, he remembered the way she'd kissed him, just at the last, the way she'd looked up at him, as if she were memorizing his face.

"She was saying goodbye," he said, almost choking on the words.

"What?"

Powell drew in a short breath. There was no time for grief now. He couldn't think of himself. He had to think of Antonia, of what he could do for her. Number one on the list was to get her to accept help. "I'm going to Arizona." He put his hat back on and turned.

"You hold on there a minute," Ben said harshly. "She's my daughter…!"

"And she doesn't want you to know what's wrong with her," Powell retorted, glaring over his shoulder at the man. "I'll be damned if I'm going to stand around and let her do nothing! She can go to the Mayo Clinic. I'll take care of the financial arrangements. But I'm not going to let her die without a fight!"

Ben felt a glimmer of hope even as he struggled with his own needs, torn between agreeing that it was better not to let her know that he was aware of her condition and wanting to rush to her to offer comfort. He knew that Powell would do his best to make her get treatment; probably he could do more with her than Ben could. But Powell had hurt her so badly in the past….

Powell saw the hesitation and relented. He could only imagine how Ben felt about his only child. He wasn't close enough to his own daughter to know how he might react to similar news. It was a sobering, depressing thought. "I'll take care of her. I'll phone you the minute I can tell you something," he told Ben quietly. "If she thinks you know, it will tear her up. Obviously she kept it quiet to protect you."

Ben grimaced. "I figured that out for myself. But I hate secrets."

"So do I. But keep this one for her. Give her peace of mind. She won't care if I know," he said with a bitter laugh. "She thinks I hate her."

Ben was realizing that whatever Powell felt, it wasn't hate. He nodded, a curt jerk of his head. "I'll stay here, then. But the minute you know something…!"

"I'll be in touch."

* * *

Powell drove home with his heart in his throat. Antonia wouldn't have told anyone. She'd have died from her stubborn refusal to go ahead and have treatment, alone, thinking herself unwanted.

He went upstairs and packed a suitcase with memories haunting him. He'd have given anything to be able to take back his harsh accusations.

He was vaguely aware of eyes on his back. He turned. Maggie was standing there, glowering again.

"What do you want?" he asked coldly.

She averted her eyes. "You going away again?"

"Yes. To Arizona."

"Oh. Why are you going there?" she asked belligerently.

He straightened and looked at the child, unblinking. "To see Antonia. To apologize on your behalf for costing her her job. She came back here because she's sick," he added curtly. "She wanted to be with her father." He averted his eyes. The shock was wearing off. He felt real fear. He couldn't imagine a world without Antonia.

Maggie was an intelligent child. She knew from the way her father was reacting that Miss Hayes meant something to him. Her eyes flickered. "Will she die?" she asked.

He took a breath before he answered. "I don't know."

She folded her thin arms over her chest. She felt worse than ever. Miss Hayes was dying and she had to leave town because of Maggie. She lowered her eyes to the floor. "I didn't know she was sick. I'm sorry I lied."

"You should be. Furthermore, you're going to go with me to see Mrs. Jameson when I get back, and tell her the truth."

"Yes, sir," she said in a subdued tone.

He finished packing and shouldered into his coat.

Her wounded blue eyes searched over the tall man who didn't like her. She'd hoped all her young life that he'd come home just once laughing, happy to see her, that he'd catch her up in his arms and swing her around and tell her he loved her. That had never happened. Julie had that sort of father. Maggie's dad didn't want her.

"You going to bring Miss Hayes back?" she asked.

"Yes," he said flatly. "And if you don't like it, that's too bad."

She didn't answer him. He seemed to dislike her all over again now, because she'd lied. She turned and went back into her room, closing the door quietly. Miss Hayes would hate her. She'd come back, but she wouldn't forget what Maggie had done. There'd be one more person to make her life miserable, to make her feel unloved and unwanted. She sat down on her bed, too sad even to cry. Her life had never seemed so hopeless before. She wondered suddenly if this was how Miss Hayes felt, knowing she was going to die and then losing the only job she could get in town, so she had to go live in a place where she didn't have any family.

"I'm really sorry, Miss Hayes," Maggie said under her breath. The tears started and she couldn't stop them. But there was no one to comfort her in the big, elegant empty house where she lived.

Powell found Mrs. Bates and told her that he was going to Arizona, but not why. He left at once, without seeing Maggie again. He was afraid that he wouldn't be able to hide his disappointment at what she'd done to Antonia.

He made it to Tucson by late afternoon and checked into a hotel downtown. He found Antonia's number in the telephone directory and called it, but the number had been disconnected. Of course, surely she'd had to give up her apartment when she went back to Bighorn. Where could she be?

He thought about it for a minute, and knew. She'd be staying with Dawson Rutherford's stepsister. He looked up Barrie Bell in the directory. There was only one B. Bell listed. He called that number. It was Sunday evening, so he expected the women to be home.

Antonia answered the phone, her voice sounding very tired and listless.

Powell hesitated. Now that he had her on the phone, he didn't know what to say. And while he hesitated, she assumed it was a crank call and hung up on him. He put the receiver down. Perhaps talking to her over the phone was a bad idea, anyway. He noted the address of the apartment, and decided that he'd just go over there in the morning. The element of surprise couldn't be discounted. It would give him an edge, and he badly needed one. He got himself a small bottle of whiskey from the refrigerator in the room and poured it into a glass with some water. He didn't drink as a rule, but he needed this. It had occurred to him that he could lose Antonia now to something other than his own pride. He was afraid, for the first time in his life.

He figured that Antonia wouldn't be going immediately back to work, and he was right. When he rang the doorbell at midmorning the next day after a sleepless night, she came to answer it, Barrie having long since gone to work.

When she saw Powell standing there, her shock gave

him the opportunity to ease her back into the apartment and close the door behind him.

"What are you doing here?" she demanded, recovering.

He looked at her, really seeing her, with eyes dark with pain and worry. She was wearing a sweatshirt and jeans and socks, and she looked pitifully thin and drawn. He hated the pain he and Maggie had caused her.

"I talked to Dr. Harris," he said shortly, bypassing her father so that she wouldn't suspect that Ben knew about her condition.

She went even paler. He knew everything. She could see it in his face. "He had no right…!"

"You have no right," he snapped back, "to sit down and die!"

She took a sharp breath. "I can do what I like with my life!" she replied.

"No."

"Go away!"

"I won't do that, either. You're going to the doctor. And you'll start whatever damn treatment he tells you to get," he said shortly. "I'm through asking. I'm telling!"

"You aren't telling me anything! You have no control over me!"

"I have the right of a fellow human being to stop someone from committing suicide," he said quietly, searching her eyes. "I'm going to take care of you. I'll start today. Get dressed. We're going to see Dr. Claridge. I made an appointment for you before I came here."

Her mind was spinning. The shock was too sudden, too extreme. She simply stared at him.

His hands went to her shoulders and he searched

her eyes slowly. "I'm going to take Maggie to see Mrs. Jameson. I know what happened. You'll get your job back. You can come home."

She pulled away from him. "I don't have a home anymore," she said, averting her face. "I can't go back. My father would find out that I have leukemia. I can't do that to him. Losing Mother almost killed him, and his sister died of cancer. It was terrible, and it took a long time for her to die." She shuddered, remembering. "I can't put him through any more. I must have been crazy to try to go back there in the first place. I don't want him to know."

He couldn't tell her that her father already knew. He shoved his hands into his pockets and stared at her straight back.

"You need to be with people who care about you," he said.

"I am. Barrie is like family."

He didn't know what else to say, how to approach her. He jingled the loose change in his pocket while he tried to find ways to convince her.

She noticed his indecision and turned back to him. "If you'd made this decision, if it was your life, you wouldn't thank anyone for interfering."

"I'd fight," he said, angry with her for giving up. "And you know it."

"Of course you would," she said heavily. "You have things to fight for—your daughter, your wealth, your businesses."

He frowned.

She saw the look and laughed bitterly. "Don't you understand? I've run out of things to fight for," she told him. "I have nothing! Nothing! My father loves me, but he's all I have. I get up in the morning, I go to work, I try to educate children who'd rather play than do homework. I come home and eat supper and read a book and go to bed. That's my life. Except for Barrie, I don't have a friend in the world." She sounded as weary as she felt. She sat down on the edge of an easy chair with her face propped in her hands. It was almost a relief that someone knew, that she could finally admit how she felt. Powell wouldn't mind talking about her condition because it didn't matter to him. "I'm tired, Powell. It's gaining on me. I've been so sick lately that I'm barely able to get around at all. I don't care anymore. The treatment scares me more than the thought of dying does. Besides, there's nothing left that I care enough about to want to live. I just want it to be over."

The terror was working its way into his heart as he stared at her. He'd never heard anyone sound so defeated. With that attitude, all the treatment in the world wouldn't do any good. She'd given up.

He stood there, staring down at her bent head, breathing erratically while he searched for something to say that would inspire her, that would give her the will to fight. What could he do?

"Isn't there anything you want, Antonia?" he asked slowly. "Isn't there something that would give you a reason to hold on?"

She shook her head. "I'm grateful to you for coming all this way. But you could have saved yourself the trip. My mind is made up. Leave me alone, Powell."

"Leave you alone…!" He choked on the words. He wanted to rage. He wanted to throw things. She sounded so calm, so unmoved. And he was churning inside with the force of his emotions. "What else have I done for nine long, empty damn years?" he demanded.

She leaned forward, letting her long, loose blond hair drape over her face. "Don't lose your temper. I can't fight anymore. I'm too tired."

She looked it. His eyes lingered on her stooped posture. She looked beaten. It was so out of character for her that it devastated him.

He knelt in front of her, taking her by the wrists and pulling her toward him so that she had to look up.

His black eyes bit into her gray ones from point-blank range. "I've known people who had leukemia. With treatment, you could keep going for years. They could find a cure in the meantime. It's crazy to just let go, not to even take the chance of being able to live!"

She searched his black eyes quietly, with an ache deep inside her that had seemed to have been there forever. Daringly, her hand tugged free of his grasp and found his face. Such a beloved face, she thought brokenly. So dear to her. She traced over the thick hair that lay unruly against his broad forehead, down to the thick black eyebrows, down his nose to the crook where it had been broken, over one high cheekbone and down the indented space to his jutting chin. Beloved. She felt the muscles clench and saw the faint glitter in his eyes.

He was barely breathing now, watching her watch him. He caught her hand roughly and held it against his cheek. What he saw in her unguarded face tormented him.

"You still love me," he accused gruffly. "Do you think I don't know?"

She started to deny it, but there was really no reason to. Not anymore. She smiled sadly. "Oh, yes," she said miserably. Her fingers touched his chiseled, thin mouth and felt it move warmly beneath them as he reacted with faint surprise to her easy admission. "I love you. I never stopped. I never could have." She drew her fingers away. "But everything ends, Powell. Even life."

He caught her hand, pulling it back to his face. "This doesn't have to," he said quietly. "I can get a license today. We can be married in three days."

She had to fight the temptation to say yes. Her eyes fell to his collar, where a pulse hammered relentlessly. "Thank you," she said with genuine feeling. "That means more to me than you can know, under the circumstances. But I won't marry you. I have nothing to give you."

"You have the rest of your life," he said shortly. "However long that is!"

"No." Her voice was weaker. She was fighting tears. She turned her head away and tried to get up, but he held her there.

"You can live with me. I'll take care of you," he said heavily. "Whatever you need, you'll get. The best doctors, the best treatment."

"Money still can't buy life," she told him. "Cancer is…pretty final."

"Stop saying that!" He gripped her arms, hard. "Stop being a defeatist! You can beat anything if you're willing to try!"

"Oh, that sounds familiar," she said, her eyes misting over with memory. "Remember when you were first starting to build your pedigree herd up? And they told you you'd never manage it with one young bull and five heifers. Remember what you said? You said that anything was possible." Her eyes grew warm. "I believed you'd do it. I never doubted it for a minute. You were so proud, Powell, even when you had nothing, and you fought on when so many others would have dropped by the wayside. It was one of the things I admired most about you."

He winced. His face clenched; his heart clenched. He felt as if he was being torn apart. He let her go and got to his feet, moving away with his hands tight in his pockets.

"I gave up on you, though, didn't I?" he asked with his back to her. "A little gossip, a few lies and I destroyed your life."

She studied her thin hands. It was good that they were finally discussing this, that he'd finally admitted that he knew the truth. Perhaps it would make it easier for him, and for her, to let go of the past.

"Sally loved you," she said, making excuses for her friend for the first time. "Perhaps love makes people act out of character."

His fists clenched in his pockets. "I hated her, God forgive me," he said huskily. "I hated her every day we were together, even more when she announced that she was pregnant with Maggie." He sighed wearily. "God, Annie, I resent my own child because I'm not even sure she's mine. I'll never be sure. Even if she is, every time I look at her, I remember what her mother did."

"You did very well without me," she said without malice. "You built up the ranch and made a fortune doing it. You have respect and influence…."

"And all it cost me was you." His head bowed. He laughed dully. "What a price to pay."

"Maggie is a bright child," she said uncertainly. "She can't be so bad. Julie likes her."

"Not recently. Everybody's mad at her for making you leave," he said surprisingly. "Julie won't speak to her."

"That's a shame," she said. "She's a child who needs love, so much." Antonia had been thinking of what had happened the past few weeks, and Maggie's role in it.

He turned, scowling. "What do you mean?"

She smiled. The reasons for Maggie's bad behavior were beginning to be so clear. "Can't you see it in her? She's so alone, Powell, just like you used to be. She doesn't mix with the other children. She's always apart, separate. She's belligerent because she's lonely."

His face hardened. "I'm a busy man…"

"Blame me. Blame Sally. But don't blame Maggie for the past," she pleaded. "If nothing else comes out of this, there should be something for Maggie."

"Oh, God, St. Antonia speaks!" he said sarcastically, because her defense of his daughter made him ashamed of his lack of feeling for the child. "She got you fired, and you think she deserves kindness?"

"She does," she replied simply. "I could have been kinder to her. She reminded me of Sally, too. I was holding grudges of my own. I wasn't deliberately unkind, but I made no overtures toward her at all. A child like Julie is easy to love, because she gives love so generously. A child like Maggie is secretive and distrustful. She can't give love because she doesn't know how. She has to learn."

He thought about that for a minute. "All right. If she needs it, you come home with me and teach me how to give it."

She searched over his rigid expression with eyes that held equal parts of love and grief. "I'm already going downhill," she said slowly. "I can't do that to her, or to you and my father." Her eyes skimmed over his broad shoulders lovingly. "I'll stay with Barrie until I become a liability, then I'll go into a hospice...Powell!"

He had her up in his arms, clear off the floor, his hot face buried in her throat. He didn't speak, but his arms had a fine tremor and his breathing was ragged. He held her so close that she felt vaguely bruised, and he paced the floor with her while he tried to cope with the most incredible emotional pain he'd ever felt.

"I won't let you die," he said roughly. "Do you hear me? I won't!"

She slid her arms around his neck and let him hold her. He did care, in his own way, and she was sorry for him. She'd had weeks to come to grips with her condition, but he'd only had a day or so. Denial was a very real part of it, as Dr. Claridge had already told her.

"It's because of the night you took me to the bar, isn't it?" she asked quietly. "There's no need to feel guilty about what you said. I know it hasn't been an easy nine years for you, either. I don't hold any more grudges. I don't have time for them now. I've put things into perspective in the past few weeks. Hatred, guilt, anger, revenge...they all become so insignificant when you realize your time is limited."

His arms contracted. He stopped pacing and stood holding her, cold with fear.

"If you take the treatments, you have a chance," he repeated.

"Yes. I can live, from day to day, with the fear of it coming back. I can have radiation sickness, my hair will fall out, the very quality of my life will be impaired. What there is left of it, that is."

He drew in a sharp breath, rocking her against him. His eyes, if she could have seen them, were wide and bleak in a face gone rigid with grief.

"I'll be there. I'll help you through it! Life is too precious to throw away." His mouth searched against her throat hungrily. "Marry me, Annie. If it's only for a few weeks, we'll make enough memories to carry us both into eternity!"

His voice was husky as he spoke. It was the most beautiful thing he'd ever said to her. She clung, giving way to tears at last.

"Yes?" he whispered.

She didn't speak. It was too much of a temptation to resist. She didn't have the willpower to say no, despite her suspicion of his motives.

"I want you," he said harshly. "I want you more than I've ever wanted anything in my life, sick or well. Say yes," he repeated insistently. "Say yes!"

If it was only physical, if he didn't love her, was she doing the right thing to agree? She didn't know. But it was more than she could do to walk away from him a second time. Her arms tightened around his neck. "If you're sure...if you're really sure."

"I'm sure, all right." His cheek slid against hers. He searched her wet eyes. His mouth closed them and then slid down to cover her soft, trembling, tear-wet mouth. He kissed her tenderly, slowly, feeling her immediate response.

The kisses quickly became passionate, intense, and he drew back, because this was a time for tenderness, not desire. "If you'll have the treatments," he said carefully, "if it's even remotely possible afterward, I'll give you a child."

As bribery went, it was a master stroke. She looked as if she thought he was going insane. Her pale eyes searched his dark ones warily.

"Don't you want a child, Antonia?" he asked curtly. "You used to. It was all you talked about while we were engaged. Surely you didn't give up those dreams."

She felt the heat rush into her cheeks. It was an intimate thing to be talking about. Her eyes escaped his, darting down to the white of his shirt.

"Don't," she said weakly.

"We'll be married," he said firmly. "It will all be legal and aboveboard."

She sighed miserably. "Your daughter won't like having me in the house, for however long I have."

"My daughter had better like it. Having you around her may be the best thing that ever happened to her. But you keep harping on my daughter—I told you before, I don't even think Maggie's mine!"

Her eyes came up sharply.

"Oh, you think you're the only one who paid the price, is that it?" he asked bluntly. "I was married to an alcoholic, who hated me because I couldn't bear to touch her. She told me that Maggie wasn't mine, that she'd been with other men."

She tried to pull away, but he wouldn't let her. He put her back on her feet, but he held her there in front of him. His eyes were relentless, like his hold on her. "I told you that I believed Sally about George, but I didn't. After that one, she told so many lies...so many...!" He let go of her abruptly and turned his back, ramming his hands into the pockets of his slacks as he went to look out the window that overlooked the city of Tucson with "A" Mountain in the distance. "I've lived in hell. Until she died, and afterward. You said you couldn't bear Maggie in your class because of the memories, and I accused you of cruelty. But it's that way with me, too."

The child's behavior made a terrible kind of sense. Her mother hadn't wanted her, and neither did her father. She was unloved, unwanted. No wonder she was a behavioral problem.

"She looks like Sally," she said.

"Oh, yes. Indeed she does. But she doesn't look like me, does she?"

She couldn't argue that point, as much as she might have liked to reassure him.

She joined him at the window. Her eyes searched his. The pain and the anguish of his life were carved into his lean face, in deep lines and an absence of happiness. He looked older than he was.

"What stupid mistakes we make, Antonia, when we're young. I didn't believe you, and that hurt you so much that you ran away. Then I spent years pretending that it wasn't a lie, because I couldn't bear to see the waste and know that I caused it. It's hard to admit guilt, fault. I fought it tooth and nail. But in the end, there was no one else to blame."

She lowered her eyes to his chest. "We were both much younger."

"I never used you to get loans on your father's name," he said bluntly. "That was the furthest thing from my mind."

She didn't answer him.

He moved closer, so that as she stared at the floor, his legs filled her line of vision. They were long legs, muscular and powerful from hours working in the saddle.

He took her cold hands in his. "I was a loner and a

misfit. I grew up in poverty, with a father who'd gamble the food out of a baby's mouth and a mother who was too afraid of him to leave. It was a rough childhood. The only thing I ever wanted was to get out of the cycle of poverty, to never have to go hungry again. I wanted to make people notice me."

"You did," she said. "You have everything you ever wanted—money and power and prestige."

"There was one other thing I wanted," he said, correcting her. "I wanted you."

She couldn't meet his eyes. "That didn't last."

"Yes, it did. I still want you more than any woman I've ever known."

"In bed," she scoffed.

"Don't knock it," he replied. "Surely by now you've learned how passion can take you over."

She looked up. Her eyes were guileless, curious, totally innocent.

He caught his breath. "No?"

She lowered her gaze again. "I stopped taking risks after you. Nobody got close enough to hurt me again. In any way."

He caught her small hand in his and rubbed his thumb slowly over its delicate back. He watched the veins in it, traced their blue paths to her fingers. "I can't say the same," he replied quietly. "It would have been more than I could bear to go without a woman for years."

"I suppose it's different for men."

"For some of us," he agreed. He clasped her fingers tight. "They were all you," he added on a cold laugh. "Every one was you. They numbed the pain for a few minutes, and then it came back full force and brought guilt with it."

She reached out hesitantly and touched his dark hair. It was cool under her fingers, clean and smelling of some masculine shampoo.

"Hold me," he said quietly, sliding his arms around her waist. "I'm as frightened as you are."

The words startled her. By the time she reacted to them, he had her close, and his face was buried in her throat.

Her hands hovered above his head and then finally gave in and slid into his hair, holding his cheek against hers.

"I can't let you die, Antonia," he said in a rough whisper.

Her fingers smoothed over his hair protectively. "The treatments are scary," she confessed.

He lifted his head and searched her eyes. "If I went with you, would it be so bad?" he asked softly. "Because I will."

She was weakening. "No. It wouldn't be…so bad, then."

He smiled gently. "Leukemia isn't necessarily fatal," he continued. "Remission can last for years." He traced her mouth. "Years and years."

Tears leaked out of her eyes and down into the corners of her mouth.

"You'll get better," he said, his voice a little rough with the control he was exercising. "And we'll have a baby together."

Her lips compressed. "If I have to have radiation, I don't think I can ever have children."

He hadn't wanted to think about that. He took her

hand and brought it hungrily to his mouth. "We'll talk to the doctor. We'll find out for certain."

It was like being caught in a dream. She stopped thinking and worrying altogether. Her eyes searched his and she smiled for the first time.

"All right?" he prompted.

She nodded. "All right."

Dr. Claridge was less than optimistic about pregnancy, and he said so. "You can't carry a child while you're undergoing the treatment," he explained patiently, and watched their faces fall. He hated telling them that.

"And afterward?" she asked, clinging to Powell's strong hand.

"I can't make any promises." He looked at her file, frowning. "You have a rare blood type, which makes it even more dangerous...."

"Rare blood type?" she echoed. "I thought Type O positive was garden variety."

He stared at her. "Yours is not O positive—it's much more rare."

"It is not!" she argued, surprised. "Dr. Claridge, I certainly do know my own blood type. I had an accident when I was in my teens and they had to give me blood. You remember," she told Powell. "I wrecked my bike and cut a gash in my thigh on some tin beside the house."

"I remember," he said.

She looked back at Dr. Claridge. "You can check with Dr. Harris. He'll tell you I'm Type O."

He was frowning as he read the test results again. "But, this is your file," he said to himself. "This is the

report that came back from the lab. The names match."
He buzzed his nurse and had her come in and verify
the file.

"Have we ever done a complete blood profile on
Antonia in the past?" he asked. "There's no record of
one here."

"No, we haven't," the nurse agreed.

"Well, do one now. Something is wrong here."

"Yes, sir."

The nurse went out and came back a minute later
with the equipment to draw blood. She drew two vials.

"Get a rush on that. Get a local lab to do it. I want to
know something by morning," he told her.

"Yes, sir."

The doctor turned back to Antonia. "Don't get your
hopes up too high," he said. "It might be a misprint on
the blood type and everything else could still be correct. But we'll double-check it. Meanwhile," he added,
"I think it would be wise to wait until tomorrow to make
any more decisions. You can call me about ten. I should
know something then."

"I'll do that. Thank you."

"Remember. Don't expect too much."

She smiled. "I won't."

"But, just on the off chance, has anyone you've been
in contact with had infectious mononucleosis lately?"

She blinked. "Why, yes. One of my female students
had it a few weeks ago," she said. "I remember that her
mother was very concerned because the girl had played
spin the bottle at a party. Ten years old, can you imagine…?" She laughed nervously.

He went very still. "Did you come into contact with
any of her saliva?"

She chuckled weakly. "I don't go around kissing my girls."

"Antonia!"

"We shared a soda," she recalled.

He began to smile. "Well, well. Of course, there's still the possibility that we're no better off, but mono and leukemia are very similar in the way they show up in blood work. A lab technician could have mixed them up."

"It might have been a mistake?" she asked hopefully.

"Maybe. But only maybe. We can't discount the other symptoms you've had."

"A maybe is pretty good," she said. "What are the symptoms of mononucleosis?"

"Same as leukemia," he confirmed. "Weakness, sore throat, fatigue, fever..." He glanced at Powell and cleared his throat. "And highly contagious."

Powell smiled crookedly. "I wouldn't care."

The doctor chuckled. "I know how you feel. Well, go home, Antonia. We'll know something in the morning. The labs are careful, but mistakes can happen."

"If only this is one," she said huskily. "Oh, if only!"

When they were outside, Powell held her hand tight in his, and paused to bend and kiss her very gently on her mouth.

"I can't think of anything I'd rather have than mononucleosis," he remarked.

She smiled tearfully. "Neither can I!"

"You're sure about that blood type."

"Positive."

"Well, we'll cross our fingers and pray. Right now, let's get some lunch. Then we might go for a drive."

"Okay."

He took her back to his hotel for lunch and then they drove out of town, through the Saguaro National Monument and looked at the giant cacti. The air was cold, but the sun was out and Antonia felt a little more hopeful than she had before.

They didn't talk. Powell simply held her hand tight in his and the radio played country and western music.

Barrie was home when they drove up to her apartment building. She was surprised to see Powell, but the expression on his face and on Antonia's made her smile.

"Good news, I hope?" she asked.

"I hope so," Antonia said.

Barrie frowned, and then Antonia realized that she didn't know what was going on.

"We're getting married," Powell said, covering for her.

"We are?" Antonia asked, shocked.

"You said yes, remember? What else did you think I meant when I started talking about children?" he asked haughtily. "I won't live in sin with you."

"I didn't ask you to!"

"Good. Because I won't. I'm not that kind of man," he added, and he smiled at her with a new and exciting tenderness.

Antonia caught her breath at the warmth in the look he gave her, tingling from head to toe with new hope. *Please God,* she thought, *let this be a new beginning.*

Barrie was smiling from ear to ear. "Do I say congratulations?"

"Does she?" Powell asked Antonia.

Antonia hesitated. She knew that Powell only wanted her; maybe he felt sorry for her, too. He hadn't really had time to get used to the possibility that she might die. His motives disturbed her. But she'd never stopped loving him. Would it be so bad to marry him? He might learn to love her, if there was enough time.

"I'll tell you tomorrow," she promised.

He searched her eyes quietly. "It will be all right," he promised. "I know it."

She didn't. She was afraid to hope. But she didn't argue.

"There's a nice film on television tonight, if you're staying," Barrie told Powell. "I thought I'd make popcorn."

"That's up to Antonia," he said.

Antonia smiled at him. "I'd like you to stay."

He took off his hat. "I like butter on my popcorn," he said with a grin.

Chapter 9

It was the longest night of Antonia's life. Powell went to his hotel at midnight, and she went to bed, still without having told Barrie what she had to face in the morning.

After Barrie went to work, Antonia got dressed. When Powell came for her at nine, she was more than ready to sit in the doctor's waiting room. She wasn't about to trust the telephone about anything that important. And apparently, neither was he.

They drove around until ten, when they went to Dr. Harris's office for their appointment. They sat in his waiting room and waited patiently through an emergency until he invited Antonia into his office, with Powell right behind her.

They didn't need to ask what he'd found. He was grinning from ear to ear.

"You're garden variety Type O," he told her without preamble, smiling even wider at her delight as she hugged an equally jubilant Powell. "Furthermore, I called the lab that did the blood work before, and they'd just fired a technician who kept mixing up test results. Yours was one he did. The other assistants turned him in, apparently. They're very professional. They don't tolerate sloppy work."

"Oh, thank God!" Antonia burst out.

"I'm very sorry for the ordeal you've had because of this," he added.

"I hid my head in the sand," she said. "If I'd come right in for treatment, and you'd done more blood work, you'd have discovered it sooner."

"Well, there is some bad news," he added with a rueful smile. "You really do have mononucleosis."

Dr. Claridge explained the course of the disease, and then warned them again about how contagious mono was.

"I've seen this run through an entire school in the cafeteria in the old days," he recalled. "And sometimes people spend weeks in bed with it. But I don't believe that'll be necessary in your case. I don't think you will lose a lot of work time."

"She won't have to worry about that," Powell said. "She's marrying me. She won't have to work. And I don't think she'll mind a few days in bed, getting rid of the infection."

She looked up at his suddenly grim face and realized that he was going through with the marriage regardless of her new diagnosis. It didn't make sense for a minute, and then it made terrible sense. He'd given his word. He wouldn't go back on it, no matter what.

His pride and honor were as much a part of his makeup as his stubbornness.

"We'll talk about that later," she said evasively. "Dr. Claridge, I can't thank you enough."

"I'm just happy to be able to give a cheerful prognosis on your condition now," he said with genuine feeling. "These things happen, but they can have tragic consequences. There was such a lab work mix-up in a big eastern city many years ago...it caused a man to take his own life out of fear. Generally I encourage people to have a second blood test to make sure. Which I would have certainly done in your case, had you come back to see me sooner," he added deliberately.

She flushed. "Yes. Well, I'll try to show a little more fortitude in the future. I was scared to death and I panicked."

"That's a very human reaction," Dr. Claridge assured her. "Take care. If you have any further problems, let me know."

"We'll be going back to Bighorn," Powell said. "But Dr. Harris will be in touch if he needs to."

"Good man, Harris," Dr. Claridge said. "He was very concerned about you when he contacted me. He'll be happy with the new diagnosis."

"I'm sure he will. I'll phone him the minute I get home and tell him," Antonia added.

They left the doctor's office and Antonia paused on the sidewalk to look around her with new eyes. "I thought I'd lost everything," she said aloud, staring with unabashed delight at trees and people and the distant mountains. "I'd given up. And now, it's all new, it's all beautiful."

He caught her hand in his and held it tight. "I wish I'd known sooner," he said.

She smiled faintly. "It was my problem, not yours."

He didn't answer that. He could tell from her attitude that she was going to try to back out of their wedding. Well, he thought, she was going to find that it was more difficult than she imagined. He had her. He wasn't letting go now.

"If you're hungry, we can have something to eat. Late breakfast or early lunch, whichever you like. But first, we'll get these filled," he added, putting the prescriptions into his pocket.

They filled the prescriptions and then went straight to Powell's hotel, and up in the elevator to his luxurious suite overlooking the Sonoran Desert.

"We can eat up here, and we can talk in private," he said, "without prying eyes. But first, I want to phone your father."

"My father? Why?"

He picked up the telephone, got an outside line and dialed. "Because he knew," he said.

"How?"

He glanced at her. "I made him phone Dr. Harris. We both felt that something was wrong. He wanted to rush down here, but I didn't want you to know… Hello, Ben? There was a mix-up at the lab. She has mononucleosis, not cancer, and she'll be back on her feet in no time." He smiled at the excitement on the other end of the line. "He wants to talk to you," he said, holding out the receiver.

"Hi, Dad," Antonia said softly, glaring at Powell. "I didn't know you knew."

"Powell wouldn't rest until he had the truth. It is the truth, this time?" Ben asked sharply. "It really was a mistake?"

"It really was, thank God," she said with genuine relief. "I was scared to death."

"You weren't the only one. This is wonderful news, girl. Really wonderful news! When are you coming back? Powell tell you Maggie was going to tell the truth? You can get your old job back."

She glanced at Powell warily. He was listening, watching, intently. "Nothing's definite yet. I'll phone you in a day or two and let you know what I decide to do. Okay?"

"Okay. Thank God you're all right," he said heavily. "It's been a hell of a couple of days, Antonia."

"For me, too. I'll talk to you soon. Love you, Dad."

"Love you."

She hung up, turning to glare at Powell. "You had to interfere!"

"Yes, I did," he agreed. "I agree with your father—I don't like secrets, either."

He took off his hat, holding her gaze the whole time. He looked incredibly grim. He slipped off his jacket and his tie, and loosened the top buttons of his shirt, exposing a dark, muscular chest thick with black hair.

The sight of him like that brought back long-buried needs and hungers.

"What are you doing?" she asked when his belt followed the rest and he'd dropped into a chair to shed his boots.

"Undressing," he said. He got back up again and moved toward her.

She started to sidestep, but she was seconds too late. He picked her up and carried her into the bedroom. He threw her onto the bed, following her down with a minimum of exertion.

With his arms on either side of her supporting his weight, she was trapped.

"Powell..."

His black eyes were faintly apologetic. "I'm sorry," he murmured as his mouth eased down against hers.

In the old days, their lovemaking had been passionate, but he'd always been the one to draw back. His reserve was what had convinced her later that he hadn't loved her.

Now, there was no reserve at all, and he was kissing her in a way he never had. His lips didn't cherish, they aroused, and aroused violently. He made her tremble with longings she'd never felt, even with him. His hands were as reckless as his mouth, touching, invading, probing against her naked skin while the only sounds in the room were his quick, sharp breaths and the thunder of his heart beating against her bare breasts.

She didn't even realize he'd half undressed her. She was too involved in the pleasure he was giving her to care about anything except that she wanted him to have access to her soft, warm skin. She needed the feel of his mouth on her, ached for it, hurt to have it. She arched up against him, moaning when the pleasure became more than she could bear.

Vaguely she was aware that a lot of skin was touching other skin. She felt the warm strength of his body against hers and there didn't seem to be any fabric separating them anymore. The hair on his long legs brushed her bare ones as he separated them and moved so that he was lying completely against her in an intimacy they'd never shared.

She panicked then, freezing when she felt his aroused body in intimate contact with her own.

His mouth softened on hers, gentled, so tender that she couldn't resist him. His hands smoothed up and down her body, and he smiled against her lips.

"Easy," he whispered, lifting his head so that he could see her wet, dazed eyes. His hips moved and she stiffened. "Does that hurt?" he asked softly.

She bit her lower lip. Her hands clenched against his hard arms. "It…yes."

"You're embarrassed. Shocked, too." He brushed his lips against hers as he moved again, tenderly, but even so, the pain was there again and she flinched. His eyes searched hers and the look on his face became strained, passionate, almost grim. "I guess it has to hurt this time," he said unsteadily, "but it won't for long."

She swallowed. "It's…wrong."

He shook his head. "We're going to be married. This is my insurance."

"In…surance?" She gasped, because he was filling her…

"Yes." He moved again, and this time she gasped because it was so sweet, and her hips lifted to prolong it. "I'm giving you a baby, Antonia," he breathed reverently, and even as the words entered her ear, his mouth crushed down over hers and his body moved urgently, and the whole world dissolved in a sweet, hot fire that lifted her like a bird in his arms and slung her headlong up into the sky…

* * *

He didn't look guilty. That was her first thought when his face came into vivid focus above her. He was smiling, and the expression in his black eyes made her want to hit him. She flushed to the very roots of her hair, as much from the intimacy of their position as from her memories of the past few hectic, unbelievably passionate minutes.

"That settles all the arguments you might have against marriage, I trust?" he asked outrageously. He drew a strand of damp blond hair over her nose playfully. "If we'd done this nine years ago, nothing could have come between us. It was sweeter than I dreamed it would be, and believe me, I dreamed a lot in nine years."

She sighed heavily, searching his black eyes. They were warm and soft now and she waited for the shame and guilt to come, but it didn't. It was very natural to lie naked in his arms and let him look at her and draw his fingers against her in lazy, intimate caresses.

"No arguments at all?" he asked at her lips, and kissed her gently. "You look worried."

"I am," she said honestly. Her wide eyes met his. "I'm midway between periods."

He smiled slowly. "The best time," he mused.

"But a baby so soon...!"

His fingers covered her lips and stopped the words. "So late," he replied. "You're already twenty-seven."

"I know, but there's Maggie," she said miserably. "She doesn't like me. She won't want me there at all... and a baby, Powell! It will be so hard on her."

"We'll cross bridges when we come to them," he said. His eyes slid down her body and back up and desire kindled in their black depths again. His face began to tauten, his caresses became arousing. When she shivered and a soft moan passed between her parted lips, he bent to kiss them with renewed hunger.

"Can you take me again?" he whispered provocatively. "Will it hurt?"

She slid closer to him, feeling the instant response of his body, feeling him shiver as she positioned her body to accept his. She looked into his eyes and caught her breath when he moved down.

He stilled, watching her, his heartbeat shaking them both. He lifted and pushed, watched. Her eyes dilated and he eased down again, harder this time, into complete possession.

She gasped. But her hands were pulling at him, not pushing. He smiled slowly and bent to cover her mouth with his. There had never been a time in his life when he felt more masculine than now, with her soft cries in his ear and her body begging for his. He closed his eyes and gave in to the glory of loving her.

Eventually they had lunch and went to Barrie's apartment when she was due home. One look at them told the story, and she hugged Antonia warmly.

"Congratulations. I told you it would work out one day."

"It worked out, all right," Antonia said, and then told her friend the real reason why she'd come back to Arizona.

Barrie had to sit down. Her green eyes were wide, her face drawn as she realized the agony her friend had suffered.

"Why didn't you tell me?" she burst out.

"For the same reason she didn't tell me," Powell murmured dryly, holding Antonia's hand tight in his. "She didn't want to worry anyone."

"You idiot!" Barrie muttered. "I'd have made you go back to the doctor."

"That's why I didn't tell you," Antonia said. "I would have told you eventually, though."

"Thanks a lot!"

"You'd have done exactly the same thing, maybe worse," Antonia said, unperturbed, as she grinned at Barrie. "You have to come to the wedding."

"When is it?"

"Ten in the morning, day after tomorrow, at the county courthouse here," Powell said with a chuckle. "I have the license, Dr. Claridge did the blood work this morning and we're going back to Bighorn wearing our rings."

"I have a spare room," Barrie offered.

Powell shook his head. "Thanks, but she's mine now," he said possessively, searching Antonia's face with quick, hungry eyes. "I'm not letting her out of my sight."

"I can understand that," Barrie agreed. "Well, do you have plans for the evening, or do you want to take in a movie with me? That new period piece is on at the shopping center."

"That might be fun," Antonia said, looking up at Powell.

"I like costume dramas," he seconded. "Suits me."

Besides, he told Antonia later, when they were briefly alone, she wasn't going to be in any shape for what he really wanted for another day or so. That being the case, a movie was as good as anything to pass the time. As long as they were together, he added quietly. If she felt like it. He worried about not keeping her still. She ignored that. She could rest when they got back to Bighorn, she informed him.

Antonia clung to his hand during the movie, and that night, she slept in his arms. It was as if the past nine years had never happened. He still hadn't said anything about love, but she knew that he wanted her. Perhaps in time, love would come. Her real concern was how they were going to cope with Maggie's resentment, especially if their passion for each other bore fruit. It was too soon for a baby, but Powell's ardor had been too headlong to allow for precautions, and his hunger for a child with her was all too obvious. He wasn't thinking about Maggie. He was thinking about all those wasted years and how quickly he could make up for them. But Antonia worried.

The wedding service was very small and sedate and dignified. Antonia wore a cream-colored wool suit to be married in, and a hat with a small veil that covered her face until the justice of the peace pronounced them man and wife. Powell lifted the veil and looked at her face for a long moment before he bent and kissed her. It was like no kiss he'd ever given her before. She looked into his eyes and felt her legs melt under her. She'd never loved him so much.

Barrie had been one of their witnesses and a sheriff's deputy who was prevailed upon by the justice of the peace was the other. The paperwork was completed, the marriage license handed back with the date and time of the wedding on it. They were married.

* * *

The next day they were on the way to Bighorn in Powell's Mercedes-Benz. He was more tense than he'd been for three days and she knew it was probably because her body was still reeling from its introduction to intimacy. She was better, but any intimacy, even the smallest, brought discomfort. She hated that. Powell had assured her that it was perfectly natural, and that time would take care of the problem, but his hunger for her was in his eyes every time he looked at her. At this stage of their new relationship, she hated denying him what he craved. After all, it was the only thing they did have right now.

"Stop looking so morose," he taunted when they neared the Wyoming border hours later. "The world won't end because we can't enjoy each other in bed again just yet."

"I was thinking of you, not me," she said absently.

He didn't reply. His eyes were straight ahead. "I thought you enjoyed it."

She glanced at him and realized that she'd unintentionally hurt his ego. "Of course I did," she said. "But I think it must be more of a need for a man. I mean…"

"Never mind," he mused, glancing at her. "You remembered what I said, didn't you—that I can't go for a long time without a woman? I was talking about years, Antonia, not days."

"Oh."

He chuckled softly. "You little green girl. You're just as you were at eighteen."

"Not anymore."

"Well, not quite." He reached out his hand and she put hers into it, feeling its comforting strength. "We're on our way, honey," he said gently, and it was the first time that he'd used an endearment to address her. "It will be all right. Don't worry."

"What about Maggie?" she asked.

His face hardened. "Let me worry about Maggie."

Antonia didn't say anything else. But she had a bad feeling that they were going to have trouble in that quarter.

They stopped by her father's house first, for a tearful reunion. Then they dropped the bombshell.

"Married?" Ben burst out. "Without even telling me, or asking if I wanted to be there?"

"It was my idea," Powell confessed, drawing Antonia close to his side. "I didn't give her much choice."

Ben glared at him, but only for a minute. He couldn't forget that Powell had been more than willing to take on responsibility for Antonia when he thought she was dying. That took courage, and something more.

"Well, you're both old enough to know what you're doing," he said grudgingly, and he smiled at his daughter, who was looking insecure. "And if I get grandkids out of this, I'll shut up."

"You'll have grandchildren," she promised shyly. "Including a ready-made one to start with."

Powell frowned slightly. She meant Maggie.

Antonia looked up at him with a quiet smile. "Speaking of whom, we'd better go, hadn't we?"

He nodded. He shook hands with Ben. "I'll take care of her," he promised.

Ben didn't say anything for a minute. But then he smiled. "Yes. I know you will."

Powell drove them to his home, palatial and elegant, sitting on a rise overlooking the distant mountains. There were several trees around the house and long, rolling hills beyond where purebred cattle grazed. In the old days, the house had been a little shack with a leaking roof and a porch that sagged.

"What a long way you've come, Powell," she said.

He didn't look at her as he swung the car around to the side of the house and pressed the button that opened the garage.

The door went up. He drove in and closed the door behind them. Even the garage was spacious and clean.

He helped Antonia out. "I'll come back for your bags in a few minutes. You remember Ida Bates, don't you? She keeps house for me."

"Ida?" She smiled. "She was one of my mother's friends. They sang together in the choir at church."

"Ida still does."

They went in through the kitchen. Ida Bates, heavy-set and harassed, turned to stare at Antonia with a question in her eyes.

"We were married in Tucson," Powell announced. "Meet the new lady of the house."

Ida dropped the spoon in the peas she was stirring and rushed to embrace Antonia with genuine affection. "I can't tell you how happy I am for you! What a surprise!"

"It was to us, too," Antonia murmured with a shy glance at her new husband, who smiled back warmly.

Ida let her go and cast a worried look at Powell. "She's up in her room," she said slowly. "Hasn't come out all day. Won't eat a bite."

Antonia felt somehow responsible for the child's tor-

ment. Powell noticed that, and his jaw tautened. He took
Antonia's hand.

"We'll go up and give her the news."

"Don't expect much," Ida muttered.

The door to Maggie's room was closed. Powell didn't
even knock. He opened it and drew Antonia in with
him.

Maggie was sitting on the floor looking at a book.
Her hair was dirty and straggly and the clothes she was
wearing looked as if they'd been slept in.

She looked at Antonia with real fear and scrambled
to her feet, backing until she could hold on to the bedpost.

"What's the matter with you?" Powell demanded
coldly.

"Is she…real?" she asked, wide-eyed.

"Of course I'm real," Antonia said quietly.

"Oh." Maggie relaxed her grip on the bedpost. "Are
you…real sick?"

"She doesn't have what we thought," Powell said
without preamble. "It was a mistake. She has something
else, but she's going to be all right."

Maggie relaxed a little, but not much.

"We're married," Powell added bluntly.

Maggie didn't react at all. Her blue eyes lifted to Antonia and she didn't smile.

"Antonia is going to live with us," Powell continued.
"I'll expect you to make her feel welcome here."

Maggie knew that. Antonia would certainly be welcome, as Maggie never had been. She looked at her father with an expression that made Antonia want to cry.
Powell never even noticed the anguish in it.

Pick her up, she wanted to tell him. Hold her. Tell

her you still love her, that it won't make any difference that you've remarried. But he didn't do that. He stared at the child with an austerity that made terrible sense of what he'd said to Antonia. He didn't know if Maggie was his, and he resented her. The child certainly knew it. His attitude all but shouted it.

"I'll have to stay in bed for a while, Maggie," Antonia said. "It would be nice if you'd read to me sometimes," she added, nodding toward the book on the floor.

"You going to be my teacher, too?" Maggie asked.

"No," Powell said firmly, looking straight at Antonia. "She's going to have enough to do getting well."

Antonia smiled ruefully. It looked as if she was going to have a war on her hands if she tried to take that teaching job back.

"But you and I are still going to see Mrs. Jameson," he told his daughter. "Don't think you're going to slide out of that."

Maggie lifted her chin and looked at him. "I already done it."

"What?" he demanded.

"I told Mrs. Jameson," she said, glaring up at him. "I told her I lied about Miss Hayes. I told her I was sorry."

Powell was impressed. "You went to see her all by yourself?" he asked.

She nodded, a curt little jerk of her head. "I'm sorry," she said gruffly to Antonia.

"It was a brave thing to do," Antonia remarked. "Were you scared?"

Maggie didn't answer. She just shrugged.

"Don't leave that book lying there," Powell instructed, nodding toward it on the carpet. "And take a bath and change those clothes."

"Yes, Daddy," she said dully.

Antonia watched her put the book away, and wished that she could do something, say something, interfere enough that she could wipe that look from Maggie's little face.

Powell tugged her out of the room before she could say anything else. She went, but she was determined that she was going to do something about this situation.

Antonia and Maggie had not started out on the right foot, because of what had happened in the past. But now Antonia wanted to try with this child. Now that she saw the truth in Powell's early words—that Maggie had paid a high price. That price had been love.

Maggie might not like her, but the child needed a champion in this household, and Antonia was going to be her champion.

Chapter 10

When they were in the master bedroom where Powell slept, Antonia went close to him.

"Don't you ever hug her?" she asked softly. "Or kiss her, and tell her you're glad to see her?"

He stiffened. "Maggie isn't the sort of child who wants affection from adults."

His attitude shocked Antonia. "Powell, you don't really believe that, do you?" she asked, aghast.

The way she was looking at him made him uncomfortable. "I don't know if she's mine." He bit off the words defensively.

"Would it matter so much?" she persisted. "Powell, she's lived in your house since she was born. You've been responsible for her. You've watched her grow. Surely you feel something for her!"

He caught her by the waist and pulled her to him.

"I want a child with you," he said quietly. "I promise you, it will be loved and wanted. It will never lack for affection."

She touched his lean cheek. "I know that. I'll love it, too. But Maggie needs us as well. You can't turn your back on her."

His eyebrows went up. "I've always fulfilled my responsibilities as far as Maggie is concerned. I've never wanted to see her hurt. But we've never had a good relationship. And she isn't going to accept you. She's probably already plotting ways to get rid of you."

"Maybe I know her better than you think," she replied. She smiled. "I'm going to love you until you're sick of it," she whispered, going close to him. "Love will spill out of every nook and cranny, it will fill you up. You'll love Maggie because I'll make you love her." She drew his head down and nibbled at his firm mouth until it parted, until he groaned and dragged her into his arms, to kiss her hungrily, like a man demented.

She returned his kisses until sheer exhaustion drained her of strength and she lay against his chest, holding on for support.

"You're still very weak," he remarked. He lifted her gently and carried her to the bed. "I'll have Ida bring lunch up here. Dr. Claridge said you'd need time in bed and you're going to get it now that we're home."

"Bully," she teased softly.

He chuckled, bending over her. "Only when I need to be." He kissed her softly.

Maggie, passing the door, heard him laugh, saw the happiness he was sharing with Antonia, and felt more alone than she ever had in her young life. She walked on, going down the stairs and into the kitchen.

"Mind you don't track mud in here," Ida Bates muttered. "I just mopped."

Maggie didn't speak. She walked out the door and closed it behind her.

Antonia had her lunch on a tray with Powell. It was so different now, being with him, loving him openly, watching the coldness leave him. He was like a different man.

But she worried about Maggie. That evening when Ida brought another tray, this time a single one because Powell had to go out, she asked about Maggie.

"I don't know where she is," Ida said, surprised. "She went out before lunch and never came back."

"But aren't you concerned?" Antonia asked sharply. "She's only nine!"

"Little monkey goes where she pleases, always has. She's probably out in the barn. New calf out there. She likes little things. She won't go far. She's got no place to go."

That sounded so heartless. She winced.

"You eat all that up, now. Do you good to have some hot food inside you." Ida smiled and went out, leaving the door open. "Call if you need me!"

Antonia couldn't enjoy her meal. She was worried, even if nobody else was.

She got up and searched in her suitcases for a pair of jeans, socks, sneakers and a sweatshirt. She put them on and eased down the stairs, through the living room and out the front door. The barn was to the side of the house, a good little walk down a dirt road. She didn't think about how tired she was. She was worried about

Maggie. It was late afternoon, and growing dark. The child had been out all day.

The barn door was ajar. She eased inside it and looked around the spacious, shadowy confines until her eyes became accustomed to the dimness. The aisle was wide and covered in wheat straw. She walked past one stall and another until she found a calf and a small child together in the very last one.

"You didn't have anything to eat," she said.

Maggie was shocked. She stared up at the woman she'd caused so much trouble for and felt sick to her stomach. Nobody else cared if she starved. It was ironic that her worst enemy was concerned about her.

Her big blue eyes stared helplessly up at Antonia.

"Aren't you hungry?" Antonia persisted.

Maggie shrugged. "I had a candy bar," she said, avoiding those soft gray eyes.

Antonia came into the stall and settled down beside the calf in the soft, clean hay. She touched the calf's soft nose and smiled. "Their noses are so soft, aren't they?" she asked. "When I was a little girl, I used to wish I had a pet, but my mother was allergic to fur, so we couldn't have a dog or cat."

Maggie fidgeted. "We don't have dogs and cats. Mrs. Bates says animals are dirty."

"Not if they're groomed."

Maggie shrugged again.

Antonia smoothed the calf's forehead. "Do you like cattle?"

Maggie watched her warily. Then she nodded. "I know all about Herefords and black Angus. That's what my daddy raises. I know about birth weights and weight gain ratios and stuff."

Antonia's eyebrows arched. "Really? Does he know?"

Maggie's eyes fell. "It wouldn't matter. He hates me on account of I'm like my mother."

Antonia was surprised that the child was that perceptive. "But your mother did have wonderful qualities," Antonia said. "When we were in school, she was my best friend."

Maggie stared at her. "She married my daddy instead of you."

Antonia's hand stilled on the calf. "Yes. She told a lie, Maggie," she explained. "Because she loved your daddy very much."

"She didn't like me," Maggie said dully. "She used to hit me when he wasn't home and say it was my fault that she was unhappy."

"Maggie, it wasn't your fault," Antonia said firmly.

Maggie's blue eyes met hers. "Nobody wants me here," she said stiffly. "Now that you're here, Daddy will make me go away!"

"Over my dead body," Antonia said shortly.

The child sat there like a little statue, as if she didn't believe what she'd heard. "You don't like me."

"You're Powell's little girl," she replied. "I love him very much. How could I possibly hate someone who's part of him?"

For the first time, the fear in the child's eyes was visible. "You don't want to make me go away?"

"Certainly not," Antonia said.

She nibbled on her lower lip. "They don't want me here," she muttered, nodding her head curtly toward the house. "Daddy goes off and leaves me all the time, and she," she added in a wounded tone, "hates having to stay with me. It was better when I could stay with Julie, but she hates me, too, on account of I got you fired."

Antonia's heart went out to the child. She wondered if in all her life any adult had taken the time to sit down and really talk to her. Perhaps Mrs. Donalds had, and that was why Maggie missed her so much.

"You're very young to try to understand this," she told Maggie slowly. "But inadvertently it was because I lost my job that I went back to the doctor and discovered that I didn't have cancer. Your dad made me go to the doctor," she added with a reflective smile. "He came after me when I left. If he hadn't, I don't know what might have happened to me. Things seem fated sometimes, to me," she added thoughtfully. "You know, as if they're meant to happen. We blame people for playing their part in the scheme of things, and we shouldn't. Life is a test, Maggie. We have obstacles to overcome, to make us stronger." She hesitated. "Is any of this making sense to you?"

"You mean God tests us," the child said softly.

Antonia smiled. "Yes. Does your dad take you to church?"

She shrugged and looked away. "He doesn't take me anywhere."

And it hurt, Antonia thought, because she was beginning to understand just how much this child was enduring. "I like going to church," she said. "My grandparents helped build the Methodist Church where I went when I was little. Would you…" She hesitated, not wanting to lose ground by rushing the child.

Maggie turned her head and looked at her. "Would I…?" she prompted softly.

"Would you like to go to church with me some-times?"

The change the question made in that sullen face was remarkable. It softened, brightened, with interest. "Just you and me?" she asked.

"At first. Your dad might come with us, eventually."

She hesitated, toying with a piece of wheat straw. "You aren't mad at me anymore?" she asked.

Antonia shook her head.

"He won't mind?"

She smiled. "No."

"Well..." She shifted and then she frowned, glancing up at the woman with sad eyes. "Well, I would like to," she said. "But I can't."

"Can't? Why not?"

Maggie's shoulders hunched forward. "I don't got a dress."

Tears stung Antonia's gray eyes. Hadn't Powell noticed? Hadn't anybody noticed?

"Oh, my dear," she said huskily, grimacing.

The note in her voice got the child's attention. She saw the glitter of tears in the woman's eyes and felt terrible.

"Antonia!"

The deep voice echoed through the barn. Powell saw them together and strode forward.

"What the hell are you doing out of bed?" he demanded, lifting her to her feet with firm hands. He saw the tears and his face hardened as he turned to the child on her knees by the calf. "She's crying. What did you say to her?" he demanded.

"Powell, no!" She put her hand across his lips. "No! She didn't make me cry!"

"You're defending her!"

"Maggie," Antonia said gently, "you tell your dad what you just told me. Don't be afraid," she added firmly. "Tell him."

Maggie gave him a belligerent glare. "I don't got a dress," she said accusingly.

"Don't have a dress," Antonia corrected her belatedly.

"I don't have a dress," Maggie said obligingly.

"So?" he asked.

"I want to take her to church with me. She doesn't have anything to wear," Antonia told him.

He looked down at his daughter with dawning realization. "You haven't got a dress?"

"No, I don't!" Maggie returned.

He let out a heavy breath. "My God."

"Tomorrow after school you and I are going shopping," Antonia told the child.

"You and me?" Maggie asked.

"Yes."

Powell stared from one of them to the other with open curiosity. Maggie got to her feet and brushed herself off. She looked up at Antonia warily. "I read this fairy tale about a woman who married a man with two little kids and she took them off and lost them in the forest."

Antonia chuckled. "I couldn't lose you, Maggie," she told the child. "Julie told me that you could track like a hunter."

"She did?"

"Who taught you how to track?" Powell demanded.

Maggie glared at him. "Nobody. I read it in a Boy Scout manual. Jake loaned me his."

"Why didn't you ask your dad to buy you one of your own?" she asked the child.

Maggie glared at him again. "He wouldn't," she said. "He brings me dolls."

Antonia's eyebrows lifted. She looked at Powell curiously. "Dolls?"

"She's a girl, isn't she?" he demanded belligerently.

"I hate dolls," Maggie muttered. "I like books."

"Yes, I noticed," Antonia said.

Powell felt like an idiot. "You never said," he muttered at his daughter.

She moved a little closer to Antonia. "You never asked," she replied. She brushed at the filthy sweatshirt where wheat straw was sticking to it.

"You look like a rag doll," Powell said. "You need a bath and a change of clothes."

"I don't got no more clothes," she said miserably. "Mrs. Bates said she wouldn't wash them because I got them too dirty to get clean."

"What?"

"She threw away my last pair of blue jeans," Maggie continued, "and this is the only sweatshirt I got left."

"Oh, Maggie," Antonia said heavily. "Maggie, why didn't you tell her you didn't have any other clothes?"

"Because she won't listen," the child said. "Nobody listens!" She looked at her father with his own scowl. "When I grow up, I'm going to leave home and never come back! And when I have little kids, I'm going to love them!"

Powell was at a complete loss for words. He couldn't even manage to speak.

"Go and have a bath," Antonia told the child gently. "Have you a gown and robe?"

"I got pajamas. I hid them or she'd have throwed them away, too," she added mutinously.

"Then put them on. I'll bring up your supper."

Powell started to speak, but she put her hand over his mouth again.

"Go ahead, Maggie," she urged the child.

Maggie nodded and with another majestic glare at her father, she stalked off down the aisle.

"Oh, she's yours, all right," Antonia mused when she'd gone out of the barn and they were alone. "Same scowl, same impatient attitude, same temper, same glare…"

He felt uncomfortable. "I didn't know she didn't have any damned clothes," he said.

"Now you do. I'm going to take her shopping to buy new ones."

"You aren't in any shape to go shopping or to carry trays of food," he muttered. "I'll do it."

"You'll take her shopping?" she asked with mischief twinkling in her gray eyes.

"I can take a kid to a dress shop," he said belligerently.

"I'm sure you can," she agreed. "It's just the shock of having you volunteer to do it, that's all."

"I'm not volunteering," he said. "I'm protecting you."

She brightened. "Was that why? You sweet man, you."

She reached up and kissed him softly, lingeringly, on his hard mouth. He only resisted for a split second. Then he lifted her clear off the ground, and kissed her with muted hunger, careful not to make any more demands on her than she was ready for. He turned and carried her down the aisle, smiling at her warmly between kisses.

* * *

Mrs. Bates was standing in the middle of the floor looking perplexed when they walked in, although she smiled at the sight of the boss with his wife in his arms.

"Carrying her over the threshold?" she teased Powell.

"Sparing her tired legs," he corrected. "Did Maggie go through here?"

"Indeed she did," Mrs. Bates said with a rueful smile. "I'm a wicked witch because I threw away the only clothes she had and now she has to go shopping for more."

"That's about the size of it," he agreed, smiling at Antonia.

"I didn't know," Mrs. Bates said.

"Neither did I," replied Powell.

They both looked at Antonia.

"I'm a schoolteacher," she reminded them. "I'm used to children."

"I guess I don't know anything," Powell said with a heavy sigh.

"You'll learn."

"How about taking a tray up to Maggie?" Powell asked Mrs. Bates.

"It's the least I can do," the older woman said sheepishly. "I'll never live that down. But you can't imagine the shape those jeans were in. And the sweatshirts!"

"I'm taking her shopping tomorrow after school," Powell said. "We'll get some new stuff for her to wear out."

Mrs. Bates was fascinated. In all the years she'd worked here, Powell Long hadn't taken his daughter anywhere if she wasn't in trouble.

"I know," he said, reading the look accurately. "But there has to be a first step."

Mrs. Bates nodded. "I guess so. For both of us."

Antonia just smiled. Progress at last!

Powell felt out of place in the children's boutique. The saleslady was very helpful, but Maggie didn't know what to get and neither did he.

They looked at each other helplessly.

"Well, what do you want to buy?" he demanded.

She glared at him. "I don't know!"

"If I could suggest some things," the saleslady intervened diplomatically.

Powell left her to it. He couldn't imagine that clothes were going to do much for his sullen child, but Antonia had insisted that it would make a difference if he went with her. So far, he didn't see any difference.

But when the child went into the dressing room with the saleslady and reappeared five minutes later, he stared at her as if he didn't recognize her.

She was wearing a ruffled pink dress with lace at the throat, a short-skirted little thing with white leggings and patent leather shoes. Her hair was neatly brushed and a frilly ribbon sat at a jaunty angle in it beside her ear.

"Maggie?" he asked, just to be sure.

The look on her dad's face was like a miracle. He seemed surprised by the way she looked. In fact, he smiled. She smiled back. And the change the expression made in her little face was staggering.

For the first time, he saw himself in the child. The eyes were the wrong color, but they were the same shape as his own. Her nose was going to be straight like his—

well, like his used to be before he got it broken in a fight. Her mouth was thin and wide like his, her cheekbones high.

Sally had lied about this, too, about Maggie not being his. He'd never been so certain of anything.

He lifted an ironic eyebrow. "Well, well, from ugly duckling to swan," he mused. "You look pretty."

Maggie's heart swelled. Her blue eyes sparkled. Her lips drew up and all at once she laughed, a gurgle of sound that hit Powell right in the heart. He had never heard her laugh. The impact of it went right through him and he seemed to see down the years with eyes full of sorrow and regret. This child had never had a chance at happiness. He'd subconsciously blamed her for Sally's betrayal, for the loss of Antonia. He'd never been a proper father to her in all her life. He wondered if it was going to be too late to start now.

The laughter had changed Maggie's whole appearance. He laughed at the difference.

"Hell," he said under his breath. "How about something blue, to match her eyes?" he asked the saleslady. "And some colorful jeans, not those old dark blue things she's been wearing."

"Yes, sir," the saleslady said enthusiastically.

Maggie pirouetted in front of the full-length mirror, surprised to see that she didn't look the way she usually did. The dress made her almost pretty. She wondered if Jake would ever get to see her in it, and her eyes brightened even more. Now that Antonia was back, maybe everyone would stop hating her.

But Antonia was sick, and she wouldn't be teaching. And that was still Maggie's fault.

"What's the matter?" Powell asked gently. He went

down on one knee in front of the child, frowning. "What's wrong?"

Maggie was surprised that he was concerned, that he'd even noticed her sudden sadness. He didn't, usually.

She lifted her eyes to his. "Miss Hayes won't be teaching. It's still my fault."

"Antonia." He corrected her. "She isn't Miss Hayes anymore."

A thought occurred to her. "Is she…my mom, now?"

"Your stepmother," he said tersely.

She moved closer. Hesitantly she reached out and put her hand on his shoulder. It barely touched and then rested, like a butterfly looking for a place to light. "Now that she's back, you don't…hate me anymore, do you?" she asked softly.

His face contorted. With a rough sound, deep in his throat, he swept her close and held her, standing with her in his arms. He hugged her and rocked her, and she clung to him with a sound like a muffled sob.

"Please don't…hate me…anymore!" She wept. "I love you, Daddy!"

"Oh, dear God," Powell whispered huskily, his eyes closed as he weighed his sins. His arms contracted. "I don't hate you," he said curtly. "God knows, I never hated you, Maggie!"

She laid her head on his shoulder and closed her own eyes, savoring the newness of a father's arms, a father's comfort. This was something she'd never known. It was so nice, being hugged. She smiled through her tears.

"Say," he said after a minute, "this is nice."

She gurgled.

He put her down and looked into her uplifted face. Tears were streaming down it, but she was smiling.

He dug in his pocket and cursed under his breath. "Hell. I never carry handkerchiefs," he said apologetically.

She wiped her eyes on the back of her hands. "Me, neither," she said.

The saleslady came back with an armload of dresses. "I found a blue suit," she said gaily, "and another skirt and top in blue."

"They're very pretty!" Maggie said enthusiastically.

"Indeed they are. Why don't you try them on?" he said invitingly.

"Okay!"

She danced off with the saleslady and he watched, astonished. That was his child. He had a very pretty daughter, and she loved him in spite of all the mistakes he'd made. He smiled reflectively. Well, well, and they said miracles didn't happen. He felt in the middle of one right now. And somehow, it all went back to Antonia, a cycle that had begun and ended with her in his life. He smiled as he thought about the process that had brought them, finally, together and made such a vital change in the way things had been. He glanced at himself in the mirror and wondered where the bitter, hard man he'd been only weeks before, had gone.

Chapter 11

Maggie ran into Antonia's bedroom ahead of her father, wearing the blue dress and leggings and new shoes.

She came to a sudden stop at the side of the bed and seemed to become suddenly shy as she looked at the pink-clad woman in the bed. Antonia's blond hair was around her shoulders and she was wearing a pink lacy gown with an equally lacy bed jacket. She looked fragile, but she also looked welcoming, because she smiled.

"Oh, how nice," Antonia said at once, wondering at the change in the child. "How very nice! You look like a different girl, Maggie!"

Maggie felt breathless. "Daddy got me five new outfits and jeans and shirts and sweatshirts and shoes," she sputtered. "And he hugged me!"

Antonia's face lit up. "He did?"

Maggie smiled shyly. "Yeah, he did!" She laughed. "I think he likes me!"

"I think he does, too," Antonia said in a loud whisper.

Maggie had something in her hand. She hesitated, glancing warily at Antonia. "Me and Daddy got you something," she said shyly.

"You did?" she asked, too surprised to correct the child's grammar.

Maggie moved forward and put it into Antonia's hands. "It plays a song."

It was a small box. Antonia unwrapped it and opened it. Inside was a music box, a fragile, porcelain-topped miniature brass piano that, when wound and opened, played "Clair de Lune."

"Oh," she exclaimed. "I've never had anything so lovely!"

Maggie smiled crookedly.

"Did your dad pick it out?" she asked, entranced by the music.

Maggie's face fell.

Antonia saw the expression and could have hit herself for what she'd asked. "You picked it out, didn't you?" she asked immediately, and watched the child's face brighten again. She would have to be careful not to do any more damage to that fragile self-esteem. "What wonderful taste you have, Maggie. Thank you!"

Maggie smiled. "You're welcome."

Powell came in the door, grinning when he saw Antonia with the music box. "Like it?" he asked.

"I love it," she replied. "I'll treasure it, always," she added with a warm glance at Maggie.

Maggie actually blushed.

"You'd better put your clothes away," Powell said.

Maggie winced at the authority in his tone, but when she looked up at him, he wasn't angry or impatient. He was smiling.

Her eyes widened. She smiled back. "Okay, Dad!"

She glanced again at Antonia and darted out the door.

"I hear we're handing out hugs today," Antonia murmured dryly.

He chuckled. "Yes, we are. I could get to like that."

"She could, too."

"How about you?" he asked with a speculative glance.

She held out her arms. "Why don't you come down here and find out?"

He laughed softly as he tossed his hat into the chair and eased down on the bed beside her, his arms on either side of her to balance him. She reached up to draw him down, smiling under the warm, slow crush of his mouth.

He kissed her hungrily, but with a tenderness she remembered from their early days together. She loved the warmth of his kisses, the feel of his body against her. She writhed under his weight suggestively and felt him tense.

"No," he whispered, easing to one side.

She sighed wistfully. "Heartless man."

"It's for your own good," he said, teasing her lips with his forefinger. "I want you to get well."

"I'm trying."

He smiled and bent to nuzzle her nose against his. "Maggie looks pretty in blue," he murmured.

"Yes, she does." She searched his black eyes. "You noticed, didn't you?"

"Noticed what?"

"How much she favors you. I saw it when she smiled. She has the same wrinkles in her face that you have in yours when you smile. Of course, she has your nasty temper, too."

"Curses with the blessings." He chuckled. His eyes searched hers and he drew in a heavy breath. "I never dreamed when I went off to Arizona to find you that it would end up like this."

"Is that a complaint?"

"What do you think?" he murmured and kissed her again.

He carried her down to the table, and for the first time, he and Antonia and Maggie had a meal together. Maggie was nervous, fidgeting with the utensils because she didn't know which one to use.

"There's plenty of time to learn that," Powell said when he saw her unease. "You aren't under the microscope, you know. I thought it might be nice to have a meal together for a change."

Maggie looked from one adult to the other. "You aren't going to send me away, are you?" she asked her father.

"Idiot," he muttered, glaring at her.

She glared right back. "Well, you didn't like me," she reminded him.

"I didn't know you," he replied. "I still don't. That's my fault, but it's going to change. You and I need to spend more time together. So suppose instead of riding the bus, I take you to and from school all the time?"

She was elated and then disappointed. Jake rode the bus. If she didn't, she wouldn't get to see him.

Powell didn't know about Jake. He scowled even more at her hesitation.

"I'd like to," Maggie said. She blushed. "But…"

Antonia remembered what Julie had told her. "Is there someone who rides the bus that you don't want to miss seeing?" she asked gently, and the blush went nuclear.

Powell pursed his lips. "So that's it," he said, and chuckled. "Do I know this lucky young man who's caught my daughter's eye?"

"Oh, Daddy!" Maggie groaned.

"Never mind. You can go on riding the bus," he said, with a wicked glance at Antonia. "But you might like to come out with me some Saturdays when I'm checking up on my cattle operation."

"I'd like to do that," Maggie said. "I want to know about your weight gain ratios and heritability factors."

Powell's fork fell from his fingers and made a clanging noise against his plate. To hear those terms coming from a nine-year-old floored him.

Maggie saw that, and grinned. "I like to read about cattle, too. He's got these herd books," she explained to Antonia, "and they have all the statistics on proper genetic breeding. Do you breed genetically, Daddy?"

"Good God," he said on a heavy breath. "She's a cattleman."

"Yes, she is," Antonia agreed. "Surprise, surprise. Speaking of genetics, I wonder who she inherited that from?"

He looked sheepish, but he grinned from ear to ear. "Yes, I do breed genetically," he told his daughter. "If you're that interested, I'll take you around the operation and show you the traits I'm breeding for."

"Like easy calving and low birth weight?" Maggie asked.

Powell let out another breath, staring at his daughter with pure admiration. "And here I was worried that I wouldn't have anyone to leave the ranch to."

Antonia burst out laughing. "It looks as if you're going to leave it in the right hands," she agreed, glancing warmly at Maggie.

Maggie blushed and beamed, all at once. She was still in shell shock from the sudden change of her life. She owed that to Antonia. It was like coming out of the darkness into the sunshine.

Antonia felt the same when she looked at her ready-made family.

"That reminds me," she said. "Your granddad would like to take you with him on an antique-buying binge next weekend. He's going to drive over to an auction in Sheridan."

"But I don't got a granddad," Maggie said, perplexed.

"Don't have," Antonia corrected her. She smiled. "And yes, you do have one. My father."

"A real granddaddy of my own?" Maggie asked, putting down her fork. "Does he know me?"

"You went to see him with your dad. Don't you remember?"

"He lived in a big white house. Oh, yes." Her face brightened, and then it fell. "I was scared and I didn't speak to him. He won't like me."

"He likes you very much," Antonia said. "And he'll enjoy teaching you about antiques, if you'd like to learn. It's his hobby."

"That would be fun!"

"I can see that you're going to be much in demand

from now on, Maggie," Antonia said, smiling. "Will you mind?"

Maggie shook her head. She smiled a little unsteadily. "Oh, no, I won't mind at all!"

Antonia was half asleep when Powell slid into bed beside her with a long sigh and stretched.

"She beat me," he said.

Antonia rolled over, pillowing her head on his bare, hair-roughened chest. "At what?" she murmured drowsily.

"Checkers. I still don't see how she set me up." He yawned. "God, I'm sleepy!"

"So am I." She curved closer. "Good night."

"Good night."

She smiled as she slipped back into oblivion, thinking as she did how lucky they were to have each other. Powell had changed so much. He might not love her as she loved him, but he seemed very content. And Maggie was friendly enough. It would take time, but she felt very much at home here already. Things looked bright.

The next morning, she was afraid she'd spoken too soon. Maggie went off to school, and Powell went to a cattle sale, leaving Antonia at home by herself on what was Mrs. Bates's day off. The persistent ringing of the doorbell got her out of bed, and she went downstairs in a long white robe, still half asleep, to answer it.

The woman standing on the other side of the door came as a total shock.

If Antonia was taken aback, so was the gorgeous redhead gaping at her with dark green eyes.

"Who are you?" she demanded haughtily.

Antonia looked her over. Elegant gray suit, pink camisole a little too low-cut, short skirt and long legs. Nice legs. Nice figure. But a little ripe, she thought wickedly. The woman was at least five years older than she was; perhaps more.

"I'm Mrs. Powell Long," Antonia replied with equal hauteur. "What can I do for you?"

The woman just stared at her. "You're joking!"

"I'm not joking." Antonia straightened. "What do you want?"

"I came to see Powell. On a private matter," she added with a cold smile.

"My husband and I don't have secrets," Antonia said daringly.

"Really? Then you know that he's been at my house every night working out the details of a merger, don't you?"

Antonia didn't know how to answer that. Powell had been working late each night, but she'd never thought it was anything other than business. Now, she didn't know. She was insecure, despite Powell's hunger for her. Desire wasn't love, and this woman was more beautiful than any that Antonia had ever seen.

"Powell won't be home until late," Antonia said evasively.

"Well, in that case, I won't wait," the redhead murmured.

"Can I take a message?"

"Yes. Tell him Leslie Holton called to see him," she replied. "I'll, uh, be in touch, if he asks. And I'm sure he will." Her cold eyes traveled down Antonia's thin body and back up again with faint contempt. "There's really no understanding the male mind, is there?" she mused aloud and with a nod, turned and walked back to her late-model Cadillac.

Antonia watched her get in it and drive away. The woman even drove with an attitude, haughty and efficient. She wished and wished that the car would run over four big nails and have all four tires go flat at once. But to her disappointment, the car glided out of sight without a single wobble.

So that was the widow Holton, who was trying to get her claws into Dawson Rutherford and Powell. Had she succeeded with Powell? She seemed very confident. And she was certainly lovely. Obviously he hadn't been serious about marrying the widow, but had there been something between them?

Antonia found herself feeling uncertain and insecure. She didn't have the beauty or sophistication to compete with a woman like that. Powell did want her, certainly, but that woman would know all the tricks of seduction. What if she and Powell had been lovers? What if they still were? Antonia hadn't been up to bouts of lovemaking, since that one long night she'd spent with Powell. Was abstinence making him desperate? He'd teased her about not being able to go without a woman for long periods of time, and he'd said years, not weeks. But was he telling the truth or just sparing Antonia's feelings? She had to find out.

Late that afternoon, another complication presented itself. Julie Ames came home with Maggie and proceeded to make herself useful, tidying up Antonia's bedroom and fluffing up her pillows. She'd come in with a bouquet of flowers, too, and she'd rushed up to hug Antonia at once, all loving concern and friendliness.

Maggie reacted to this as she always had, by withdrawing, and Antonia wanted so badly to tell her that Julie didn't mean to hurt her.

"I'll go get a vase," Maggie said miserably, turning.

"I'll bet Julie wouldn't mind doing that," Antonia said, surprising both girls. "Would you?" she asked Julie. "You could ask Mrs. Bates to find you one and put water in it."

"I'd be happy to, Mrs. Long!" Julie said enthusiastically, and rushed out to do as she was asked.

Antonia smiled at Maggie, who was still staring at her in a puzzled way.

"Whose idea was it to pick the flowers?" she asked knowingly.

Maggie flushed. "Well, it was mine, sort of."

"Yes, I thought so. And Julie got the credit, and it hurt."

Maggie was surprised. "Yes," she admitted absently.

"I'm not as dim as you think I am," she told Maggie. "Just try to remember one thing, will you? You're my daughter. You belong here."

Maggie's heart leaped. She smiled hesitantly.

"Or I'm your stepmother, if you'd rather…"

She moved closer to the bed. "I'd rather call you Mom," she said slowly. "If…you don't mind."

Antonia smiled gently. "No, Maggie. I don't mind. I'd be very, very flattered."

Maggie sighed. "My mother didn't want me," she said in a world-weary way. "I thought it was my fault, that there was something wrong with me."

"There's nothing wrong with you, darling," Antonia said gently. "You're fine just the way you are."

Maggie fought back tears. "Thanks."

"Something's still wrong, isn't it?" she asked softly. "Can you tell me?"

Maggie looked at her feet. "Julie hugged you."

"I like being hugged."

She looked up. "You do?"

She smiled, nodding.

Maggie hesitated, but Antonia opened her arms, and the child went into them like a homing pigeon. It was incredible, this warm feeling she got from being close to people. First her own dad had hugged her, and now Antonia had. She couldn't remember a time when anyone had wanted to hug her.

She smiled against Antonia's warm shoulder and sighed.

Antonia's arms contracted. "I do like being hugged."

Maggie chortled. "So do I."

Antonia let her go with a smile. "Well, we'll both have to put in some practice, and your dad will, too. You're very pretty when you smile," she observed.

"Here's the vase!" Julie said, smiling as she came in with it. She glanced at Maggie, who was beaming. "Gosh, you look different lately."

"I got new clothes," Maggie said pointedly.

"No. You smile a lot." Julie chuckled. "Jake said you looked like that actress on his favorite TV show, and he was sort of shocked. Didn't you see him staring at you in class today?"

"He never!" Maggie exclaimed, embarrassed. "Did he?" she added hopefully.

"He sure did! The other boys teased him. He didn't even get mad. He just sort of grinned."

Maggie's heart leaped. She looked at Antonia with eyes brimming with joy and discovery.

Antonia felt that same wonder. She couldn't ever regret marrying Powell, regardless of how it all ended up. She thought of the widow Holton and grew cold inside. But she didn't let the girls see it. She only smiled, listening to their friendly discussion with half an ear, while she wondered what Powell was going to say when she told him about their early-morning visitor.

He said nothing at all, as it turned out. And that made it worse. He only watched her through narrowed black eyes when she mentioned it, oh, so carelessly, as they prepared for bed that night.

"She didn't tell me what she wanted to discuss with you. She said that it was personal. I told her I'd give you the message. She did say that she'd be in touch." She peered up at him.

His hard face didn't soften. He searched her eyes, looking for signs of jealousy, but none were there. She'd given him the bare bones of Leslie's visit with no emotion at all. Surely if he meant anything to her, it would have mattered that he was carrying on private, personal discussions with another woman. And Leslie's name had been linked with his in past years. She must have known that, too.

"Was that all?" he asked.

She shrugged. "All that I remember." She smiled. "She's a knockout, isn't she?" she added generously. "Her hair is long and thick and wavy. I've never seen a human being with hair like that…it's almost alive. Does she model?"

"She was a motion picture actress until the death of her husband. She was tired of the pace so when she inherited his fortune, she gave it up."

"Isn't it boring for her here, in such a small community?"

"She spends a lot of time chasing Dawson Rutherford."

That was discouraging, for Barrie, anyway. Antonia wondered if Barrie knew about her stepbrother's contact with the woman. Then she remembered what her father had said about Dawson.

"Does he like her?" she asked curiously.

"He likes her land," he replied. "We're both trying to get her to sell a tract that separates his border from mine. Her property has a river running right through it. If he gets his hands on it, I'll have an ongoing court battle over water rights, and vice versa."

"So it really is business," she blurted out.

He cocked an eyebrow. "I didn't say that was all it was," he replied softly, mockingly. "Rutherford is a cold fish with women, and Leslie is, how can I put it, overstimulated."

Her breath caught in her throat. "How overstimulated is she?" she demanded suddenly. "And by whom?"

He pursed his lips and toyed with his sleeve. "My past is none of your concern."

She glared at him and sat upright in the bed. "Are you sleeping with her?"

His eyebrows jumped up. "What?"

"You heard me!" she snapped. "I asked if you were

so determined to get that land that you'd forsake your marriage vows to accomplish it!"

"Is that what you think?" he asked, and he looked vaguely threatening.

"Why else would she come here to the house to see you?" she asked. "And at a time when she knew you were usually home and Maggie was in school?"

"You're really unsettled about this, aren't you? What did she say to you?"

"She said you'd been at her house every evening when you were supposedly working late," she muttered sharply. "And she acted as if I were the interloper, not her."

"She wanted to marry me," he remarked, digging the knife in deeper.

"Well, you married me," she said angrily. "And I'm not going to be cuckolded!"

"Antonia! What a word!"

"You know what I mean!"

"I hope I do," he said quietly, searching her furious eyes. "Why don't you explain it to me?"

"I wish I had a bottle, I'd explain it," she raged at him, "right over your hard head!"

His dark eyes widened with humor. "You're so jealous you can't see straight," he said, chuckling.

"Of that skinny redheaded cat?" she retorted.

He moved closer to the bed, still grinning. "Meow."

She glared at him, her fists clenched on the covers. "I'm twice the woman she is!"

He cocked one eyebrow. "Are you up to proving it?" he challenged softly.

Her breath came in sharp little whispers. "You go lock that door. I'll show you a few things."

He laughed with sheer delight. He locked the door and turned out the top light, turning back toward the bed.

She was standing beside it by then, and while he watched, she slid her negligee and gown down her arms to the floor.

"Well?" she asked huskily. "I may be a little thinner than I like, but I…"

He was against her before she could finish, his arms encircling her, his mouth hungry and insistent on her lips. She yielded at once, no argument, no protest.

He laid her down and quickly divested himself of everything he was wearing.

"Wait a minute," she protested weakly, "I'm supposed to be…proving something."

"Go ahead," he said invitingly as his mouth opened on her soft breast and his hands found new territory to explore.

She tried to speak, but it ended on a wild little cry. She arched up to him and her nails bit into his lean hips. By the time his mouth shifted back to hers and she felt the hungry pressure of his body over her, she couldn't even manage a sound.

Later, storm-tossed and damp all over from the exertion, she lay panting and trembling in his arms, so drained by pleasure that she couldn't even coordinate her body.

"You were too weak," he accused lazily, tracing her mouth with a lazy finger as he arched over her. "I shouldn't have done that."

"Yes, you should," she whispered huskily, drawing his mouth down over hers. "It was beautiful."

"Indeed it was." He smiled against her lips. "I hope

you were serious about wanting children. I meant to stop by the drugstore, but I forgot."

She laughed. "I love children, and we've only got one so far."

He lifted his head and searched her eyes. "You've changed her."

"She's changed me. And you." Her arms tightened around his neck. "We're a family. I've never been so happy. And from now on, it will only get better."

He nodded. "She's very forgiving," he replied. "I've got to earn back the trust I lost along the way. I'm ashamed for what I've put her through."

"Life is all lessons," she said. "She's got you now. She'll have sisters and brothers to spoil, too." Her eyes warmed him. "I love you."

He traced the soft line of her cheek. "I've loved you for most of my life," he said simply, shocking her, because he'd never said the words before. "I couldn't manage to tell you. Funny, isn't it? I didn't realize what I had until I lost it." His eyes darkened. "I wouldn't have wanted to live, if you hadn't."

"Powell," she whispered brokenly.

He kissed away the tears. "And you thought I wanted the widow Holton!"

"Well, she's skinny, but she is pretty."

"Only on the outside. You're beautiful clean through, especially when you're being Maggie's mom."

She smiled. "That's because I love Maggie's dad so much," she whispered.

"And he loves you," he whispered back, bending. "Outrageously."

"Is that so?" she teased. "Prove it."

He groaned. "The spirit is willing, but you've worn

out the flesh. Besides," he added softly, "you aren't up to long sessions just yet. I promise when you're completely well, I'll take you to the Bahamas and we'll see if we can make the world record book."

"Fair enough," she said. She held him close and closed her eyes, aglow with the glory of loving and being loved.

Chapter 12

The new teacher for Maggie's class found a co-operative, happy little girl as ready to help as Julie Ames was. And Maggie came home each day with a new outlook and joy in being with her parents. There were long evenings with new movies in front of the fire, and books to look at, and parties, because Antonia arranged them and invited all the kids Maggie liked— especially Jake.

Powell had done some slowing down, although he was still an arch rival of Dawson Rutherford's over that strip of land the widow Holton was dangling between them.

"She's courting him," Powell muttered one evening. "That's the joke of the century. The man's ice clean through. He avoids women like the plague, but she's angling for a weekend with him."

"Yes, I know. I spoke to Barrie last week. She said he's tried to get her to come home and chaperone him, but they had a terrible fight over it and now they're not speaking at all. Barrie's jealous of her, I think."

"Poor kid," he replied, drawing Antonia closer. "There's nothing to be jealous of. Rutherford doesn't like women."

"He doesn't like men, either."

He chuckled. "Me, especially. I know. What I meant was that he's not interested in sexual escapades, even with lovely widows. He just wants land and cattle."

"Women are much more fun," she teased, snuggling close.

"Barrie might try showing him that."

"She'd never have the nerve."

"Barrie? Are we talking about the same woman who entertained three admirers at once at dinner?"

"Dawson is different," she replied. "He matters."

"I begin to see the light."

She closed her eyes with a sigh. "He's a nice man," she said. "You don't like him because of his father, but he's not as ruthless as George was."

He stiffened. "Let's not talk about George."

She lifted away and looked at him. "You don't still believe…!"

"Of course not," he said immediately. "I meant that the Rutherfords have been a thorn in my side for years, in a business sense. Dawson and I will never be friends."

"Never is a long time. Barrie is my friend."

"And a good one," he agreed.

"Yes, well, I think she might end up with Dawson one day."

"They're related," he said shortly.

"They are not. His father married her mother."

"He hates her, and vice versa."

"I wonder," Antonia said quietly. "That sort of dislike is suspicious, isn't it? I mean, you avoid people you really dislike. He's always making some excuse to see Barrie and give her hell."

"She gives it right back," he reminded her.

"She has to. A man like that will run right over a woman unless she stands up to him." She curled her fingers into his. "You're like that, too," she added, searching his black eyes quietly. "A gentle woman could never cope with you."

"As Sally found out," he agreed. His fingers contracted. "There's something about our marriage that I never told you. I think it's time I did. Maggie was born two months premature. I didn't sleep with Sally until after I broke our engagement. And I was so drunk that I thought you'd come back to me," he added quietly. "You can't imagine how sick I felt when I woke up with her the next morning and realized what I'd done. And it was too late to put it right."

She didn't say anything. She swallowed down the pain. "I see."

"I was cruel, Antonia," he said heavily. "Cruel and thoughtless. But I paid for it. Sadly, Sally and Maggie paid with me, and so did you." He searched her eyes. "From now on, baby, if you tell me green is orange, I'll believe it. I wanted to tell you that from the day you came back to your father's house and I saw you there."

"You made cutting remarks instead."

He smiled ruefully. "It hurts to see what you've lost," he replied. "I loved you to the soles of your feet, and I couldn't tell you. I thought you hated me."

"Part of me did."

"And then I found out why you'd really come here to teach," he said. "I wanted to die."

She went into his arms and nuzzled closer to him. "You mustn't look back," she said. "It's over now. I'm safe, and so are you, and so is Maggie."

"My Maggie," he sighed, smiling. "She's a hell of a cattlewoman already."

"She's your daughter."

"Mmm. Yes, she is. I'm glad I finally realized that Sally had lied about that. There are too many similarities."

"Far too many." She smiled against his chest. "It's been six weeks since that night I offered to prove I was more of a woman than the widow Holton," she reminded him.

"So it has."

She drew away a little, her eyes searching his while a secret smile touched her lips. But he wasn't waiting for surprises. His lean hand pressed softly against her flat stomach and he smiled back, all of heaven in his dark eyes.

"You know?" she whispered softly.

"I sleep with you every night," he replied. "And I make love to you most every one. I'm not numb. And," he added, "you've lost your breakfast for the past week."

"I wanted to surprise you."

"Go ahead," he suggested.

She glared at him. "I'm pregnant," she said.

He jumped up, clasped his hands over his heart and gave her such a look of wonder that she burst out laughing.

"Are you, truly?" he exclaimed. "My God!"

She was all but rolling on the floor from his exaggerated glee. Mrs. Bates stuck her head in the door to see what the commotion was all about.

"She's pregnant!" he told her.

"Well!" Mrs. Bates exclaimed. "Really?"

"The home test I took says I am," she replied. "I still have to go to the doctor to have it confirmed."

"Yes," Powell said. "And the results from this test won't be frightening."

She agreed wholeheartedly.

They told Maggie that afternoon. She was apprehensive when they called her into the living room. Things had been so wonderful lately. Perhaps they'd changed their minds about her, and she was going to be sent off to school…

"Antonia is pregnant," Powell said softly.

Maggie's eyes lit up. "Oh, is that it!" she said, relieved. "I thought it was going to be something awful. You mean we're going to have a real baby of our own?" She hugged Antonia warmly and snuggled close to her on the sofa. "Julie will be just green, just green with envy!" she said, laughing. "Can I hold him when he's born, and help you take care of him? I can get books about babies…."

Antonia was laughing with pure delight. "Yes, you can help," she said. "I thought it might be too soon, that you'd be unhappy about it."

"Silly old Mom," Maggie said with a frown. "I'd love a baby brother. It's going to be a boy, isn't it?"

Powell chuckled. "I like girls, too," he said.

Maggie grinned at him. "You only like me on account of I know one end of a cow from another," she said pointedly.

"Well, you're pretty, too," he added.

She beamed. "Now, I'll have something really important to share at show and tell." She looked up. "I miss you at school. So does everybody else. Miss Tyler is nice, but you were special."

"I'll go back to teaching one day," Antonia promised. "It's like riding a bike. You never forget how."

"Shall we go over and tell your granddad?" Powell asked.

"Yes," Maggie said enthusiastically. "Right now!"

Ben was overwhelmed by the news. He sat down heavily in his easy chair and just stared at the three of them sitting smugly on his couch.

"A baby," he exclaimed. His face began to light up. "Well!"

"It's going to be a boy, Granddad," Maggie assured him. "Then you'll have somebody who'll appreciate those old electric trains you collect. I'm sorry I don't, but I like cattle."

Ben chuckled. "That's okay, imp," he told her. "Maybe some day you can help teach the baby about Queen Anne furniture."

"He likes that a lot," Maggie told the other adults. "We spend ever so much time looking at furniture."

"Well, it's fun," Ben said.

"Yes, it is," Maggie agreed, "but cattle are so much more interesting, Granddad, and it's scientific, too, isn't it, Dad?"

Powell had to agree. "She's my kid. You can tell."

"Oh, yes." Ben nodded. He smiled at the girl warmly.

Since she'd come into his life, whole new worlds had opened up for him. She came over sometimes just to help him organize his books. He had plenty, and it was another love they shared. "That reminds me. Found you something at that last sale."

He got up and produced a very rare nineteenth-century breed book. He handed it to Maggie with great care. "You look after that," he told her. "It's valuable."

"Oh, Granddad!" She went into raptures of enthusiasm.

Powell whistled through his teeth. "That's expensive, Ben."

"Maggie knows that. She'll take care of it, too," he added. "Never saw anyone take the care with books that she does. Never slams them around or leaves them lying about. She puts every one right back in its place. I'd even lend her my first editions. She's a little jewel."

Maggie heard that last remark and looked up at her grandfather with an affectionate smile. "He's teaching me how to take care of books properly," she announced.

"And she's an excellent pupil." He looked at Antonia with pure love in his eyes. "I wish your mother was here," he told her. "She'd be so happy and proud."

"I know she would. But, I think she knows, Dad," Antonia said gently. And she smiled.

That night, Antonia phoned Barrie to tell her the news. Her best friend was overjoyed.

"You have to let me know when he's born, so that I can fly up and see him."

"Him?"

"Boys are nice. You should have at least one. Then you'll have a matched set. Maggie and a boy."

"Well, I'll do my best." There was a pause. "Heard from Dawson?"

There was a cold silence. "No."

"I met the widow Holton not so long ago," Antonia remarked.

Barrie cleared her throat. "Is she old?"

"About six years older than I am," Antonia said. "Slender, redheaded, green-eyed and very glamorous."

"Dawson should be ecstatic to have her visiting every weekend."

"Barrie, Dawson really could use a little support where that woman is concerned," she said slowly. "She's hard and cold and very devious, from what I hear. You never know what she might do."

"He invited her up there," Barrie muttered. "And then had the audacity to try and get me to come play chaperone, so that people wouldn't think there was anything going on between them. As if I want to watch her paw him and fawn all over him and help him pretend it's all innocent!"

"Maybe it is innocent. Dawson doesn't like women, Barrie," she added. "They say he's, well, sexually cold."

"Dawson?"

"Dawson."

Barrie hesitated. She couldn't very well say what she was thinking, or what she was remembering.

"Are you still there?" Antonia asked.

"Yes." Barrie sighed. "It's his own fault, he wants that land so badly that he'll do anything to get it."

"I don't think he'd go this far. I think he just invited Mrs. Holton up there to talk to her, and now she thinks he had amorous intentions instead of business ones and he can't get rid of her. She strikes me as the sort who'd be hard to dissuade. She's a very pushy woman, and Dawson's very rich. It may be that she's chasing him, instead of the reverse."

"He never said that."

"Did you give him a chance to say anything?" Antonia asked.

"It's safer if I don't," Barrie muttered. "I don't know if I want to risk giving Dawson a whole weekend to spend giving me hell."

"You could try. He might have had a change of heart."

"Not likely." There was a harsh laugh. "Well, I'll call him, and if he asks me again, I'll go, but only if there are plenty of people around, not just the widow."

"Call him up and tell him that."

"I don't know…"

"He's not an ogre. He's just a man."

"Sure." She sounded unconvinced.

"Barrie, you're not a coward. Save him."

"Imagine, the iceman needing saving." She hesitated. "Who told you they called him that?"

"Just about everybody I know. He doesn't date. The widow is the first woman he's been seen with in years." Antonia's voice softened. "Curious, isn't it?"

It was, but Barrie didn't dare mention why. She had some ideas about it, and she wondered if she had enough courage to go to Sheridan and find out the truth.

"Maybe I'll go," Barrie said.

"Maybe you should," Antonia agreed, and shortly afterward, she hung up, giving Barrie plenty to think about.

Powell came to find her after she'd gotten off the

phone, smiling at her warmly. "You look pretty in pink," he remarked.

She smiled back. "Thanks."

He sat down beside her on the sofa and pulled her close. "What's wrong?"

"The widow Holton is giving Dawson a hard time."

"Good," Powell said.

She glared at him. "You might have the decency to feel sorry for the poor man. You were her target once, I believe."

"Until you stepped in and saved me, you sweet woman," he replied, and bent to kiss her warmly.

"There isn't anybody to save Dawson unless Barrie will."

"He can fight his own dragons. Or should I say dragonettes?" he mused thoughtfully.

"Aren't you still after that strip of land, too?"

"Oh, I gave up on it when we got married," he said easily. "I had an idea that she wanted more than money for it, and you were jealous enough of her already."

"I like that!" she muttered.

"You never had anything to worry about," he said. "She wasn't my type. But, I had an idea she'd make mischief if I kept trying to get those few acres, so I let the idea go. And I'll tell you something else," he added with a chuckle. "I don't think Dawson Rutherford's going to get that strip, either. She may string him along to see if she can get him interested in a more permanent arrangement, but unless he wants to propose…"

"Maybe he does," she said.

He shook his head. "I don't like him," he said, "but he's not a fool. She isn't his type of woman. She likes to give orders, not take them. He's too strong willed to suit her for long. More than likely, it's because she can't get him that she wants him."

"I hope so," she replied. "I'd hate to see him trapped into marriage. I think Barrie cares a lot more for him than she'll admit."

He drew her close. "They'll work out their own problems. Do you realize how this household has changed since you married me?"

She smiled. "Yes. Maggie is a whole new person."

"So am I. So are you. So is your father and Mrs. Bates," he added. "And now we've got a baby on the way as well, and Maggie's actually looking forward to it. I tell you, we've got the world."

She nestled close to him and closed her eyes. "The whole world," she agreed huskily.

Seven months later, Nelson Charles Long was born in the Bighorn community hospital. It had been a quick, easy birth, and Powell had been with Antonia every step of the way. Maggie was allowed in with her dad to see the baby while Antonia fed him.

"He looks like you, Dad," Maggie said.

"He looks like Antonia," he protested. "You look like me," he added.

Maggie beamed. There was a whole new relationship between Maggie and her father. She wasn't threatened by the baby at all, not when she was so well loved by both parents. The cold, empty past was truly behind her now, just as it had finally been laid to rest by her parents.

Antonia had asked Powell finally what Sally had written in the letter she'd sent back, so many years ago. Sally had told him very little about it, he recalled, ex-

cept he recalled one line she'd quoted from some author he couldn't quite remember: Take what you want,
says God, and pay for it. The letter was to the effect
that Sally had discovered the painful truth of that old
proverb, and she was sorry.

Too late, of course. Much too late.

Sally had been forgiven, and the joy Antonia felt
with Powell and Maggie grew by the day. She, too,
had learned a hard lesson from the experience, that one
had to stand and fight sometimes. She would teach that
lesson to Maggie, she thought as she looked adoringly
up at her proud husband, and to the child she held in
her arms.

* * * * *

SPECIAL EDITION

Life, Love and Family

You have just read a
Harlequin® Special Edition book.

Discover more heartfelt tales of **family, friendship** and **love** from the
Harlequin Special Edition series. Be sure to look for all six Harlequin Special Edition books every month.

SPECIAL EDITION

Life, Love and Family

Use this coupon to save

$1.00

on the purchase of any
Harlequin® Special Edition book.

Available wherever books are sold, including most bookstores, supermarkets, drugstores and discount stores.

Save $1.00

on the purchase of any Harlequin® Special Edition book.

Coupon valid until December 16, 2014. Redeemable at participating retail outlets in the U.S. and Canada only. Limit one coupon per customer.

Canadian Retailers: Harlequin Enterprises Limited will pay the face value of this coupon plus 10.25¢ if submitted by customer for this product only. Any other use constitutes fraud. Coupon is nonassignable. Void if taxed, prohibited or restricted by law. Consumer must pay any government taxes. Void if copied. Millennium1 Promotional Services ("M1P") customers submit coupons and proof of sales to Harlequin Enterprises Limited, P.O. Box 3000, Saint John, NB E2L 4L3, Canada. Non-M1P retailer—for reimbursement submit coupons and proof of sales directly to Harlequin Enterprises Limited, Retail Marketing Department, 225 Duncan Mill Rd., Don Mills, ON M3B 3K9, Canada.

U.S. Retailers: Harlequin Enterprises Limited will pay the face value of this coupon plus 8¢ if submitted by customer for this product only. Any other use constitutes fraud. Coupon is nonassignable. Void if taxed, prohibited or restricted by law. Consumer must pay any government taxes. Void if copied. For reimbursement submit coupons and proof of sales directly to Harlequin Enterprises Limited, P.O. Box 880478, El Paso, TX 88588-0478, U.S.A. Cash value 1/100 cents.

52611940

5 65373 00076 2   (8100)0 11982

® and TM are trademarks owned and used by the trademark owner and/or its licensee.
© 2014 Harlequin Enterprises Limited

HSEINCCOUP1014

*Attorney Maggie Roarke's one-night stand with rancher
Jesse Crawford was completely out of character—
and resulted in pregnancy! The once-burned cowboy
proposes a marriage of convenience, but Maggie longs
for true romance. Will their holiday baby-to-be bring
them to a fairy-tale ending?*

***

"I should probably be on my way."

"Oh." She forced a smile and tried to ignore the sense of disappointment that spread through her. "Okay."

She followed him to the door.

He paused. "Thanks again for dinner."

"You're welcome," she said. "And if you ever need a fictional girlfriend to get you out of a tight spot, feel free to give me a call."

He lifted a hand and touched her cheek, the stroke of his fingertips over her skin making her shiver. "I don't want a fictional girlfriend, but I do want to kiss you for real."

She wasn't sure if he was stating a fact or asking permission, but before she could respond, he'd lowered his head and covered her mouth with his.

This time, he was in control right from the beginning— she didn't have a chance to think about what he was doing or brace herself against the wave of emotions that washed over her.

For a man who claimed he didn't do a lot of dating, he sure knew how to kiss. His mouth was warm and firm as it moved over hers, masterfully persuasive and seductive. Never before had she been kissed with such patient thoroughness. His hands were big and strong, but infinitely gentle as they slid up her back, burning her skin through the silky fabric of her blouse as he urged her closer.

She wanted him to touch her, and the fierceness of the want was shocking. Equally strong was the desire to touch him—to let her hands roam over his rock-hard body, exploring and savoring every inch of him. He was so completely and undeniably male, and he made everything that was female inside of her quiver with excitement.

Eventually, reluctantly, he eased his mouth from hers. But he kept his arms around her, as if he couldn't bear to let her go. "I should probably be on my way before the sheriff gets home."

"He won't be home tonight," she admitted. "He and Lissa went to Bozeman for the weekend."

He frowned at that. "You're going to be alone here tonight?"

She held his gaze steadily. "I hope not."

He closed the door and turned the lock.

***

We hope you enjoyed this sneak peek from award-winning author Brenda Harlen's
THE MAVERICK'S THANKSGIVING BABY,
the next installment in the six-book continuity
MONTANA MAVERICKS: 20 YEARS IN THE SADDLE!,
coming in November 2014 from Harlequin® Special Edition!

HSEINCEXP1014